Praise for Valerie Hansen and her novels

"*The Troublesome Angel* by Valerie Hansen is a tender, well-written story of forgiveness, God's great sense of humor and how falling in love is never easy."
—*Romantic Times BOOKreviews*

"Valerie Hansen's tale is both charming and inspirational from first page to last."
—*Romantic Times BOOKreviews* on *Samantha's Gift*

"*Second Chances* by Valerie Hansen will put a smile on your face…A great spontaneous little romance!"
—*Romantic Times BOOKreviews*

"The fourth book in the Davis Landing series is an excellent read. Valerie Hansen's *The Hamilton Heir* is a great book."
—*Romantic Times BOOKreviews*

VALERIE HANSEN

Blessings of the Heart

❦

Samantha's Gift

Steeple Hill®

Published by Steeple Hill Books™

STEEPLE HILL BOOKS

Steeple
Hill®

Recycling programs
for this product may
not exist in your area.

ISBN-13: 978-0-373-65126-9
ISBN-10:   0-373-65126-0

BLESSINGS OF THE HEART AND SAMANTHA'S GIFT

BLESSINGS OF THE HEART
Copyright © 2003 by Valerie Whisenand

SAMANTHA'S GIFT
Copyright © 2003 by Valerie Whisenand

www.SteepleHill.com

Printed in U.S.A.

CONTENTS

Books by Valerie Hansen

Love Inspired

*The Wedding Arbor
*The Troublesome Angel
*The Perfect Couple
*Second Chances
*Love One Another
*Blessings of the Heart
*Samantha's Gift
*Everlasting Love
The Hamilton Heir
*A Treasure of the Heart

*Serenity, Arkansas

Love Inspired Suspense

*Her Brother's Keeper
The Danger Within
*Out of the Depths
Deadly Payoff
*Shadow of Turning
Hidden in the Wall
*Nowhere to Run

Love Inspired Historical

Frontier Courtship
Wilderness Courtship

VALERIE HANSEN

was thirty when she awoke to the presence of the Lord in her life and turned to Jesus. In the years that followed she worked with young children, both in church and secular environments. She also raised a family of her own and played foster mother to a wide assortment of furred and feathered critters.

Married to her high school sweetheart since age seventeen, she now lives in an old farmhouse she and her husband renovated with their own hands. She loves to hike the wooded hills behind the house and reflect on the marvelous turn her life has taken. Not only is she privileged to reside among the loving, accepting folks in the breathtakingly beautiful Ozark mountains of Arkansas, she also gets to share her personal faith by telling the stories of her heart for all of Steeple Hill's Love Inspired lines.

Life doesn't get much better than that!

BLESSINGS OF THE HEART

If I take the wings of the morning and dwell
in the uttermost parts of the sea; even there shall
thy hand lead me, and thy right hand shall hold me.
—*Psalms* 139:9–10

To Joe, for having the courage and strength
of character to walk away from a lucrative,
prestigious job and come chase rainbows with me.

Chapter One

"If I take the wings of the morning and dwell in the uttermost parts of the sea; even there shall thy hand lead me and thy right hand shall hold me."

—Psalm 139:9-10

Startled, Brianne Bailey froze. Listened. Straightened. Who in the world could be making such an awful racket?

She'd been in her kitchen, peacefully raiding the refrigerator for a quick afternoon snack, when she'd heard the first whack. Before she could determine the source, repeated pounding had built to a deafening crescendo and was echoing through the enormous house. It sounded as if a herd of rampaging elephants was trampling down her substantial mahogany front door. That, or she was being accosted by a psychopathic door-to-door salesman who knew she was there alone and hoped to frighten her into buying his wares!

Both ideas were so ludicrous they made Bree chuckle as she hurried down the hall to answer the knock. "Boy, I've been living in a world of fiction for too long," she muttered. "I'm beginning to think like the crazy characters in my stories." *Which wouldn't be too bad if I were writing at the time,* she added, smiling.

The hammering intensified. "Okay, okay, I'm coming," Brianne shouted. "Don't you break the stained glass in the top of that door, whoever you are. I'll never be able to replace it."

She grabbed the knob and jerked open the door, ready to continue scolding her would-be intruder. Instead, she took one look at the cause of the disturbance and gasped, slack-jawed.

The man standing on the porch with his fist raised to continue his assault on her helpless door was dirty, sweaty, scratched and bleeding, as if he'd just plunged through a green-briar thicket. He was also remarkably handsome in spite of his disheveled appearance. Left speechless, she wasn't having a lot of luck sucking in enough air for adequate breathing, either.

Her visitor looked to be in his mid-thirties, with

dark, wavy hair and darker eyes beneath scowling brows. Standing there, facing her, he seemed larger than life. As if the pounding hadn't been enough, his reddened face was added proof of his anger, although what had upset him was a mystery to Bree. Far as she knew, she didn't have an enemy in the world.

"Can I help you?" She managed to speak.

"It's your pond," the man said, looking directly into her wide, blue eyes and pointing with a thrust of his arm. "It's cut off all my water!"

Brianne held up one hand in a calming gesture. "Whoa. There's no need to get upset. I'm sure we can work things out. Just tell me exactly what water you're talking about?"

"From the spring. Over there," he explained. "You built your new pond between my place and the spring."

"My pond? Oh, dear. Did I do something against the law?"

"I don't know. What difference does it make? By the time we finally get enough rain to finish filling that enormous hole of yours and spill over into the creek bed again, I'll be an old man."

Oddly, his comment amused her. She smiled, smoothed the hem of her knit shirt over her shorts and said, "I imagine that will be quite a long time."

"This isn't funny. I need water for my cabin."

"Which is, I take it, downhill from here?"

"Brilliant deduction."

Certain the man wouldn't appreciate her growing humor, Bree fought a threatened eruption of giggles. "Thanks. I'm trying."

"Well?" he asked, scowling.

"Well, what? I had that valley explored before I made any changes in the landscaping up here. We did find one old cabin, but these hills are full of abandoned homesteads. Surely, you can't be talking about that decrepit old place."

"I certainly am."

"Oops. Sorry." Her smile turned apologetic. "You live there?"

"I do now."

"I see. What about your well?"

"Don't have a well. Or running water. Never have." He held up the bucket he was carrying. "That's what I've been trying to tell you."

"Why didn't you say so?"

"I thought I just did."

"Not hardly," Bree argued. "If you'd knocked on my door politely and explained your problem we could have handled this without everybody getting upset."

"Who said I was upset?"

She arched an eyebrow as she eyed him critically. "Some things are self-explanatory, Mr...."

"Fowler. Mitch Fowler."

"All right, Mr. Fowler. You can take all the water you need from my well. Will that satisfy you?"

"I guess that's my only choice." Some of the tension left him. "My Uncle Eldon and Aunt Vi used to live in the same old cabin. Maybe you knew them."

"I'm afraid not. I'm Brianne Bailey. Bree, for short." She politely offered to shake hands, waiting while Mitch wiped his on his jeans. "I'm not from around here. I…"

The moment Mitch's hand touched hers she forgot whatever else she was going to say. Staring at him, she realized that he was returning her gaze with a look of equal amazement. Now that he was no longer irate, his glance seemed warmer, more appealing. It reminded her of a cup of dark, rich coffee on a cold winter's morning.

Brianne didn't know how long she stood there holding the stranger's hand, because time had ceased to register. She didn't come to her senses until she heard him clear his throat.

"I'm sorry I came on so strong just now," Mitch said, finally letting go and stepping away. "When I discovered we had no water it threw me for a loop."

"I'm sure it did." Bree eyed the bucket. "Before I get back to work I suppose I should show you where to fill that."

"That won't be necessary. It's too hot to come outside if you don't need to. Just point me in the right direction, and I'll get out of your hair."

The mention of temperature and hair together made her unconsciously lift her long, honey-blond tresses off her neck to cool her skin. Even in shorts and a sleeveless blouse she was feeling the heat, too.

"Nonsense," she said. "You look like you had to fight your way through a pack of wildcats to get up here. The least I can do is walk you out to the hose. Besides, I was taking a break, anyway."

"A break? Do you work at home?"

"Yes. I'm a writer." She waited for the usual questions about her publishing history. When they didn't come, she relaxed, smiled amiably and pointed. "This way. I need to water the new flower beds over there again, anyway. Sure wish we'd get some decent rain. It's been awfully dry lately."

"I know. At first I was afraid the spring had dried up."

Mitch stepped back to give her room to pass, then walked beside her as she led the way down the stone steps and along the path that took them around the east wing of the sprawling dwelling. In the distance lay the offending pond. Closer to the house, a bright yellow hose stood out against the green of the perfectly groomed lawn.

"You have a nice place here," Mitch said.

"Thanks. I like it."

"I do a little building, myself."

She noticed that he was assessing the newest addition to the house as they walked. "Would you like to wander around and look the place over? I don't mind."

"I'd love to but I need to get home. I didn't expect to be gone this long when I left the boys."

"Boys?" Brianne couldn't picture him as a scout-master leading a camp out or a Sunday school teacher taking his class on a field trip, which left only one other likely probability—fatherhood. The notion of having one man living close by didn't bother her nearly as much as the idea of his children running rampant all over the hills, whooping and hollering and disturbing the otherwise perfect solitude she'd created in which to work.

"I have two sons," Mitch said.

"Congratulations." There was an embarrassing pause before she went on. "I can't imagine coping with any children, let alone boys."

"It isn't easy." Mitch bent to fill the bucket, not looking at her as he spoke. "Especially alone."

Curiosity got the better of her. "Oh? Are you divorced?"

"No." Mitch straightened, his expression guarded. "My wife died recently."

Open mouth, insert foot, chew thoroughly. "I'm so sorry. I shouldn't have asked. It's none of my business."

The hint of a smile lifted one corner of his strong mouth. "It's no secret that I'm single, if that's what you want to know. And I'm not grieving. Liz and I had separated long before her accident. I hadn't seen her in ages."

"Then what about—?" Brianne broke off and cast a telling glance down the wooded slope in the direction of his cabin. No more questions. She'd already said enough dumb things for one day.

Mitch, however, supplied the answer to her unspoken query. "Liz took the boys away with her when she left me. It took almost three years to track them down."

The poignancy of his situation touched her heart. "What an awful thing to go through."

"Yeah, no kidding. I've got my work cut out for me now, that's for sure, which is why I'd better get a move on. Even kids who are used to living by strict rules can get into trouble, and mine haven't had much discipline lately. Ryan—he's eight—says he's used to looking after his younger brother, but that doesn't mean they won't both be swinging from the chandeliers by the time I get home."

She was incredulous. "Wait a minute. You have no water—but you have chandeliers in your cabin?"

"No, ma'am." Mitch chuckled. "That was just a figure of speech." Glancing toward the mansion, he added, "I think you've been surrounded by luxury too long. You're out of touch with how the rest of the world lives."

She sighed. "I suppose you could be right. I find this whole area very confusing. There aren't any neighborhoods like I'm used to back home. People just seem to build whatever kind of house they want, wherever they want it, no matter what the places next door look like." Realizing how that comment had sounded, she pulled a face. "Sorry. No offense meant."

"Don't worry about it. You can't help it if you have more money than good sense." He followed his comment with a smile so she'd realize he'd been joking.

"Hey, I'm not that wealthy."

Mitch's smile grew. "Good. Maybe there's hope for you yet. Are you famous? Maybe I've read something you wrote."

Delayed reaction but predictable questions? "I doubt that. I write women's fiction. And I didn't get rich doing it. My father passed away several years ago, and I inherited a bundle. After that, I left Pennsylvania and moved down here to Arkansas to get away from the sad memories."

Mitch hefted the heavy bucket with ease and

started toward the edge of the lawn where the forest began. "Can't run from those," he said wisely. "I ought to know. No matter where you go, your past goes with you, mistakes and all."

A jolt of uneasiness hit her as she fell into step beside him. "I hope you're wrong."

"Not about that. Experience is a great teacher," he said soberly. "Well, nice to have met you, Ms. Bailey, and thanks for the water. If you ever feel like slumming, just follow this streambed about half a mile. You'll find us at the bottom of the draw." He smiled. "Bye. Gotta go."

She raised her hand tentatively in reply. She'd have done more, but a flock of butterflies had just launched themselves en masse at the sight of his dynamic parting grin, and she was busy wondering if his last glimpse of her was going to feature her keeling over in a dead faint. The notion wasn't very appealing.

"Phooey. I don't swoon," Bree whispered, wresting control of her body from her topsy-turvy emotions. "I'm just a little woozy from the heat and humidity, that's all. I've never fainted and I never will."

Besides, that poor man is saddled with two little kids, she added, silently reinforcing her growing conviction that Mitch was anything but appealing. Children. Eesh! And the oldest was only eight! What a nightmare!

Bree shivered. As far as she was concerned, the man might as well have confessed to being in league with the devil himself!

By the time Mitch got to his cabin, he'd managed to spill half the contents of the bucket. Considering the rough, overgrown terrain he'd had to cover on his trek down the hill he was surprised to have salvaged that much.

As he approached the cabin, he could hear shouts and squeals of laughter. That might not be a good sign but at least it proved the boys hadn't mutinied and wandered off in his absence.

The minute he pushed open the door, his children froze in mid-motion, looking as if they were sure they were guilty of some awful crime and expected him to mete out immediate punishment.

Instead, Mitch set the bucket down and paused to assess the mayhem. Ryan had pulled the narrow end of a flat sheet over his shoulders and tied the corners so the fabric draped behind him like a long cape. Bud had apparently been trying to sit on the part that dragged the floor while his big brother pulled him around the room. Bud's raggedy old teddy bear was perched on the sidelines like an audience at a sporting event.

Judging by the swirls of dust on the wooden flooring and the boys' grubby faces and hands, they'd been playing their little game for some time. Their expressions were priceless!

Mitch wanted desperately to laugh. They were just typical kids having a good time. He wasn't about to play the ogre and spoil their fun.

He pointed. "You missed a couple of places."

"Huh?" Ryan frowned.

"That's an ingenious way to sweep the floor but it doesn't do the corners very well. I suggest we use a mop for those."

"Uh, okay."

Mitch could tell the boy's mind was working, struggling to comprehend Mitch's surprising parental reaction. Finally, Ryan's thin shoulders relaxed, and he untied his makeshift cape.

"Little kids get bored real easy," the eight-year-old said. "You have to keep 'em busy or they get into trouble."

"I can see that."

For an instant Mitch glimpsed the child behind his eldest son's tough-guy facade. It couldn't have been easy for Ryan to act as a pseudo parent while his flaky mother, Liz, ran around doing as she pleased. There was no telling how often she'd gone off on a tangent and left the boys alone much longer than she'd originally intended. Still, that lack of responsibility on her part may have been a blessing in disguise because it had led to them not being with her when she'd had the horrible accident that had taken her life.

"I may need you to help me understand your brother," Mitch said. "Especially since I haven't seen either of you for such a long time. I'm not used to having kids around. I've really missed you guys."

"Then why didn't you come get us?"

Ah, so that was what was eating at Ryan. "Because I didn't know where your mother had taken you," Mitch explained. "Even the police couldn't find you. I spent every cent I could lay my hands on to hire private detectives. I'll say this for your mom, she hides really good."

"We moved a lot," the boy replied, eyes downcast.

"It's okay. I won't bug you about it," Mitch promised. "But if you ever do decide you want to talk about anything that happened while you were gone, I'm willing to listen, okay?"

"Yeah. Sure."

Mitch would have pursued the subject if there hadn't been a strange scratching noise at the door. He immediately assumed it was a marauding raccoon or possum, but before he had time to warn the boys, Bud had run to the door and thrown it wide open.

"Don't!"

Mitch started to shout, then stopped, startled,

when he realized their visitor was a puppy. At least he thought it was. There was so much mud and so many leaves and twigs stuck in its dull brown coat that its age wasn't the only thing in question.

Mitch's protective instincts came to the fore. "Close the door. You don't know where that thing has been. It could be sick."

The advice came too late. Bud was already on his knees beside the pitiful little dog, and Ryan was patting it on the head while it shook and whimpered. Whether Mitch approved or not, it looked like his boys had themselves a pet.

He strode quickly to the doorway and scooped up the skinny pup so he could look it over. Poor thing. He could feel every one of its ribs beneath the matted fur. Chances were good it was covered with fleas, too. If any stray ever needed a home, this one sure did.

"Okay. First things first," he said firmly. "Ryan, you grab a rag and wipe down all the furniture with clean water from the bucket. Bud, you help him. And do a good job of it, guys, because you'll only get one chance. As soon as you're done we're going to use the rest of the wash water to give this dog a bath."

Hearing the boys' mutual intake of breath he added, "That is, if you want it to live inside with us. Of course, if you don't…"

"We do!" Ryan shouted. Grabbing Bud by the

hand, he hurried him off with a breathless command, "Come on," leaving Mitch and the dog behind.

"You guys found him. What do you want to name him?" Mitch called after them.

Bud grabbed Ryan's arm and leaned close to whisper in his ear.

Ryan nodded sagely. "Barney."

Bud agreed, "Yeah!"

At the shrill sound of their voices the little dog's trembling increased. Mitch felt so sorry for it, he held it closer in spite of its dirty coat. "Shush. You're scaring him."

They immediately quieted down, looking at their father with awe. In their eyes, he had apparently become an instant expert on dogs.

Soberly, Mitch gazed at the skinny, quivering ball of filthy fur he was cradling in his arms, hoping with all his heart that he'd be wise enough, caring enough, to salvage all three of the neglected waifs he was now responsible for.

Chapter Two

With darkness came a midsummer thunderstorm. Mitch figured out how hard it was raining by listening to the torrent pounding against the peaked tin roof and running off the steep slope to fall in a solid sheet of water along both sides.

Before long, he felt a drop hit him on the head. It didn't startle him because he was already wide awake. As soon as the thunder and lightning had started, Bud had climbed into his bed with him, stuffed bear and all. That wasn't so bad until a wide-eyed Ryan showed up carrying a battery-powered lantern and their new dog.

"Barney is scared, too," the eight-year-old said. "Can we get in bed with you?"

"Sure." Mitch scooted over as far as he could to make room and promptly fell off the narrow mattress onto the floor with a thump and an ouch.

That brought giggles from the boys.

"Tell you what," he said, raising himself up to peer over the edge of the bed, "how about we put a couple of these beds together to make one bigger one? Then we can all sleep close without pushing your poor daddy onto the floor."

No one answered. Mitch got to his feet and took charge. "Okay. Everybody out. The roof is leaking over here, and I don't know how much worse the rain will get, so the first thing we're going to do is move my bed to a drier place." He motioned. "Ryan, you push the foot of the bed in that direction. I'll get the end with the headboard."

"I have to go potty," Bud announced.

"In a minute," Mitch promised. "Right now we're getting Daddy's bed out of the way so it won't get wet."

Ryan shot him a knowing look. "That's not the only thing that'll be wet if you don't take him to the bathroom. When he says he has to go, he has to go."

"Okay, okay."

It suddenly occurred to Mitch that the facilities were outside and it was pouring. He glanced at Ryan. The boy was sporting a sly grin.

Mitch frowned. "Did you take your brother to the outhouse before dark, like I told you?"

"Yup." Ryan's eyes twinkled with mischief. "But he'd never seen one before. He was scared to go in."

"Why didn't you go in with him?"

"It was too crowded." His smile spread from ear to ear. "Guess you'll have to make the trip, huh?"

Mitch sighed, vowing to add a portable commode to the list of supplies he intended to get the next time he drove into town. He reached for his jeans and pulled them on over his pajamas, then slid his bare feet into his boots. "I guess I will. Help your brother put his shoes on."

He grabbed a waterproof plastic poncho, slung it over his head and held the front part out of the way while he hoisted his youngest son in his arms and covered him with it.

"I'll take Bud now. Ryan, you fix the beds while I'm gone. When I come back I'll help you. Okay?"

Ryan nodded compliantly.

Looking terribly smug, he handed his father a flashlight.

The humidity gathering beneath the plastic gear had already brought up beads of sweat on Mitch's forehead.

The moment Ryan opened the door for him, the rain gusted in, soaking the floorboards and puddling on the uneven surface. Lightning illuminated the yard as if a floodlight had been turned on. Thunder crashed and rolled, echoing across the hills.

If Mitch hadn't been obliged to make a mad dash for the outhouse he would have stopped then and there and told his eldest son a few things about following orders in the future. As it was, he figured he would be doing well to keep his balance and get there and back in one piece. Discipline would have to wait.

From her second-story vantage point, Bree could see the recently dug pond that had caused her new neighbor such consternation. Every time there was a flash of lightning the water level looked higher. If this deluge kept up, the creek he'd mentioned was probably going to start flowing again very soon.

"I think I'll still run a pipe from our well so they'll have decent drinking water all the time," she told herself. "That's only fair." Besides, doing that would keep the neighbors from disturbing her solitude by hiking up the hill to fetch water day after day. She made a disgusted face. Did having an ulterior motive cancel out the benefits of doing a good deed? "I sure hope not."

As she watched, the water level in the pond continued to rise, then appeared to stabilize even though the rain was still coming down hard. Her brow furrowed, and she peered into the darkness, hoping for another bright burst so she could see better. When it did finally come, she could have sworn there was less water in the pond than before. How strange.

Puzzled, she watched the anomaly for a few more minutes, then pulled a light cotton robe over her nightgown and went downstairs to make sure her computer was disconnected in case of a lightning strike. There wasn't much point in going back to bed while the storm raged. She'd never be able to sleep when the flashes were so bright she could see them through her closed eyelids!

Bree got herself a glass of milk and settled into a chair at the kitchen table. She noticed that her hands were trembling slightly. Undue concern during bad weather was a new phenomenon for her. There seemed to be something particularly disconcerting about the ferocity of Arkansas summer storms. Maybe it was the stories her part-time housekeeper, Emma, had told about that kind of weather spawning tornadoes. Or maybe it was simply the fact that Bree was alone in the enormous house with no one to talk to. Most of the time, that was exactly how she wanted it. Tonight, however, she almost wished it was time for Emma to drive out from Serenity and clean the place again.

Thunder rattled the windows. Bree winced. "Guess I'm not much of a country girl," she murmured. "I'd sure like to ask somebody a few questions right about now."

Mitch had pulled on his leather boots without lacing them, and they were totally soaked. Thanks to the blowing rain and stifling humidity, the rest of him wasn't much drier.

Bud had obviously never had to rough it before. Consequently, their foray into the storm had taken far longer than Mitch had anticipated.

By the time he returned Bud to the cabin, Mitch was furious with Ryan. Pulling off his slicker, he glared at the boy. "You knew this would happen, didn't you?"

"I didn't know it was going to rain," Ryan answered, acting subdued under his father's ire. "It's not my fault this place is a dump. It's worse than going to camp. At least they had the bathrooms in the same building."

"You went to camp?"

"Yeah. Once. Mom sent us. I didn't like it much."

"No doubt." Mitch noticed that Ryan was fidgeting more than usual. Since the sound of running, dripping water had been serenading them for hours, he suspected the power of suggestion was getting to Ryan the same way it already had to Bud.

"You wouldn't happen to have to use the bathroom, too, would you?" Mitch asked with a slow drawl.

"Me? Naw."

"You sure? I could lend you my poncho. You wouldn't get too wet."

Ryan eyed him with obvious misgivings. "You mean you wouldn't come with me?"

"Nope. One of us has to stay in here and watch your brother. If you go, that means I stay." He could see the indecisiveness in his son's face turn to stubborn resolve.

"Fine. Gimme the raincoat. I'm out of here."

Mitch watched him don the man-size slicker and pick up the flashlight. The only thing that hinted at anxiety was a slight pause in Ryan's stride as he opened the door and faced the storm. Then he slammed the door and was gone.

The kid has guts, Mitch told himself with pride. He hadn't been nearly that brave when he was only eight. Of course, he hadn't been compelled to care for a younger sibling, either. That responsibility had undoubtedly forced Ryan to grow up way before his time—which was a real shame. If possible, Mitch was going to teach the poor kid to enjoy being a child again.

Warmer thoughts of Ryan had just about blotted out the last of Mitch's rancor when the door burst open and his son ran in, shouting, "Look out! It's a flood!"

If it hadn't been for the wild look in his son's eyes, Mitch might have doubted his truthfulness. Instead, he joined him at the door and shined the flashlight on the yard to assess the situation for himself.

"It's just runoff water," Mitch assured the frightened boy. "Nothing to worry about."

Ryan grabbed the light and pointed it toward the creek bed. "Oh, yeah? How about over there?"

"That's just…" Reality struck, bringing Mitch's heart to his throat and making his pulse race. He whispered, "Dear God."

"You told me not to cuss."

"That wasn't a curse. See the debris in the water? Those are whole trees, not twigs. I didn't know it was raining hard enough to do that." He whirled. "Come on. We're getting out of here. Follow me. I'll get Bud."

"Want your raincoat?" Ryan held it out.

"Forget it. I'd rather be wet than get caught by that water coming down the canyon."

Mitch scooped up his youngest son and ran for the front door. Bud immediately started to bawl.

Racing toward the car, Mitch belatedly realized that Ryan wasn't right behind him. He tossed Bud into the back seat and was about to return to the house for his other son when Ryan appeared, leaning into the wind and struggling to make headway through the pelting rain.

"Had to stop and get the bear," the boy shouted.

Mitch was already standing in mud and water up to his ankles. Fortunately, Ryan was able to get the passenger door open without his help.

Sliding behind the wheel, Mitch leaned over and pulled Ryan into the car beside him, then started the motor while the boy struggled to shut the heavy door against the force of the gale.

"Where's the dog? Who's got the dog?" Mitch shouted over the combined furor of the storm and his upset children.

"I don't know," Ryan hollered back. "Want me to go see?"

"No. Stay right where you are. I'll get him."

The moment Mitch opened the driver's door the soggy little dog jumped in, bounded across his feet and scrambled over the back of the front seat as if he'd always done it that way.

The boys cheered.

"Belt yourselves in!" Mitch ordered.

He put the car in reverse, praying the tires wouldn't slip in the slimy mud and wishing he'd had enough foresight to bring his four-wheel-drive pickup truck instead of the cumbersome passenger car.

Gently, evenly, he pressed the accelerator. Every instinct screamed for him to gun the motor, to race onto the paved road as fast as he could. But he knew better than to try.

The rear wheels slipped, spun. Mitch eased up on the gas, and they finally caught. He prayed a silent thanks to his heavenly Father, then added a fervent, soul-deep plea for further help, just as he had every single day and night his sons had been missing.

Nothing like a disaster to bring out the spiritual side of a man, was there? Well, at least *something* good had come out of that time of horrible worry and loneliness.

Mitch's hands clenched the wheel.

The heavy vehicle slipped and slid in and out of ruts as it inched backward out of the valley.

Even if there had been room to turn the car around, he wouldn't have tried the maneuver in this weather. Too much chance of going off the road and getting mired in one of the ditches that ran along both sides.

He hardly had time to think about that danger before they skidded off the road and were mired up to their axles! Terrific. Now what? He glanced at his sons.

Ryan gave him a cynical look in reply. "Smooth move, Dad."

Under other circumstances Mitch would have countered that comment, but right now he had more important things on his mind than the boy's pessimism. He had to decide quickly what to do with his wet, shivering kids and the soggy dog. Given the current conditions, staying in the car was out of the question.

It didn't take a genius to see that a short hike to the estate up the hill was the only sensible course of action. For the sake of the kids, he'd have to swallow his pride and ask for help. Again.

Too bad he hadn't tried to make a better impression on the wealthy woman who lived there the first time he'd knocked on her door.

Getting Bud and Ryan up the hill was a lot harder for Mitch than climbing with the bucket had been. It was also dark and wet, and everybody was clammy and slippery.

Mitch finally slung the smaller boy under one arm like a sack of potatoes so he could carry him and still have one hand free to grab low-hanging tree branches to aid his ascent.

Ryan tried valiantly to keep up but made little forward progress while he was trying to hold on to the soggy dog. Finally, he set Barney down to fend for himself and concentrated on toting only the drenched teddy bear while Mitch struggled along with Bud.

By the time they topped the rise and came out of the forest onto the lawn of the estate, Mitch was so exhausted he dropped to his knees.

Fighting to catch his breath, he set Bud on his feet, "Okay. You can walk now."

Though the rain had slackened some, it was still falling. Gusting wind made it feel colder. He pointed toward the house, thankful a few lights were on inside so the boys could see it clearly. "That's where we're going. It's not much farther."

Ryan drew up beside his father and whistled. "Whoa. Cool. Why didn't you bring us here in the first place?"

"Look, the only reason we're here tonight is because we need shelter and a dry place to sleep," Mitch explained. "In the morning we'll head back down to the cabin and see what kind of shape it's in."

"Bummer."

"Get over it." Mitch stood. "Come on, fellas. I don't know about you, but I'm freezing. Grab the dog and let's go."

Chapter Three

Brianne was still sitting in the kitchen when she thought she heard a knock on the front door. Chalking it up to her imagination, she didn't move. As isolated as the house was, she hardly ever had company, even on a nice day. On a wretched night like this it was unheard of.

A second knock made her jump. "Who in the world can that be?" There was only one way to find out—answer the door. But what if it was a burglar?

"A burglar wouldn't knock," she countered, chuckling softly. Just in case, however, she'd leave the chain fastened till she saw who it was. Too bad she didn't have a baseball bat handy.

"Sure, then if it is a burglar I can ask him if he wants to play a few innings?" Bree taunted herself.

She was still smiling at the amusing idea as she

unlocked the front door and opened it far enough to see if she really did have callers.

Oh, my! She certainly did! Not only was Mitch Fowler standing on her porch big as life—he had two dripping wet children at his side. The pose reminded her of a mother hen corralling her chicks to shelter them beneath her wings. How adorable!

Brianne quickly undid the chain and threw the door wide. "You look awful. Get in here where it's dry."

"You sure?"

"Of course!"

"Thanks. We got flooded out, and I didn't know where else to go. The kids are pretty cold."

Ushering his boys through the door without delay, he ran his hands over his wet hair to smooth it back, apparently trying to make himself present-able.

Bree thought he looked absolutely endearing. The tender way he was hovering over his children touched her heart and created a never-to-be-forgot-ten picture of true parenting. When she was little she would have given anything to see that kind of love in her father's expression. The thought brought a melancholy smile.

Mitch's glance met hers and lingered. "I hate to be a bother. Have you got a couple of extra blankets we could borrow? And maybe some spare towels?"

"Of course." Blushing and pulling her cotton robe around her more tightly, she said, "Stay right where you are. Don't move. I'll go get them."

She frowned momentarily at the water puddling on her shiny marble foyer floor, then hurried down the hall. In moments she was back and handing out towels. "Here. These will get you started."

"Thanks. I'm really sorry about this, Ms. Bailey. I hadn't intended to bother you again."

"Please, call me Bree."

"Bree? Okay. This is Ryan." Mitch laid a hand on the boy's thin shoulder, then touched his sibling in turn. "And this is Bud. The little furry one Ryan's holding is named Barney. He's new to our family."

"How—sweet." Though the whole group was dripping, the dog was definitely the dirtiest. Clearly, she wasn't going to be able to dry off her guests and then send them packing. Therefore, they'd have to make other arrangements. Ones that would keep the current mess confined to a small area.

"I guess I should see what I can find for the boys to wear until their clothes and shoes are dry. As for you..." A blush warmed her cheeks when she scanned Mitch's full height. "You're much bigger than I am. I'm afraid you'll have to rough it."

"No problem—as long as my kids are okay. We really appreciate your hospitality, ma'am. We'll be out of here as soon as possible."

Bree shivered. The whole idea of having them stay, even temporarily, was so unsettling it made her insides tremble as she doled out more fluffy bath towels. And to think she'd just been yearning for some company because of the storm! What a stupid idea. Being lonesome was starting to look better by the minute.

Mitch's hand accidentally brushed hers when he accepted the last towel. Startled, she pulled back and folded her arms across her chest in a defensive posture.

He gave her a concerned look. "You okay?"

"Storms make me nervous," she replied.

"Not me. At least not until the one tonight. I've never seen that creek by Eldon's rise so high or move so fast. I was afraid it might take out the whole cabin."

"Is that what you meant by a flood?"

"Yeah." Mitch draped another towel around Bud's neck and proceeded to tousle his hair to dry it. "I tried to drive out to the main road, but we never made it."

"Dad backed into a ditch and we got stuck," Ryan piped up, wiggling and squirming. "Can I take a bath? I think I've got mud in my shorts."

"Ryan! That's enough. Mind your manners."

Amused, Brianne pointed. "Sounds like a good idea to me. The downstairs bathroom is right around that corner. It has a large shower and linen closet. Take your family through there and down the tiled hall so you won't get muddy tracks on the carpet. If you drop everybody's wet clothes outside the bathroom door I'll see that they're washed and dried."

"Gotcha. Thanks."

Bending slightly, Mitch began to herd his little group of soggy refugees in the direction she'd indicated. All except one, that is.

In order to hold on to his towel, Ryan had had to put Barney down. The curious pup was busy sniffing his way across the foyer. Behind him, a line of smudged paw prints stood out prominently on the highly polished black marble floor.

"Uh-oh. Trouble," Mitch muttered. Then louder, "Hey! Dog. Over here." He began to whistle repeatedly while the children also called.

Barney ignored everything except the interesting scent he was tracking, which wasn't too surprising since he'd only been with the family for a few hectic hours.

Mitch was about to leave the boys and go chasing after the wayward animal when Bree screeched, "Oh, no!" and dashed madly across the smooth floor.

She was really moving when her bare feet hit the rain puddle he and the boys had left. She started to slide, arms thrown out for balance, looking for all the world like a surfer hanging ten only without a surfboard or wave.

Mitch shouted, "Look out!"

Ryan punched the air over his head and hollered, "All right!" Bud clutched his teddy bear to his chest and wailed, "Barney! Barney!"

Brianne's slide ended abruptly when she came to the edge of the slippery area. She staggered forward and almost fell flat on her face.

To Mitch's relief, she regained her balance in time to overtake the shaggy little dog before it had walked three paces onto the cream-colored carpeting. He breathed a sigh.

The sense of relief didn't last a millisecond. Barney was cringing. Poor pup must have been scared to death by all the noise, and now…

"Careful! Don't scare him!" Mitch shouted. The warning came too late.

The moment Brianne reached down to grab the little dog he whimpered, shied and made a fresh puddle of his own. Right on her precious carpet!

Fortunately, by biting the inside of his lower lip, Mitch was able to keep from laughing out loud. Just barely.

By the time Mitch got his children showered and dressed in the makeshift outfits Bree had delivered to the luxurious bathroom, he was totally exhausted. He was also the only one who wasn't clean, which meant he and the dog were probably still persona non grata in the rest of the house.

His biggest problem was what to do next. He'd already offered to shampoo the soiled carpet, but he couldn't even do that much until he got himself clean and dry or he'd only make matters worse.

The boys were whooping it up so loudly he almost missed hearing the knock on the bathroom door.

He shushed them. "Yes?"

"It's me, Mr. Fowler. Brianne. I've looked everywhere and I can't find anything for you to wear. What if I wash your wet things with the other clothes and get them back to you as soon as possible?"

"I suppose that beats staying in here till morning," he answered. "Hold on. I'll toss them out."

"Hey, Dad, can we go with her?" Ryan asked. "There's nothin' fun to do in here."

Mitch was about to deny his request when Bree said, "If the boys are showered and dressed they're welcome to come out. I have cookies in the kitchen, and it's no trouble at all to make up some hot chocolate."

"Well… I don't know."

"I'm sure they'll be fine without you for an hour or so."

Although he was anything but certain she was right, he gave in to the chorus of pleas that followed the mention of cocoa and cookies. "All right. Simmer down. You can go. But Barney stays here. And if you guys cause any trouble you'll have to settle with me the minute I get my clothes back. Is that understood?"

Two small heads nodded soberly. That wasn't nearly enough to negate Mitch's misgivings, but it would have to do.

"Okay."

He stripped off his muddy jeans and wadded them into a ball with his pajama top, grateful he'd left his pajama bottoms on underneath the jeans when he'd dressed in such a hurry.

Hiding behind the bathroom door, Mitch peered around it far enough to toss his clothes onto the pile with the other washing.

Bree waited nearby.

He smiled at her. "If the kids give you any grief, march them right back in here, and I'll take over."

"It's a deal."

She was amazed when she saw the boys parading out. They looked positively angelic! Their hair was slicked back, their feet were bare, and the shorts and T-shirts she'd found for them were so roomy they made the children seem even smaller than they actually were.

The contrast between the way they looked now and the way they'd looked when they'd arrived was truly miraculous. The younger one was holding a scruffy teddy bear, which had obviously had a bath, too.

She paused and smiled, assessing the boys looking at her with such expectant expressions. How darling! Mitch Fowler must be awfully cynical to imagine that such cute kids would cause trouble. He probably didn't have a clue how to handle them properly, the poor little things.

"Come on. This way," Bree said, starting off. Ryan, Bud and Bud's teddy bear followed obediently.

When they got to the kitchen, Bree helped Bud crawl into a chair, then smiled with satisfaction. This wasn't so bad, was it? Maybe their short stay wasn't going to upset her routine as much as she'd thought. After all, she didn't dare use her computer during inclement weather anyway, and as soon as the skies cleared they'd all go home, and she could get back to work without any more distraction.

Satisfied, she placed a napkin in front of each boy and laid two cookies in the center. "Hot chocolate coming up."

"I want whipped cream on mine," Ryan ordered.

"Sorry, I don't have any whipped cream."

To Bree's surprise, Bud immediately began to

whimper while his brother made a sour face and turned sullen. Apparently, the boys' cute, agreeable phase was over already. Oh, well.

"I like to float those little tiny marshmallows in my hot chocolate," she said brightly. "I'll put some in your cups, and you can tell me if you like them, too."

"I hate mush mellows," Ryan said.

"Not mush. Marshmallows."

Crossing to the table, she dropped several of the small, rounded balls of candy fluff onto the napkins with the boys' cookies. "There you go. That's what they look like. You can eat them just like that. When they're floating in hot cocoa they melt and get really good and gooey."

The children were still sitting there, pouting and staring at the napkins, when Bree set their mugs on the table. "Okay. Here's your drink. It's hot. Sip it slowly so you don't burn yourselves. And be careful not to get melted marshmallow stuck to the end of your nose. That always happens to me."

She sipped at the contents of her mug with theatrical relish, then licked her lips and set the drink aside.

"I'm going to go start the washing machine so you can have your regular clothes back," she said. "I won't be gone long."

Eyeing Ryan's defiant expression, she decided it

would be prudent to add, "If you move off those chairs or do anything except eat and drink while I'm out of the kitchen, I'll have to put you back in with your daddy like he said. Got that?"

Neither boy spoke, but Bree was certain they both understood. Headstrong Ryan was giving her a dirty look, and Bud was clutching his teddy bear so tightly it was leaving a damp spot on the front of his T-shirt.

As soon as Mitch was alone he wasted no time stripping and jumping into the shower. Thanks to the raging storm, the kids had only picked up a few ticks on their trek up the hill, but as far as he was concerned, one was too many. No doubt the boys would be itching like crazy by tomorrow. The power of suggestion was already doing a number on him.

He soaped and scrubbed from head to foot. If he couldn't dig his car out of the mud in the morning he'd borrow transportation and run into town to buy something to kill whatever bugs had taken up residence in Barney's thick coat—and in the cabin. Until then, he'd see that the little dog stayed confined to this one room of his hostess's home to avoid contaminating it, too.

Mitch was chuckling when he stepped out of the shower and began to towel himself dry.

Panting, the little dog looked at him with shining ebony eyes and cocked its head.

"Yes, I was thinking about you," Mitch said. That was all the attention it took for the pup to begin wagging its tail so hard its whole rear end wiggled with delight. "You, and the lady who owns this place. I'll bet she'd have a fit if she knew we'd probably brought bugs into her fancy house."

Barney whirled in tight circles at Mitch's feet.

"Yeah, yeah, I know. You're so adorable you can get away with just about anything. Like those kids of mine. I hate to have to start out by being tough with them but I know they need discipline. Desperately."

The little dog's antics heightened to include a frenzied dash around the room. Mitch said, "Whoa. Come here." He held out his hand, and the dog skidded to a stop and looked at him with clear devotion.

He bent to pet it. Barney threw himself on the floor at the man's feet and rolled onto his back in complete surrender.

Mitch laughed as he scratched the dog's exposed belly. "Now that's the kind of love and respect I want from my boys. I wish they were as easy to win over as you are, little guy."

Barney licked his hand.

"Yeah, all I have to do is figure out a way to show them how much I care, prove how much I've missed them, and make them behave—all at the same time."

He snorted in derision. "The way things have been going, I figure that shouldn't take more than twenty or thirty years."

When Bree returned, the cookies and cocoa were gone and Bud was sporting a sticky chocolate mustache. She could tell the children were fighting sleep.

"Okay, guys. Time for bed," she said. "Use your napkins to wipe off your faces and hands, and let's go upstairs." Thankfully, there was no suggestion of rebellion this time.

Ryan made the choice of sleeping arrangements for himself and his brother. "We don't need separate beds. We're used to sleepin' together," he said matter-of-factly. "He'd get scared if he woke up and I wasn't there. You know how it is."

Brianne smiled. "Actually, I don't. I never had any brothers or sisters."

"Who'd you play with?" The eight-year-old looked astounded. Mimicking her motions, he turned down one edge of the embroidered coverlet while Bree did the same on the opposite side of the double bed.

"I had a few friends I used to hang out with," she said. "We'd jump rope or swim or maybe go shopping together."

"Girl stuff. Didn't you ever wrestle or play ball on a team or nothin'?"

"Afraid not. My father tried to teach me to play baseball like a boy, but I never managed to please him."

"Bet you didn't even have a dog, huh?"

"No. My father didn't like animals very much, either." She grew pensive. "There was a stray cat I made friends with once. It was gray, with white paws and a white star on its chest. By being very patient, I finally managed to get it to trust me enough to take food out of my hand."

"What happened to it?"

"I don't know. It disappeared."

"Probably died," he said sagely. Pausing, he lowered his voice and added, "So did our mother."

"I know. Your father told me. I'm sorry."

The boy opened his mouth as if to speak, then quickly shut it and looked away.

Brianne helped Bud climb into bed. She stood aside so Ryan could join him before she carefully pulled the sheet over them both. Bud curled into a ball around his teddy bear, his eyes tightly shut. Ryan looked at her.

She tenderly stroked his damp hair off his forehead. "If you ever decide you want to talk about your mother, I'll be glad to listen."

"There's nothin' to talk about. She's dead. That's all there is to it."

Bree could see his lower lip quivering in spite of

his tough-guy affectation. Of course he was hurting. He was a little boy who'd spent the past few years of his short life mostly with his mother. And now she was gone. Forever. There must be some way to comfort him.

"Maybe you'll see your mother in heaven some day," she offered. To her chagrin, Ryan's eyes began to fill with tears.

"That stuff's for suckers," he said, swallowing a sob.

Perched on the edge of the bed, Brianne took his small hand and gazed at him. No matter how lost, how far from God she'd felt since her mother's death, she knew she should try to give the child some semblance of hope. "Oh, honey, Jesus said heaven was real. Who told you it wasn't?"

"My mama."

"How about your daddy? What does he think?"

Ryan shook his head. "Mama said he was stupid 'cause he believed all that ch-church stuff."

"I see."

Brianne's vision misted with tears of empathy, of sympathy, for everyone involved. She wished mightily for the words to reassure the grieving child but found none. There was no way to go back and change things for Ryan and his brother, any more than she could change the painful facts of her mother's demise, no matter how much she wanted to. All she could do at this point was continue to offer honest compassion and hope for the best.

She leaned down to kiss his cheek, then stood. "Go to sleep, honey. You've had a rough night. I'll see you in the morning, okay?"

The child sniffled and nodded.

"Good. Sleep tight."

Fleeing the room, Bree barely made it to the hallway before tears spilled out to trickle down her cheeks. She leaned against the wall and dashed them away.

"Those poor children. What can I do? How can I help them?"

Thoughts of turning to prayer immediately assailed her. She disregarded the urge. All the prayers in the world hadn't helped her come to grips with her mother's suicide. Where had God been when she'd been a lost, grieving twelve-year-old, weeping for the one person who had truly loved her? How could she hope to help anyone else cope with tragedy when she hadn't been able to help herself?

The only positive thing was what Ryan had said about his father. If Mitch Fowler was committed to Christ enough to raise his late wife's ire, that was a definite plus. At least he'd be able to counsel his children based on his personal faith, which was a whole lot better than the self-centered reactions she'd gotten from her father in the midst of her despair.

Bree didn't see the Bible as a magical cure-all the way some people did, as in, "Take two verses and call the doctor in the morning," but she did believe it could be useful for sorting out life's problems, including how best to raise kids. And judging by what she'd learned so far, Mitch was going to need all the help he could get, human or otherwise.

Bree pushed away from the wall and straightened. Though she didn't understand what her part in the children's healing might be, she felt included somehow.

That, alone, was a miracle.

A rather disturbing one.

Chapter Four

Deep in thought and barely watching where she was going, Bree almost crashed into Mitch at the base of the stairway. "Oh! You startled me!"

"I didn't mean to," Mitch said. He grinned amiably and propped one shoulder against the archway leading into the kitchen. "I heard the buzzer on the dryer. Nobody seemed to be around so I fished my clothes out, got dressed and came looking for the boys."

"They're upstairs, asleep."

"Which is where you'd be, too, if we hadn't showed up. I really am sorry."

"It's okay," Bree said.

The only clear thought she could muster was that it should be illegal for any man to look as casually appealing as Mitch Fowler did at that moment. His dark hair was tousled. His jeans were snug from the clothes dryer. And his clean short-sleeve pajama top left altogether too much arm muscle showing.

"I still feel responsible. At least let me clean up the mess we made by the front door."

"That's not necessary. I already soaked up the water. I have a woman who comes in twice a week to clean. She'll polish all the floors when she comes on Thursday. Nobody but me will see them till then."

"You live here all alone?" He was frowning. "In this great big house?"

"Yes."

Bree hurried past him into the kitchen, knowing without a doubt that he'd follow. She opened the refrigerator to check her food supplies, using the door as a convenient physical barrier between them. "Do you think you'll be staying for breakfast?"

"I hadn't thought about it. Are we invited?"

"If you like pancakes, you are," she said, leaning in. "I usually eat an omelette, but I seem to be a bit short of eggs."

"You're sure we won't be a bother?"

Bree had been bending to peer behind a carton of milk and hadn't heard him clearly when he'd spoken. The low rumble of his voice had, however, sent a shiver zinging up her spine. She straightened abruptly to ask, "What?" and found him standing close behind her. Very close.

Acting on instinct, she held her breath to listen for his answer. If her pulse hadn't been hammering in her head like the percussion section of an overzealous high school band, she might have been able to hear what he was saying. Not that her befuddled brain could have translated his words into relevant concepts.

Her senses were bombarded by his clean, masculine scent, his overpowering presence and his exhilarating voice. Plus, his warm breath was tickling the tiny hairs behind her ear. Considering all that, Brianne figured she was lucky to remain standing, let alone hope to make sense of anything he said.

Awed by her reaction to his innocent nearness, she wanted to climb into the refrigerator and pull the door shut behind her. Instead, she sidled away and rounded the center island workstation to put something more solid between her and the attractive man.

Mitch paused and watched her, his stance wide, his arms folded across his broad chest. "I'm not dangerous, you know."

"Of course you're not! Whatever gave you the idea that I thought so?"

"You did. The way you're acting. I had no idea you were here all alone. And I didn't cook up some nefarious plan to steal the silver or kidnap the rich heiress, if that's what you're thinking. Believe me, I'd much rather be back home in my cabin, sleeping peacefully and listening to the rain drumming on the tin roof."

"I—I'm sure you would."

"Then if you'll just tell me where my boys are, I'll go and join them."

He sounded put out. Brianne did her best to keep her voice pleasant. "First door on the right, top of the stairs. There are two double beds in that room. I hope it's okay. Ryan picked it out."

"It'll be fine."

"The boys are sharing. If you need more room, the sofa makes into another bed, and there's extra linen on the shelves in the walk-in closet. Make yourself at home."

"Thanks." Mitch started to leave, then paused. "Forget about breakfast. We'll be out of your hair first thing in the morning."

"There's no need to rush off."

"Thanks, but now that I think about it, I want to see how badly the cabin is damaged and dig my car out so I can go to town for more supplies. The earlier I get started, the better. That is, providing the rain has stopped by then."

"Wait a minute. What about the boys? You don't intend to drag them around in the woods with you like you did tonight, do you? I can watch them for you." Bree couldn't believe the idiotic offer she'd just blurted out!

"They're not babies."

Oh, well, in for a penny, in for a pound. "They're still way too young to be traipsing up and down hills with you like they're on some lost safari."

"Good point." Mitch considered alternatives for a moment while he searched for truth in Brianne's beautiful blue eyes. Maybe she hadn't been trying to get rid of him the way he'd thought. She *was* right about some things, like the boys' physical limitations.

"Okay," he said, "I might have breakfast here, then go out alone, if you wouldn't mind keeping the kids for a couple of hours."

"Of course not," she said, amazed that she honestly meant it. "They were wonderful tonight."

Mitch snorted a wry chuckle. "Are we talking about the same two—an eight-year-old with a giant chip on his shoulder and a six-year-old with a teddy-bear fixation?"

"Sounds like the ones I met. What I don't understand is how you could let their mother just take them away from you the way she did."

"It's a long story."

"I have all night."

He decided it wouldn't hurt to at least try to explain. "When I met Liz I thought she was the most amazing woman I'd ever known, always fun to be with, always exciting. I didn't realize she was also unstable and flighty. Unfortunately, once she got it into her head that she'd be happier away from me, she was almost impossible to locate. She was too unpredictable."

Even from halfway across the room, Bree could see the muscles of his jaw clenching. Perhaps she shouldn't have probed so deeply but she was interested in learning more about the children's lives. "That's it?"

"Pretty much."

"What about school? Didn't Ryan go to school?"

"Not often. He'll have some catching up to do this year but he's smart. He can do it. Bud was too young until recently, so he didn't miss as much."

"How about getting them a tutor?"

"Why? Were you planning on funding a private recovery effort?" There was a stubborn edge to his voice when he added, "I assure you, Ms. Bailey, I can take care of my family without anybody else's help."

If he had been the only one involved, Bree wouldn't have considered speaking her mind. It would have been easier to simply give up and walk away. It would also have been wrong. Like it or not, she found herself in a position to aid those poor little boys, and she intended to take every advantage of it. If that included alienating their hardheaded father for their sakes, so be it.

She boldly rounded the end of the workstation island and approached him. "It's not what you think that matters, Mr. Fowler. What's important is what's best for your sons. Don't let your pride keep you from accepting whatever assistance comes your way."

Mitch made a rumbling sound low in his throat and shook his head. "Since you seem to have all the answers, suppose you tell me how to get those three years of my boys' lives back."

"Believe me, if I had the ability to fix the past, your children aren't the only ones I'd help."

"You think I need fixing, too, I suppose?"

"Actually, you may," Bree said with the lift of an eyebrow and a wry smile, "but I happened to be referring to myself just now."

"Oh?"

"Never mind. It's not important."

Heading for the doorway, she'd planned to walk out past him. If the overhead lights hadn't flickered at that moment she would have kept going. Instead, she hesitated and sucked in a quick breath. "What was that?"

"The storm is probably causing power problems," Mitch said calmly. "It's not unusual up here in the hills."

Losing her electricity and having to grope around in a pitch-dark house alone didn't frighten her one bit. Having to do it with Mitch Fowler underfoot, however, was a decidedly unsettling thought!

"Everything is unusual here," she said. "For such beautiful country, the Ozark Mountains certainly have a lot of drawbacks."

"That's a matter of opinion. If you had a gas generator for backup, like I do, you wouldn't have to worry about whether or not you lost power."

Bree huffed in mock disgust. "I don't suppose you brought your generator with you."

"It's much too heavy to carry," Mitch said as if explaining to a simpleton. "Don't you have a flashlight?"

"Yes! I know there's one around here somewhere. Let me see…" Turning in a slow circle, Brianne frowned. "I think I may have put it in the pantry."

"Then I suggest you go get it." He looked at the lights as they flickered repeatedly. "Soon."

Bree had traveled less than three paces when the lights flashed one more time. Then everything went black.

"Don't move," Mitch warned. "Let your eyes adjust to the darkness first."

"I know that." Tension was making her sound waspish.

"Excuse me. I was just trying to help."

"I know that, too," Bree said. "You stay put. I'm used to this place. I can find my way around."

"Make use of the lightning. You'll be able to see a little better when it flashes. It'll help you get your bearings."

"Is that more of your homesteading wisdom?"

Mitch chuckled softly. "No. Just plain male logic. Something women don't understand."

She was glad he couldn't see the exasperated face she was making at him. "Next, you'll be telling me that female logic is an oxymoron."

"Isn't it?"

If Mitch hadn't known he was in the company of a well-bred, refined lady he'd have sworn he heard her give him a raspberry!

The sky outside the kitchen windows was alive. Clouds glowed a misty gray, dimming and brightening unevenly as if lit from behind by some monstrous, out-of-control searchlight.

Brianne knew which direction to walk, she just wasn't sure how many steps remained between her and the pantry. Extending her arms in front of her so she wouldn't hit anything headlong, she groped her way toward the door.

Mitch waited and watched as best he could. She reminded him of a sleepwalker being illuminated by a strobe light, and he wasn't comfortable with what little he could discern. What was she doing? Didn't she see the door?

He blurted, "Look out!"

"What?" Bree turned her head in his direction. That moment's inattention was a mistake. Before another flash came to guide her, she'd jammed the end of her middle finger into the leading edge of the half-open pantry door.

"Ouch!"

"That's what I was trying to warn you about," Mitch said. He reached her side quickly, touched her arm lightly. "Are you all right?"

"No. It hurts."

"I figured that much," he said wryly. "Let me see it."

Brianne allowed him to take her hand, but only because it would have been silly to pitch a fit or try to evade him in the dark. "See it? How do you propose to see anything? In case you haven't noticed, there's no light in here."

To her dismay he began using his hands instead of his eyes to survey her sore finger, bring another ouch.

"Does it hurt when I do this?"

"It hurts, period," she said, tugging against his firm grasp. "Quit trying to help so much, okay?"

"You are the most stubborn woman I've ever met."

His exasperation amused her. "Thank you. I do my best."

"You should put ice on that finger, just in case,"

Mitch said, caressing her hand as he spoke. "The joints might be swollen by morning if you don't."

It was all she could do to continue to sound flippant while he was stroking her injury so tenderly. "I'll live. But thanks for your concern."

The overhead lights suddenly came on, temporarily blinding her. She blinked, squinted against the glare, looked down. Her finger didn't appear to be injured at all, now that she could see it.

Before Mitch could argue, she jerked her hand from his grasp and held it up. "I'm fine. See? Well, I'd better run while the lights are working."

"What about the flashlight?"

"Don't need it now."

"What if you do later?"

Already through the door into the hall, she ignored his question and called, "Good night."

Mitch stood there dumbfounded, watching her retreat and wondering why she was in such an all-fired hurry. What made her tick, anyway?

Pondering that thought, he frowned. She had sounded serious when she'd talked about the past, about wishing she could go back and fix her old problems, but given what he already knew about her, her negative attitude didn't make any sense. The past was past. Gone. Beyond changing. Everybody knew that.

Besides, what kind of terrible problems could a beautiful, wealthy woman like Brianne Bailey possibly have? Certainly none as serious as the ones he'd been dealing with for the past three years. No kidding!

Comparing their lives, he pictured her and smiled. The woman had everything—looks, money, a career, a beautiful place to live. Yes, she was alone, but she didn't have to be. She seemed to prefer solitude.

Boy, not him. Mitch knew he wouldn't trade having his boys with him for all the money in the world. Finding them had cost him dearly, both emotionally and monetarily, yet he'd do it all again, and then some, if necessary.

His gut clenched. God, he loved those kids. Being separated from them had been the worst thing that had ever happened to him.

And it had also been one of the best, he added with chagrin. When he'd been at the end of his rope, at the end of his endurance with nowhere to turn, he'd looked to God for strength and answers. He shuddered to think what would have become of him if he hadn't decided to trust the Lord then. There had been times when he'd doubted, sure, but over time he'd come to realize that things really were going to work out for the best.

Maybe not the way he'd imagined. Maybe not as

fast as he'd have wanted, either. But they had worked out. He and the boys were together. Life was good. From here on out, it could only get better.

Chapter Five

Distant, shrill yapping woke Brianne at dawn. Talk about a short night! Between listening to the awful storm and worrying about her houseguests, she doubted she'd gotten three hours rest.

She rubbed sleep out of her eyes, padded barefoot to her bedroom window and gazed at the wide expanse of lawn. Thankfully, the rain had stopped. Mitch and Ryan were romping on the damp grass with their dog.

Good thing somebody had remembered to let that little monster out, Bree thought. She'd been so distracted by her late-night encounter with Mitch Fowler she'd forgotten all about Barney. She hoped the guest bathroom wasn't going to have to be redecorated after serving as a temporary kennel.

Brianne dressed quickly, concerned that Bud was

also awake and might be running around the house unsupervised. By the time she reached the head of the stairs, however, she realized she needn't have worried. The children's bed was empty, and laughter was drifting up from the first floor. Above the giggles she could hear the musical sound of television cartoons.

Already planning breakfast in her head, Bree went directly to the kitchen and began assembling the basic ingredients for pancakes. Thankfully, the instructions were written on the box of mix, or she'd have been lost.

She'd rarely cooked for anyone but herself, nor had she ventured beyond the most simple fare. If she wanted a more elaborate meal she waited until one of Emma's regular visits and had the accomplished housekeeper fix a big dinner with plenty of leftovers that would last for several days. Not only did it simplify Brianne's daily chores, it gave her nutritious food to fall back on if, as often happened, she got so engrossed in her writing that she forgot to defrost anything.

Now, however, she was faced with feeding a full-grown man who looked like he could easily consume three times the amount she usually did, and two boys who were so fussy they might refuse to eat anything at all. Given those considerations, she hoped plain pancakes were going to be satisfactory.

She had the batter mixed and was heating the griddle when Mitch and Ryan returned from exercising the dog.

"Smells great," Mitch said with enthusiasm.

"I'm not cooking anything yet."

"You will be." His grin warmed her from head to toe. "How's your hand this morning? Any soreness?"

"No. I'd forgotten all about it."

"Good. Can I help you do anything?"

The offer took Bree aback. So did his dazzling smile. "Oh, well… I suppose you could set the table. My everyday dishes are in that cupboard over there."

"Gotcha. I'll find 'em." He handed Barney off to his eldest son. "Go put the dog in the bathroom and wash your hands while you're in there. Then get your brother."

To Bree's surprise, Ryan didn't argue. She arched a brow as she watched him quickly leave the kitchen. "That was easy."

Mitch chuckled. "We'll see. He hasn't followed my directions yet. I need to wash, too, so I'll go check on him. Be right back."

Her instinctive, unspoken retort was, Don't hurry. It was hard enough to concentrate on cooking when she was alone. Having Mitch underfoot made it a hundred times harder. That was one of the reasons she'd chosen to make pancakes. They were simple. You just fried them and stacked them up. No sweat.

She spread a thin coating of oil on the griddle, then poured four circles of batter. So far, so good. Maybe she wasn't going to botch breakfast after all. Hurrah!

It had occurred to her to wonder briefly why she was so concerned about making a favorable impression. Her guests had arrived looking and acting like shipwreck survivors. Under those circumstances they could hardly find fault with her hospitality, even if she didn't feed them anything fancy. So cooking was not her forte. So what? As far as she was concerned it was far better to provide well-prepared, simple fare than to try to make something complicated and chance failure.

The stack of cooked pancakes had grown so tall by the time Mitch and the boys returned, Brianne had put one plate on the table and started to fill another. Mitch immediately went to work setting the table and assigning seats.

"The syrup is in the pantry," she told him. "It's that room over there. Where I hit my finger last night."

Ryan jumped to his feet. "I'll go get it!"

"No. You sit. I'll get it as soon as I pour your milk," his father said.

"Aw."

Flipping the pancakes that were sizzling on the grill, Bree had to chuckle to herself. That sounded more like the Ryan Fowler she knew. The kid was a study in defiance. Attached to his personality, the word *stubborn* took on a much more intense meaning.

"I made a pot of coffee, too," Bree told Mitch. "I didn't know if you liked it or not, but I do."

"Me, too."

His voice seemed farther away and muffled. She glanced over her shoulder. The pantry door stood open, and he was nowhere to be seen.

A second later, he stuck his head out. "Where did you say the syrup was?"

"It's in there somewhere. I'm not sure exactly. I don't eat pancakes that often."

Mitch disappeared again. "I don't see it. But I did run across the flashlight we were looking for last night. It's on the shelf just to the left of the door, about shoulder height, in case you want it."

"I want syrup," Ryan whined.

Frustrated, Bree left the stove and hurried across the kitchen. "I know the bottle's in there. It has to be."

"Okay." With a shrug, Mitch stepped aside. "Show me."

It didn't help that the pantry was barely big enough to accommodate them both. Bree sidled past him, rapidly scanning the shelves and wondering why the room temperature had suddenly risen dramatically.

She brushed her hand across her damp forehead to push back her bangs and made a sound of disgust. "This can't be. Syrup bottles don't just walk off." In the background she could hear Ryan complaining. Mitch, however, seemed amused at her predicament.

"We can always eat them with butter and sugar," he suggested. "That should taste good."

Brianne rolled her eyes. "I have regular maple syrup. Somewhere. All I have to do is figure out where."

"Hey, Dad," Ryan shouted.

Mitch answered, "In a minute. We're still looking."

"Dad!"

"Not now, Ryan."

"But, Dad…"

"Ryan, if you don't…"

Mitch stuck his head out the door for emphasis, then bolted from the pantry with a guttural noise that reminded Bree of his attitude the first time he'd banged on her door. That was when she smelled the smoke.

Her first thought was that the boys had set her kitchen on fire. One quick peek, however, told her that the error was hers.

Black smoke was billowing from the griddle and what was left of the pancakes she'd temporarily forgotten to tend. Mitch had grabbed a towel and wrapped it around the handle so he could move the flat pan off the stove and into the sink without getting burned. If the ventilating fan hadn't already been turned on to clear the air as she cooked, they probably wouldn't have been able to see across the room.

So much for the perfect breakfast. Disappointed, Bree stood there and shook her head. Bedlam reigned. Ryan was screeching. Bud was sobbing. Mitch was muttering to himself and running cold water over the steaming, smoking mess as well as using the stream to cool his smarting fingers.

It was in the midst of all the distraction that Bree remembered where she'd last seen the syrup bottle. In the refrigerator. With a sigh she retrieved it and set it in the middle of the table.

"Leave that for later," she told Mitch. "I found the syrup. Come and eat."

He turned with a scowl. "Where was it?"

"In the fridge."

"Terrific."

"My sentiments, exactly. It probably won't surprise you to hear that I don't cook often."

"No kidding."

"You don't have to rub it in."

"Sorry." A smile began to lift one corner of his mouth. "Are you through cooking for now, or shall I go get the garden hose and bring it inside just in case?"

"I'm through." She put on a mock pout.

"In that case, I guess it's safe for me to sit down." Taking the only empty chair, Mitch proceeded to serve the boys, then pass a platter to Bree.

She took two cakes and handed it back to him. "Can I get you some coffee? I made plenty."

"Thanks. I take it black."

"Coming up."

She'd poured Mitch's cup and was about to add a dash of cream to her own when she saw Ryan reach for more syrup and tip over his glass of milk. He let out a screech that sounded like a deranged owl caught under a lawnmower.

The white puddle spread rapidly across the table, pooled around the bases of glasses and disappeared under the plates.

Mitch immediately jumped to his feet, juggling the boys' breakfasts to rescue them and glaring at his son.

Bree grabbed a handful of paper towels and rushed to the source of the mess. She righted the empty tumbler and dabbed at the milk.

While she was mopping up Ryan's place, a rivulet of spilled milk reached the far edge of the round table and began to dribble into Bud's lap. When he saw that his resident teddy bear was getting wet he clutched it to his chest and screeched in pure anguish.

Mitch shifted both plates to one hand long enough to grab the back of the boy's chair and slide it away from the table. That helped. Milk continued to drip, but Bud was no longer directly in its path.

The paper towels Bree had started with were thoroughly saturated. She held them in place like a dam and reached her free hand to Mitch.

"Get me more towels. Quick! Before this runs all over the floor."

"Too late," he said, glancing at the spattered tile. "Don't worry. Ryan will clean it up."

"It wasn't my fault the stupid milk fell over," the boy argued.

Mitch was about to contradict him when he noticed movement below. He blinked, stared, shouted, "Hey! Who let the dog out?"

"The what?" Bree peered under the table. Her eyes widened. Barney was not only licking up the spill, he was standing directly beneath a waterfall of milk that was splashing his head and back. "What's he doing in here?"

Ryan jumped down, dropped to his hands and knees and went into action. "No sweat, lady. I'll get him."

"No! Don't chase him, he'll…"

The dog darted through the archway and disappeared in a blur. Ryan was in hot pursuit.

Left behind, Bree shouted, "Don't you dare let him shake!"

By this time, Bud had quieted down. He was making questionable use of his napkin, alternating between drying his bear and wiping his runny nose.

"Paper towels! Now!" Bree yelled at Mitch.

His answer didn't sound a bit amiable. "Stop screaming."

"How else can I make myself understood with all this noise? I've never heard anything like it."

"Hey, the kids didn't set the place on fire. You did."

"Only because I got distracted helping you," she argued. "I'll take care of this mess. You go help Ryan catch that blasted dog before he trails milk all over the house."

Mitch stiffened and gave her a mock salute. "Yes, ma'am. Don't throw the extra pancakes away while I'm gone. We'll put sugar on them, roll them up and take them outside to eat."

"I wish you'd thought of that in the first place," Bree grumbled.

Scowling, he nodded. "Yeah. Me, too."

The impromptu picnic took place half an hour later. Mitch had buttered the pancakes, warmed them in the microwave, then added sugar before rolling them up and wrapping one end in a paper napkin.

His children seemed relieved to be eating outside. He certainly was. The less time he was forced to spend inside Brianne Bailey's oh-so-perfect house, the better he'd like it. No wonder the boys couldn't seem to stay out of trouble. Hanging around the estate was like trying to live in a pristine model home without giving away your presence.

Everything was arranged artistically, from the books on the coffee table to the pots and pans hanging in the kitchen. Little wonder she lived alone. No one else would be able to put up for long with her suffocating ideals.

Mitch saw that the dog was starting to wander off toward the forest, followed closely by both boys, so he called, "Hey! Don't go too far."

Naturally, all three ignored him. He wasn't surprised about Barney, but the other two were supposed to listen. Rather than bellow at them when he didn't have to, he decided to follow and see what they were up to.

They'd halted at the edge of the pond Mitch had objected to when he'd met Bree. The first thing he noticed was that Ryan was teaching his brother how to pitch rocks into the void.

The second thing he noted was the void. After the storm they'd had last night, that pond should have been full, or nearly so. Instead, it was little more than a brown puddle in the bottom of a clay-walled crater.

Mitch's heart sank. The dam hadn't held. And his

cabin was at the bottom of that hill. At least it had been. No wonder the water had come at them so fast and hard!

Brianne was still cleaning up the aftermath of the disaster in her kitchen when Mitch burst through the door. Startled by the wild look on his face, she froze in mid-motion. "What's wrong?"

"Remember that new pond? The one I was complaining about when we first met?"

"Yes." Keeping her wet hands suspended over the sink, Brianne scowled. "What about it?"

"It's gone. Empty. Your dam's got a hole in it big enough to drive a bus through."

"That's impossible. I hired a professional to do the grading. He came highly recommended."

"Oh, yeah? Well, it looks like the wind knocked a big tree onto the spillway. The water backed up till it was forced out the wrong side of the dam. Without any natural vegetation to strengthen that clay bank once it started to wash, nothing could have stopped it."

"Oh, no." Brianne's heart felt like it was lodged in her throat. Hands trembling, she looked out the door past the angry man. "Where are the kids?"

"Outside. I'll need you to watch them while I hike down to the cabin—or what's left of it. Looks like that water cleared everything out of the canyon.

You can still see where some of the tree roots pulled right up out of the ground."

Brianne closed her eyes for a moment and tried to imagine the probable results of an onslaught like that. "What about your cabin? Do you think it's okay?"

Shaking his head, Mitch answered without hedging. "Not a chance. That's why I want to go check it out by myself. No sense scaring the kids if I don't have to."

"Of course not."

His shoulders sagged momentarily. "We must have a real busy guardian angel. If we'd stayed home last night we'd have gotten a lot muddier than we were when we showed up here."

Reading the veiled anxiety in his gaze before he turned away, Bree knew exactly what he meant. Mitch's whole family could have been wiped out while they slept. And because it was her dam that had failed, their loss would have been her fault!

She dried her hands and followed him outside. "If it turns out as bad as you think, I'll make full restitution, I promise."

The look he gave her was unreadable. He said, "Lady, possessions don't matter to me. All I care about is my boys. Just look after them for a little while and try not to set your house on fire while I'm gone. Okay?"

* * *

What do you do with two restless little boys and a hyperactive dog? Bree found the answer to that question by letting them continue to play outside. Unfortunately, it began to drizzle before a half hour had passed.

She called, "Over here!" motioned for them to follow, and ran for cover beneath the patio overhang.

"We can't play in the rain," she said, gathering her ragtag little group together. "We'll wait here for a few minutes and see if it stops, okay?"

To her relief, no one argued. Bud hunkered close beside her to shelter himself and his bear. Ryan shrugged and plopped down in a nearby garden chair.

Barney, however, was not happy to be still for more than a few seconds. Springing off the ground, he grabbed Bud's teddy bear in his sharp little teeth and took off running.

Suddenly bearless, Bud let out a squeal that sounded like a baby piglet abruptly separated from its mama. Before Bree could do more than bend down to comfort the hysterical child, his older brother had darted into the rain, wrestled the stuffed toy away from the dog and returned it.

Brianne smiled at the eight-year-old. "Thanks."

"No problem. The kid's nuts about that bear, so I help him keep an eye on it."

"I can see he is." She laid her hand on Bud's damp curls and absently stroked the hair off his forehead. "I suppose it's natural for you boys to want to hang on to things that make you feel secure. It must be rough coming to live with your daddy after such a long time."

"It's okay," Ryan muttered, shrugging as he spoke. "Not like we had a choice or anything."

"I don't think your father did, either," Bree reminded him.

The boy made a guttural sound of disgust. "He didn't have to sell our house and make us live in a dump."

"You mean in the cabin?"

"Yeah. It doesn't even have a bathroom."

"Well, then, maybe it was for the best that you had problems last night. I'll bet there's something better waiting for you."

"Right."

She couldn't have missed the boy's sarcasm if she'd been blindfolded and wearing earplugs. "Sounds like you don't think so. Why not?"

"'Cause Dad spent all his money lookin' for us."

"How do you know?"

"He said so."

Brianne's stomach knotted. That was exactly the kind of dire economic situation she'd feared Mitch Fowler was in. The probable loss of his cabin and its contents was the final straw. If anybody ever needed financial aid, he did. The hardest part would be convincing him to accept it. As soon as he came back for the boys, she planned to have a serious talk with him.

Barney started barking, then ran and hid behind Ryan. Bree attributed the dog's nervousness to distant thunder, but in seconds the real reason was clear.

Soaking wet, Mitch lunged out of the forest, made a noise like a bear suffering a migraine and threw down an armload of muddy supplies. His face was even redder than it had been the first time Bree had seen him, meaning he was either totally spent from his hard climb or he was even more furious than before. Both theories were plausible. Either was likely.

Ordering the children to stay put, Brianne jogged across the wet lawn to speak with him privately.

"I'm glad you're back. The kids were getting bored. I'm surprised you made the trip so fast."

"It wasn't hard." Scowling, he wiped his muddy hands on his jeans and eyed the meager pile of belongings he'd brought up the hill. "See that? That's all there is left. I was lucky to salvage that much."

"Was there a lot of water damage to your cabin?"

"What cabin?"

"It's gone?" Until then, Bree had refused to let herself consider total destruction.

"Along with everything except what you see in front of you. Looks like a couple of big trees washed down the canyon and pushed the cabin off its foundation. After that, there was no way it could withstand the flood."

"It's all my fault. I'm so very sorry."

The intensity of the rain was increasing, and she paused to wipe her face with her hands and push her wet bangs out of her eyes. When she looked at Mitch he was bending over, picking up a handful of rags.

"We should get inside. Want me to help you carry that stuff?" she asked.

"No. I'll handle it. I'm already dirty, and you're not. But you're right about going back to the house. I've been hearing thunder in the distance. The way my luck's been running lately I'll probably be struck by lightning if I stay out here."

If he could make jokes in the midst of such a hopeless situation, he was probably not as angry as she'd thought. That was a good sign. It meant he'd be in a better frame of mind to accept the aid she planned to offer.

She led the way toward the overhang where the Fowler boys waited. Ryan had picked up the raggedy dog and had taken charge of his brother, too. All were present and accounted for. Even Bud's bear.

Rather than go inside through the French doors by

the patio and track mud into her library, Brianne circled to the rear of the house and stopped at the kitchen.

"Leave your wet shoes out here by the door and give your daddy the dog," she told the boys. "You can go turn the television on again if you want, just be sure you stick to watching kid shows."

As soon as she was sure they were following her orders she glanced at Mitch, wondering how to tactfully suggest that he hose down the dog—and himself—before coming inside. Her gaze settled on the muddy rags he was holding. "I'll dispose of that trash for you. Just drop it out there."

"Humph!" He snorted. "If I did I'd be throwing away the only extra clothes the kids and I have."

"Those are your clothes?"

"Yes. At least they'll give us a change. I figured that would beat my being stuck in your guest bathroom again. Old Barney's not much of a conversationalist."

"I suppose not."

Kicking clumps of red-clay mud off the sides of his boots, Mitch said, "I guess I should be thankful he's outgrown the chewing stage. So, tell me where the washing machine is, and I'll start a load."

"It's..." Purposely blocking the doorway, Brianne couldn't make herself move out of his way. She pulled a face as she scanned his full length. "Never mind. You can't come in like that. Take your boots off and leave them out here. I'll bring you a towel and washcloth." Her mouth twisted tighter at one corner. "Those jeans will just have to do until something else is washed and dried."

"You want me to stand out here in the rain? You really are picky, aren't you?"

"It's not picky to have an immaculate house and want to keep it that way. I wouldn't dream of coming into your house if I wasn't spotlessly clean."

Chuckling and shaking his head, Mitch sat on a step and started to unlace his hiking boots. "I don't think that'll be much of a problem for a while. At the moment, I don't seem to have a house to worry about getting dirty."

Chapter Six

Brianne measured the proper amount of laundry detergent into her gleaming white washing machine, then yielded to a strong impulse to add more soap.

Planning ahead while she worked, she closed the lid on Mitch's recovered clothes. The first thing she'd need to do was make a few calls and find him another place to live. Then she'd either offer to drive him down to get his car or arrange for a tow truck to pull it out so he'd have wheels again.

What if I can't find a new house for him right away? she asked herself. Don't say it. Don't even think it. Whatever happened, they weren't staying here. No way. The whole Fowler family was one big disaster waiting to get worse.

Brianne started toward her office while she mulled over the events that had dropped Mitch Fowler and his kids in her lap. The image of having two children sitting on her lap was amusing. And scary. As far as she could recall, this was the first time in her life she had ever imagined herself anywhere near children— anybody's children—let alone rambunctious little boys.

Makes me feel sticky already, Brianne thought. She suspected she'd be finding smears of pancake syrup here and there for months to come, and little maple-flavored fingerprints. How those kids managed to get any nourishment was a mystery. It seemed like most of their meal had wound up spilled on the table, the chair seats, the floor or the lawn. And no telling how much their scruffy dog had gobbled up. Or soaked up!

Having Mitch's family as guests in her home had certainly been interesting. It was going to take weeks to get the place straightened up and running smoothly again. Thank heavens their visit was almost over!

She seated herself at her desk, picked up the telephone and held the receiver to her ear. No dial tone. Hmm. Well, there was always the cellular phone she carried in her purse. She dug it out and began to dial.

When Mitch got himself cleaned up and came looking for her, she was in her office. The door was ajar so he knocked on the jamb. When Bree gazed at him, he could have sworn her eyes had the mesmerized look of a deer staring blankly into the headlights of an oncoming car.

"What's wrong?" he asked.

"I couldn't find you another house."

"Is that all? Hey, don't worry. We'll make do. I've got a little…"

"No—no road."

"Sorry. I don't understand." Concerned, he approached her desk. "Take it easy. Whatever it is, it can't be as bad as what's already happened."

"Yes, it can." Recovering from her shock, she stared at him. "The people at the Realtor's office say there's no road. Not anymore. The stretch between here and Serenity was washed out by the storm. Nobody can go to town and nobody can get up here to rescue us. We're stranded."

"That's impossible."

"Oh, yeah?" Bree held out the phone. "Here. Call somebody and ask them yourself."

Apparently, she was serious. "I don't believe this."

"You don't believe it?" Bree snapped. "It's my worst nightmare."

"Well, thanks a lot."

Thunderstruck at first, Mitch quickly began to consider alternatives. Finally he said, "Look. This can't be as serious as you make it sound. I'm sure we'll be able cope for a little while longer."

"How?"

"By using our heads. All we have to do is set up some sensible rules and make sure everybody abides by them. You'll see. It won't be so bad."

Bree was tempted to throttle him, especially when he picked up a pencil from her desk, handed it to her and said, "Here. Make some notes. Where shall we start?"

That was an easy question for her. "With the muddy dog. It stays outside. Period." She focused on Mitch, and her scowl deepened. "Where did you leave it this time?"

"In the guest bathroom, like before."

The resolute look on the man's face dared her to challenge him. Bree stared back with the same rigid resolve.

Mitch yielded first. "Look. Barney is terrified of storms. He was shaking all over when I brought him in. I wouldn't dream of leaving him outside, alone, in weather like this. The poor little guy hasn't hurt a thing, and he's scared to death."

"Well, you don't have to act like I was trying to be mean," she countered. "I simply want my house to stay reasonably clean. If you'll be responsible for Barney, I suppose he can live in that bathroom for a little while longer."

"You're all heart."

"Remember, I am the one who invited you in out of the rain in the first place."

"And I'm grateful. Just keep in mind that you're also the reason I have no home. I wouldn't be here if I had any other choice, you know."

"I know." Being reminded of her part in their current dilemma helped Bree gain control of her temper. "I am glad you came to me for help. Now, what other rules can we jot down? How about, everybody takes his shoes off at the door? I imagine little boys love to run in and out of the house. If there's a mud puddle within miles they're sure to find it."

"You've got that right," Mitch said. It was going to be a real challenge to keep this woman satisfied about the condition of her fancy house, rules or no rules. How sad that she gave material possessions such undue importance.

Mitch's conscience kicked him in the gut. It couldn't be easy for her having his family underfoot. And as long as the bad weather persisted there wasn't a thing he could do about leaving, although he found it hard to believe they were stranded. The Ozarks weren't that primitive. There had to be options they were overlooking.

He held out his hand. "Give me that cell phone."

"The battery's almost dead."

"What about the other phone?"

"The regular one isn't working. I imagine the line is down. Why? What are you going to do?"

"Call the fire department and tell them we need rescuing."

"Oh, no, you don't," Brianne said. "I won't let you report a false emergency. If things are as bad as I think, the police and fire departments have their hands full already."

"I never said I was going to claim this is an emergency," Mitch insisted. "I just want to explain the situation up here and get put on their waiting list." One eyebrow lifted. "You certainly can't object to that."

"Of course not."

"Then charge up your cell phone and let's get to it. After all, you don't want to be stuck with us any longer than necessary."

Put that bluntly, her attitude sounded really hostile. Okay, so she wasn't crazy about muddy shoes and dogs with fleas. That didn't mean she was necessarily at odds with the people who owned them, even if she had inadvertently implied as much.

If that truly was the impression she'd given— and apparently it was—she owed Mitch Fowler an apology. With him standing so close, however, she found she was unable to sort her random thoughts into any semblance of order, let alone form a coherent sentence. If she intended to explain without making matters worse, there was only one thing to do.

Marshaling what was left of her willpower, Brianne seized upon the need to recharge the cellular phone as an excuse to move away from him.

"I didn't mean to sound unfriendly," she said, busying herself fitting the phone into its charger. "It's just that this house is very special to me. Why can't you understand that?"

"Oh, I understand, all right. Lots of people like to put on a show to impress their neighbors."

"Being wealthy is not a sin." Bree was adamant. "Neither is having nice things and enjoying them."

"That depends on what level of importance you give to your possessions." Mitch folded his arms across his chest, his stance wide and off-putting. "My late wife had that problem. When I couldn't give her everything she wanted, she left me cold."

"If all she cared about was money, why take the boys? Why not keep in touch so she could collect child support?"

Mitch shook his head slowly, solemnly, and stared into the distance. "I've asked myself the same question a thousand times."

"You must have been frantic. Was that when you sold the house Ryan told me about?"

"Yes. That's what I've been trying to explain to

you. No amount of money matters when more critical needs are at stake. My boys mean everything to me. Possessions can be replaced. People can't. Nothing is more important than family."

"I suppose that's true in some families."

Studying her closed expression, Mitch decided to press her for details. The worst that could happen was that she'd refuse to answer. "Not in yours?"

"Not that you'd notice. My parents fought all the time."

"Do they still do it?"

"No, but only because they're both dead."

"I'm sorry," Mitch said.

"Hey, it's okay. My mother took the coward's way out. She swallowed enough sleeping pills to go to sleep forever. After that, I'd kind of hoped Dad would mellow, but he got even meaner. He didn't have Mother to argue with anymore so he started trying to pick fights with me. When I'd refuse to play his mind games he'd get furious and start to throw things—usually Mother's good china or one of the beautiful little ceramic statues she'd collected."

"That was his problem, not yours. Did he die of natural causes?"

"My father died of meanness," Bree said flatly. "He was in the middle of delivering a tirade to some of his so-called friends when he collapsed. They called an ambulance but it was no use. He never regained consciousness."

"Like I said, I'm really sorry."

"Don't be. My parents made their own choices."

Moisture began to blur Bree's vision. She averted her gaze. This was the first time since the night her father had died that she'd cried for him. And she'd run out of tears for her mother long before that. Showing this much emotion was foreign to her. Doing so in front of a stranger was unthinkable, yet there was something about Mitch Fowler that had made her open her heart and bare her most painful secrets.

Sighing deeply, Mitch nodded and said, "This time, I know exactly what you mean. We aren't responsible for the wrong choices of others, you know."

Bree didn't stop to analyze whether it was his gentle tone of voice or their empathetic words that drew her to him. All she knew was that Mitch reached out to her and she responded.

One moment they were standing there commiserating, and the next they were sharing a tender embrace. She couldn't remember the last time a man had hugged her to offer comfort with no strings attached.

The feeling was one of peace, yet exhilaration; innocence, yet awareness; solace, yet perplexity. Listening to the sure, solid thudding of his heart as her cheek lay against his chest, Bree was certain of only one thing. She didn't want to let go.

Minutes passed. No one spoke. They didn't step apart until they heard the sound of approaching footsteps and the clicking of tiny claws on the tiled hall.

By the time the children and Barney appeared in the doorway, Brianne was on one side of the room, and Mitch was on the other.

"Hey, Dad, can we have a cookie?" Ryan asked.

"You'll have to ask Ms. Bailey. This is her house. And put that dog in the bathroom. I told you he has to stay there."

"Okay, okay."

The boy turned sparkling dark eyes to her. "Can we have cookies? Please?"

"I suppose so. If you eat them at the kitchen table," Bree said. The bouncy little dog had ducked beneath her desk and disappeared from sight. She circled to the opposite side and bent to try to keep an eye on it.

"Aw. We'll miss cartoons," Ryan whined. "Mama used to let us eat on the floor by the TV."

Mitch took over the conversation. "There were a lot of things your mother let you do that I don't intend to permit. Might as well get used to it. We're guests in this house, and I expect you to behave that way. If you want cookies, you'll eat them when and where Ms. Bailey says. The choice is yours."

"Okay. The TV's been actin' funny, anyway. It keeps goin' on and off by itself. We'll go watch till it quits again, then we'll have cookies. Come on, Bud. Come on, Barney."

The adults glanced at each other across her desk as the two boys sped down the hall.

"Have you noticed any fluctuations in the electricity since last night?" Mitch asked.

"No. But I probably wouldn't in the daylight. I threw the circuit breaker that powers my computer early last night when the storm started brewing. I haven't turned the computer on since, so I don't have any easy way to tell. That wouldn't be why the regular telephone didn't work just now, would it?"

"No. Phone lines are separate. Better leave your computer disconnected, though. If we are having power surges they could fry your appliances."

She wrinkled her nose. "Speaking of frying, I still smell burned pancakes."

"Are you sure that's not the odor of wet dog?" Mitch paused, sniffing and scowling. "I didn't see Barney leave with the kids, did you?"

"No. The last time I saw him he was crawling under my desk. By the time I came around here to check, he was gone."

"Well, he has to be somewhere. Stand back. I'll find him for you."

Bree wasn't about to leave the search to Mitch.

After all, her office was her personal sanctuary. She looked about the room, chasing shadows. Her random survey led her to the cellular phone charger, where she paused. That was funny.

"Hey, Mitch. Why did you move the phone? It can't be fully charged yet."

"What are you talking about? I didn't move the phone. It's right over…" Puzzled, he stared at the empty receptacle. "That's impossible. Nobody's been in here but you and me."

"And the boys. But they stayed by the door." Bree's gaze locked with Mitch's. Together they said, "Barney!"

Brianne dropped onto her hands and knees.

Mitch did the same on the opposite side of the desk. "There he is! Got him!" he shouted.

"The phone. Does he have the phone?" By the time she clambered to her feet and joined Mitch, he had the dog tucked under one arm and was wiping the telephone on his jeans. Bree's only comment was, "Yuck."

"It'll be okay," Mitch assured her. "It's just a little wet, that's all. He didn't have it long enough to do any damage."

"I thought you said he didn't chew things."

"This is the first time."

"That you know of," she said, holding out her hand. "Give it to me. Let me look."

Mitch obliged. "See? I told you. No real damage."

"Oh?" Bree said sarcastically. "Then maybe you'd like to tell me how to make this thing work without an antenna."

He mumbled under his breath, then set his jaw. "Okay. Don't panic. That can't be our only option. What else have you got?"

"Nothing. Just the normal telephone on the desk."

"I don't believe it! A first-class place like this, and you don't have a satellite connection?"

"Hey, don't yell at me. I never needed anything else until you showed up."

"What if you had a real emergency up here? What would you do then, hike down the mountain yourself to bring help?"

"Don't be ridiculous."

He regarded her with derision. "I'll bet you don't even have any hiking boots, do you?"

"I do so. I've worn them once, too."

"Wow. I'm impressed. How did you manage to do that without getting them dirty?"

"You don't have to be sarcastic. If you must know, I didn't leave the yard. I wouldn't have bought boots in the first place if Emma hadn't insisted I needed them to keep from being bitten by snakes."

"Not during the winter. Only at this time of the year," Mitch said. "You know, you really should get out more. Walk through the woods. Enjoy God's country. You miss the real beauty of this area by not exploring the wilds. In the spring and summer you can spot new varieties of wildflowers every week. Some of them are so tiny you'd miss them if you weren't watching where you stepped."

"Meaning, I need to stop and smell the roses?"

"Something like that."

"Point taken." Bree looked from Mitch to the ruined phone and back again. "Well, what's Plan B? Do we just sit here and stare at each other while we wait for rescue or is there something we can do to help ourselves?"

"I'm still willing to walk down the road as far as I can and check out the damage. If I can work my way around the washed-out places on foot, I'll come back for the boys, and we'll try to make it to the highway."

"And then what?" Bree asked. "Hitchhike? That's a dumb idea under the best of circumstances. You're not going to put those poor little kids in danger like that. I won't let you."

Mitch's eyebrows lifted. "Well, well. How come you're suddenly being so protective?"

"Survival instinct, I guess. I may not be mother material but I'm not stupid. It's miles to the highway. Assuming it's open at all, what makes you think you'd catch a ride easily? And suppose you slipped and were injured trying to navigate the washed-out parts of the dirt roads on the way? Who would take care of your boys and lead them to safety then?"

"When you're right, you're right." He gave her a wry smile and nodded for emphasis. "In that case, what do you suggest I do to keep the kids occupied? They won't be happy just sitting and staring at cartoons for a whole day. They'll get restless."

"So, take them outside and play hide-and-seek."

"No way. Even if it wasn't drizzling out there, all I'd need is for one of them to leave the yard and get himself lost in the woods. And don't forget the snakes. Copperheads can be especially nasty."

Her eyes widened in disbelief as she anticipated his thoughts. "Oh, no. You aren't suggesting they play in the house, are you? Of all the idiotic notions!"

"Not a fast game like hide-and-seek," Mitch said. "Do you happen to have any crayons?"

"I have markers."

"No way. Too permanent. Your rugs would never survive if we let them use ink."

He brightened. "How about a treasure hunt? You could set the rules, pick which rooms they're allowed to look in, stuff like that. And we could each supervise one hunter to keep him out of trouble. How about it?"

"Well… I suppose that might be all right, providing we watched them carefully." Bree figured she must be getting bored, too, because she was beginning to warm to his crazy idea. "You could pick something to hide, tell me where it is, and then I could use the markers to draw a map for the kids to follow. I've always been good at art."

Mitch grinned. It was nice to see the wealthy woman loosening up a little. A change in her neat-freak attitude would be a welcome relief. And the boys definitely did need something to do. They hadn't caused much trouble so far, but it was only a matter of time until their bottled-up energy bubbled over and got out of hand. Like the dog's had.

"I have a good idea," he said. "Let's hide a little bag of cookies so they'll have a real reward when they find their treasure."

"Great!" Brianne eyed the dog in his arms. "Go get rid of that monster and meet me in the kitchen. I'll find you a sandwich bag to put the cookies in. Emma made a big batch of peanut butter and raisin the last time she was here."

Following her directions and rejoining her took Mitch only a few minutes. "Okay. Ready," he said.

"Good." She handed him a small plastic bag and pointed to the cookie jar. "Go for it."

Smiling, he took the bag and filled it, then held it up for inspection. "Okay. Now what? Where do you want me to hide these?"

"I don't know. Someplace easy to get to but hard to see. And low to the ground. We don't want the kids climbing all over the furniture."

He hesitated. "Now that I think about it, this may not be such a good idea, after all. You sure you want to go ahead with it?"

Being totally honest, Bree had to admit the game sounded like a welcome diversion. "Of course I do. You and I will be right there. What can go wrong?"

He shot her a lopsided grin, his dark eyes twinkling.

"What's so funny?"

"Oh, nothing. I was just picturing you saying the same kind of thing about your pond before it went south and wiped me out."

Bree made a face at him. "All the more reason for me to make you and your children feel welcome here. Now go stash those cookies and come tell me where you put them so I can get started on the treasure maps. And hurry up, before I have time to change my mind."

Chapter Seven

From her sanctuary in the kitchen, Brianne was putting the finishing touches to her homemade maps when she heard squeals of glee followed by the light slap of small bare feet in the tiled hallway. Ryan burst into the kitchen with Bud on his heels. There was something contagious about his eager, expectant expression.

"Okay, fellas," she said, smiling and holding out two sheets of paper. "Here are your treasure maps. To be fair to Bud, I drew pictures so you wouldn't have to read any words."

She bent over and pointed. "See? This is where we are now. And here at the big X is where you'll find your cookies. Are you ready?"

Both boys nodded soberly.

"Okay, then. Your daddy will go with Ryan, and I'll help Bud in case he gets lost. Let's go."

Ryan was out of the room like a shot. Holding the teddy bear by an ear, Bud clutched his map in his other hand and gave Bree a look that was half adoration, half heartfelt plea.

She smiled at him. "How about letting me carry your bear for you so you'll have one hand free? We'll be right here with you. Promise."

To her delight, the shy child hesitated only an instant before passing her the precious stuffed toy. Touched by his show of trust, she cradled the teddy as if it were a real baby.

"I think we should go this way," she told him quietly, pointing first to the map, then to the hallway. "I know a shortcut."

Mitch wasn't as personally involved in Ryan's quest as Brianne was in Bud's, so he kept his distance and let the boy work out the puzzle alone. All he was concerned about was being in the right place at the right time to keep his excited son from wrecking the place during his search.

Standing back and observing, Mitch let his mind ramble through memories of the past few hours. The more he learned about their hostess's background, the more he could sympathize with her desire to protect her expensive possessions. It couldn't have been easy being a teenager without a mother and being raised by the kind of father she'd described.

Thank God his childhood had normalized once he'd come to live with Uncle Eldon and Aunt Vi. It was his adulthood that had turned out disappointing.

No, that wasn't entirely right, he argued. He had great kids. They were both his past and his future, a future he could honestly look forward to. Perhaps that was what had led him to embrace Bree when he'd learned of her loneliness. All the money in the world couldn't take the place of somebody who cared.

Mitch was so preoccupied he barely noticed Ryan entering the dining room. What did catch his attention, however, was the sight of Barney bounding along beside him.

"Hey! Who let that dog out again?"

"He's helping me," Ryan said brightly. "Dogs can find anything. Especially cookies."

"He's done enough damage for one day. Put him back in the bathroom," Mitch ordered. "Right now."

"Aw, Dad…"

"Now!" Mitch's voice was gruff.

"But, Dad—"

"Now!"

The commotion seemed to give the little dog an added boost of adrenaline. Barking and leaping, he ran around and around the dining room table with Ryan in hot pursuit.

Mitch made a lunge as they passed, missing them both. Suddenly, the little dog slowed, sniffed, then put his shiny black nose to the ground and made a beeline for the rear of the china cabinet.

Uh-oh. Instinct told Mitch to move closer. He was circling the dining table when Barney gave a yap and dived into the narrow space behind the cabinet.

The little dog would have been fine if he'd been able to grab the sack of cookies and continue out the opposite side. Unfortunately, he got stuck, panicked and began howling in misery and fright. The shrill sound reminded Mitch of a cross between a pack of lonesome coyotes and an ambulance siren.

"I'll get him," Ryan shouted.

Mitch yelled, "No!"

The boy ignored him.

After that, things went to pieces so rapidly it was impossible to tell exactly what sequence the events took. All Mitch knew for sure was that the heavy cabinet started to teeter. He put up his hand to steady it, assuming that Ryan would realize what was wrong and stop trying to rescue the dog single-handedly. He didn't.

In the background, Brianne screamed and dropped the stuffed bear.

Mitch raised both hands to stop the cabinet's forward fall, realizing too late that its contents were sliding toward him with nothing to stop their descent but two narrow door frames containing panes of glass.

He barely had time to worry about breaking glass before he noticed the doors weren't fastened closed.

Bree lunged beneath him, slapped the flat of her hands against the loose doors and banged them shut. The clatter was awful. When the edges of the sliding china met the glass, it sounded like everything had shattered.

The front feet of the cabinet shifted toward the wall, then stopped abruptly.

Mitch stood there, breathing hard and waiting to see what else could possibly go wrong.

When nothing moved he took a deep breath, let his temper have its way and roared, "Ryan!"

Adding to the chaos, Bud had decided to hide under the mahogany dining table. He was clutching his rescued bear and weeping inconsolably while Barney dashed circles around everyone, yapping as if he was certain they were all in danger.

Bree could hear Ryan cursing. She could only make out snatches of what Mitch was muttering in reply, but the few words she could discern were colorful enough to remind her of her father in the midst of one of his infamous tirades.

Clearly, Bree was the only one with enough remaining self-control to make sensible decisions. No one seemed to be listening to anything she said, however, so she gave up trying to talk, pursed her lips and whistled.

The shrill sound echoed off the walls and high ceiling and had an even greater effect than she'd hoped. Everyone froze, staring at her as if she'd suddenly become someone else.

"I learned how to do that at camp," she said, immediately taking charge. "Okay. Kids, get over there away from the glass. Ryan, you grab that dog and take him, too. Mitch, hang in there."

He made a disgusted sound. "No kidding. Where could I go?"

"Good point." Trapped in the narrow space between the man and the glass doors, Bree had a similar problem. She'd created a human sandwich, with Mitch and the cabinet as the bread and herself as the filling. If she hadn't been so worried about saving her precious china, she would never have put herself in such a tenuous position.

"Okay," Bree said. "Get ready. We push on the count of three. One…"

Mitch interrupted. "Wait. That won't work. The front of the cabinet slid closer to the wall when it started to tip over. There's not enough room left between it and the wall to stand it back up. I tried."

"Well, we're going to get pretty tired of holding it like this. If we need to drag it farther away from the baseboard, let's do it."

"Can't. There's not enough room to back up. We're too close to the table."

"Okay, smarty. What would you suggest?"

"I don't know."

"Well, I do." She glanced over her shoulder at the children. "Ryan, do you think you and Bud can move the chairs away and pull the big table in your direction? It should slide pretty easily on this rug."

When there was no answer from the boys, their father turned his head far enough to peer at them. "Well? You heard her. Give it a try. I'll shove with my legs from this side."

Ryan said, "Yes sir," and tucked Barney into the front of his baggy shirt. Bud did the same with his precious teddy bear.

As soon as they were in position at the far end of the table, Mitch called, "Now!" and began straining to help.

The table stuck at first, then let go and slid toward the boys about a foot before stopping.

Mitch sounded out of breath. "Oof! I hope that's enough."

"It'll have to be," Bree said. "I can't hold these doors closed much longer." She was losing patience with everyone, including herself. "It's going all the way up this time. One, two, three, push!"

The cabinet passed its center of balance on their initial effort, paused for an instant, then got away from them and slammed against the dining room wall before anyone could stop it.

Bree's breath caught. She was afraid to assess the damage closely for fear it would be worse than she'd imagined. Even though fine porcelain china was more durable than it looked, it could only stand so much rough handling.

Cautious, ready to react again if necessary, Mitch slowly stepped away, his hands raised. "I'm really sorry. The boys and I will replace anything that's broken."

With what? Bree wanted to scream. Do you have any idea how much a place setting of Limoges costs? "Would you like to tell me what happened in here?"

"It was Barney's fault," Ryan said.

A stern look from his father ended his supposed helpfulness while Mitch explained. "It did all start when Ryan let the dog out again. I told you where I was going to hide the cookies. Neither one of us dreamed anything could tip over a piece of furniture that heavy."

"Barney knocked it over?"

"Not exactly. He figured out where the cookies were and decided to go after them. Only he got stuck. Ryan tried to wedge himself behind there to save him. I saw the thing start to fall forward. At that point, the only thing I could do was try to stop it from crashing into the table and doing even more damage. That's when you came in."

"Terrific. Why weren't you watching Ryan like you were supposed to be?"

"I was. Things just went to pieces too fast."

"Pieces?" She eyed the mess inside her china cabinet. "You can say that again."

"I said I was sorry."

"I know. It's as much my fault as yours, I suppose. I should have known better. Okay. Everybody out. Leave. I can take care of this by myself."

"Let me help," Mitch offered.

"No way. You've helped enough."

He didn't argue. He escorted his children out of the room by shooing them like a gaggle of geese. Ryan was silent, but Bud punctuated their departure with shuddering breaths.

Finally alone, Bree slowly and cautiously eased open the glass doors to the cabinet. Stacks of dinner and salad plates had slid forward as a unit. So had most of the saucers. The cups and serving dishes, however, were piled haphazardly wherever they'd landed. Some were broken.

Bree picked up a chipped cup and carefully turned it in her hands. The graceful, translucent shape was perfectly accentuated by its hand-painted floral design. This was the kind of delicate ceramic beauty her mother had treasured. The poor woman had always wept whenever a piece from her collection was broken. Brianne remembered her father purposely smashing her mother's favorite pieces, then laughing at the emotional trauma he'd caused.

After her mother's death, Bree had tried to preserve some of the woman's fragile treasures, but her father had found out where she'd hidden them and had hurled them against a wall, one by one, until there were none left.

That was when Bree had made up her mind that she'd never let anyone else rob her of the things she loved. Nor would she ever bring children into a world that could be so cruel. People might disappoint you, leave you, abuse you, but beautiful objects that were loved and well cared for remained unchanged. Predictable.

Sadly noting the cup's cracked handle, she sighed. She'd made it her life's work to protect those treasures that had been placed in her care. It was her way of showing appreciation for the gifts she'd been given, of upholding fond memories of her mother in spite of everything.

Nothing had happened since her unhappy childhood to change her mind about that one iota.

"So, what's the verdict?" Mitch had approached so quietly his question made Brianne jump.

She turned from the cabinet to face him. "Could be worse."

"How much worse?"

"Actually, quite a bit. You saved most of the cups and all the plates when you stopped the whole thing from hitting the ground."

"Hitting the table, you mean." He'd paused in the doorway, his hands stuffed into the pockets of his jeans.

"I stand corrected. Where's the rest of your wild bunch?"

"Sleeping in front of the TV. Except for Barney, that is. I put him in the bathroom. And I've warned Ryan that if he lets him out again, he'll be keeping him company in there for the rest of the day."

Brianne gave him an exaggerated scowl. "I hope he's learned to follow the rules this time."

"Yeah, well… Ryan was trying to catch the dog to put him back when they had their accident. Would it do me any good to say I'm sorry again, or are you sick of hearing it?"

"I think you've groveled enough," Bree said with a weary sigh. "I still can't believe what happened."

"I can. I should have anticipated something going wrong." He swung his arm in an arc that encompassed that room and part of the next. "Look at this place. It's no wonder the kids had such a hard time staying out of trouble in here. Anybody would."

"Why? What's wrong with it?"

"Well, for starters, the carpet is practically white. So is the furniture."

"Ecru," Brianne informed him proudly. "The carpet is ivory, and the damask upholstery is ecru."

"Gesundheit."

"Very funny."

"I thought so."

"You would. Well, if you'll excuse me, I have to go get supper started."

"You're cooking? After this morning?"

"Somebody has to." She raised an eyebrow at him. "Unless you're volunteering."

"I boil a mean egg. And I can roast weenies on a stick over a campfire. Does that count?"

"Not for much." She pushed past him and led the way down the hall toward the kitchen. "How did you expect to feed your kids if you can't cook? They'd get pretty sick of peanut butter sandwiches if they had to eat them every day."

"I wasn't worried. Little boys eat anything—except maybe fried liver or Brussels sprouts."

"Oh, what a shame," Bree teased, watching his face so she could enjoy the result. "That's exactly what I was planning to fix for supper tonight."

Chapter Eight

Brianne found a package of chicken strips in the freezer and defrosted them in the microwave. She was fairly well acquainted with the way Emma had arranged the kitchen cupboards and drawers, which helped her function considerably better than Mitch did.

He was so intent on helping her prepare the evening meal he drove her crazy. Finally, after turning around to fetch something and almost crashing into him for the umpteenth time, she decided to banish him.

"Look, I appreciate your efforts. I really do. I'd just rather do this by myself. Okay?"

"Okay. If you insist. Let me get one more thing and…" Moving while he spoke, Mitch wound up trying to enter the pantry at the same time Bree was on her way out. They met in the narrow doorway, jostling for room.

Suddenly breathless, she managed to speak, "Excuse me."

He chuckled but failed to give ground. "What's the matter with you? I'd think you'd have figured out by now that I'm not going to hurt you."

"I know that!"

"Then why do you keep acting scared whenever I get anywhere near you?"

"I'm not scared. You're just in my way, that's all."

"There must be more to it than that," he drawled. "I think we should stand here like this until you decide to tell me what's really bothering you."

"Don't be silly. There's nothing to tell."

Mitch's grin spread, his eyes twinkling with mischief. "You might as well give in and tell me what's wrong. I've got all day—maybe several. Come to think of it, so do you."

"Unfortunately."

He'd placed one hand on the doorjamb on either side of her head. Hoping to escape, she tried to duck under his raised arm.

Mitch was quicker. He caught her neatly and spun her to face him, holding tight in spite of her half-hearted struggles. "Oh, no, you don't."

"Let go of me. I don't want to play games."

"I'm beginning to think you do," he said.

"Well, you're wrong."

"Am I?" He bent to place a chaste kiss on her forehead, then grasped her shoulders and held her away so he could better study her expression.

"Yes," she insisted.

"Liar."

That accusation took her aback. Was it possible he could be right? Truth to tell, it was getting harder and harder to convince herself she should continue to try to evade him. Worse, he seemed to be reading that fact in her upturned gaze.

Mitch's hold on her shoulders softened. "I'm not a bad guy once you get to know me. I'll admit that having the boys underfoot right now is a drawback, but I can't do anything about that until we're rescued. Then, after things settle down, I'd like to start seeing you."

"Dating me?"

"Yes, dating you. Is that so strange?"

"Actually, yes."

"Why? You don't look like a hermit." He was leaning slightly as if inspecting her. "No long gray beard or anything."

She pulled a face. "I don't get out much, that's all. I've isolated myself up here because I have to have peace and quiet in order to concentrate on my writing. I'm not much for the social scene. Never have been."

"Well, you have to get away from your computer sometime. Besides, I haven't dated in years. The idea of starting again feels pretty awkward to me, too."

"Really?"

"Really. After Liz left me I considered myself still married so I didn't look for anyone else. Then, when I found out I was getting my boys back, there was so much to do I didn't have time to think about women." The color of his cheeks deepened. "Not much, anyway."

"Why start now?"

Mitch laughed. "I don't know. It doesn't sound like such a bad idea to me. Matter of fact, I'm beginning to like the thought of having someone besides the boys in my life. Maybe you and I were meant to meet like this."

"I sincerely doubt that."

"Why? Don't you believe in divine intervention?"

"Truthfully? I can't say I believe in divine anything. Not anymore."

Softly, he said, "That's a shame. You miss a lot of blessings that way."

"I doubt it."

Certain he was going to back off and let her walk away, Brianne stopped staring into his eyes. That's why she didn't realize he was going to cup her face in his hands until he was cradling her cheeks in his warm, callused palms. At that point, she wouldn't have been able to make herself pull away if someone had yelled that the house was on fire.

Slowly, gently, Mitch tilted her face up as he leaned closer.

Brianne held her breath and waited for his kiss. In her heart she knew it would be wonderful.

She was right. Instead of grabbing her and pressing his mouth hard against hers the way other men had, he kept himself in check, barely brushing her lips with his before easing away.

Was he trembling? Yes! Her eyes widened, and her lips parted slightly as she studied Mitch's face, searching for answers to questions she was afraid to ask. When he looked at her there was a unique intensity to his gaze that left her weak-kneed and reeling.

With her emotions fluctuating wildly and every cell of her body attuned to the man who was still gently caressing her face, all Bree could do was stand there and absorb the precious moments. She pictured herself as a desert wanderer, dying of thirst, who had accidentally stumbled upon an oasis that held the sweetest, most refreshing water imaginable. And she wasn't ready to force herself to stop drinking in that sweetness and turn to face the wasteland. Not yet.

Without conscious thought, Bree raised her hand and mirrored Mitch's actions, drawing her fingers over his jaw and feeling the beginnings of the beard that gave the lower portion of his face a shadowy roughness. To her surprise, he clasped her wrist and stopped her.

"Don't," he warned with unusual hoarseness.

Part of Brianne wanted to remind him that their present encounter was his doing, that she was merely the blameless victim of his silly game.

Another part of her, however, was taking the whole incident far more seriously. Judging by the intensity of Mitch's gaze and the way he was holding her wrist so tightly, she wasn't the only one who had sensed that something important was happening between them.

They stared into each other's eyes for long moments until Bree's brain finally provided an observation that was lucid enough—and innocent enough—to give voice to.

"You need a shave," she said simply.

Mitch released her wrist and stepped back, rubbing his cheeks with his palms and appearing relieved. "Apparently so. I've had other things on my mind lately. Know where I can find a sharp razor?"

Her nervousness remained so heightened it was all she could do to stifle the giggles welling up in her throat. "A sharp one? Picky, aren't you?"

"Well, if I'm going to court you, the least you can do is help me make myself presentable."

"What's your hurry? I thought you said you were going to wait until everything was back to normal."

"I don't want to grow a beard in the meantime," Mitch said with his characteristic lopsided smile. "Not that I expect us to be stuck up here long enough for that."

"Heaven forbid!"

He laughed. "I thought you didn't believe that the Lord might have thrown us together."

"It was a figure of speech," she countered, making a grumpy face to add emphasis. "You'll find disposable razors in the cabinet in the guest bathroom. Help yourself."

"Thanks, I will."

He glanced to where the elements of their evening meal waited. "Sure you can handle this okay without me? I'll be glad to stay and help you get organized."

"Being unorganized is one problem I've never had," Bree said proudly. "Why don't you go shave? And while you're at it, see if the boys are okay, too. I'd hate to ignore them and then hear another crash."

"You and me both." Mitch pointed to the counter. "I left the spices lined up over there on that end. The marinade for the chicken is in the blue bowl by the recipe card. It smells great."

"Good. Thanks. Bye."

"I'm going, I'm going," he said, finally making his exit.

Bree sighed. She didn't want to hurt his feelings when all he was trying to do was be helpful, but she knew if he'd continued to hover over her, watching her every move and getting in the way, she'd have had a terrible time concentrating on anything, especially since their surprising kiss.

No kidding! For some reason, being near Mitch Fowler was making Bree feel more and more like a radio that was only partially tuned in. The signal was there, it just wasn't clear.

Which reminded her. Serenity had its own radio station. She could probably get some idea of what was going on in the immediate area by listening to it.

Encouraged, Bree flicked on the portable radio. A newscaster was speaking. "Flooding is widespread, especially in Fulton, Izard and Sharp counties. Disaster teams are being pushed to the limit. According to state records, the Strawberry River is at its highest level in forty years. Scattered showers are expected to continue through tomorrow. And in the daily farm report, corn futures for October are up a tenth, soybeans are…"

Brianne let her mind drift. Considering all the terrible things that had been happening in the lowlands, she felt ashamed that she'd been so hard on her houseguests. After all, Mitch couldn't help being stranded any more than she could. And his kids probably weren't acting any differently than most children would if they were cooped up in a strange house.

Bree continued to measure spices and stir them into the marinade for the chicken strips. Her thoughts centered on Mitch. She could still see him supporting the weight of her china cabinet, his arm muscles bulging with superhuman effort.

Though she hadn't been conscious of it at the time, she was able to relive the awesome feeling of warmth and power that had radiated from him as she'd helped him right the cabinet. And she remembered with chagrin how she'd berated him afterward. She wished she hadn't been quite so cranky.

Staring at the measuring spoon in her hand, she had to laugh at herself. She could apparently remember minute details of every moment spent with Mitch Fowler, yet she wasn't sure whether she'd added the two teaspoons of red pepper flakes the recipe called for.

The bowl of dark, thick marinade didn't seem to have any flakes in it. Besides, now that she thought about it, it would probably be best to limit the hot spices for the sake of the children.

Brianne measured half the recommended amount of pepper, stirred it into the liquid, then submerged the chicken breasts and put them in the refrigerator. There. That wasn't so hard. As her mother had always said, anyone who could read well could cook well.

Bree studied the rest of the recipe card. Interpretation of Emma's handwritten directions seemed to be the hardest part of the process. Nowhere did the instructions say what to do with the meat after it had been soaked in the spices. If Bree hadn't remembered that her housekeeper had recently prepared the dish, she wouldn't have had a clue that the chicken was supposed to be baked.

Pleased with her progress so far and feeling quite confident, Brianne paused for a relaxing cup of herb tea and straightened up the mess she'd made in the kitchen while the meat marinated.

Then she took out a Pyrex baking dish and carefully arranged the chicken pieces in the bottom. They looked drier than she remembered, so she poured the extra marinade over them before covering the dish with aluminum foil and slipping it into the double oven. Later, she'd bake some potatoes in the second oven.

Smiling, she took off the makeshift apron she'd donned at the outset of her foray into cooking. If this was all there was to feeding a big family, she certainly didn't know what all the fuss was about.

Chapter Nine

By dinnertime, the aroma permeating the house was so wonderful she didn't even have to call her guests to the table. One by one they gravitated toward the kitchen, drawn there by hunger.

Bree tucked a tea towel into her belt to serve as an apron, the way she had before, and greeted them graciously. "The table's all set. Just take your usual places. I'll have everything ready in a jiffy."

"Need any help now?" Mitch asked.

"If you'd get everyone a drink it would be nice," she told him. "Ice water for me, please."

"Coming up."

"I want soda!" Ryan whined. "I always have soda."

Mitch ignored him and set about pouring two small glasses of milk. Bud was silent. He looked as if he was going to burst into tears when his father put a glass of milk by his plate.

Busy peeling the foil off the top of the casserole dish, Bree asked, "When you finish there, will you get the baked potatoes, please? They're in the top oven."

"Okay. That sure smells great."

"Thanks. Actually, I changed the recipe a little. I was afraid there'd be too much red pepper in it for the kids so I cut the amount in half."

Holding an empty dish to put the baked potatoes on, Mitch cleared his throat. "Uh, excuse me? Did you say you added more red pepper?"

"No, I added less. Why?"

"Because I told you the marinade was ready when I left the kitchen. You didn't need to add a thing to it."

"What? You did not tell me that!"

"Yes, I did. I distinctly recall pointing out that it was already in the blue bowl."

"Well, sure, but you also said you'd laid out all the spices. What was I supposed to think?"

"I don't know. If you hadn't thrown me out of the kitchen you could have asked me."

"If I hadn't let you into the kitchen in the first place we wouldn't have a problem to ask about. I told you I could make dinner by myself."

"Fine." Disgruntled, Mitch turned toward the oven

to retrieve the potatoes. When he opened the door, a cloud of steam and smoke billowed out. "What the…"

"What did you do?" Bree demanded.

"Me? Nothing." He waved the fumes away with his hand and began lifting the remains of the potatoes with an oven mitt. "I'll bet you didn't prick the skins before you baked these."

"How was I supposed to know to do that? There's nothing in Emma's files about baking potatoes."

"That's probably because it's so elementary." Mitch stared at her. "Haven't you ever cooked anything before?"

"Not like this. And not lately, except for tonight."

"I wanna send out for pizza," Ryan hollered.

His father was not in the mood to fight with him, too. "That's enough. We can't send out for pizza because we don't have a phone that works—thanks to you and your dog. And the road is washed away so the delivery guy couldn't get it here, anyway."

"I'm not gonna eat that," the boy insisted, pointing at the remains of the potatoes. "It looks gross!"

"Oh, I don't know," Mitch said. "I kind of like exploding food, as long as it's done blowing up before I try to eat it."

Bree was not amused. "You don't have to rub it in." She studied the oddly shaped remnants of skin and fluffy white potato. "They look kind of like they're double baked, only a lot rougher around the edges."

"They do, don't they? Wonder if they'd be good with cheese melted on top?" Mitch put the dish aside and went to the refrigerator to look for a wedge of Cheddar.

Brianne stood back, watching. At the mere mention of melted cheese the younger boy had brightened up. She could tell that Ryan, too, was happy about the cheese idea, though he tried not to show approval. Well, fine. She wasn't trying to starve the poor kids. If they didn't want to eat her potatoes without doctoring them, that was okay with her.

While the cheese and milk were heating in the microwave to make a quick sauce, Mitch got busy scraping the marinade off portions of chicken and cutting them into bite-size pieces for the boys. He cautioned them to wait politely until everyone had been seated before beginning to eat.

Brianne brought a hot dish of canned corn to the table and took her place. Having all of them together at the small kitchen table made things crowded but doable. After what had happened at breakfast she certainly didn't intend to serve the children in the formal dining room and spend all her time worrying about drips on the rug. And she could hardly throw them outside again, since the rain had resumed.

As soon as Mitch returned with the cheese sauce and sat down, Bree took the first bite of her chicken. The initial taste was delicious. By the time several seconds had passed, however, her tongue started to prickle.

That was just the beginning. In less than ten heartbeats the roof of her mouth was on fire. When she breathed, her sinuses felt like she was inhaling pure flame and being seared from the inside out.

Eyes tearing, she grabbed her glass of water and gulped it dry, looking at Mitch just in time to see him sample his entrée. He raised one eyebrow and saluted her with his fork, evidently surprised that it tasted so good.

By the time Bree said, "Don't!" it was too late. His face reddened, his dark eyes widened and his nostrils flared.

Bree couldn't tell if his expression was one of shock, aggravation, panic—or none of the above, since he'd covered his mouth with his napkin and was snorting like a walrus with a bad cold.

One thing was certain. Even though Mitch had scraped the extra marinade off the chicken he'd cut up for the children, they mustn't be permitted to taste it.

Brianne moved to snatch their plates an instant before Mitch did. That set up a clamor from the hungry boys reminiscent of a henhouse being raided by a ravenous fox.

Ignoring the ruckus, Bree and Mitch made a mad dash for the sink and began gulping down cold water. She glanced at him, expecting a tirade. To her surprise, he looked amused.

"I—I'm sorry," she blurted, chancing a smile.

Mitch drew another glassful of water. "No problem."

There was something about the mischievous twinkle in his watering eyes and the twitch at the corners of his mouth that made her giggle. That was all it took to set him off.

He began to roar. Brianne joined him. They chuckled and snickered and laughed and hooted until both were gasping for air.

Tears rolled down Bree's cheeks. She drew a shuddering breath and said, "Oops," which started Mitch off again, nearly doubling him up.

Finally, he managed to regain his self-control. Laying a hand on Brianne's shoulder, he said, "Maybe you'd better retire from cooking while we're still on our feet."

"The exploding potatoes were a nice touch," she countered, bringing more chuckles.

Together, they looked at the table. Both boys were sitting there, unmoving, holding their empty forks in their small fists and staring at the adults with bewildered expressions.

"Maybe we'd better get clean plates for their

potatoes," Bree said, reaching into the cupboard. "Will that be enough supper? All they had for lunch was peanut butter and jelly sandwiches."

"It'll be fine. Put gobs of cheese on his food and any kid will be satisfied," he said. "They could live on the stuff. That, and peanut butter."

Bree winked at Mitch. "Peanut butter on baked potatoes? Yuck."

"Hey," he said, "if I had the choice of another helping of your special chicken or a peanut butter flavored spud, I wouldn't have any trouble choosing."

"You'd pick the potato?"

"Oh, yeah." He nodded solemnly. "No contest."

Mitch had his children bathed and in bed by nine. Ryan was the only one who had argued, and even he had started to doze off almost immediately.

As soon as Mitch was sure they were both sleeping soundly he went downstairs. He'd convinced himself that he was merely looking for something with which to make a list of the items he'd need to replace or repair.

Pen and paper he found easily. When he continued to wander through the downstairs rooms, he was forced to admit he also wanted to see Brianne.

Noticing a light in the library, he headed in that direction. Bookshelves blanketed three walls. On the fourth, French doors opened onto the covered terrace where Bree had taken the children when they'd been caught in the rain while playing outside.

Could that really have been less than twenty-four hours ago? Mitch marveled. How time flew when you were having fun!

The heavy library door was ajar. He cautiously gave it a push, and it glided open effortlessly, quietly. Mitch smiled as Brianne looked up. "Hi. Mind if I join you?"

"No. Not at all."

She was seated on one end of a leather sofa, her feet bare, one leg tucked partially beneath her. She closed the book she'd been reading and laid it aside, then leaned out to peer past him. "Are you alone?"

"Yes. Even Barney's sleeping, thank goodness."

As Bree watched the tall man saunter across the room, she got goose bumps wondering if he was going to join her on the couch. When he chose to sit in a chair, she wasn't sure whether to be relieved or disappointed. Given the choice, she opted for disappointed.

Mitch leaned back, stretched his legs out in front of him with his ankles crossed and sighed. "Boy, what a day this has been. I'm beat."

"I know what you mean."

"So, what were you reading? A cookbook?"

"Very funny. Actually, I don't own a cookbook—which was part of my problem tonight. This book is a mystery." Come to think of it, so is cooking, she thought.

"Ah. Is that the kind of book you write?" he asked.

"Not exactly. My stories are mostly romantic, although I do occasionally work in an element of suspense."

"Love stories? You write love stories?"

"You don't have to sound so shocked."

"I didn't mean anything by it," Mitch assured her. "I'm sure the folks who write science fiction haven't been to outer space, either." The moment the words were out of his mouth he regretted them. "I mean... I didn't mean..." He began to mutter to himself and shake his head.

"I'm not that naive, Mr. Fowler."

"I'm sure you're not." Flustered, he realized he'd insulted her again.

The absurd look on his face made Bree laugh. "I think you're bumfuzzled."

"I'm what?"

"It's one of Emma's favorite expressions. Near as I can tell, it means something between frazzled and confused."

"Sounds about right. Think I should go out and

come in again so we can start this conversation over?"

"That won't be necessary." She eyed the paper in his hand. "What are you doing?"

"Making a list. I want you to tell me exactly what was broken."

"Why?"

"Because I intend to replace the busted pieces." His face reddened slightly. "And I'll probably have to buy you a new bathroom door, too, thanks to Barney. He's scratched the inside pretty badly."

"I've been afraid to look."

"Don't. It's not a pretty sight. You'll be glad to hear that the rest of the room is okay, though. Apparently, the only thing he likes to chew is telephones."

"I suppose I should be thankful."

"I sure am." Mitch paused, pen poised, waiting for her to answer his original question. "Well? Which dishes were broken?"

Hearing the fine French china referred to as *dishes* amused Bree. "You don't want to know."

"Yes, I do. I'm serious about this."

"Okay. Let me put it this way. A few years ago, hand-painted Limoges plates were selling for well over five hundred dollars."

"Each?"

"Each. And that's if you can find any for sale that

match the original set. Of course, the ones signed by the artist can go for double that amount."

"Oh, boy."

"I told you, you didn't want to know."

"You're right," Mitch said, shaking his head. "No wonder you were so concerned. Looks like my son's going to be working off that bill until he's fifty or sixty years old."

"I don't think that's really fair."

"I have to teach him responsibility."

"Within reason," she countered.

Mitch smiled. "Why are you defending him? I thought you didn't like kids."

"I don't."

"You may think you don't. But I've seen you dealing with my boys, and you certainly don't hate them. The dog, maybe, but not the kids."

"Even the stupid dog was starting to grow on me—until he ate the cell phone antenna," she admitted with a wry smile.

"Then liking the children can't be far behind."

"Why? Because they're little animals, too?"

That brought his full-bodied laugh. "You do have an odd way of looking at things, lady."

"I've been told that before."

"I imagine you have." Staring at her, he sobered. "Have I ever told you how beautiful you are?"

"No." It was barely a whisper.

"Then I'm a fool. And to prove it for sure, I'm going to come over there and kiss you again."

Brianne knew she should tell him not to. She also knew that if she put off doing anything for a few seconds there would be no need. It would be too late. What was the matter with her? Where was her common sense? She was beginning to think and act just like one of the lovesick heroines in her novels.

She closed her eyes. What would she do if she were writing this scene instead of living it? That was the easiest question she'd asked herself in a long time. The first thing she'd do was go back to the beginning of the story and make sure there were no children in the picture. Marriage was hard enough without adding the complications of off-spring. She ought to know. She'd overheard her father and mother scream at each other often enough about having a daughter they didn't want. The memory made her suddenly feel queasy.

"Mitch." She opened her eyes. "We need to talk."

He sat next to her, whispered, "Later," and gently stroked her long, golden hair.

Their lips were almost touching, his breath warm on her face. Trembling, Bree waited. The feather-light kiss she was expecting came, followed without pause by a heavier, more insistent pressure.

Her heart leaped, danced, raced. It was as if Mitch had breached her soul through that simple contact.

She wrapped her arms around his neck, meeting him with an eagerness that rivaled his.

Being so near to him left her breathless, and when he pulled her even closer, she wondered if the world had suddenly tipped off its normal axis. *Her* world certainly had! It didn't seem to matter what kind of touch, what kind of kiss, Mitch bestowed upon her. Everything he did was so astounding, so amazingly perfect, she could hardly believe she wasn't dreaming.

Lost in the moment, Brianne was surprised and flustered when he broke contact and set her away from him without warning. This wasn't the way a perfect love scene was supposed to turn out!

She blinked to clear her vision. Mitch was standing there, staring at her as if he'd never seen her before.

"I'd better go," he said, his voice raw with emotion.

"Why?"

"Because it's getting late."

The lame excuse hurt so much she couldn't bring herself to argue. "I suppose you're right."

"See you in the morning, then?"

"I'll try to have breakfast ready around eight, if that's not too late."

Frustrated, tense, Mitch combed his fingers through his hair. "Eight is fine. After we get the kids fed I think I'll go ahead and hike down the dirt road a ways, like I said before. Maybe I can see enough to tell how bad the damage is. It's possible a four-by-four could get us out of here if anybody knew we were stranded."

Are you in that much of a hurry to leave? she wondered. She refused to swallow her pride and ask. Instead, she said, "That's a good idea. I keep checking the telephone. The line is still dead."

"Too bad we messed up your cell phone."

A lot of things are too bad, Bree mused. Like the fact that we'll have nothing in common, nothing to hold us together once this calamity is over.

Mitch was edging toward the library door. Brianne wanted to reach out to him, to beg him to take her in his arms, to kiss her again. Instead, she remained quiet and let him go.

She'd known him for what—two days at the most? Yet she was yearning for him like a silly teen with her first crush. That wasn't sensible. Nor was it normal. At least not for her.

Slowly shaking her head, she sighed. It might not make any sense, but it was a fact. She was so enamored of Mitch Fowler, constant thoughts of him were driving her crazy. It had been bad enough before he'd kissed her. Now that he had, she wondered how she was going to cope, how she was going to resist making a blithering fool of herself around him.

A vivid image popped into Bree's mind and immediately struck her funny. She saw herself clad in a long, flowing white gown. Beautifully hued ribbons were streaming from her hair, and she was leaping through a field of wildflowers in slow motion like a ballerina, eventually throwing herself headlong into Mitch's strong, open arms.

The exaggerated spectacle reminded her of the reunion of long-lost lovers in an old movie— combined with a recent TV commercial for the latest allergy medicine!

"May cause unwelcome side effects," she quoted. "And may be habit forming!" No kidding.

There was no use arguing with herself about that. She was already having to deal with plenty of unwelcome side effects when Mitch was nearby, like fluttering heartbeats, sweaty palms and an inability to form sane thoughts. The only good thing about being so dithered was that those strong feelings would eventually help her write better love scenes.

As for the idea that she'd already gotten in the habit of having Mitch underfoot, could that possibly have happened in such a short time?

The answer was a resounding, disconcerting yes.

Chapter Ten

Brianne had never been one to stand by and let circumstances run her life. This time was no exception. When she finally gave up and went to bed that night, she'd narrowed her choices of action to two that were workable.

The way she saw it, she could either try to keep Mitch and his family with her long enough for their initial attraction to wear off, or she could hurry his departure and save herself the heartache she was afraid would eventually come once he realized how incompatible they were.

A soft sound in the hallway outside her bedroom caught her attention. She strained to listen. She couldn't tell if she was hearing a child's sniffling or if Barney had escaped and was nosing around. Either way, the situation called for investigation.

She pulled a light cotton robe over her gown, went to her door and eased it open. Bud was standing there, barefoot, clad in a T-shirt that was miles too big, hugging his bear and wearing the most pitiful expression she'd ever seen.

Brianne smiled and instinctively dropped to her knees so they'd be at the same eye level. "Hi, honey. What's the matter? Couldn't you sleep?"

He shook his tousled head, his lower lip quivering.

Maybe his silence was due to her lack of rapport with small children, but as far as Bree could recall, the little boy had never talked much in her presence. Considering the trauma he'd been through recently, it wasn't surprising he was shy.

Unsure how to comfort him, she decided to start with the obvious. "Are you hungry?"

Again, he shook his head.

"Then what's the matter? Can you tell me?"

Tears began to fill Bud's limpid eyes, making them seem larger and more expressive than ever.

The little boy looked so small, so lost, Bree couldn't resist reaching out to him.

The moment she opened her arms, Bud dropped his teddy bear and threw himself at her, clinging as if he were adrift at sea and she held the only lifeline. His little arms went around her neck and clasped tightly as he buried his face against her shoulder.

"Oh, baby," she crooned. "It's okay. Don't be scared. I've got you. I've got you."

Limitless love poured from her soul and bathed them both in its grace. Brianne couldn't believe what was happening. There wasn't a maternal bone in her body, so what was she doing on her knees in the middle of the night, hugging a frightened, lonely little boy? This experience with the Fowlers was certainly getting complicated.

She began to rock in place, soothing Bud with softly uttered sounds while she mulled over the kinds of support she'd already decided to offer. Helping Ryan would be easy. All she had to do was arrange for tutoring to bring him up to grade level. And Mitch would benefit from her generosity in regard to his lost cabin and personal possessions, so he was taken care of. The question was, what in the world could she hope to do for Bud?

The unspoken answer filled her heart and mind. You're doing it. Just love him.

I can't love him, Bree argued. I can't. It's not in me. I don't understand children. I never have. Look at the way I was brought up. I'd ruin any kid I tried to raise. I know I would.

Tears misted Bree's vision as she held the needy six-year-old close and kissed the top of his tousled head. This was all wrong! She had her future sensibly planned. It wasn't supposed to include any children.

Maybe I can buy Bud a bicycle or something, she reasoned.

Immediately, her conscience twitched uncomfortably. Shame on you. This is not about money, this is about love.

How could she argue? Apparently, she'd needed a visual aid to convince her this kind of love was possible, because there was no mistaking what was going on. The proof was clinging to her with complete trust and unqualified affection.

"Oh, dear." Brianne started to sniffle the way the child had when he'd first come to her. "Oh, dear, oh, dear."

That was enough to get Bud's attention. He loosened his hold on her neck, then bent to pick up his teddy bear.

He held it out. "Here," he said, clearly yet softly. "He'll make it all better."

She had to fight to keep from weeping out loud. This tenderhearted child, whom she hardly knew, was offering to share his most precious possession. There was no way she'd refuse such a kindness.

"Thank you, honey." Smiling through her tears, she included the worn teddy bear in their mutual hug. "I feel better already."

"Told ya."

"You sure did."

Still cradling the raggedy toy, she got to her feet

and held out her hand to Bud. "What do you say you and I go downstairs and see if we can find some cookies?"

"Okay. Only my bear doesn't like cookies. I'll have to eat his for him."

Brianne laughed and played along. "You're the expert. Shall we bring some back for your brother, too?"

"Naw," Bud said. "He doesn't like cookies, either." His grin spread wide.

"Are you sure about that?"

"Uh-huh."

"Then I guess you'll have to eat his, too, right?"

The little boy muffled a high-pitched giggle with his free hand before he answered, "Yup. I guess I will."

Mitch was already frying bacon when Brianne wandered into the kitchen the following morning.

She yawned. "Do you always get up this early?"

"I like mornings."

"Me, too," she muttered, heading for the coffee-pot, "as long as they start around nine or ten."

He laughed. "That's almost noon to me."

"Fine. Then skip breakfast and start with lunch." Another yawn was followed by a sigh. "I told you I'd start cooking around eight, and you said that was fine. If you wanted to eat earlier you should have said so. What time is it, anyway?"

"Around six-thirty." Her resulting groan brought a chuckle from him. "If you wouldn't spend half the night raiding the cookie jar, maybe you wouldn't be so tired."

Her head snapped around so fast she sloshed her coffee. "How do you know about that?"

"My first clue? The crumbs I found in my bed," Mitch said. "Bud crawled in with me sometime during the night and brought a fistful of extra cookies with him. When I asked him about it, he said you and he had been having a late-night snack."

"Us and the bear. So, you didn't actually see us?"

"No. Why?"

"No particular reason. I just wondered." Until she was able to sort out her confusing sentiments she didn't want to get into a discussion about the merits of motherhood versus a life without offspring. And she certainly didn't want to influence Mitch by playing up her newly discovered affinity for one of his children.

She carried her cup to the table and plopped down. "If I'd realized how early it was I wouldn't have gotten dressed. I'm glad you've decided to cook. I'm beat."

"You look like it," he teased, taking in her light-weight jeans and shirt appreciatively. The blue color almost matched her eyes.

Bree made a face. "Thanks a heap."

"It might help if you combed your hair."

"I did. Didn't I?" She started to smooth her long hair back from her face with her fingers, realized he was right and frowned. "Oops. Guess I forgot. I told you I was tired."

"Don't worry about it. You look kind of cute all mussed like that. It's a good thing you're not trying to cook our breakfast, though. It was interesting enough when you were making dinner wide awake."

"I'd have done fine if you hadn't tried to help."

"The potatoes were good."

"Sure, thanks to your pouring cheese all over them. I told you I didn't know anything about what kids liked."

"You did okay with the cookies last night."

Brianne took a careful sip of her coffee, stalling while she tried to think of another snappy comeback. Before she could come up with one, Ryan dashed into the kitchen, slid to a stop and confronted her.

"Where's the bear?" he hollered. "What'd you do with it?"

Taken aback by his hostility, Bree stared at him. "What?"

"My brother's bear. Where is it? I want it back. Now!"

To her relief, Mitch placed a hand on the boy's shoulder and said, "Knock it off, Ryan. That's no way to talk to Ms. Bailey."

"But—"

"I said, knock it off." Mitch looked to Brianne. "Do you know what he's talking about?"

"Sure. Bud loaned me his bear, that's all. It's fine. I tried to give it back to him last night, but he wouldn't take it."

Ryan stiffened. "You didn't lose it?"

"Of course not. It's right upstairs in my room."

Twisting out of his father's hold, the eight-year-old dashed from the kitchen without further comment.

Puzzled, Bree focused on Mitch. "Okay. You understand kids. What just happened here?"

"Beats me. I've had a hiatus from parenting, remember?"

"At least you were a little boy once. I never was."

"I must confess, I already had that much figured out."

The look Bree gave him in response was so comical he almost burst out laughing.

"What's so funny, mister?"

"You are. I think one of us ought to follow Ryan and make sure he doesn't get into anything that's none of his business. I shouldn't leave the bacon right now. Do you mind doing it?"

"Not at all." Rising, Brianne smoothed her tangled hair. "I have to go upstairs, anyway, and make myself more presentable. The new chef we hired has complained that I'm unfit to grace his kitchen."

"Don't misquote me. I said you were cute that way."

"Cute is for puppies and kittens and little kids. I'd rather look like I have it together, thank you."

"Whatever." With a nonchalant shrug, Mitch turned his back to her and appeared to give the sizzling bacon his full attention. Much of his mind, however, was busy trying to figure out why Brianne seemed unwilling to accept a sincere compliment because she wasn't precisely groomed. Didn't she know how endearing she was when she relaxed and stopped trying to prove whatever it was she was trying to prove?

Then again, maybe it was normal for a woman to think she had to have every hair in place. Personally, he didn't care whether Bree was dressed up or running around the house barefoot. All he wanted to do was look at her, be with her. She was doing everything she could to discourage him, yet he couldn't get her out of his mind for even a few minutes. No wonder he understood kids so well. He was acting like a child. The one thing he'd been told he couldn't possibly have was the one he wanted most.

Brianne met Ryan coming out of her room. "I see you found Bud's bear."

"Yeah."

"I told you it was okay."

His icy glare was unnerving. She refused to be cowed. "Would you like to tell me why you were so worried?"

"No."

"Then how about telling me something about the bear? Where did Bud get it?"

"From our mother. Why?"

"I just wondered."

"It's none of your business," the boy muttered. He tucked the toy under his arm and disappeared down the hall before she could think of a suitable reply.

Astonished, Bree returned to the kitchen.

"Did he find it?" Mitch asked.

"Yes."

"Then why are you frowning?"

"Kids," she said. "I don't understand them at all."

"Welcome to the club. What happened up there?"

"Ryan is furious with me."

"Why?"

"I don't know. He acted like he thought I'd stolen the bear from Bud. It was weird."

"No kidding?" Mitch took the hot frying pan off the burner so he could give Brianne his full attention. "What, exactly, did you say to him?"

"Nothing much. I just asked where Bud got the bear."

"And?"

"That was all. Ryan said it came from their mother."

"You're positive he was mad at you?"

Bree arched her eyebrows. "Oh, yeah. Does his reaction make any sense to you?"

"Maybe." Mitch nodded slowly, thoughtfully. "Ryan hasn't told me much about the years he spent with his mother. I do know he was left in charge of Bud a lot of the time. Maybe he got to thinking of his brother as his personal responsibility. Even so, that's no reason to be rude to you. I'll have a talk with him."

"Forget it. I'm already on his bad side. If he thinks I ratted on him, he'll be positive I'm one of the bad guys."

Mitch gave her a lopsided smile. "Guess he doesn't know about the cookie spree you and Bud went on last night, huh?"

"I guess not. Sorry about the crumbs in your bed. I told Bud he could take some cookies upstairs with him. I didn't realize that I should have explained he wasn't supposed to sleep with them."

"Kids take things literally," Mitch said. "If you leave out details, they'll assume there are no restrictions. I'm just thankful you didn't give him something messier."

"Like ice cream." She laughed softly. "He asked for some of that, too."

"Which reminds me. We need to check our food

supplies and make sure we ration the important stuff. Just in case."

She didn't even want to consider the possibility of long-term isolation. "I've already looked through the pantry and the freezer. Surely we won't be stuck here long enough to run out of food."

"I'll know more after I've hiked down the road a ways and scoped it out. I want to take a list with me so I'll know what extras to pick up in case I make it as far as Burnham's store."

"Where's that? I've never heard of it."

"It's a couple of ridges to the west of here. When I was a kid, I used to run errands over that way for my aunt. I hope the old place is still there." He smiled in fond remembrance. "Chances are she didn't need the stuff from Burnham's nearly as much as she needed to get me out of the cabin—and out of her hair."

"You mean you weren't a lovable little boy like Bud?"

"No. I was more like Ryan—or rather, he's like me. Had a chip on my shoulder the size of a full-grown oak. And just as hard. If it hadn't been for Uncle Eldon taking me in and straightening me out, starting when I was thirteen, I'd probably have wound up in serious trouble."

"That's too bad."

"No, it isn't. It gives me insight into what makes Ryan tick. Right now, he's angry at everybody and everything. Plus, he's disappointed in adults. I can relate to that."

Bree smiled slightly. "I'm with you so far. When I was little I remember wishing that the neighbors were my parents."

"At least you had somebody. My folks decided having a kid around was too much trouble, so they tossed me out on my ear."

"That may have been a blessing in disguise. Your uncle sounds like he was a wonderful influence."

"He was. Vi and Eldon both were. I intended to teach my kids the same lessons by bringing them out here to the woods. That plan hasn't worked real well so far."

"Don't worry. You'll be compensated fairly for your cabin."

Mitch was slowly shaking his head. "Money's not my biggest problem right now. I was fooling myself to think things would be the same up here now as they used to be. It wasn't just living out in the woods that made the difference in me, it was my aunt's and uncle's kindness, their faith and unconditional love."

"I have faith in you, too," Bree said. "You'll be able to win back your boys once they get used to you again. Remember, three years is a long time."

"Yeah." Mitch sobered. "In their case it's practically a whole lifetime."

* * *

Breakfast went off without a hitch. Later, Bree was sitting in the den, reading and watching the boys enjoy morning cartoons, when Mitch joined them.

"Kitchen's all cleaned up," he said. "If I hurry I can be down the hill and back before the kids get hungry again."

Bree smiled at him. "We should be okay till tonight. I found a couple packages of hot dogs in the freezer. I'm positive I can manage to boil a pot of water to cook them in."

"You sure?"

"Absolutely."

"I wish you could come with me." He glanced at the children for emphasis.

Bree understood. "I don't see how. I'll be fine here. I haven't had a good excuse to watch cartoons since I was a kid."

Ryan's attention was diverted. He gave his father a stormy look. "Why do we have to stay with her?"

"Because." Mitch met the boy's animosity with a stern look of his own. "Remember. No running in the house, no noisy games and absolutely no Barney while I'm gone. I want you to behave yourselves just like you would if I was right here."

"Yeah, sure." The sullen child went back to watching television.

Bree followed Mitch from the den and didn't comment until they were out of earshot. "Has he always been so belligerent?"

"No. The Ryan I remember used to be a lot easier to get along with."

"Well, I wouldn't be too hard on him. I imagine his mother told him all kinds of bad things about you to justify her leaving. Being back with you must be a difficult adjustment for him, especially after so long."

"I hope that's all that's wrong," Mitch said. "If he's scared, I'll cut him some slack. On the other hand, if he's just being a brat, I can't let him get away with it."

"I'm glad it's your problem, not mine."

Mitch heaved a noisy sigh. "Yeah. I've got a lot to keep praying about, all right."

"For your sake, I hope it helps," she said solemnly.

"Always does."

"Does it? The first night you stayed here, Ryan told me his mother thought you were crazy to believe in God."

"And you agree with her."

"I didn't say that."

"No, but you were thinking it." Mitch smiled benevolently. "Funny how it all worked out in my case. In the beginning, any faith I had came from living out here with Vi and Eldon. They lugged me to their homey little country church when I was so hostile they practically had to hog-tie me to get me in the door. It's a wonder the whole congregation didn't line up to paddle me. I deserved it."

"What *did* they do?"

"Treated me like a decent human being, mostly. That was a whole new experience for me." He shrugged. "Then again, everything up here in the Ozarks was new to me. I'd never seen a live deer before. Or a rabbit, or a nesting bird, or a wild terrapin, or a turkey, or…"

Brianne cut in. "Or ticks, or chiggers, or copperheads and water moccasins, or hail the size of baseballs, or rainstorms that would make old Noah so nervous he'd start building another ark. I still can't believe what happened to your cabin. I'm so, so sorry."

"Don't be. Picturing what might have happened to us if we hadn't made a run for it has put the whole incident into perspective. The old place was in pretty bad shape, anyway. When the boys get a little older, maybe we'll rebuild it together."

"That would be nice. Go on about your aunt and uncle. How long did it take you to quit resisting going with them on Sunday mornings?"

"Sunday mornings?" Mitch laughed. "It was Sunday morning and Sunday night, Wednesday evenings, volunteer work parties for senior citizens and widows, extra Bible study after I finished my school homework and chores, dinner-on-the-ground once a month or more, pie suppers to raise funds for all kinds of charity projects, gospel sings, revivals in a brush arbor—one thing after another. If it hadn't been for doings at church they wouldn't have had any social life at all."

"Where did you fit into it all?"

"It took about four years for them to win me over. I was sixteen when all of a sudden the whole thing made sense to me. I hotfooted it up that aisle so fast one morning when the preacher gave the invitation, I think I scared him silly."

"Do you still go to the same little church?"

Mitch shook his head slowly. "No. It's long gone. Until my family fell apart, I hadn't been in any church for years."

"And then?"

"Then I had nowhere else to turn. I fell back on my raising, as they say. My belief in God and Christ is stronger now than it ever was. Until this week I hadn't missed a Sunday in church for a long time."

"I'm happy for you," Bree said wistfully. "I wish I could say the same. I went to Sunday school when I was little. It didn't stick. When my mother died, so did my faith."

"Lots of people question their beliefs after a trauma. If you aren't in the habit of looking to the Lord for help and trusting Him to work things out, it's easy to go the other way. That doesn't mean you can't choose to turn yourself around."

"And stir up all those terrible feelings again? No, thanks."

"I guess it is easier to stay mad at God."

"I never said that."

"Am I wrong?"

"Dead wrong," she insisted, her jaw set with determination. "Listen. My father went to church all the time, and he was one of the meanest men I've ever known. I have no desire to be around people like that, thank you."

"I'm sorry you feel that way. Just be sure you're not confusing church membership with genuine commitment to Christ. They're not necessarily the same thing. Anybody can warm a pew on Sunday morning without actually belonging. It's like a woodstove with no fire in it. It's still a stove. It looks the same. It can even be stuffed full of firewood and kindling. It just won't function the way it was meant to until you put a lighted match to it."

"Any spiritual fire I ever had is long gone," Bree said.

Mitch smiled knowingly. "That's because no flame will continue to burn unless it's well tended.

If you don't want to go back to church, at least consider picking up the Bible once in a while. You might be surprised."

That was what she was afraid of. The disconcerting turn of their conversation had left her unsettled and jittery. As a child, she'd expected messages from God to be delivered to her the same way they had been in biblical times. Angels were supposed to swoop down. Or a finger was supposed to write on the wall. Or bright lights and flames were supposed to miraculously appear and speak.

It was beginning to occur to Brianne that an important part of her psyche may have failed to mature after her mother's death. If that were true, then it was also possible that Mitch Fowler had been sent to awaken her dormant faith.

The whole idea gave her goose bumps. If she accepted that premise, then she'd also have to accept the existence of a God who cared, who watched over His own.

That concept brought her thoughts full circle and slammed them hard against the brick wall she'd built around her heart. If there was a God, He hadn't cared enough to save her mother, so how could she ever hope to trust Him again?

Mitch had been studying Brianne's changing expression as they'd walked and talked. Clearly, she was too overwrought to look after his rambunctious children. Mitch knew Ryan. He'd sense her unsettled state and capitalize on it the minute he got the chance, which would only make matters worse. That left Mitch with only two options. He could either stay at the house with the others or take them all along. He chose the latter.

"Look," he said, lightly touching Bree's arm to get her attention. "Why don't you go dig out those boots you said you had, and we'll all take a hike down the road? The kids need to get out of the house, and so do you. How about it? I promise we won't be gone too long."

The look in his eyes was so kind it brought a lump to her throat. Seeking to distract herself, to keep from taking him too seriously, she made a joke. "You sure you're not trying to get me out into the woods so you can ditch me?"

Mitch chuckled. "If I was going to ditch anybody it would be good old Barney."

"Now you're talking," she said with a silly grin. "Okay. You go break the news to the kids, and I'll put on my boots. Meet you back here in five minutes."

Starting away, she paused to add, "And I like your other idea, too. Don't forget to bring the dog!"

Chapter Eleven

Mitch led. Sullen Ryan was second. Bud was hanging on to his bear for dear life and Bree was plodding along in her heavy hiking boots, bringing up the rear. Only Barney seemed totally thrilled with their outing. He raced in circles, his tiny feet barely touching the ground.

Reaching the end of the driveway where the dirt road began, Mitch paused to let them close ranks, turned and smiled. "Okay. Ready?"

Though Bree knew he'd been asking if they were ready to hike along the damaged road, she couldn't help relating the question to her personal life. Was she ready for Mitch Fowler? For what she might find if she gave herself permission to fall in love with him? Moreover, was she ready to throw away all her previously sensible decisions about her future for his sake and the sake of his children?

Not yet, she insisted, hurrying to keep pace with his longer strides. Not yet.

Soon? her rebellious subconscious asked.

All Brianne could truthfully promise herself was, maybe. That would have to suffice. Under the present trying circumstances, she figured she was doing well to think reasonably, let alone try to adhere to the inflexible ideals she'd set for her prospective mate.

Inside, she was laughing at herself. There wasn't a thing about Mitch Fowler that even remotely qualified him to become her husband. He was the last—the very last—man she should be attracted to.

Yet he was the first who had ever gotten this close to capturing her heart and soul.

Progress was slow because of the children. There was so much mud sticking to the bottoms and outer edges of Bud's sneakers he had to lift his knees in a march step to even walk.

Ryan did better only because he continually stamped his feet. That threw globs of mud against anything within three or four feet of him, including his legs, but at least he was able to keep up with his father.

Bree was not only as encumbered as poor Bud,

she had more trouble keeping her balance than he did. She was toying with the idea of taking him with her and turning back when she noticed with a start that Mitch and Ryan were no longer visible.

"Where'd your daddy go?" she asked the younger boy.

"Over there."

Arms held out for balance, she drew up next to him. "Where? Show me."

He pointed. "I think they fell down."

"Oh, no. Surely not."

That suggestion was enough to flip Bree's stomach into her throat and send her heart on a runaway ride. Grasping the child's hand, she hurried him along. Up ahead the road seemed to vanish. Until they reached that place, there was no way to tell if the drop-off was dangerous.

To her relief, the distance to the bottom of the gully was barely fifteen feet, with a gentle slope. It looked, however, as slick as any plastic slide at a water park.

Mitch smiled from the bottom and held out his hand when he saw her peering over the edge. "Come on. It's easy."

"No way. It's too slippery."

"Don't worry. I'll catch you. If Ryan and Barney and I can do it, you can."

"What about Bud? I can't just leave him up here."

"You're right. Send him down first, then come yourself."

She crouched next to the little boy, sensing his fright. "I guess we're going to have to do this, or Ryan and your daddy will think we're chicken."

A shake of his head was his only comment.

"I know how you feel," she said softly, "but we don't have much of a choice. How about doing it together? We could hold hands. Then you could help me."

To her relief that logic seemed to help. Bud took her hand again and held tight as she straightened. Together they stepped closer to the edge and took their first tentative steps onto the incline.

Brianne felt her feet begin slip almost immediately. She didn't dare let go of Bud, and with no way to stop their rapid descent she had no choice but to balance as best she could and ski directly into Mitch's open arms.

Waiting at the bottom, Mitch saw what was happening and braced himself. If he bent to catch his little boy, Brianne was liable to flatten them both. If he caught her, maybe that would be good enough. He had only an instant to decide.

Bree careened squarely into his chest.

He let out a muffled oof as he seized and steadied her, hands spanning her waist. A satisfied smile lit his face when he felt Bud's arms grabbing his leg. "Gotcha! Both!"

Ryan was jumping up and down like a cheer-leader and whooping with glee. "Good one, Dad!"

"Thanks." Mitch's grin widened. Holding his ground, he used the opportunity to gaze into Bree's wide eyes. "What happened? I thought you guys were coming down one at a time?"

"I needed Bud to help me be brave enough," she said. "I couldn't have done it without him."

"Ah, I see."

"You can let go of me now." Bree pushed the man away, stepped back and nervously ran her hands over her hips as if her jeans needed smoothing. "I shouldn't have let you bully me into trying to do that. My boots didn't help at all."

"Nothing does in slimy clay. Your biggest problem was fear. You were way too tense."

A disclaimer was definitely called for. "Who wouldn't be tense sliding down a mountain of mud?" She tentatively lifted one foot. "Look what it's done to my poor boots! They didn't have a mark on them when we left home this morning. The awful stains will never come out of this suede."

"Good. Then there won't be any reason for you to avoid walking in the woods in the future. You need to listen to the birds, appreciate the wonders all around you, instead of always worrying about every-thing being perfect."

Frowning, Bree was still examining her feet.

"Perfect? Look at the globs of gunk stuck to my soles. If I walk much farther it'll be so thick I'll be six feet tall, like Bud."

Mitch chuckled and reached down to ruffle his youngest son's hair as he untangled him from around his lower leg and carefully set him apart, bear and all. "No, you won't. It'll fall off before then. Look. Most of the mud came off Bud when he skied down the hill with you."

"Nifty. Maybe I should climb up and come down again."

"Don't do that on my account," Mitch quipped. "Catching you when you're going fifty miles an hour is hard on me."

"Poor baby."

"I knew you'd be concerned. If you want, we can wait a minute while you wipe your feet."

"With what?"

"You weren't kidding about being raised in the city, were you?" he said, grinning. "Since you won't find a boot scraper out here, I suggest you use a clump of leaves or a rock."

If Mitch had dreamed she'd start to wade into the highest grass along the edge of the road to take his advice he'd have been a lot more specific.

"Not in there!" He grabbed her arm and yanked her clear, careful to keep from flinging her into the boys. "You'll get covered with seed ticks."

"Well, make up your mind." To her consternation, he'd crouched at her feet and was closely examining the denim covering her lower legs. She was about to order him to stop when he mumbled, "Uh-oh. Too late." He began swatting at her ankle.

That didn't set well with Bree. "What do you think you're doing?"

"Saving you from weeks of itching," Mitch said. "If these little bugs have a chance to climb higher you'll be real sorry, believe me."

Bree bent over and stared. "I don't see a thing."

"Well, I do."

"Don't be ridiculous."

"Okay. If you don't want my help…"

She paused long enough to consider his evident sincerity. "Show me one, and I'll believe you."

"I thought Missouri was the *show me* state. This is Arkansas."

"Humor me."

Mitch pinched the fabric near her ankle and held up his index finger. "There. See?"

"No." Bree squinted and peered at his fingertip.

"You're looking for something too big. Think tiny. Almost invisible. Just look for movement— and hurry up. I don't want this one to decide it likes the taste of me better than it does you."

Curiosity got the best of Ryan, and he crept closer to see, too. "Oh, wow! Awesome, Dad."

Thunderstruck, Brianne realized Mitch had been telling the truth. "Oh, for…" Instantly itchy from head to toe she started stamping her feet. "Ah! Get them off me!"

"That's what I've been trying to do," he said. "Hold still. Stop wiggling around."

"I feel like they're…" Glancing at the children and beginning to blush, she broke off and began hitting herself higher on both legs, hoping to do some good. "Never mind. Just get the rest of them off. Quick!"

Mitch took another couple of hard swipes at the fabric around her ankles, then straightened. "When you get back to the house you'll need to use bleach on your legs while you shower. That should take care of any I've missed."

"What do you mean, missed? You can't miss any. They'll bite me!"

"Unfortunately. You shouldn't have waded into that long grass. Big clumps of newly hatched ticks hang on the tips of the tallest blades waiting for a victim to pass by and knock them off. That's why I pulled you out of there so fast."

"I wish you'd warned me not to get near the grass in the first place."

"I didn't realize I needed to." His grin widened as he vigorously dusted off his hands. "Even the kids know better than to do that. You mentioned ticks a while back, so I figured you knew, too."

"I do—now," Bree said with a grimace. "Can we go home soon?"

"Gladly. We're almost to where the paved road starts. I'm pretty sure that'll be intact. The bad spots the radio reported should be between here and there. We'll know in a couple more minutes. Think you're up to finishing the hike?"

Brianne didn't answer except to break away while he was still speaking and begin clomping down the middle of the rutted road. Gummy clay coated the soles of her ankle-high boots and rolled up along the sides, hampering her progress. She persisted until the worst of the accumulation had sloughed off, glob by glob.

"Hey. Slow down and wait for the kids." Mitch's longer strides brought him even with her. "This isn't a race."

"It is for me. The sooner I get out of these clothes, the better I'll like it." Cheeks flaming, she cast him a sidelong glance then lowered her voice so the boys couldn't overhear. "Don't look so smug, mister. You know what I meant."

"I'm not smug," Mitch argued. "I know exactly how you feel." It was his turn to blush. "And you know what I meant."

Brianne couldn't help smiling. "Maybe we'd better quit talking before we're both any more embarrassed." She paused, listening. "Is that a motor I hear?"

"I think so!" Mitch looked back and motioned to the plodding boys. "Come on, you guys! We hear a car!"

The road ahead was narrow and winding with a few drop-offs. It was those places that showed the worst damage, the deepest cuts. Small valleys made the sound of the engine echo, confusing the direction it was coming from. All Mitch could hope for was that the vehicle they'd heard was on the same trail they were.

Bree lagged. "Slow down. You're killing us."

"You don't want whoever it is to get away, do you?"

"Of course not. Maybe you should go on ahead. I'll bring the kids. None of us are used to running in pudding."

"Feels more like cold oatmeal to me," Mitch countered. "You know. Gummy."

"What a disgusting thought. I don't think I'll ever eat oatmeal again without thinking of this. Yuck."

"I didn't like the stuff in the first place," he said. "Give me ham and eggs any day."

"Stop. You're making me hungry again."

"That's because you didn't eat enough of the great breakfast I cooked. You don't know what you missed. Barney loved the leftovers."

"Brag, brag, brag. You're insufferable."

"Thanks."

They rounded a corner masked by a thick stand of oaks and came upon the source of the noise. A white pickup truck with a county logo on the door sat on the opposite side of a wide fissure. The driver was gunning the motor. A second man was leaning on the handle of a shovel and squinting at the mired rear of the truck.

Mitch waved and shouted at them across the mucky chasm. "Hey! Over here!"

The man with the shovel spat into the dirt and slowly made his way around the truck to join his partner. As soon as the driver shut off the truck's engine, the man cupped his hand and called, "You folks all right?"

"As all right as a person can be when he's stranded," Mitch shouted. "How soon before you guys fix this road?"

The driver climbed out and waved. "That you, Mitch?"

"Yeah. Charlie?"

"In the flesh. What're you doin' up here?" With a chuckle he added, "Never mind. I can see what you're doin'."

Embarrassed, Brianne sidled away from Mitch and folded her arms while she watched the children approach.

"It's not what it looks like," Mitch said. "My car's stuck in a ditch up on Nine Mile Ridge. Any chance you can send somebody up there to pull it out for me?"

"'Fraid not. That road's messed up worse'n this one. We should have this place fixed in a day or so, though. Gotta get some good fill dirt in here and tamp it down. If we don't have any more gully washers it won't take long."

"What do you know about the phones?"

"Not a thing. That's not our department," Charlie said. "We've got enough problems with these here roads. You wouldn't believe the mess that storm made."

Mitch frowned. "Oh, yes, I would. Remind me to tell you about it when I get to town."

"Hey, I see you got your boys," the other man said. "They okay, too?"

"Fine. We're all fine. Right now we're staying at the Bailey place."

"Don't recall anybody by that name up this way," Charlie said. "Do you, Sam?"

The other man shook his head. "Nope. Must be newcomers."

Brianne stepped forward and tapped Mitch on the shoulder. "I have an unlisted number. Give it to them in case the phones start working, and then let's get back to the house. I itch all over."

"Okay." He shouted the numbers across the void as she recited them to him.

"Got it," Charlie said. "Take care a yourself, Mitch. I'll do what I can." Pausing, he glanced at the rear of his truck and snorted in disgust. "As soon as Sam gets me dug out, that is."

Mitch waved goodbye and turned to go, finding Bree and his sons thirty feet ahead of him, and headed the way they'd come. He hurried to catch up. "Wait for me."

Busy trying to keep her balance on the uneven, slippery road, Bree barely acknowledged him until he pulled even with her and asked, "What's your hurry?"

She gave him a dirty look. "I think I feel ticks in places I didn't even know I had."

"Well, don't take it out on me. It's not my fault you were too prissy to put up with a little mud on your shoes."

Ryan's resulting giggle put her in an even worse mood. "Prissy? Ha! I'm not having trouble putting up with anything but you," she declared.

Although Mitch didn't reply, his hurt expression made her conscience twitch uncomfortably. What was wrong with her? Why was she being so unkind to him all of a sudden? When you got down to basics, their present situation wasn't really his fault any more than it was hers.

Bree slowed and held out a hand to him. "I'm sorry. I shouldn't have snapped at you. I guess I'm just frustrated about this whole thing."

"That makes two of us," he grumbled.

"I know. I said I was sorry." The hint of a smile lifted one corner of her mouth.

"What's so funny?"

"I was just thinking." The smile grew. "I've finally found something you and I have in common. We're both in a really bad mood today."

Chapter Twelve

Mitch didn't talk any more than necessary as they struggled home via a roundabout course. His thoughts, however, were loud and clear. It didn't matter how attracted he was to Bree if she refused to give herself permission to consider him, or his family, as anything other than a nuisance.

There had been a few times since they'd met when he'd imagined an equal interest on her part, but she'd always managed to counter his enthusiasm with a big dose of reality. Lots of people survived an unhappy childhood to go on and lead a normal life, yet she was apparently determined to cling to the past. The question was, why?

Why, indeed. Beneath Bree's capable, self-confident facade he'd sensed the heart of a lonely, lost little girl. It was as if she was afraid to let anyone know she cared. Or was afraid to let herself become emotionally involved in the first place. The way she was acting right now, chances of his ever finding out which were slim and none.

They crested the final hill to arrive at the broad, sweeping lawn surrounding her house. Grass along the outer edges had grown noticeably after the heavy rain. Bree picked her way carefully past the tallest clumps.

Mitch had been carrying Bud most of the way home. He set the boy on his feet next to Ryan to wait for Barney while he reassured Bree. "You're probably safe from ticks this close to the house. Whoever mows the lawn has kept it short. That discourages bugs."

"Oh, goody. I'm so glad to hear my gardener is doing it right." She was out of breath and once again sounded curt.

The perplexing conversation he'd been carrying on within himself had left him irritable. His primary urge was to grab her, hold her tight, and kiss her senseless in spite of her off-putting attitude. Taking that course of action was probably the worst thing he could do, especially in front of the boys.

Then again, Mitch wasn't feeling very smart or very rational. He was physically weary and emotionally on edge. Only one thing seemed certain. Soon, the road would be opened and he'd have no excuse to be near Bree. If she refused to see him socially, as he suspected she would, he'd never get the chance to show her how right they could be for each other.

Looking at his impulse in that light gave it more credence. He hurried to catch up with her before she reached the rear door.

"Wait!"

Startled by the urgency in his voice, she hesitated and looked back. "Why? What's wrong?"

"I forgot to give you something."

Before she could ask what, he'd reached out, pulled her into his arms and kissed her with such intensity that she felt weightless, senseless—wonderful!

Conscious thought fled, replaced instantly by intuitive response. Brianne closed her eyes, clung to him and returned his kisses with all the pent-up fervor she'd tried so hard to hide from everyone, including herself.

This isn't love, she kept insisting. It's just a normal physical reaction to being kissed so passionately.

The only problem with that premise was that she was positive she wouldn't feel the same way if any other man were delivering those gentle yet demanding kisses.

Head spinning, Brianne fought to resist the insistence of her heart that Mitch Fowler was special. It was no use. She'd lost the fight before it began. There was only one thing to do—surrender, melt into his arms and return his kiss with all her heart and soul.

She'd almost forgotten they weren't alone when Ryan's high-pitched voice intruded on her bliss. He squealed, "Eeew. Gross!"

That was jarring enough to cause Bree to break off their mutual kiss. She turned her head, pressed her palms to Mitch's chest and tried to push him away. To her surprise he held her tight. The restriction only intensified her desire for freedom.

"Mitch, no." There was muted alarm in her tone. "We can't let this go any further. Remember the children."

He frowned, stared into her eyes. "Further? I wasn't trying to seduce you, Brianne. I wouldn't treat you that way even if the kids weren't here. I care for you. Why can't you see that?"

She didn't know how to respond. Possible seduction hadn't been a conscious part of her thoughts until he'd mentioned it. Now that he had, however, the disturbing notion refused to go away. Had he been telling her he cared merely as a prelude to a physical relationship? Maybe. That was the way her manipulative father had always approached her mother after one of their terrible arguments.

The comparison made her shiver. A few seconds

ago she'd been every bit as vulnerable as her mother used to be. Doubt surfaced. "Why me?"

By this time, Mitch was at the end of his tolerance. He'd given it his best shot when he'd kissed her. If she couldn't accept or understand the feelings he had for her, there was no use beating her over the head with them.

"Because I'm nuts," he said dryly.

Brianne realized immediately that she had destroyed what had remained of their romantic mood. Somehow, her pride carried on, substituting tongue-in-cheek humor for the ache in her heart. "I could have told you that."

"I'm sure you could have." Mitch not only stepped back, he shoved his hands into his pockets to keep himself from reaching out to her and shot her a look of annoyance. "Well, I suppose we might as well go in the house."

"I suppose so."

Exasperated, he looked at his eldest son. "You. Take off everything that's muddy and leave it outside on the porch. Then march straight to the bathroom and get into the shower."

"Bud, too?"

"Bud, too. And Barney," Mitch said flatly. "You're all taking a bath. You might as well do it together."

The boy pouted. Looking from his father to Brianne and back, he muttered to himself.

"One more word out of you and you'll spend the rest of your life locked up with that dog," Mitch threatened. He realized immediately how petulant and childish the warning sounded, but at the moment he didn't care one whit.

"I wish we'd never come here," Ryan countered, glaring at Brianne.

Mitch didn't hesitate. "Yeah. Me, too."

Well, Brianne noted, the Fowlers were beginning to sound more and more like a normal family. Not that that was a positive change. The look in Ryan's eyes had made the hair on the back of her neck prickle. His animosity couldn't have been clearer if he'd been shouting curses at her through a megaphone.

Bree was curled up on the sofa in the den, reading and absently scratching a red spot on her ankle, when Mitch found her later. She'd donned shorts and a sleeveless shirt so her clothing wouldn't irritate the bites she'd gotten on their hike.

One eyebrow rose as he noticed what she was doing. "Don't scratch that. You'll make it worse."

"Considering how badly I itch, I suppose I owe you a big thanks for knocking most of the bugs off," she said.

"You're welcome."

He was looking at his feet instead of at her. Bree

thought he seemed unduly nervous. "Did you want to talk to me?"

"Yes. About what happened this afternoon—I'm sorry. I know I was wrong."

Wrong to kiss me? Or wrong to get so mad at Ryan when he interrupted us? she wondered. "I'm glad you came and found me. I've been wanting to talk to you about Ryan."

"What's he done this time?"

"Nothing. It's just that he still seems awfully angry with me. Is it normal for kids to hold a grudge like that?"

"I don't know. I remember feeling unsettled at his age, but that was because my parents kept telling me I'd ruined their lives. In spite of Liz's poor choices I know she loved the boys. And so do I."

"Have you told them?"

"Sure," Mitch said.

"In so many words?"

"Words can be overrated."

"I suppose they can. So, what's the deal with Bud's teddy bear? Do you think it's some kind of security symbol for him and Ryan? Like a tangible form of reassurance?"

Mitch combed his fingers through his hair. "Beats me. If I didn't think taking that toy away would cause more trouble than it's worth, I'd get rid of it in a heartbeat. I'm just worried that Bud would fall apart if I did. I guess I'll have to wait till he outgrows his fixation."

"Oh, sure. I can picture him going off to college with that old bear hidden in his suitcase," she said, smiling. "Especially if Ryan has anything to do with it. Do you think it would help if you came right out and asked Ryan why he's so miffed at me?"

"Does it matter?" Hopeful, Mitch paused, studying her expression.

Brianne shrugged. "A few days ago I would have told you it didn't. That's changed. I can't explain why, it just has."

"Could it be that you *like* my kids?"

"Of course I like them. Sort of. They can't help it that they're young and totally confusing to me, any more than I can help feeling lost when I try to relate to them. For kids, I suppose they're not half bad."

Mitch's smile spread into a grin. "Thanks."

"You're welcome. So, will you have a talk with Ryan for me, after all?"

"Sure. Do you want to listen in?"

"No! That's the last thing he needs. He's already sure I'm the enemy. If you make it look like you've sided with me, you'll destroy any progress you may have made toward winning his trust. At least I think you will, assuming there's any logic to kids' thoughts."

"We can hope." Mitch reached for the doorknob, then hesitated. "What about the rest? You know."

"I do?"

"Yes."

She could swear he was blushing, which meant he was probably referring to their kiss. And what a kiss it had been!

"I don't know what you're talking about," Bree said.

"Liar."

"There you go again, besmirching my character."

"At least I'm consistent," Mitch countered.

"About some things."

Mitch started to leave, then paused again. "Oh, I meant to tell you. Dinner was great."

"Thanks." She laughed softly. "If I'd managed to ruin hot dogs and canned baked beans I'd never have lived it down. Oh, well, at least the kids liked it."

"And nothing exploded," Mitch quipped. "I would have complimented you at the time, but the boys were making so much noise all I wanted to do was get them fed and out of the kitchen."

"No kidding! I can see why people with children put picnic tables in their yards. They can't stand the constant mayhem inside the house."

"We should be gone in a couple more days," he said. "Think you can keep your sanity that long?"

"I'll try."

In the back of Bree's mind was the certainty that

the Fowler children weren't *half* the threat to her well-balanced life—or to her sanity—that their father was.

She picked up her book again but found concentration difficult, so she laid it aside and turned her thoughts to her unfinished manuscript.

Silently critiquing her characters, she realized she'd have to go back and make some changes, thanks to the time she'd spent around Mitch. Although he was far too human to be considered a role model for a hero, he had awakened her to a part of her subliminal self that had been a surprise. Obviously, she'd had a warped view of the way men's minds worked. Then again, there was no guarantee she understood Mitch's motivations any better than she did those of her fictional heroes!

The urge to go turn on her computer was great. She wandered to her office and decided to chance it. There hadn't been any noticeable power fluctuations for a long time, and she backed up everything she wrote on floppy disks anyway. If, heaven forbid, her computer did get toasted by an errant jolt of electricity, it wouldn't destroy her work to date.

Bree was seated at her desk, absently staring at the monitor and waiting for the necessary programs to load, when Mitch interrupted. "May we come in?" Ryan was with him.

"Of course. I just sat down. I'm not working yet."

"Good. Ryan has something to say to you."

The boy scuffed his bare toes against the carpet and made a face as he stared at the floor. It wasn't until Mitch nudged him that he looked up and spoke. "I...I'm sorry, Miss Bailey."

Bree smiled and pushed back her swivel chair. "Apology accepted. How about some cookies?"

"No, thank you," Ryan said soberly. "I'm not allowed to have any more."

"Oh? Why not?"

"'Cause I busted your dishes."

Looking from the boy to his father, she arched an eyebrow.

Mitch was shaking his head. "There's a lot more to it than that. I've been trying to explain the difference between being truly sorry and only pretending to be in order to get rewards. I think my rationale got lost in the translation when I mentioned eating your cookies in the same breath with holding a grudge."

"Probably," she said with a light laugh. "All this talk about cookies has made me hungry, though. Suppose we go see how many are left in the jar and divvy them up evenly. That way, you and I can eat a few now, and the boys will be sure we've saved some for them. Then they'll have something to look forward to when you're ready to let them have another treat."

To Bree's surprise, Ryan didn't argue. He looked at his father and didn't say a word.

"You can go," Mitch told him. "It's almost your bedtime, anyway. Carry Barney out the back door and let him go potty, then put him in the bathroom. When you've done that, maybe you and Bud can have one cookie and a little glass of milk."

"Yes, sir."

Impressed, Brianne stood with Mitch and watched the eight-year-old walk slowly down the hall, his bare feet padding on the dark tile. "I think you're making progress," she said softly.

"It does seem like it." In a show of frustration, Mitch raked his fingers through his hair. "Trouble is, I won't know for sure if I've done things right until he's grown up, and then it'll be too late."

"He'll be fine. They both will be."

"I'm not as worried about Bud," Mitch said. "He's a different kind of kid."

"He's also younger, more impressionable," she reminded him. "Surely that makes a difference, too."

"I suppose so. What they both need is a decent mother—someone like you."

Bree held up both hands as if fending off a literal advance. "Whoa. Stop right there. You said it all when you said a decent mother. Their first one wasn't exactly mother of the year. Don't make the same mistake again."

"Meaning?"

"Meaning, I decided a long time ago that I was never going to subject any child to the kind of up- bringing I had. Period. Relationships are too tenuous, too apt to fall apart. Putting kids into the mix only makes things worse."

"Or better," Mitch countered.

"Don't count on it. People tend to repeat the same mistakes they were raised with, whether they mean to or not. That's a statistical fact. I don't intend to saddle myself with such a serious responsibility."

"You don't believe in the healing power of love? How can you write the kind of books you do if you don't buy into the illusion?"

"Illusion is the right word," Bree said. "Just because I can create a believable fantasy on paper doesn't mean I think I can do it in real life."

Mitch took a step closer, then stopped when he saw her tense up. "I think you could," he said quietly, "if you weren't afraid to try."

Chapter Thirteen

Bree would have left him standing there and retreated into her office behind closed doors if she hadn't been afraid that doing so would affirm his erroneous opinion. Instead, she put on a pleasant expression and led the way to the kitchen.

Bustling around, she set the cookie jar on the table and reached for the can of coffee. "Shall I make us a cup?"

"Only if you have decaf," Mitch said wearily. "I haven't been sleeping well. More caffeine won't help."

"Okay. Decaf it is." She went to work measuring as she continued their conversation. "You'll sleep better when you get your own roof over your head again. I wish I'd been able to find you a permanent place before your stupid dog ate my phone."

He sank into a chair at the table, his shoulders slumping, his elbows propped in front of him, fingers laced together. "If you'd bothered to ask me in the first place, I'd have told you I had a place in town. As a matter of fact, I remember trying to tell you at least once."

"When?"

"I don't know."

"Roughly?"

"I think it may have been about the time you'd run down the battery in your cell phone. You were so overwrought you wouldn't listen to a thing I said."

"Well, you could have kept trying," Bree said, annoyed. "I've been worrying myself sick about where you were going to live. Why the sob story about the cabin if you weren't homeless? Were you getting even with me?"

"Of course not." Mitch heaved a noisy sigh. "Do you always think the worst about everybody or do you save that attitude exclusively for me?"

"I'm an equal-opportunity cynic," she said. "Even Ryan had me fooled."

"About what?"

"The big house. He said you sold it to get the money to look for him and Bud, and that was why you all had to go live in the old cabin."

"That's more of his scrambled logic," Mitch

countered. "I did have an expensive house. And I did sell it. True, most of the money went into the long-term search for Liz and the kids, but I'm not desti-tute. I never said I was. Matter of fact, I distinctly remember telling you that I built houses for a living."

Brianne racked her brain. Had he? Probably. Whenever Mitch was speaking she'd constantly had to fight to keep her mind from wandering the way it did when she was formulating a plot for one of her stories.

"Okay," she admitted, "maybe you did say some-thing about having a job. But that doesn't mean I understood what you meant."

"Why not?"

"I don't know."

"I think I do," Mitch told her. "You were judging me by what you could see. You'd decided from the get-go that I was a poor hillbilly without a dime so you didn't pay attention to anything I said that might have changed your mind."

"I did nothing of the kind!"

"Oh, no? I lived in a cabin with no running water or indoor plumbing. As far as you knew, I was raising my sons there. When we got flooded out, I showed up with a handful of possessions and nothing else." He huffed in disgust. "I'm surprised you even let us in."

In retrospect, so was she. Normally she'd have

been so apprehensive of a knock on her door in the middle of a storm she'd have hesitated to answer it at all. Yet she had. And had immediately taken in the waifs on her doorstep as if she were running some kind of halfway house for soggy ragamuffins.

The analogy brought her up short. That *was* how she'd viewed Mitch and his family, wasn't it? Well, it wasn't her fault. He'd certainly looked the part both times she'd seen him.

"I suppose I should apologize," Bree finally said. "I'm still getting used to living out here in the country. Nothing is like where I came from. It's a whole new world for me."

"I don't doubt that."

"You don't have to sound so smug."

"Yeah, well, I'm sorry, too." He picked up a cookie and studied it to give himself something to do besides look at Bree. He finally took a bite and chewed slowly. "Now that I think about it, I was doing the same kind of thing with regard to you until recently."

Bree was puzzled. "You were?"

"Yes. I'd made up my mind that you and I could never get along together because of this fancy-schmancy house of yours and the way you live."

"You were right."

"Nope," he drawled. "I was wrong. If you were really as prissy as I'd thought, you'd have thrown us out on our ears long ago." He chuckled. "Especially Barney."

Mitch's good humor was affecting Bree's mood. "That had occurred to me. Often. I'd have done it, too, except I didn't want the kids to pitch a fit."

"I don't buy that. You've gone to a lot of trouble to try to convince me you don't like the boys. If that were truly the case, you wouldn't care how upset they got."

"Sure I would. I'm not mean."

An enigmatic smile lit his countenance. "My point, exactly."

By the time Bree and Mitch left the kitchen it was after ten. Yawning behind his hand, he bid her a polite good-night and said, "Guess the kids forgot their cookies and went straight up to bed. I'll go tuck them in. See you in the morning." He started up the stairs.

"Good night."

Trapped amid whirling emotions and confused thoughts, Brianne headed toward her office. There was no way she could recapture the mood to work on her book. Not tonight. Not after the disturbing conversation she and Mitch had just had. It didn't matter that he'd been dead wrong about her. Once real life intruded and she lost the feeling that she was a part of her ongoing story, her creativity vanished.

She knew she could either be sensible and quit for the night, or sit at her computer and stare blankly at the blinking cursor while her mind wandered. In other words, the lights were on but there was definitely nobody home.

The door to her office stood ajar. Pushing it all the way open, Brianne froze, puzzled. Something looked wrong. Her desk chair had been rolled up to face the computer, and although she couldn't see anyone sitting in it because its back was toward the door, she could look past it and see colorful figures dancing across the edges of her monitor screen.

She stared, openmouthed and unbelieving. Then, she launched herself across the room with a yowl that could have been heard all the way to Little Rock—and probably was.

"No! Not my computer!"

She grabbed the back of the swivel chair and spun it around. There sat Ryan, hands in the air as if he were an arch criminal who had just been caught red-handed by the police. Bud, who was squeezed into the chair beside him, puckered up to cry.

Apparently Ryan had been balancing the keyboard in his lap, because when Bree moved the chair, the short cable beneath the keyboard held it back and sent it crashing to the floor.

"I don't believe you did this!" she screeched.

"How could you? How dare you? You're supposed to be in bed!"

"It's just a game," the older boy said. "We didn't hurt your stupid computer."

"Stupid computer?" Bree howled. "It's my whole life! My business. I can't work without it."

"So?"

"So? So?"

She was so angry at the inconsiderate child she didn't know what to do or say next. Mitch appeared in the doorway just in time. Bud bailed out of the chair and ran to him. Ryan went, too, though he took his time.

Scowling, Mitch looked to Bree for answers. "I heard you screaming all the way upstairs. What happened?"

"I caught them playing with my computer!"

"Did they hurt it?"

What a stupid question. "I don't know. What difference does it make. *Nobody* touches my computer. Nobody!"

"Don't you think you should check it before you come unglued? Kids are pretty savvy about electronic gadgets these days. Chances are, it's fine."

"That's not the point."

"It's exactly the point," Mitch argued, keeping his voice even, his attitude calm. "I'm going to take the boys upstairs and put them to bed now. Then I'll come back down here. While I'm gone, I want you to carefully check your files."

Taking the boys by the hand and turning to go, he paused. "If you expect my children to be drawn and quartered for touching your computer, you're going to have to prove to me that they've actually destroyed it."

Brianne was playing computer solitaire when Mitch returned.

She glanced at him with a disgusted expression. "Everything's fine."

"I thought it would be."

"No, you *hoped* it would be. There's a big difference."

"I'll give you that one," he said, sauntering across the room and perching on the edge of her desk. "If it's any consolation, Ryan says he's sorry."

"So what else is new?"

"Well, at least he's going to get used to apologizing. I'm sure it's a skill he'll need plenty in the years to come."

"Undoubtedly." Abandoning her half-finished game, Bree scooted her chair back. "I hope I scared him good."

"You must have," Mitch said. "You terrified me. I thought for sure there'd been a murder down here or something."

Bree smiled. "There almost was."

"That's what Bud figured. He was a lot more scared than Ryan. It took me a long time to get him calmed down."

"Oh, dear." The smile faded. "I didn't mean to frighten him like that. I just saw what was going on and reacted instinctively. If anything happens to my computer I'm out of business. Did you explain that to the boys?"

Mitch chuckled under his breath. "Sort of. I think I said something about you being crazy and unstable."

"Oh, that's close. Poor little Bud." Rolling her eyes and shaking her head, she stood and headed for the door. "I'm going up there right now and explain it to him."

"Okay," Mitch said, following, "but if he's already asleep I'd appreciate it if you didn't wake him. He's had a pretty rough time the last couple of days."

"He's had it rough? What about me?"

"Okay. None of us have had an easy time of it," he agreed with a weary sigh. "But it'll all be over soon. After we're gone, I hope you'll remember us fondly."

Remember them? She'd couldn't have forgotten the Fowlers if she'd tried. Nevertheless, Bree wasn't about to let herself be drawn into another serious discussion about her personal feelings. No, sir. Especially not when a still, small voice kept insisting that she didn't really want the road to be repaired. Not soon. Maybe not ever.

Logic told her they couldn't continue the way they had been for much longer, though. To begin with, she'd soon run out of food. It was amazing how much the four of them had already consumed, even if you didn't count the meals she'd partially ruined or the leftovers she'd given the dog.

Other staples were in short supply, too. Right after Barney had dined on her cell phone, he'd decided to shred several extra rolls of toilet paper for dessert. Add laundry soap and paper towels to that list, and they'd soon be in dire need.

Climbing the stairs a few steps behind her, Mitch spoke softly, sincerely. "I want you to know, as soon as I get back to town, I'm going to make every effort to let folks know there was nothing funny going on up here."

"Funny? Like what?"

"You know. Hanky-panky."

She giggled. "Do people still use that expression?"

"They do around here. And their moral code dates back to the old days, too. Charlie's bound to mention having seen us together. I don't want anybody saying or thinking anything bad about you on my account."

"That's sweet. But you don't need to worry about my reputation. I've already told you I don't get out much. By the time I've lived here awhile they'll all be sure I'm some kind of nutty recluse, anyway. Which I am."

"That could change." Mitch had closed the distance between them, and his breath ruffled her hair as he spoke.

Barely ahead, Brianne sensed his nearness. Her steps slowed at the top landing.

After what seemed like eons, Mitch finally came closer and wrapped his arms around her. She laid her arms over his and leaned against his strong chest with a sigh.

The quiet hallway wrapped them in the cocoon of its dimness and made Bree feel as if they were the only two people in the world. If only that were so. If only her waking dreams could come true. There was a rightness, a flawlessness in Mitch's touch, in his nearness. It was the rest of their world that was all wrong.

Tears blurred her already cloudy vision. Closing her eyes, she wished she were the kind of person who could pray, believing her plea would be heard, because this was the perfect time to ask God for a miracle.

Mitch bent to place a kiss on her hair, then whispered, "I'm going to miss you, honey."

She couldn't speak, couldn't make herself respond in kind. No matter what she said it would only make matters worse. A solitary tear slid down her cheek and dropped onto his arm before she could catch it.

Once again, he leaned and nuzzled her hair, kissing her ear, her temple, the corner of her eye and finally her cheek. She was crying. For that he blamed himself. He'd pushed her too hard. Too fast. Because he'd managed to fall in love in the space of a few days, he'd made the mistake of believing it could be mutual.

He turned her in his embrace and lifted her chin with one finger so she'd have to look at him. "Ryan isn't the only one who needs to keep apologizing. I'm sorry, Bree. I wasn't trying to torment you. I just didn't want to leave here without telling you how I felt."

Mitch bent to place a chaste kiss on her trembling, moist lips, then straightened and held her away from him. "Do you understand what I'm trying to say?"

Her silent nod was his answer.

"Good. Then I think I'd better leave you now, before I have to lie to your neighbors about what did or didn't go on while I was staying with you." He managed a tenuous smile. "You can talk to the boys in the morning. We'll all feel a lot better in the daylight."

She watched him turn and walk away. Standing alone in the long hallway, she realized she'd never felt more isolated, more bereft, in her entire life.

Feel better in the daylight? Her thoughts echoed. Now that *would* be a miracle.

Chapter Fourteen

The following morning, Brianne accepted Mitch's offer to help her prepare a second meal of pancakes, but only because their food supplies were getting scarce, and she couldn't afford to make another error and waste precious ingredients.

They were both in the kitchen, sidling around and trying to work without getting too close to each other, when they heard a rumble in the distance.

She stopped in the midst of setting the table and turned to him. "Is that thunder?"

"No. I don't think so. It sounds like heavy equipment to me. Maybe Charlie and his crew have started working on that part of the road, like he said they would."

"Oh." Bree felt numb. Time was running out.

Ryan came barreling into the kitchen, almost

knocking the plates out of her hands. "Dad! Is the road fixed?"

"If it isn't, it soon will be," Mitch said. He carefully flipped the hotcakes he'd been tending. "Go get your brother and be sure your hands are clean. Breakfast is almost ready."

Ryan left the room the same way he'd entered, at a dead run, shouting, "Bud! We get to go home!"

"How long do you think the repairs will take?" Bree purposely avoided eye contact with Mitch so she wouldn't inadvertently reveal her disappointment.

"There's no way to tell. Hours, days. It'll depend on how much clay is in the soil and whether or not they have to truck in a lot of fill dirt and rocks, I suppose. Why?"

"I just wondered."

"You aren't going to miss us, are you?"

"Of course not!"

"Uh-huh. That's what I thought." Mitch knew he'd sensed a lot more emotion in her denial than she'd intended. Still, as long as she kept refusing to consider the prospect that they might be right for each other, there was nothing he could do or say that would change things between them.

Of course, there was also the possibility that he was mistaken, Mitch admitted ruefully. He'd consciously placed his whole life in God's hands before he'd gotten his boys back. Nothing had happened since then to change that unwavering commitment. Consequently, it made sense to conclude that if the good Lord had wanted him to stay with Brianne long enough to convince her they were compatible, He wouldn't have let the crew repair the road so quickly.

Mitch huffed in disgust. It was a lot easier to trust the Lord for answers to prayer when he was getting exactly what he'd prayed for, wasn't it? No kidding! It was also easier when he thought he'd figured out just what God's aim was in a particular situation. In this case, he didn't have a clue, unless… Unless he was supposed to be helping Brianne instead of the other way around!

Looking at the present dilemma in that light gave him a broader scope of ideas. As folks said, it isn't over till it's over. Therefore…

"Once the road is passable, would you mind driving us down to Serenity?" Mitch asked.

"What about your car?" She sounded disconcerted. "You can't just abandon it."

"I figured to get a few friends to help me. We can come back later and use my work truck to pull the car out."

"Oh." Bree didn't think her raw emotions could withstand the stress of a prolonged drive to town with Mitch Fowler seated next to her, yet she saw no graceful way to refuse. "Well, I suppose I can drive you. That is, providing the road is good and solid. I don't want to get my car stuck, too."

He flashed her a winning smile. "If we get stranded we can always hike back up here like we did before."

"No way. I've tromped around in enough mud to last me the rest of my life, thank you."

"Speaking of mud, I noticed that the creek below the spring is running normally again. You don't intend to rebuild your lake, do you?"

"Not a chance," she said quickly. "If I want fresh fish I'll buy it in the market."

"You like to fish?"

"You don't have to sound so surprised. Fishing was fun the few times I tried it. I figured, if I stocked the pond well, it would be a good source of natural food."

Mitch laughed at her naiveté. "Have you ever cleaned a fish?"

"No. So what? How hard can it be?"

"That's not the point," he said, continuing to chuckle. "Trust me. It's *way* too messy for you."

His smart-alecky attitude and the strain of knowing he'd soon be out of her life for good coupled to make her unduly short-tempered. "When are you going to stop assuming I'm some kind of obsessive cleanliness nut? Just because I don't happen to be a slob doesn't mean there's anything wrong with me."

"You're right," he said sagely. "There's not a thing wrong with liking nice things. Or with getting dressed up to go to town occasionally. Take Sunday mornings, for instance. I'll bet you'd feel a lot better about me if I showed up in a suit and tie when I picked you up for church."

Brianne crinkled her brow, stared at him. "What are you talking about? I never said I was going to church with you."

"No, but it's safe. And public. And it will certainly help your reputation if you let me introduce you to the folks in town that way."

"I told you. I'm not worried about my reputation. I don't want to meet a lot of new people. I like my solitude. I need to preserve it in order to work, remember?"

"So you said. What happens when you run out of ideas? Where do you go to recharge your batteries, so to speak?"

He had a point. Though books and movies were good as far as they went, it was more intellectually stimulating to interact with real people. Still, she wasn't keen on going to church with him. There was something awfully personal about it.

"Thanks, but no, thanks," Bree said.

"Are you afraid?"

Her head snapped around, her eyes narrowing. "Of course not. You don't scare me one bit."

"I wasn't talking about me," Mitch said. "I was talking about God."

"That's ridiculous."

"Is it? You told me once that you used to be a believer—until your mother died."

"So? What did I know? I was just a kid."

"When it comes to God, we all are," he argued. "There's nothing wrong with that. It's not a sin to ask questions, either. Or to doubt God's love or His wisdom when we're faced with loss. I did the same thing when my boys disappeared. The sad part is when a person gets stuck in that rut and never works through it."

"I'm not stuck in any rut," Bree said flatly.

A broad grin spread across Mitch's face. "Good. Then as soon as the boys and I are settled in town and the phones start working again, I'll call you and we'll pick a Sunday that's good for both of us."

I won't go, she assured herself. *Call all you want. I won't go. I won't go. I won't go.*

The return of the exuberant children didn't distract her. Nothing did. All during breakfast and the cleanup afterward the same declaration kept running through Brianne's mind. She nurtured it as if it alone would ensure her unwavering resolve.

Adamant, she convinced herself that if she'd had

her computer powered up she'd have programmed the negative statement into a screen saver!

Ryan was in the yard with Barney, so he was the first to spot the approach of their rescuers. He barreled into the house with a whoop that almost scared the poor dog into having another accident.

Everyone headed for the front porch to see what all the shouting was about. Bree paused just outside the door while the others ran ahead to meet the approaching vehicle. It was a medium-size truck with a light bar mounted above the cab and a second bench seat behind the driver.

Her heart lodged in her throat. She edged closer to listen to what was being said. Mitch was gesturing to the men in the mud-caked volunteer fire department rescue truck and pointing to the canyon, telling the story of what had happened to his cabin.

Three men in heavy yellow coats climbed out of the truck. Mitch shook hands with them, then looked at his children.

Bree heard him say, "Okay, boys. The firemen are going to give us a lift into town if we hurry. You guys need to go back in the house and gather up your stuff."

Then he looked at Brianne. "Guess you're off the hook. You won't need to drive us home, after all."

"Good." She lifted her chin, managed a slight

smile. "Whatever you do, don't forget to take the dog."

Chuckling, Mitch stepped closer and gently grasped her hands. "There are lots of things I won't forget, especially your kindness and tolerance."

"Or the fact that it was my fault you almost got killed."

"Nobody's perfect," he said, caressing her knuckles with his thumbs. "But I will have to admit, you're closer than most."

"Thanks. I think."

"You're welcome." Mitch released her. "Well, I guess I'd better go get my gear, too. Not that there's a lot of it. I just don't want you to have to clean up after us when we're gone."

He hesitated, looking from the house to the waiting fire truck. "Uh-oh. I just thought of something. I won't have time to scrub the spare bathroom before I go."

"That's okay," Bree said. "Now that the road is open, Emma will be coming again soon. Whatever cleaning I don't get done, she can finish."

"Okay. But that bathroom door will have to be replaced. I'll measure it the next time I'm here, then pick one up and install it for you later."

Bree couldn't stand there and allow him to talk about their nonexistent future for one more second. "That won't be necessary. I'll call the firm that remodeled the house before I moved in and have them handle it. That way, you won't have to bother, and everything will be sure to match."

Sighing in resignation, Mitch nodded. "Okay. Have it your way." Backing away he added dryly, "Perfect, as usual."

Rather than go into the house while Mitch was inside, Brianne waited on the lawn for the little family to come out. When they did, Mitch herded them past her as if she were of no more interest to him than one of her ornamental shrubs.

"Bud and Ryan, you ride in the jump seats," he was saying. "I'll take Barney with me. Let's go. Move it."

Ryan obeyed easily. Bud lagged behind, then doubled back to Brianne. There were tears in his eyes.

Overcome with more affection than she'd thought possible, she dropped to her knees and took his little hand. "You be a good boy, okay?"

Sniffling, he nodded.

Fighting her own tears, she smiled at Bud, gave him a tender hug, then set him away and kissed his damp cheek. "I love you, honey. You remember that. Okay?"

"O-kay."

"And take good care of your bear."

"Okay." Hesitating, he sniffled again and looked

at Brianne, his eyes glistening with more tears. "I want you to be my new mama."

That did it. Bree began to weep silently, unashamed. "Oh, honey, I wish I could be, but life doesn't work like that. Grown-ups have a lot of other problems to worry about. Not everybody in your family likes me the way you do. You wouldn't want them to be unhappy, would you?"

The child burst into tears and threw himself at her, clinging to her neck with fierce determination. She struggled to her feet and carried him to the rescue truck, no more willing to let go of him than he was to release his hold on her.

I won't have Mitch Fowler feeling sorry for me, she lectured herself. I can't let him see how upset I am.

While Mitch was leaning into the truck to check Ryan's seat belt, Bree handed Bud to one of the firefighters and hurried toward the house.

It would have been gracious to stand on the porch, put on a brave front and wave a friendly farewell to her accidental guests. Unfortunately, Bree knew she didn't have enough self-control left to manage it.

It hurt too much to even *think* about what was happening. Seeing Mitch and the boys driving away would be far more pain than her wounded heart could take.

* * *

"Cute dog," the youngest firefighter said. He and Mitch were leaning against the rear of the truck's cab, watching the road play out behind them while the others rode in the seats up front. Barney was curled in Mitch's lap, shivering in spite of the warm day.

"The kids found him during the storm," Mitch said, petting the dog to soothe it—and himself. "I hope nobody comes forward to claim him when I place an ad in the lost and found. We're all pretty attached to him already."

"I can see why. He does look kind of lost. Course, so do…" He stopped talking and looked away.

Mitch knew exactly what he'd left unsaid. "My boys? Yeah, I know. They've had it pretty rough lately."

"I heard Miz Fowler'd died a while back. Sorry about that. So, you and the writer lady fixin' to get together after all a this? You could do worse 'n her, that's a fact. 'Sides, I heard she's rich."

Mitch glared at him as if the other man had just spit in his face. "I suggest you keep your opinions of Ms. Bailey and me to yourself." His voice was almost a growl. "You get my drift?"

"Yes, sir, Mr. Fowler," the younger man said. "Ain't none of my business who you're living with. No, sirree. If you and her want to shack up, nobody's gonna hear about it from me."

Furious, Mitch figured it was a good thing he had to keep holding on to the dog to keep it from jumping out of the moving truck. If he'd had both hands free, he might have done something he'd have been sorry for later.

He clenched his jaw. This was exactly the kind of wild rumor he'd been worried about.

If he'd had only his welfare to consider when he learned that Brianne was living alone, he'd have left her house immediately, before anyone found out he'd even been there. Responsibility for Ryan and Bud, however, had eliminated that option.

Although he hadn't consciously made the choice to damage Brianne Bailey's reputation, he had chosen to put the health and safety of his sons first. It had been the right thing to do. Unfortunately, this was the result.

Denial of any wrongdoing would only sound like an excuse and make matters worse. If Bree didn't get out of that house of hers pretty soon and personally demonstrate the kind of upright, virtuous person she really was, there was no telling how bad the gossip would get.

Maybe she didn't care, as she'd claimed, but *he* did. She'd rescued his family, and he was going to see to it that she didn't have to pay any higher price for her good deed than she already had.

And as for himself? Mitch snorted in disgust.

The price he was paying was infinitely higher than a mere reputation. Being around Brianne had cost him his heart and soul. Whether he'd ever be able to reclaim them remained to be seen.

Chapter Fifteen

For days after everyone else had left, Brianne had wandered aimlessly through her cavernous house, unable to concentrate, unable to work. Without Mitch and the boys underfoot, the place seemed more than empty. It seemed desolate.

Everything she saw, everything she touched, reminded her fondly of them—even the cookie crumbs she'd found in the boys' bed when she'd stripped off the sheets and gathered them to be washed.

"I'm hopeless," she murmured. "Absolutely hopeless."

She paused on the upper landing of the staircase, hugging the loose bundle of sheets and remembering the last time she and Mitch had stood there together. Could he have been trying to say what she'd thought he was? Or was she reading more into his declaration than was really there because affection was what always developed in the stories she wrote?

Her sensible nature came to her rescue. There was no way two people could fall in love in just a few days. Those kinds of things only happened in fairy tales. She and Mitch might have felt some fondness for each other due to the stressful situation they'd been trapped in, but that didn't mean they'd found anything lasting. They couldn't have. They hardly knew each other.

The sound of an approaching car caught her attention. Now what?

Bree had missed out on her housekeeper's usual Thursday session because the phone lines hadn't been repaired in time for Bree to call and assure the older woman that the road was safe. By the time she'd finally reached her on Friday night, Emma had insisted she wasn't free again until the following Tuesday. Could she have taken pity on her part-time employer and come early, after all?

Hopeful, Bree listened. The car was slowing. She dropped the loose sheets in a pile on the entry floor and hurriedly threw open the front door.

An unfamiliar pickup truck with an extended cab had stopped in the driveway. A well-dressed man was getting out. It couldn't be! It was. Mitch Fowler!

She gaped in awe. His hair had been trimmed and was neatly combed. A dark blue suit accented his trim frame, making his shoulders seem even broader, his waist more narrow. He was wearing a pale blue dress shirt and silk tie. Bree was flabbergasted. If she'd passed him on the street she might not have recognized him.

Behind him, a small arm was waving to her from the rear seat of the shiny black truck. It looked like Bud. She returned the greeting. "Hi!"

Mitch smiled, eyeing her. "I like that outfit. It looks nice and cool. But I'm afraid shorts aren't really appropriate for where we're going. How long will it take you to change?"

"What are you talking about?"

"It's Sunday. We've come to take you to church."

Bree backed up, hands raised to fend him off. "Oh, no, you don't. You said you'd call first."

"You have an unlisted phone. I couldn't call."

"Hey, that's not my fault. You could have asked me for the number if you'd really wanted it. You were here long enough."

He shrugged, pushed back his cuff to check his watch. "I know. My error. So, you coming with us? The service starts in forty-five minutes."

"No way."

"Okay. But if we backslide it'll be your fault."

Mitch opened the passenger side door of his truck

and folded the front seat forward to make it easier for the boys to clamber out.

"Come on, guys. It'll get too hot to sit in there for long. You can run around on the grass while I talk to Ms. Bailey. Just try to keep your new clothes and shoes clean, will you?"

"Yeah!" Ryan shouted. Hitting the ground, he immediately raced for the back of the house with his brother in pursuit. As always, Bud's bear made it a threesome.

Mitch was removing his suit jacket and loosening his tie as Bree asked, "Where's Barney?"

"Home." He gave a short laugh. "I didn't think you'd appreciate riding with him."

"That's a pretty truck. It looks new."

"It is. I wanted something that was roomy and safe for the kids. It had to come with four-wheel drive too, so we wouldn't get stuck again. This seemed to fill the bill." Mitch laid his jacket neatly over the back of the front seat, tossed the tie in after it and slammed the door.

"Can you afford it?"

"Yes. I told you I'm not broke. So, shall we go inside?"

"Well… The place is kind of a mess."

"Never. Not your house."

Brianne pulled a face. "I missed Emma's regular Thursday session last week."

"I'll manage to tolerate the clutter, no matter how bad it is," Mitch teased. He casually looped an arm around her shoulders. "Come on. I need a big dose of that air-conditioning you keep on all the time."

What could she say? All her mental rehearsal had been in vain. He'd already thwarted her by not insisting she drop everything and attend church with him.

"All right. But one joke about lousy housekeeping and out you go."

Laughing heartily, he escorted her to the door. "I wouldn't dream of it. So, tell me…what have you cooked lately?"

Bree was in a perfect position to elbow him in the ribs, and that's exactly what she did. Mitch's resulting *oof* made her giggle. "Hush. You deserved that, and more."

"Probably." He'd released her and was feigning injury by rubbing his ribs. Then he spotted the pile of sheets on the floor and switched to visible shock. "What happened there? Did a laundry truck wreck in your foyer?"

"I warned you…"

"Okay, okay. Let's go into the kitchen so we can watch the boys from the windows. They may look like they've reformed, but believe me, the change is mostly on the outside."

"I should have complimented you," Bree

drawled, eyeing him surreptitiously as he led the way down the hall. "You cleaned up nicely."

"Told you. It's the suit."

"I meant the boys. They look really nice this morning," she said, suppressing another giggle when Mitch turned to give her a derogatory look.

She crossed to the kitchen sink and peered out the window above it. "Speaking of which, I don't see them."

"Well, they can't have gone far. Not in those shoes. They're brand new. I had to sandpaper the soles to keep them from slipping on the carpet at home."

"Did you get settled in okay? I was worried you might need some help, but I was as cut off as you were. I didn't ask for your address or phone number, either."

"I'm in the book," Mitch said absently. Leaning past her, he began to frown when he couldn't spot his children. "Excuse me a minute. I think I'd better go check on the kids."

It never occurred to Brianne to let him do it alone. Once outside, she had to half run to keep up with his long, purposeful strides.

He called, "Ryan!"

She thought she heard a faint answer from the direction of the canyon where the stream ran.

"Over there," she said, pointing.

Mitch was way ahead of her. Breaking into a run, he sped across the wide lawn, not slowing until he reached the ruptured clay knoll that was all that remained of her manmade dam. He stopped, looked over the edge.

Thirty feet below, Ryan, muddy and crying, was struggling to keep his footing on the slick slope.

Without a moment's hesitation, Mitch plunged over the edge toward the frantic boy.

So did Bree.

Brambles and sharp twigs scratched her bare legs below her shorts. Mud and slimy dead leaves squished into her sandals and between her toes. She ignored the discomfort. All that mattered was reaching Ryan and finding out what was going on.

Mitch got there first. "Where's Bud?"

Shaky sobs kept the eight-year-old from speaking clearly enough to be understood. Frantic, Mitch grabbed him by the shoulders. "Calm down. What happened? Where's your brother?"

"Down there," Ryan said. "The bear fell."

"In the water?" Mitch shouted.

Ryan nodded vigorously. "I—I tried to stop him. I told him I'd get it for him, like always, but—"

Before he'd finished speaking, Bree was on her way again. Wherever Bud ended up, she knew it would have to be lower down the slippery hill. She didn't even want to think about the possibility he might have jumped into the creek to rescue his teddy bear. The water wasn't deep, but it was swift. Dangerous. And still filled with debris from the flood.

Tree branches hung in her path and slapped her face, her bare arms. Saplings bent under the weight of her body as she passed over them, then snapped back like a whip.

She could hear Mitch crashing through the brush, gaining on her, but there was no time to worry about holding the branches to keep them out of his face. Poor little Bud was in danger. Mitch was on his own.

Breathless, she cried, "Bud! Where are you?"

There was no answering shout. Not even a whimper.

Closing in, Mitch echoed her call. His voice was hoarse, breaking with emotion. "Bud! Bud!"

Bree could see the slope easing. Ahead, the creek widened. White water boiled over the remains of a fallen oak. Its broken branches extended like claws, bare of leaves and reaching for the sky in one last, silent plea.

Her heart stopped. Was something small and brown caught in the undertow beneath the tree's battered trunk? There was only one way to be sure. Grabbing wildly at passing vegetation to slow her descent, Bree threw herself over the bank and into the racing water.

Mitch read purpose in her headlong leap. He slid to a stop, gasping for breath, and flattened himself on the ground on his stomach, one hand holding fast to a snag, the other reaching out over the water toward her. "Brianne! Do you see him?"

Her head broke the roiling surface of the icy water. She coughed, gagged. There was pathos and desperation in her eyes.

"Did you see Bud?" Mitch shouted again.

"No. Just the bear," she answered. "I felt all along the bottom. There's nothing else here."

"You sure?"

"Positive."

Mitch scrambled to his feet, staggered, slipped. Wild-eyed, he stared at the water as it cascaded down the canyon.

"Go!" Bree waved her arms and yelled at him. "Leave me. It's not deep here. I can stand. I'll be all right. Go! Go!"

To her relief, Mitch followed her orders and quickly disappeared past the fallen tree. She made one last underwater foray to satisfy herself that she hadn't overlooked any clues, then pulled herself to the bank, tossed the teddy bear onto higher ground and crawled out after it.

Remaining on her hands and knees for a moment to catch her breath, Bree shivered. It wasn't because she was chilled. It hurt to inhale, to move. Her ribs felt sore, like one of those jagged limbs might have poked them without her realizing it. Maybe it had. So what? That kind of minor injury didn't matter. Not now.

She hauled herself to her feet, pushed her wet hair from her face, then pressed a hand to her aching side, held it tight, and set off to follow Mitch down the canyon.

She couldn't see him because of the thick vegetation, but she could hear him shouting for his missing son. That was enough to keep her going.

The ground started leveling out. The streambed was lined with enormous black rocks that looked like they'd been stacked one atop the other in flat, uneven layers by some giant hand. Over time, running water had polished the exposed surfaces, making walking on the rocks treacherous.

Drawing ragged breaths, Brianne paused to listen. She could still hear Mitch in the distance. What else? Was that a child sobbing? The sound was growing louder. Bud? Anxious, she looked around, hoping, praying.

No, it was Ryan. Her heart plummeted. The older boy was running blindly along the opposite bank, weeping as he went. He was soaking wet, like her, and muddy from head to foot. Apparently, he'd been in the water, too, and had saved himself. If only Bud were big enough, strong enough, to do the same.

More frantic than ever, Bree kept pace with Ryan by staying on a parallel course. This was a nightmare. It couldn't really be happening. She hadn't felt this helpless, this defeated, this alone, since the night her mother had died.

As always, that memory triggered turbulent, unsettling emotions that filled her mind and heart. Yet this time was different. Bree was able to picture herself, not as a child but as a *parent*.

Suddenly she realized that, unlike her mother, she was capable of loving others enough to put them first, to care about them more than she cared about her needs or wants, to give them the kind of altruistic love she'd been denied as a lonely, frightened little girl. And she owed her awakening to Mitch and his boys.

None of the usual arguments surfaced to dissuade her, to make her question her conclusions. On the contrary, every beat of her heart was further affirmation that she was, indeed, a different person than she had been before she'd met the Fowlers. Before she'd accidentally fallen in love with Mitch.

It was a miracle! And the answer to her long-ago prayers for healing after her mother's untimely death. She owed her heavenly Father more thanks and praise than she'd ever be able to deliver.

Right now, however, she hoped God would understand that she had more pressing concerns. Poor little Bud was lost, maybe fighting for his life.

That thought almost made her cry out. She wanted to fall to her knees in anguish, to beat the ground with her fists and plead with God once again.

Instead, she did what she knew she must. She breathed a simple prayer and kept going. "Father, help us! Please! I'm so sorry I doubted You."

It wasn't very eloquent or very practiced, but it was the best she could do. And it was the most sincere prayer she'd ever prayed.

As if in answer, she heard Mitch shout, "Bud!" at the top of his lungs. The call didn't sound worried or plaintive, like the others had. It was the kind of triumphant cry a father would make if he'd located his missing child.

Chapter Sixteen

Brianne arrived at the muddy, rock-edged pool seconds after Ryan did. Two dark heads were bobbing together in the water. The older boy didn't hesitate. He ignored Bree's screeched command—"Ryan, no!"—and jumped in, feet first.

His splashdown was so close to his father and brother he made a wave that washed over them and temporarily kept Bree from seeing whether or not Bud was all right. It never occurred to her to sit on the creek bank and wait patiently for someone to eventually tell her.

Instead, she followed Ryan's lead, although with a lot less forward momentum.

The current wasn't nearly as swift as it had been in the steep canyon. The water came to her waist, and she waded to Mitch and the boys on leaden legs. Covering those few yards seemed to take an eternity.

Her first indication that all was well was Mitch's whoop of triumph. Holding Bud tight to his chest, he closed his eyes for a moment, then opened them to gaze at the little boy with so much love, Brianne wept for joy.

Ryan had already joined his father and brother in their mutual hug. The instant Bree was close enough, she was included, too.

It was hard for her to tell if the others were laughing or crying. Little wonder. She wasn't sure exactly what she was doing, either. But who cared? All that mattered was that Bud was safe. They were all safe. And well. Her prayers had been answered. God was so good!

Mitch's hearty laugh warmed her in spite of the icy water and the aftereffects of her fatigue. Her answering grin was so wide it made her cheeks hurt—until she decided he might be laughing at *her*.

She paddled her arms back and forth and braced her feet wide on the creek bottom to hold her position while she made a face at him. "Okay, mister. What's so funny?"

"You are. You should see yourself!"

"Well, you're not so spiffy, either," Bree countered with a toss of her head and a swipe at the bangs plastered to her forehead. "At least I started out casually dressed."

"You mean you're not still impressed with my suit and tie? How about the boys? Don't they look nice?"

"Wonderful." Bree's tone was filled with love. She reached out and ruffled Bud's hair and would have done the same to Ryan if he hadn't ducked around his father, out of her reach. "I've never seen them look more adorable."

Softening, she gazed into Mitch's eyes and added, "Their daddy looks pretty good to me, too."

"You sure? We're all awfully dirty."

"I know. I noticed. I don't suppose you guys have a change of clothes with you, do you?"

"Nope."

"That figures."

Mitch was chuckling. "I would have brought extra clothes if I'd known swimming was on today's agenda."

"Never mind trying to make plans," Bree said. "The way your family finds trouble, I think you should start carrying an overnight bag with you all the time. You're bound to need it sooner or later." She grinned. "Probably sooner."

"And maybe a life raft, too?"

"Good idea." Brianne kept listing things for his amusement. "And sunscreen, and packets of food, and bottled water, and lots of towels. Oh, and a leash."

"For Barney?" Mitch asked.

"No. For Bud's bear." She flashed a smile of encouragement at the soaking wet little boy and told him, "Your bear is fine, honey. I found him up the creek."

"You did?" The child's voice was barely audible.

"She sure did," his father assured him. "I saw her. She jumped right in and rescued him."

"I could of done it," Ryan grumbled.

Brianne was too elated, too relieved, to take his grumpy mood seriously. He was giving her his usual testy, temperamental look, and she wasn't about to let him get away with it. Not this time.

Instead of making unwarranted apologies, she raised her arm and crooned, "Oh, Ryan…"

The minute he turned his head to look at her she smacked the surface of the pool with the heel of her hand and sent a rooster tail of creek water right into his face.

Sputtering, he blew water out of his nose and mouth. His eyes widened in shock, looking bigger and darker than she'd ever seen them. Before he had a chance to recover and complain to his father, Bree splashed him again.

That second affront was all the boy could stand. He drew back his thin arm and retaliated.

Mitch had glanced over to see how Ryan was reacting to Bree's teasing. Unfortunately, the boy was so excited he failed to control his aim. Part of the spray he threw at Bree made it all the way to her face. The rest smacked into his father's head.

Feigning anger, Mitch roared and splashed Ryan. Ryan splashed him back. Bud was caught in the middle and getting well doused from both sides. He began to squeal and flail his arms, flinging droplets in no particular direction.

Bree didn't play favorites. She wildly sloshed as much water as she could at everyone. The advantage was clearly hers because she was the most mobile. Continuing to hold on to Bud gave Mitch only one free hand with which to defend himself, so she started to work her way around to his opposite side, hoping to limit his ability to strike back.

Ryan had ducked behind his father and was holding on to the man's broad shoulders, trying to use Mitch's bulk as a shield.

As soon as Mitch discovered what the boy was doing, he spun around and inundated the contentious eight-year-old. "Oh, no, you don't. Take that!"

"No, Dad, no!" He spit. Blew like a beached whale. "I give. I give!"

"Oh, yeah? We'll see about that."

"But Dad," the boy yelled. "I didn't start it."

"No, you didn't, did you?"

Mitch stopped splashing. Then suddenly, as if obeying a silent command, all three Fowlers turned on Bree.

"Get her," Mitch hollered.

Ryan was all for it. "Yeah! Drown her!"

"No!" Brianne had to keep her hands in front of her face in order to draw enough breath for a screech of protest, which meant she couldn't fight back. When she saw Mitch swing Bud around so the boy could hang on to him piggyback style, she knew it was payback time. Mitch could use both hands. She was really in for it.

He held out his arms and began to paddle water at her so fast it felt like he was dumping bucketfuls over her head. Burying her face in her hands, she squealed and turned away, heading for the nearest bank.

"Oh, no, you don't," he shouted. "Come back here."

"No!" Bree stumbled, lost her balance.

Mitch caught her from behind, closed his strong arms around her waist and lifted her half out of the shallow water. "Gotcha. Now try and get me wet."

"Let go," she begged through her giggles. "I'm sorry. I didn't mean to splash you. I'll never do it again. Honest."

"Dunk her, Dad. Dunk her," Ryan urged.

Mitch was chuckling. "How about if I kiss her, instead?"

"No!" the boy said. "Dunk her."

"I will—if she doesn't quit wiggling."

Brianne got the message. Gasping for breath, she

stopped trying to pry loose his grip and forced herself to relax. "Okay, okay. I'm not fighting you anymore. See? Truce?"

"It better last," Mitch said. "No funny stuff."

She held up her hands in exaggerated surrender. "I'll behave. I promise."

"Then what are we all standing here for?" Mitch said wryly. "Personally, I'm not crazy about becoming crawdad bait. Let's get out."

By hanging together and helping each other, they managed to reach the bank without too much slipping, sliding and tripping.

Mitch set Bud out of the water easily, then put his hands on Bree's waist and gave her a boost, intending to do the same thing for her.

Unfortunately, the bank was so slick in that particular spot she couldn't get a firm hold. Losing traction, she slid into the pool—and into Mitch's arms—with a splash and a giggle.

"Lift me a couple of inches higher, and I'll make it the next time," she said.

"You could put one foot in my hands and I could throw you up there, too, but I don't recommend it." He set her aside. "Stand right here. I'll climb up and pull you out."

Ryan had already clambered out by himself when his father breached the bank and turned to give Bree a hand, as promised.

As the furor died, Bree realized how totally spent she was. She found a flat, accommodating rock and plunked herself down on it to rest. Judging by the look on Mitch's face when he joined her, he was exhausted, too.

Bud wiggled into the narrow space between them and yawned.

"My sentiments exactly," Bree said. "I sure wish it wasn't uphill all the way to my place."

"Yeah. Me, too. But it really isn't as far as it felt like on the way down."

"Let's hope not." She sighed, stretched her legs in front of her and ran her hands over the damp skin to check for injury. To her delight, none of the scratches were deep. "That was some trip."

"Are you okay?"

"I'll live. I think the cold water actually helped. Before I got wet, my ribs were sore, too."

"We'll probably all be pretty sore tomorrow," Mitch said.

He smiled, leaned closer and put his arm around Bree's shoulders to pull her to him as he glanced at his youngest. Bud had laid his head on her lap and was already half asleep. "Except maybe for him. He wasn't quite as stressed as the rest of us were."

"Which reminds me. We need to pick up his teddy bear on our way home. I think I can remember about where I left it."

Ryan spoke. "Hey, Dad! I lost a shoe. Can I go back in the creek and look for it?"

"No way." Mitch was far too thankful to waste energy getting mad over something that trivial. Instead, he teased, "I thought I told you guys to keep your new clothes clean."

Bree gave a little giggle. "Hey, we can't get much cleaner than we are now."

"I never thought I'd see you involved in a mess like this."

"I learned everything I know about having fun from you and the boys," she told him, flipping her wet hair with a quick toss of her head. "Well, that was exciting. What shall we do next?"

"It'll be pretty hard to top our trip down the canyon. How about we quit for the day?"

"Good idea. What do you say we all go back to my house, get cleaned up and fix something to eat? I'm suddenly starving."

Ryan looked askance. "Not me. Not if she's going to cook."

Mitch laughed. "Tell you what. We'll all cook. I vote we skip the exploding potatoes this time, though. They're too hard to scrape off the oven walls."

"Picky, picky, picky." Bree scowled at father and sons while she stroked Bud's damp hair. "You guys had better be nice to me, or I'll go lock myself in the pantry and eat every cookie I can find. And when I'm done with the baked stuff, I'll start on the cake mixes."

"Looks like you'd better cool it, Ryan." Mitch's happiness was so overwhelming he spoke directly from the heart. "You don't want a mother who doesn't share her cookies."

That brought Bud to full wakefulness. He sat up. "Mother?"

"Yes, mother," Mitch said, giving his older son the sternest stare he could manage, to reinforce his decision.

Looking from Bud to Ryan, Mitch decided Bree was a lot more surprised than either boy was. He gave her another quick squeeze, then released her and raked his wet hair back to smooth it. "I guess I got a little ahead of myself again, didn't I? I was going to take you out and impress you with my gentlemanly ways before I talked more about marriage. Guess it's too late for that now." He cleared his throat. "So, will you marry me, Ms. Bailey?"

"You're asking me? Just like that?"

She'd been staring at her scraped legs and ruined sandals. She jumped to her feet, arms outstretched. "Look at me. I've just slid down a mountain. I've been dunked in a mud hole. And I'm dripping like a drowned rat. Where's the romance?"

"You're not going to make this easy for me, are you?"

"Deciding to get married isn't supposed to be easy. It's a big step, Mitch."

"You still want me to court you? After all this?"

Hands fisted on her hips, Brianne made a pretense of being upset. "A few normal dates certainly wouldn't hurt."

He couldn't keep a straight face. "Honey, with the start you and I've had, I doubt anything we do will seem normal from here on."

"Give it a shot." She stood firm, eyebrows raised, waiting.

"Okay. I'll try. Just remember, I haven't done this in a long time."

The boys were edging closer, giving both adults their rapt attention.

Mitch noticed and hesitated before saying, "Ms. Bailey, would you like to go to dinner and a movie with me?"

"That's better. When?"

"Does it matter?"

"Yes. I think the theater over in Highland is showing a full-length cartoon this weekend. If we get cleaned up and grab an early dinner we can make the first showing."

"That's your idea of a date?"

"It is now." Bree smiled benevolently. The

children had been concentrating on the conversation, their little heads snapping right and left like spectators in box seats at a tennis match.

She crouched and opened her arms to them. Bud was first to respond to the invitation for a hug, but Ryan wasn't far behind.

Brianne gave them both an affectionate squeeze. "The last thing I want is for my kids to feel left out."

"How about me? Where's my hug?" Mitch asked. "I'm beginning to feel left out."

"Poor baby."

Bree stood and patted his cheek, thoroughly enjoying the lost-little-boy look he'd put on for her benefit. If ever there was a man who was all grown up—and then some—it was Mitch Fowler.

No kidding! For her, the hardest part of their supposed courtship was going to be keeping herself from rushing into his arms, pledging her undying love and cutting their dating period very, very short.

Which was further evidence that the Lord had known exactly what He was doing when he'd brought them together like this, she reasoned. They not only had each other, their courtship came complete with two resident chaperons.

At peace, she held out her hands to the children. Bud grasped one. Ryan took the other.

Feeling more content, more maternal, than she'd

ever dreamed possible, Brianne said, "Okay kids. Come on. Let's all go home."

A week later, Brianne and Mitch were relaxing in a glider on the porch outside her library and watching the children playing a game of tag.

He put his arm around her shoulders and gave the swing another push with his feet. "So, are you ready to say you'll marry me?"

"You are in a hurry, aren't you?"

"You didn't answer my question."

She smiled him and nodded. "As ready as I'll ever be, I guess."

"Does that mean yes?"

"Yes."

"Good, because I'd hate to have to beg. It's too hard on my ego." He pulled her closer. "In case I haven't told you so in the past five minutes, I love you."

"I love you, too." She nestled against him and rested her hand on his chest, feeling the steady, rapid beat of his heart. "All three of you."

"Four, counting the dog." Mitch admired his offspring as they chased Barney and each other around the lawn. "They are great kids, aren't they?"

"Sweethearts. Like their daddy."

He kissed the top of her head. "Thanks. Hold that thought. You'll need it when you're standing at the altar pretty soon, saying *I do*."

"I've been thinking about that. I want the boys to be a part of the ceremony."

"Both of them?"

Bree looked at him, her expression filled with love. "Yes. It's not just for them. It's for me, too. They're my kids, one hundred percent. We're already a family. Leaving them out of our wedding plans is unthinkable."

Mitch couldn't help the wide grin that spread across his face or the warmth coloring his cheeks as his thoughts followed their natural course. "Okay. They can be in the wedding, as long as you don't decide we have to take them with us on our honeymoon, too."

"Well…"

"No, Brianne. No way." He studied her expression carefully, trying to decide whether or not she was serious.

She laughed. "I know. I'm just teasing you. The boys will understand. We'll promise to bring them back some great presents, and they won't hardly notice we're gone."

"You're going to spoil them."

"Sure am." She threaded her fingers through his hair and urged him closer as she whispered, "And I have every intention of spoiling their wonderful daddy, too. Any objections?"

Mitch placed a quick kiss on her lips, then left the

swing and retreated across the porch. "Nope. I'll expect you to start spoiling me as soon as you're my wife. Until then, I think I'd better go home."

Laughing gaily, Bree agreed. "I think you're right. We're already the town's favorite scandal."

"I know. I keep reminding folks that a literal act of God is what brought us together. They'll find somebody else to gossip about soon enough."

"It was, wasn't it? And act of God, I mean."

His voice gentled, his eyes misting. "You're not talking about just the storm, are you?"

"No. There was a lot more to it than a little rain. I used to believe in coincidences. No more. There's no way everything that happened to us could have been an accident."

"I agree." Mitch's dark eyes held an unspoken promise. Then he began to smile mischievously. "So, is there anything I can do for you before I leave, Ms. Bailey? Carry you over the threshold? Hug you? Kiss you senseless?"

Bree gazed at him, loving him so much she could hardly contain her elation and marveling at the overwhelming sense of God's presence or of His perfect blessing on their future.

"Soon," she promised, knowing it was true.

"How soon?"

"Very soon." A broad grin lit her face, her cheeks suddenly extra rosy. "Actually, I've picked out my dress already. As soon as we can arrange for the church and find out what dates your pastor has free, we can coordinate everything."

"Good. You're the one who's always organized, so I'll leave all those details up to you. Whatever you decide will be fine with me. I'll take care of our honeymoon plans."

Brianne gave him a quick hug then gazed at him, her blue eyes brimming with love. "Now *that's* romantic."

Epilogue

The day finally arrived.

Brianne could have had the most extravagant wedding Arkansas had ever seen—an enormous sanctuary filled with flowers, a designer gown, a catered reception and a cake big enough to feed all of Little Rock, with plenty left over.

Instead, she'd chosen a simple, fitted white satin dress and an equally simple ceremony in Mitch's home church, surrounded by the majestic beauty of the forested Ozark foothills. Wild maples had already turned bright red and orange, and oaks were beginning to show early fall color.

Bree had filled every corner of the churchyard with pots of chrysanthemums that echoed the rich, natural autumn hues. They made it look as if the whole countryside had purposely been blended into a huge, majestic backdrop painted especially for her nuptials.

At first, she'd thought it would be nice if Ryan escorted her down the aisle, but when Mitch decided to make the eight-year-old his best man, she chose to let Bud do the honors rather than walk to the altar alone.

Finding formal suits to fit the boys necessitated a trip to Batesville. A matching outfit for Bud's freshly shampooed and blow-dried bear was a little harder to come by. Bree finally settled on a black bow tie and red satin cummerbund. In spite of the rough treatment the poor teddy had gotten recently, he looked absolutely elegant, as did his proud owner.

Holding her bouquet in one hand, she stood at the back of the church and reached out to Bud with the other. "You ready, honey?"

"Uh-huh."

"Is your bear ready, too?" It was tucked in the crook of his other arm.

"Uh-huh."

Bud grasped Bree's hand and grinned at her with pure adoration. He'd lost a baby tooth the day before, and the gap made his smile look even more endearing.

"Okay. It's almost time," Bree told him. "See? There's your daddy and Ryan standing up front. We can go, too, as soon as the right music starts."

The delay seemed interminable. Her mouth got dry, her palms damp. Even the sight of her beloved Mitch, waiting with the preacher in front of the congregation and smiling encouragement, wasn't enough to calm her jitters. She was doubly glad she had little Bud for company. Worrying about his possible nervousness helped take her mind off the butterflies holding a convention in her stomach.

The boy squeezed her hand and gave it a tug to get her attention. "Bree?"

"Yes, honey?" She leaned closer to listen.

"Are you my mama yet?"

"Almost." Tears of joy misted her vision. The wedding march began to echo through the small sanctuary, and she stepped forward. "Just a few more minutes, and I will be."

"Good," Bud whispered. "'Cause my bear's hungry. We really want some more cookies."

Bree clasped her new husband's arm as they left the church as husband and wife. In spite of the crowd of well-wishers surging around them, they had eyes for only each other.

Mitch covered her hand with his. "You okay?"

"I will be, as soon as all this is over. I never realized how nervous I'd be."

"Me, too. I kept worrying that the kids would decide they were tired of being good and start acting up."

"Not a chance. They were little angels. Even Ryan was on his best behavior." Fondness for both children made her smile. "I almost cried when Bud asked me how soon I'd be his mother."

"When was this?"

"While we were waiting to walk down the aisle. The only thing that kept me from bursting into tears was the reason he gave."

Mitch arched an eyebrow. "I'm almost afraid to ask what it was."

Laughing, her eyes sparkling, Bree said, "He told me he and the bear were hungry and they wanted cookies. I guess he figured mothers were the best people to get them from."

"I told you those kids were bright."

"And cute."

"Like their daddy?"

"Yes." Bree cooed the word. "Just like their daddy."

"No second thoughts?"

"None. I still can't believe I'm married, though. I was sure it would never happen. I was never going to have kids, either, and all of a sudden I'm the mother of two. I hope I'm up to the challenge."

"You're perfect. The Lord knew what He was doing when He threw us together. I'm thankful He made sure we were stuck with each other long enough for both of us to realize what we'd been missing."

"I just wish it hadn't cost you your cabin."

"Hey, I told you stuff like that doesn't matter."

"I know. I agree, but…"

"No buts. Buildings aren't important. Families are. You, me, the boys, we're all starting over at the same time. We'll make a home wherever we are because we're together."

Given the earnestness of their conversation, he was taken aback by Bree's nervous titter. "What's so funny?"

"Me," she said. "You're being so sweet and serious. I'm ashamed of the notion that just popped into my head. It was really silly."

"What?"

"If I tell you, you'll laugh."

"I hope so. Some of the happiest times I've had lately have been when we've shared a good laugh."

"This has *nothing* to do with my baked chicken recipe," she insisted. "Or with setting pancakes on fire.

"That's a relief." Mitch was already chuckling. He paused long enough to take her in his arms and pull her closer. "Better hurry if you're going to tell me. The photographer's about to have a conniption. It looks like he wants us to go into the fellowship hall. Probably wants to take pictures of us cutting the cake."

"Okay. Then let's go."

Mitch wasn't through studying her indefinable

expression. "Wait a minute. First, tell me what you were thinking about that made you laugh."

"It wasn't important." Bree tried to break away.

"Then why are you blushing?"

"Blushing? Me?"

"Yes, you. I'm your husband, remember? You can confide in me. You *should* confide in me."

"Well… Okay." Bree raised on tiptoe, cupped her hand around her mouth and whispered in his ear. "All of a sudden, I remembered that old joke about a woman who married a man who already had children because she was too lazy to have them herself."

"That's it? That's all?" Mitch gave her a puzzled look. "What's so funny about that?"

"I think it must have lost something in the translation," Brianne said. "Either that or I'm so uptight I'd laugh at anything right now."

"Maybe. Unless…"

Cocking his head, he bent to speak so that only she could hear. "This is probably not the time or the place to bring this up, Mrs. Fowler, but I have wondered. Are you trying to tell me that you think the boys might need a little sister?"

"Well…" Bree felt suspended in air, as if her feet had suddenly left the ground. She hadn't brought up the subject of their having children together because she'd been afraid Mitch might change his mind about marrying her if she did. Obviously, he already had all the family he'd ever need. He'd as much as said so. She just wanted…

Her cheeks flamed. Her gaze locked with her husband's. The perceptive look on Mitch's face told her he knew *exactly* what she wanted.

As his expression softened, he leaned down and kissed her, much to the delight of their guests.

When he straightened there was a broad grin on his face. Slipping his arm around Bree's waist, he said, "I love you, honey, but first things first. Come on. Let's go cut the cake and get our pictures taken."

"Okay. Then what?" Bree's heart was pounding so hard and fast she could feel her pulse in her temples without touching them.

"Then, we'll sneak off by ourselves so we can have a nice, long, private talk about you being such a terrible lazybones."

"I can try to improve," she said happily.

Mitch's grin widened. "Honey," he said, "I'm counting on it."

* * * * *

Dear Reader,

As you've probably gathered by now, especially if you've read my earlier Love Inspired titles, I love rural life in the Ozark Mountains.

We moved out here in the country to escape, just as Brianne does in my story. Only, we did it for different reasons. We weren't running away from anything, we were running toward it. A city had grown up around us where we'd lived before and our life had become too fast-paced and complicated as a result. Yes, wages there were high and jobs were plentiful, but without peace of mind and good physical health, what difference did that make?

So we left. Some of our friends thought we were crazy to follow our dream all the way from Southern California to the backwoods of Arkansas. Others envied us. It took guts and faith to do what we did, but we've never been sorry.

There have been a few interesting surprises along the way, too. I knew I could continue to write no matter where I lived but I'd never imagined how much finding a good country church, a Bible-preaching pastor and dozens of new Christian friends would reshape and refocus my faith.

I had to come here as preparation for the books I'm writing now. I just didn't know it ahead of time!

I invite your letters at P.O. Box 13, Glencoe, AR 72539-0013, e-mails at valw@centurytel.net or visit my Web site for the latest news, www.ValerieHansen.com.

Blessings,

Valerie Hansen

SAMANTHA'S GIFT

For He shall give His angels charge over thee,
to keep thee in all thy ways.
—*Psalms* 91:11

My sister Audrey has suggested that I dedicate this book to our mother, Helen Hansen, who was a stickler for correct spelling and grammar, and probably taught me a lot more than I cared to admit, especially in my student days. Mom was also the one who laid the foundation of faith by taking us to Sunday school. So this one's for her. I wish she were here to read it.

Chapter One

Rachel Woodward's spirits soared the moment she stepped out the supply room door into the clear, warm Ozark morning. Pausing in appreciation, she took a slow, deep breath of fresh mountain air, noted the spicy, familiar aroma of the crayons and colored construction paper piled high in her arms, and smiled.

Another day in paradise. Life was as close to perfect as it could get.

Working with young children and seeing the world through their eyes made Rachel feel as if she were discovering new wonders every day. Their innocent enthusiasm was contagious. Why, if she were six instead of twenty-six, she might even give in to the urge to skip happily down the sidewalk all the way to her classroom!

She clasped the stack of supplies closer to her chest and looked around furtively. Did she dare? What would it hurt as long as no one saw her? Few students arrived this early in the morning and the other teachers were either in the staff lounge discussing their summer vacations or already in their rooms finishing last-minute preparations. The coast was clear.

Rachel's grin widened. Why not? It seemed like a sin to suppress all the elation she was feeling, simply because society dictated that adults should behave more sedately.

Who wanted to be a stuffy adult, anyway? Certainly not *her*.

The moment she gave in and began to skip, her joy took flight. Her skirt skimmed her calves and her shoulder-length dark hair swung with every hop.

Squinting against the bright sunshine, she blinked slowly, reverently. *Thank you, Father, for finding me a job that blesses me so much.*

That instant's inattention was a mistake. A large figure loomed suddenly in her path! She tried to dodge. Momentum foiled the effort. She smashed into a man's broad, solid chest with a *thump* and a stifled screech.

Boxes of crayons and loose drawing paper sailed into the air. The whole mess rained down on them. Crayons rolled all over the sidewalk, making a solid footing nearly impossible.

"Look out!" he shouted belatedly.

Everything happened so fast that it took Rachel a few seconds to realize why she hadn't fallen when they'd collided. Her vivid blue eyes widened and focused on the stranger whose warm, strong hands were clamped on her upper arms, steadying her.

Since Rachel was barely five-foot-two and slight, she'd often found herself at a size disadvantage. This instance, however, was much worse than usual. This man was so tall, so broad shouldered, so obviously muscular, she felt like the captive of a giant. Hopefully, a *friendly* one.

Her mouth suddenly went dry. Heart pounding, she fought to catch her breath and compose herself in spite of the nervous fluttering in her stomach. She knew it was normal for people to feel a surge of adrenaline when they were startled the way she'd just been, but this was ridiculous. She was not one of those faint-of-heart women who swooned every time an attractive man looked her way.

And speaking of looking… The man's chest, covered in a pale shirt and navy blazer, fell at her eye level. Following the line of his tie upward she saw a square jaw, firm mouth, hazel eyes—and an expression clearly filled with amusement.

She was too embarrassed to mirror his good humor. With a stubborn lift of her chin she did her best to appear unruffled as she asked, "Where did *you* come from?"

"Cleveland." A half smile lifted one corner of his mouth.

"I meant just now," Rachel told him. "I didn't see a soul in the hall before you ran into me."

"*I* ran into *you?*"

"Yes." She tried unsuccessfully to pull away. When he continued to hold on to her, she asserted her independence clearly. "That's enough. You can let go of me now."

"Okay."

The man released her so abruptly, she staggered and almost wound up sitting at his feet amid the spilled crayons. Wouldn't *that* have been cute! As if being caught skipping wasn't bad enough.

"I didn't mean for you to throw me down," she said.

"Make up your mind." He stuffed his hands into the pockets of his slacks and struck a nonchalant pose.

Rachel studied his face and frowned, trying to place him. "Who are you, anyway?"

Watching the movement of her eyes, he must have guessed that she was casting around for something with which to write; he stooped and came up with a blue crayon and a piece of the drawing paper she'd dropped.

"I'm Sean Bates. But you don't have to bother reporting me, ma'am. I work here."

"You do?" She paused, crayon poised. "Since when? I didn't see you at the in-service meetings last week."

"That's because I just moved from up north."

"You really are from Cleveland? It wasn't a joke?"

He laughed. "Not to me."

So, this was the new school counselor she'd heard so much about. No wonder all the single women on staff were figuratively lining up to vie for his attention. He was not only good-looking, he had a charisma that was almost irresistible—to anyone but her, of course. She wasn't susceptible to that kind of romantic insanity anymore.

Smiling up at him, Rachel said, "Well then, welcome to Serenity Elementary. If I can be of any assistance, please let me know."

"Thanks. I do have one question."

"Sure. Anything."

"Okay. Why were you skipping down the hall like a kid?"

"Shh." She blushed, looked around furtively. "You weren't supposed to notice that."

"It was kind of hard not to."

"Then, why didn't you get out of my way?"

"I tried. Guess I was so surprised, I didn't move quite fast enough. Sorry."

"Me, too." Pulling a face, she lamented the

supplies scattered at their feet, then gathered the hem of her skirt at her knees, holding it bunched in one hand so she could crouch down safely. "My poor crayons. They were brand new. I'll bet half of them are broken."

Sean squatted to help her gather up the spill. "Hey, these are those big fat crayons. I haven't seen any of those since kindergarten."

"Makes sense. That's what I teach."

"You're a teacher?"

"Yes, I'm a teacher. Why?"

"No special reason. You don't fit my memories of the teachers I had when I was a boy, that's all."

Rachel knew better than to acknowledge the backhanded compliment and open their conversation to more of his personal opinions. There was nothing he could say about her diminutive appearance that she hadn't heard many times before.

She continued to stack paper, barely glancing at him. "Do you have children coming to our school, too, Mr. Bates?"

"No. No kids."

The answer was simple. It was the off-putting tone that drew and held her attention. The man had sounded as if he didn't even like children, which was a definite drawback since he was about to start a job where he'd be up to his elbows in them.

"You *are* the new counselor, aren't you?"

"Yes."

Silent, she studied his profile, trying to determine if she'd read him correctly. He looked to be about thirty or thirty-five, with reddish brown hair and compelling green eyes.

He raised them to meet hers. "What?"

"Nothing. I was just wondering what brought you to a little town like Serenity. Being from the city, you're liable to have quite an adjustment to make."

"I'll cope. It wasn't a spur-of-the-moment decision." Straightening with an armload of loose supplies, he changed the subject. "Lead the way to your room, Teacher. I'll carry these for you."

"I can manage by myself."

"I know you can." He lifted an eyebrow. "I just had a demonstration of how well. But I've already got this stuff balanced. If I try to hand it to you and you fumble it again, you'll have even more busted crayons. Let's go."

That logic overcame Rachel's misgivings. She gathered up the last of the paper and started off. "Okay. Come on. I'm in building A. You may as well start learning the layout of the campus. Where's your office, anyway?"

"So far, I don't have one."

"I'm not surprised. We aren't used to having a full-time counselor on staff."

"I'm not exactly full time. Not yet. I've told the

boss I can fill in as a substitute bus driver, too, if they need me."

Confused, she glanced back over her shoulder at him. "Bus driver? Why? I thought you were a psychologist."

"Hey, I'm a versatile guy."

"If you say so." She paused to unlock the door to her classroom, then pushed the door open with her hip and swept through ahead of Sean.

"I do say so." He cast around for the best place to dump his load of crayons and settled on the top of a low cabinet. "Actually, I put myself through college by driving a school bus."

She studied him further, frowning and questioning her deductions regarding his age. "How long did that take?"

Sean laughed. "It's a little complicated. Let's just say that counseling wasn't my first career."

"Hmm. I was sure I wanted to be a teacher from the time I was seven," Rachel said.

"I envy you. Most people aren't that decisive, even as adults."

He looked her up and down as he spoke. She was petite, pretty, and so thin she looked like she'd blow away in a strong wind—unless she happened to be tethered to the jungle gym. When he'd steadied her in the hallway, he'd noticed that he could easily encircle her upper arm with one hand. Good thing she'd chosen to teach very young children. The thought made him smile.

"What's so funny?"

"Sorry. I was just thinking." His gaze traveled around the room. "Kindergarten was a good choice."

"Why? Because children are so loving at that age?"

"No. Because you don't look like you could hold your own in a pillow fight against anybody much bigger."

Rachel's smile faded. "You'd be surprised what I can do." She hustled him to the door, opened it and practically shoved him through. "Thanks for your help, Mr. Bates. Now, if you'll excuse me, I have a lot of work to do before class starts."

"Sure. No problem. Have a good day."

Rachel closed the door behind him and leaned against it, eyes shut tight.

Not hold her own? Ha! She might not look tough on the outside, but inside she knew she was made of steel. Tempered steel. And the pain of the tempering process lingered. It probably always would.

An unexpected call summoned Rachel to the office right after the dismissal bell. She was anything but thrilled. The first few days of every school year were very tiring, and the last thing she wanted was to have to face the principal this late in the afternoon. Refusal, however, was not an option.

Sean was coming out of a classroom as she passed by. He beamed at the sight of her. "Hi."

"Hi. So far, so good?" Rachel asked pleasantly, trying to ignore the jolt of awareness she'd felt the moment she spied him again.

"No problems," Sean said.

"Good."

"You okay? You look kind of funny."

Did her unwarranted reaction show? Oh dear! Hedging, she made a silly face at him. "Thanks—I think."

"Actually, you remind me a lot of a condemned man on the way to the gallows."

"Oh, that." *What a relief.* "Probably because I feel like one. I've been called to Principal Vanbruger's office and I don't have the slightest idea why. That kind of thing always gives me butterflies in my stomach."

"Is there a problem?"

"Who knows. It's a little too early in the year for me to have earned a commendation for exemplary teaching, so I have to assume that's not why he wants to see me."

"You never know. Maybe you're about to get a blue ribbon for your skipping skills."

"Let's hope not."

He fell into step beside her. "I'm headed your way. Mind if I walk along? Keep you company?"

"Aren't you afraid to be associated with a terrible rule-breaker like me?"

"Not as long as I don't catch you running with scissors," he quipped. "I do have my limits."

"Glad to hear it."

Rachel couldn't help chuckling softly. The man seemed to have the kind of nature that lifted a person's spirits. That quality made him more appealing to her than any superficial attributes, like the fact that he was every bit as handsome as her friends had insisted during lunch, when she'd carelessly mentioned having met him.

She and Sean reached the door to the school office. Rachel paused. "Well, this is it. Here I go."

"Want me to hang around till you're done?"

She was amazed at his sensitivity. "No. I'll be fine. I just hate the idea of hearing that I'm not perfect."

Sean arched an eyebrow. "I don't know. You look pretty good to me. Tell you what. If that guy Vanbruger picks on you, tell me, and I'll go let the air out of the tires on his bicycle so he knows better the next time."

Amused, Rachel looked up into his kind face and caught a glimmer of deeper concern. He'd apparently been trying to distract her with his silly banter and was now waiting to see if he'd been successful.

She assumed a pseudo-serious expression, made

a fist and punched him lightly in the upper arm as she said, "Thanks, buddy. It's good to know you're standing by in case I need avenging. But I don't think he rides a bicycle, so that's out. Guess I'll just have to take my chances."

Turning, she reached for the doorknob. So did Sean.

His hand closed gently over hers. Their inadvertent touch sent tingles zinging up Rachel's arm and prickled in the tiny hairs at the nape of her neck.

She quickly slipped her hand from beneath his, hoping he couldn't tell how bewildered her unexpected, fervent response had left her. Or how close she'd come to actually shivering just now!

"Allow me," Sean said, gallantly opening the office door for her and stepping back with a bow.

Rachel took a deep breath and held it. She sidled through the open door without looking up or glancing back at Sean. Principal Vanbruger wasn't the main reason for her nervousness anymore. Sean Bates was.

Not only were her original butterflies still having a riotous party in her stomach, but the moment Sean had accidentally touched her hand, they'd invited all their friends—and a few hundred moths, to boot!

Rachel's bumfuzzled state of mind became of secondary importance the moment she entered the principal's office and saw who, and what, was waiting for her.

Her gaze lingered a moment on the two adults, then went to a withdrawn-looking little girl sitting on a chair in the corner, lower legs and feet dangling.

The child's shorts and T-shirt were faded and much too big for her, but that wasn't the saddest part. Everything, from her posture to her placement in the room, screamed *lonely,* immediately capturing Rachel's heart.

Principal Vanbruger rose from behind his desk. "Ah, good. Ms. Woodward, I believe you know Ms. Heatherington, from Health and Human Services in Little Rock."

Rachel nodded. "Yes." She shook the social worker's hand formally. "We've met."

He gestured toward the child. "And this is Samantha Smith. Samantha, this is your new teacher, Ms. Woodward."

"Please, call me Miss Rachel," she told the shy little waif. "All the other children do." Wide, pale blue eyes stared up at her from a cherubic face surrounded by unkempt blond curls.

Approaching slowly and pausing in front of the child, Rachel said, "I see we're all out of my favorite kind of chair. Can I share yours? I'm pretty little. There should be room for both of us."

Samantha's only answer was to scoot to one side.

Rachel perched on the edge of the seat at an angle and laid her arm across the chair's low, curved back. That not only helped her balance, it formed a pose of guardianship, offering unspoken protection in a world of staid, intimidating adults.

"Samantha's parents died," the social worker said. "She's in foster care right now. I'm working on getting her placed with relatives in Colorado, so I doubt you'll have to bother with her for long. She hasn't been behaving very well, I'm afraid. Just try to keep her out of trouble and make the best of it till the paperwork comes through and we can send her out of state."

Tactful, as always. Rachel wanted to jump up and scream, *How dare you be so matter-of-fact? Can't you see how frightened the poor thing is?*

Instead, Rachel settled back into the chair, lowered her arm and pulled the little girl against her as if they were already fast friends. The glare of animosity she sent across the room belied her casual posture.

"I can read all the details in the files later, Ms. Heatherington. There's no need to discuss any of it now."

Without waiting for a reply, Rachel leaned down and whispered in Samantha's ear, then stood, holding out her hand. "If you'll excuse us—we're going to see my classroom."

The social worker opened her mouth to object and was silenced by the righteous anger in Rachel's backward glance.

"I'm going to show Samantha the playground, too. Then she'll know where everything is when she gets here tomorrow."

Wisely, Principal Vanbruger shooed them on their way with a wave of his hand and a firm "Fine. Go. I'll take care of things here."

Rachel was thankful he had interceded. If she'd been forced to stay in that woman's presence much longer she was afraid she might have expressed a very un-Christian opinion. That wouldn't do. It was bad enough to be thinking it in the first place.

Chapter Two

Proceeding down the sidewalk to the double doors that would take them to the interior halls of one of the low, nondescript buildings, Rachel kept up a friendly banter.

"It's not far to my room. Here we are. Look. First you go in these glass doors by the big letter *A*." Pointing, she led the way. "Then you find the room with a green door. It's right here. See the *K* on it? That stands for *Kindergarten*. I put a smiley face in the window, too, so all the kids can be sure this is the right place. Can you see that?"

The five-year-old nodded solemnly.

"I like to smile big like that. It makes my whole face happy," Rachel said as she reached for the doorknob. "Let's go inside and see where your seat is going to be. I have new crayons and pencils for you, too." She felt the child's grip on her hand tighten. "Do you like to draw and color?"

Another nod.

"Good. Me, too."

Rachel swung the door open and ushered her new student into the colorfully decorated classroom. One whole wall was plastered with letters of the alphabet, arranged amid the flowers and vegetables of a cartoon-like garden. In the foreground, a bunny made of the letter *B* was nibbling on a carrot that was bent to resemble a *C*. On the opposite side of the room there was a sink, bookcase and bright blue cabinet with banks of cubbyholes. Red, blue and yellow plastic chairs surrounded four low, round work tables and echoed the same vivid colors.

Above the chalkboard, Rachel had fastened gigantic numbers, one through ten, and a more sedate version of the *ABC*s. No flat, vertical surface remained undecorated. It had taken days to pin the pictures and cutout letters to the bulletin boards. Judging by the look of amazement and awe on the child's face, the effort had been well worth it.

"Did you go to preschool?" Rachel asked.

"Uh-uh."

She talked! *Thank You, God!* Rachel felt like cheering. Instead, she kept her tone deliberately casual. "That's okay. We'll learn our letters and numbers here in my class, together."

"I'm five," Samantha said softly.

"I'm a little older than that," Rachel countered with a grin.

"Teachers are supposed to be old."

"That's right. You're very smart."

The child beamed. "I know."

At least she hasn't lost her sense of self-worth, Rachel mused. That was a big plus. Obviously, someone in Samantha Smith's past had done a wonderful job of making her feel worthwhile. That confidence would help her adjust to whatever troubles came her way, the loss of her parents being the worst one imaginable. It was hard enough growing up *with* parents, let alone coping without them.

Except maybe in the case of my own mother. The thought popped into Rachel's head before she had time to censor it. There were some people who could give advice in a way that made the recipient glad to follow it. Then there was Rachel's mother, Martha. When Martha Woodward spoke, she acted as if everyone should be thrilled to profit from her superior wisdom. To disagree with her opinions was to invite condemnation. Rachel was, unfortunately, very good at doing that.

As she reflected on the strange twists and turns her private life had taken lately, she stood aside and watched the curious child explore the classroom. The sight brought a smile and a sigh of contentment.

Teaching was Rachel's God-given gift and she relished every moment of it. Moreover, when she got a chance to help an emotionally needy child like Samantha, even for a short time, the blessing was magnified.

Rachel hoped that someday, if she was patient enough, Martha would finally accept the fact that her only daughter was single by choice. That her happiness came from loving other people's children as if they were her own.

If that happened, it would be a direct answer to prayer. And if not? Well, that would be an answer of another kind, wouldn't it?

The playground was deserted when Rachel finally took Samantha outside to the play equipment. It was grouped according to size. That which was assigned to the youngest children was naturally the smallest. The stiff, canvaslike seats of those swings were so tiny that even a person as diminutive as Rachel couldn't fit into them safely. Knowing that, she led the way to the next larger size.

Samantha strained on tiptoe to make herself tall enough to scoot back into one of the higher swings.

Rachel sat next to her and pushed off with her feet, swinging slowly, as if they were simply two friends sharing a recess. "I like to do this, don't you?"

"Uh-huh." Because she could no longer reach the

ground, the little girl wiggled and kicked her feet in the air, managing to coax very little back and forth motion out of the swing. "Will you push me?"

"Okay. But first, watch how I move my legs. See? I pull them in when I go backward, then lean back and stick them out to go forward."

The child made a feeble try, failed, and pulled a face. "It doesn't work."

"It will. You just need to practice. Watch again. See?"

Instead of listening, Samantha jumped down and stalked away, kicking sand and muttering to herself, "Dumb old swing. I hate swings."

So much for the buddy system, Rachel thought. It served her right. She'd taken one look at Samantha Smith, sensed her loneliness, identified with her, and promptly broken her own rule against blurring the line between teacher and pupil.

"Okay. Fun's over," she said. "Time for you to go back to the office so Ms. Heatherington can drive you home."

Samantha whirled. "No!"

"Yes." Rachel cocked her head to one side, raised an eyebrow and held out her hand. "Come on."

Tears blurred the little girl's wide, blue eyes. "I wanna stay here. With you."

"When you come back tomorrow morning you'll be in my class all day."

"No!" The child spun around and took off at a run.

Surprise made Rachel hesitate. Samantha was already disappearing down an exterior hallway when she came to her senses and started in pursuit.

She didn't dare shout. If Heatherington happened to look out the window and see what was happening she might decide to move Samantha to another class for the short time she had left before being sent out of state. That was the last thing Rachel wanted.

At the corner where the sidewalk made a T, Rachel skidded to a stop. Which way? Left? Right? The hall was deserted.

Breathless, she prayed, "Where is she? Help me? Please, Lord?"

A commotion to the right caught her attention. Though the sounds were muffled, Rachel was certain she heard a childish squeal, followed by a definitely masculine "Oof."

She dashed toward the noise, rounded a blind corner and nearly slammed into the doubled-over figure of Sean Bates! This time, he wasn't laughing.

"Which way?" Rachel demanded.

Breathless, Sean pointed. "What's going on?"

"Tell you later."

"You'd better believe it."

He straightened slowly, painfully, watching Rachel race down the hall in pursuit of the little blond monster that had plowed into him. It had been moving so fast that he wasn't even sure whether it was a girl or a boy. When he saw Rachel returning, holding the child in front of her with its arms and legs thrashing, he still wasn't sure. Not that it mattered.

"Want some help?" he asked.

"Oh, no. I'll just hang on like this until she gets tired. Or until she kills me."

"You don't have to be sarcastic. I said I'd help."

"Sorry. It's been a rough day."

"Tell me about it."

He eyed the red-faced child. Rachel had grabbed her from behind, rendering her kicks useless. If he approached from the front, however, he was liable to be very, very sorry—again.

"I just did tell you," Rachel said. "This is Samantha Smith. She's going to be in my class. I think."

"You sure you want that?" Eyebrows cocked, Sean gave her a lopsided grin.

"Of course I do. Samantha and I just have to come to an understanding first." Rachel raised her voice, speaking slowly, plainly. "If she doesn't decide to settle down and behave pretty soon, I may have to ask Ms. Heatherington to take her to another school. I really don't want to do that."

The little girl gasped, froze in midmotion and stared past Sean's shoulder in the direction of the office. Then she wilted like a plucked blossom on a hot summer day.

Relieved, Rachel relaxed and eased her to the ground so she could stand. "Whew. That's better."

Sean was braced for another escape attempt. It didn't come.

Instead, the girl gazed up at her teacher with new respect. "I— I'm sorry. You won't tell, will you?"

"Not unless I have to. It's my job to keep you safe and teach you how to get along with others. That means you have to listen to me and do as I say. Will you do that from now on?"

The child peered off into the distance one more time, then looked back up at Rachel and nodded solemnly. "Uh-huh."

"Okay. We have a deal."

Rachel held out her hand and Samantha took it. Together, they started to walk back toward the office.

Sean watched them go. He had to admit he'd been wrong to judge the pretty, diminutive teacher on appearance alone. Rachel Woodward was definitely special. One of a kind. Not only was she physically stronger than she looked, she had an indomitable will and a tender, empathetic heart that were impossible to deny.

He smiled to himself. With "credentials" like that, it was no wonder her unconventional form of child psychology had worked so well.

* * *

Driving home that evening, Rachel couldn't get memories of Sean Bates out of her mind, so she forced herself to concentrate on her newest student instead. Thinking about Samantha kept her from reliving her recent close encounters with Sean, at least temporarily. She was getting pretty disgusted with herself about that. There was certainly no good reason for her to get the shivers every time she pictured his smile and sparkling eyes.

Rachel was glad she'd paused to examine her innermost thoughts regarding Samantha, because they revealed a truly deep concern. As long as that little girl remained in her class, Rachel knew she'd have to be careful to avoid showing favoritism. All students deserved equal treatment, as much as it was within a teacher's ability to provide it, and getting emotionally attached to one or two individuals made impartiality that much harder.

Rachel pulled into the driveway of her modest, white-painted house. Boy, was she glad to be home. She'd bought the house on Old Sturkie Road at auction and had fixed it up to suit her eclectic taste. Now that she was well settled in, she couldn't imagine ever wanting to move. The place had everything: quaint heritage charm, combined with all the modern conveniences such as running water, indoor plumbing, electricity and telephone. In the winter, Rachel could even supplement her regular heating system by lighting the woodstove that still sat by the chimney in her living room.

In the summer, however, there was nothing she'd rather do than relax in the shade of the covered front porch overlooking her peaceful neighborhood.

The phone was already ringing when she flung open the back door and grabbed the receiver. Between her delay at work and the fact that she'd stopped at the market on the way home to pick up a few things for supper, she was running late. Which meant she had a very good idea who was calling.

"Hi, Mom."

"How'd you know it was me?"

"Lucky guess."

"You didn't call," Martha chided.

"I just walked in the door."

"Hard day?"

"The first ones always are. You know how it is."

"It took you a long time to get home tonight. I've been trying to reach you for over an hour."

Rachel chuckled cynically. "Well, unless you expect Schatzy or Muffin to answer, you'll have to give me time to get here."

Hearing his name, the little black-and-tan dachshund danced at Rachel's feet, circled a couple of times, then ran over to give the lazy, gray angora cat a lick across its face. Muffin showed her displeasure by hissing.

"Stop that," Rachel said.

Confused, Martha asked, "Who? Me?"

"No, not you, Mom. The cat."

"Oh. I never could abide animals in the house, myself. Too messy. All that hair!"

"I keep them brushed. Anyway, Schatzy hardly sheds." Rachel surveyed her homey living room with a contented smile.

"You and your animals."

Here it comes, Rachel thought. She tensed, waiting for her mother to seize the opportunity to point up the difference between keeping pets and raising children.

Instead, Martha said, "I had my hair done today. Mercy Cosgrove was in the beauty shop the same time I was. She says her granddaughter, Emily, is getting married."

"I know."

"Why didn't you tell me?"

"I only found out today. She's marrying Jack Foster."

"Hard to believe, isn't it? I mean, there was a time when she could have had a doctor for a husband. Sam Barryman was ripe for the picking."

"So you've reminded me. Often," Rachel drawled. "Didn't he finally run off and marry Sheila Something-or-other?"

"That's old news," Martha said. "They're getting a divorce."

"Too bad. But it doesn't surprise me. My one date with good old Dr. Sam was enough to cure me—pun intended."

"What about the new guy at your school? I understand he's single. And cute, too."

"News travels fast."

Rachel knew better than to offer additional information about Sean. All she'd have to do was give her mother a hint that she might be interested in him and Martha's wild imagination would take off. Pretty soon, she'd have convinced herself that Rachel was practically engaged to the poor guy, when nothing could be further from the truth.

"Well, have you met him yet?" Martha asked.

"I, uh, I did run into him," Rachel said, laughing to herself and picturing the shocked look on Sean's face when she'd crashed into his broad chest. The vivid memory of his strong hands steadying her followed instantly, leading to an all-over tingle and another little shiver. Maybe she was catching a summer cold or something.

"You wait too long and there won't be any good ones left," Martha said.

"There weren't all that many to start with, Mother."

"I still don't know why you had to break up with that nice Craig Slocum."

Because that nice Craig Slocum dumped me when I told him I might not be able to have kids, Rachel countered silently. She said, "These things happen. Look, Mom, I'm really beat and I have to put my groceries away before they spoil. Can I call you back later?"

"There's no need. I just wanted to hear your voice, to make sure my little girl was okay."

"I'm fine, Mom," Rachel said. "I'm all grown up, remember?"

"You'll always be my little girl, honey."

She laughed lightly. "I can just see us now. I'll be seventy and you'll be ninety-five and you'll still expect me to phone you every day to tell you I'm okay."

"Not a chance," Martha said. "By that time, I'll either be living with you and your family or you'll at least have a husband to look after you so I can quit worrying."

What a choice! Rachel was glad her mother couldn't see the way she was rolling her eyes. "You wouldn't like living in my house, Mom. Animals make you sneeze, remember?"

Martha snickered. "I'll hold my breath. At ninety-five, that shouldn't be hard. It's the breathing in and out part that might get a little tricky."

Rachel wasn't too weary to appreciate her mother's dark humor. "You're amazing."

"You, too, honey. Talk to you tomorrow."

"I'll call you as soon as I get home from work. Don't panic, okay? You know I'm always late when school first starts."

"You shouldn't let them take advantage of you."

"I'm the one who's taking advantage, Mom. I let them pay me for something I'd gladly do for free."

"So, swallow your pride and marry a rich man. Then you can afford to be a volunteer."

"I'd rather eat dirt."

Rachel could hear the smile in her mother's voice when she replied, "I hear dirt is pretty tasty if you pour enough red-eye gravy over it."

Chapter Three

If Samantha had been added to her class after the group had been together longer, Rachel would have made a special point of introducing her. Since it was only the second day of the school year, however, that wouldn't be necessary. Or advisable. The less fuss, the better.

Parents had already escorted many of the other children to the classroom door. It was amusing how often the parent was the one reluctant to let go, while the child was eager to join in the excitement of finally starting school.

Wearing a favorite lightweight summer shirt with a softly draped skirt, Rachel stood in the doorway of her room to welcome her students and gently encourage their parents to leave. She glanced up at the clock on the wall as the final morning bell rang. One child hadn't arrived yet.

A few latecomers rushed by. Concerned, Rachel was about to give up and close the door when she saw a man and a small, blond girl approaching hand-in-hand. It was Samantha!

Rachel's breath caught. Sean Bates was bringing her.

"Thank You, God," she whispered.

Watching their approach she couldn't have said which of the two she was most delighted to see. Each was certainly a welcome sight. And together they made her heart sing.

Unfortunately, the little girl was wearing the same faded T-shirt and baggy blue shorts she'd had on the day before. In contrast to the new school clothes her classmates were sporting, she made a sad figure, indeed. Rachel made a mental note to remedy that situation ASAP. If Heatherington wouldn't see to it that Samantha had proper clothing and shoes for school, she'd do it herself. There was no excuse for sending the little girl out into the world looking like an urchin—even if she was one.

Rachel greeted the latecomers with a broad grin. "Good morning! I'm so glad to see you, Samantha. Did you ride the bus to school?"

Sean spoke up. "I think so. I found her standing out front on the lawn. It looked like she was waiting for directions, so I brought her on over. I hope that's okay."

"Of course. Thank you for helping. We all try to watch out for each other around here." She crouched down to be on the little girl's level and asked again, "Did you ride the bus?"

Samantha nodded.

"Then, it's my fault you had trouble finding my class. I should have shown you how to get here from the place where the buses stop. I'm sorry you had trouble. But I am glad you met Mr. Bates yesterday and that he knew where to bring you."

Instead of paying attention to what Rachel was saying, Samantha gazed up at Sean with evident adoration, then leaned to one side so she could peer at his back.

With a questioning frown, Rachel straightened. Her intense blue gaze wordlessly asked him what was going on.

Sean shrugged, palms out. "That's the third time she's done that." He turned. "Did somebody stick a 'Kick Me' sign on my back when I wasn't paying attention?"

"No. There's nothing there," Rachel assured him. "It's clean." And broad and strong and impressive and… *Oh, stop it,* her conscience demanded, bringing her up short before she had time to give in to the idiotic urge to dust invisible lint off the shoulders of his jacket.

"That's a relief," he said.

Rachel swallowed hard. "Yeah. Well, thanks again for helping Samantha find her class."

"You're quite welcome." He gave a slight bow and grinned at the little girl. "I'll watch tomorrow, too. Okay? After that, I'm sure you'll be able to get here all by yourself."

"I know she'll be fine." Pausing to give the loitering parents—and Sean—a look that clearly meant she was taking charge, Rachel added, "It's time for class. All the grown-ups have to go, now."

It wasn't until she'd guided Samantha through the door and closed it behind her that she realized her hands were shaking. That third cup of coffee she'd had for breakfast must have provided more caffeine than she'd thought.

To Rachel's relief, the only tears she'd seen that morning had been those of the parents left outside. Some years the opposite was true. Snifflers weren't so bad because they were fairly easy to distract. Screamers were another story. Occasionally, there would be a child who was so afraid of separation from mommy or daddy that hysteria ensued. Not only was the wild sobbing distracting, it tended to spread an unwarranted sense of dread to the others. This year, however, it looked as if the adjustment was going to be peaceful.

Suddenly, an indignant *whoop* disturbed the calm. Children froze and stared. Rachel immediately zeroed in on the cause and hurried to help.

She bent over the screeching little boy. "What's wrong?" *Name—name—what was his name?* And where was the name tag she'd carefully pinned on him when he'd first arrived?

Other children had huddled in small groups, looking on as if expecting dire consequences to spill over onto them.

Rachel guessed. "It's Jimmy, isn't it? What's the matter, Jimmy? Did you hurt yourself? Can you tell me what happened so I can fix it?" By keeping her voice soft she forced the child to quiet down to hear what she was saying.

Jimmy drew a shuddering breath and pointed to a nearby knot of boys. "He hit me."

The knot instantly unraveled as children scattered.

Rachel took charge. "All right. I need everyone to sit down on the rug so we can talk about keeping our hands to ourselves." She pointed. "Jimmy, there's a box of tissues over there. You can go get one and wipe your nose before you come sit with us."

Choosing the adult-size chair at the head of the class, Rachel waited for the children to comply. All but two did. The tearful boy was doing as he'd been told and blowing his nose. Samantha had gone with him.

Rachel was about to remind the little girl that she was a part of the class and needed to behave just like the others, when she noticed something that gave her pause. Although Samantha was whispering to the sniffling boy, her excitement was evident. She waved. She pointed across the room. She held out her arms as if mimicking a bird and smiled so broadly her eyes were squeezed almost shut. Or were they actually closed? Rachel couldn't tell for sure. All she knew was that Jimmy had forgotten about being upset and was giving Samantha his rapt attention.

So, Samantha wanted to play mother. Rachel smiled. That was a good sign. The child obviously needed to feel needed. Looking after the other children would give her a positive purpose, not to mention a boost in morale.

And anybody who can calm a screamer like that is okay in my book, she thought. There was a tender-hearted peacemaker in the class. This was going to be a good year.

A very good year.

The day flew by so fast that it was over before Rachel had time to notice how tired she was. At two-thirty she lined up all her students and marched them out to the lawn in front of the school to make sure each one was handed over to a parent or had boarded the right bus.

Samantha stood by Rachel's side and watched each classmate depart, until only she was left.

"Which bus did you come on?" Rachel asked her, wiping sweat from her own brow and wishing she could escape the sultry southern afternoon by heading back to her air-conditioned classroom.

"I don't know."

"What was the number on it?"

"I don't know." Clearly, the child was about to cry.

"Well, did it have a lady driver or a man?"

"I don't remember."

Terrific. "Okay. Let's go check in the office."

As she turned to lead the way, the little girl gave a happy squeal, shouted, "There! That one," and took off running toward the last bus in line.

Rachel paused, unconvinced. An older child might remember suddenly, but five-year-olds were more likely to remain confused.

She started to follow, then decided to check the office records first. If Samantha had chosen the right bus after all, Rachel didn't want to do anything to undermine her self-confidence. If not, there would be plenty of time to correct the error before the buses pulled out.

She hurried into the office, glad for a temporary

respite from the heat and humidity of the September afternoon. "I need to see the Samantha Smith file, Mary." Breezing past the receptionist, she headed straight for the upright filing cabinet.

"I don't think I've finished that one yet. It's probably still here in this pile on my desk." Mary gestured toward a messy stack. "Sorry. We've been swamped. I don't know why so many folks wait till the last minute to register their kids."

"In Samantha's case, I don't think there was a choice. Any idea where her file might be? Top, bottom, middle?" Rachel was already paging through the folders.

"Near the top, I think. Why? Didn't you already see it?"

"Yes, but I don't recall what it said about the foster home placement. She needs to ride a bus and I don't know which one."

"Oops. Maybe we should phone and ask Ms. Heatherington."

"No way. I'd rather spend an hour listening to my mother complain than to have to say two words to that woman."

"She is kind of stuffy. Is that why you dislike her?"

"No. It's her attitude about the children she deals with that makes me mad. She acts like it's their fault that their families fell apart and she got stuck helping them."

"The little Smith girl's an orphan, isn't she?"

"Yes, which makes it even harder. That's why it's so important to be sure she's on the right bus. Life has to be frightening enough for her already."

"Well, you'd better get a move on. It's almost time for those buses to leave."

"I know. I'm hurrying."

Rachel fumbled a file folder and almost dropped it, just as a mother burst through the door and shouted, "There you are. I want to talk to you. Now!"

It took Rachel a moment to realize she was the object of the woman's ire. Her first clue was the small, round-faced boy who was clutching his mother's pudgy finger and rubbing his runny nose with his other hand. It was Jimmy.

"I'll be right with you, Mrs.—"

"Andrews," she said crisply. "My son, James, is in your class, as you well know."

"Yes, ma'am. We can go talk in my room. I just have to take care of—"

"I'm not going anyplace where you can make excuses in private," the woman said. "I want to know, right here and right now, where you get off telling my son that there are *angels* in his classroom?"

"What?" Rachel was totally confused.

"Angels. He says there are guardian angels flying all over the kindergarten room."

"I never told him that."

"Well, somebody sure did."

"Maybe one of the other children." A light went on in Rachel's head. Of course! Samantha hadn't been pretending to be a bird when she'd comforted Jimmy, she'd been demonstrating her ideas about angels! *How sweet.*

Rachel nodded, convinced of her conclusions. "I think I know what happened to confuse your son. Children have wonderful imaginations. One of the girls must have told him about angels this morning while she was helping him blow his nose."

Mrs. Andrews wasn't placated. "Well, what if she did? You're the teacher. What are you going to do about it?"

"Nothing. No harm's been done," she said calmly. "Now, if you'll excuse me, I have to go hold the buses until I can be sure one of my students is on the right one."

"Well! I never…"

The woman was still muttering to herself when Rachel brushed past and headed for the curb. Her eyes widened in disbelief.

The buses were already gone!

After a hurried search of the hallways and her own classroom, Rachel returned to the office, gave in and telephoned Heatherington's office.

When she hung up, Mary asked, "Well?"

"Samantha's living with the Brodys on Squirrel Hill Road. I saw her get on bus number seven. I think she belonged on five." Rachel began pacing. "It's my fault. I should have kept her with me until I knew for sure."

"She'll be okay. Surely, the driver will notice and… Oh-oh. Seven, did you say?"

"Yes. Why?"

"Because we have a sub driving that one this afternoon."

"Don't tell me. Let me guess. Sean Bates is driving seven, right?"

"No, Maxwell Eades is." Mary frowned. "Why would you think it was Sean Bates?"

"Because Samantha knows Sean. I figured she'd choose that bus if she saw him behind the wheel."

"Nope. Sorry. We can't use Bates until he gets an Arkansas license. Mr. Vanbruger did suggest he ride along to familiarize himself with the routes, though. He could have decided to start with any of them."

"Give me maps of all the routes," Rachel ordered. "Then please get on the phone and alert some of the parents who live along seven. Ask them to tell Max to keep Samantha from getting off."

Mary handed her copies of hand-drawn maps. "Gotcha. What are you going to do?"

"Jump in my car and try to catch the bus before that poor kid gets herself totally lost."

"Isn't that above and beyond the call of duty?"

"Not for me it isn't. And definitely not where Samantha Smith is concerned. The minute I saw her I knew I was meant to look after her. So far I haven't done a very good job of it. From now on, I intend to do a lot better."

Rachel was familiar with the rural area where the Brody family lived, but since Samantha's bus wasn't headed that way, the knowledge was no help. The only sensible thing to do was trace the bus route, mile by mile, until she overtook number seven.

And what if Samantha's already gotten off before I catch up to her? Rachel's heart sped. *Or what if she changed buses at school while I was stuck in the office?*

Stomach in knots, Rachel tightened her grip on the wheel of her compact car, sweating in spite of the air-conditioning. She mustn't think such negative thoughts. They only made everything seem worse.

Prayer would be a much better choice, yet she was unable to force her worried mind to concentrate enough to come up with a lucid plea. Finally, she resorted to a misty-eyed *Please, God,* and left it at that.

She made good time until she turned off the highway onto the narrow, winding road that ran between Glencoe and Heart. According to old-timers, Heart had once been a thriving little town. It had even had its own post office inside a mom-and-pop grocery store. For decades, that had been a favorite local gathering place, especially on Friday nights when weekly paychecks needed to be cashed. Now, however, Heart consisted of a couple of isolated houses and a community center building that was used mainly on Wednesdays by a quilting club.

This was Tuesday. If Samantha got off the school bus in Heart, she wouldn't meet a soul who could help her.

Rachel chewed on her lower lip. "Calm down. Stop imagining the worst. You'll find her."

Head spinning, thoughts churning, Rachel pictured possible scenarios. If Samantha truly had boarded that particular bus because Sean was on it, she'd want to stay near him. She wouldn't be likely to get off at all! Then again, if she hadn't...

The pavement ended abruptly. Rachel slowed and pulled over in front of the Heart Community Center to double-check her map. She frowned. She'd seen kindergartners draw clearer diagrams.

The building sat in a rocky, dusty triangle at the confluence of the roads. One track was supposed to lead to Saddle, one to Salem with a cutoff to Camp, and the other to Agnos. Bus seven should be headed for Camp, which meant the first thing she needed to find was the branch of the road that led toward Salem.

She peered west. *That one.* It had to be that one. She could see the red lights flashing on the radio station antennae atop the hill called the Salem Knob.

Decision made, Rachel tromped the accelerator. Her car's wheels spun in the loose gravel and dirt, leaving behind a cloud of powdery red dust. It was a blessing that Max was driving the bus, because he knew where he was going. She'd lived around here all her life and she still sometimes got turned around when she left the highway. An inexperienced person like Sean, using the same map she'd been given, would be likely to get lost.

Seeing more dust ahead was encouraging. Rachel cautiously increased her speed. She didn't want to go too fast. The roads had recently been scraped by county graders, making the center smoother but un-covering and scattering enough sharp rocks to make driving more hazardous than usual. Previous vehicles had left tracks in passing; Rachel tried to keep her tires in those same ruts to avoid unneces-sary risk.

Rounding a corner she came upon a sight that made her heart pound. Bus seven! Now, all she had to do was get it to pull over so she could be certain Samantha was still safely aboard.

Approaching the slow-moving bus she flashed her lights and honked. Small faces peered out the bus's rear windows at her, grinning and waving. She signaled as best she could, but the children apparently thought she was merely being friendly because they returned her greeting with renewed vigor.

According to the map, it was miles before the next bus stop. Rachel was too frustrated to wait that long to learn Samantha's fate, yet it was unsafe to pass the lumbering bus on such a treacherous road.

"Give me patience, Lord, and hurry," she muttered, laughing at the contradiction. *God is in charge, God is in charge,* she reminded herself.

Finally, she laid on the horn and held it. That worked. Max pulled the bus over. Rachel stopped behind it, jumped out and was immediately enveloped in a noxious cloud of exhaust fumes and unsettled dust.

Ignoring the discomfort, she forged ahead, waving her arms wildly, and circled to the front of the bus. Max had already opened the folding doors.

Sean was standing on the top step, steadying himself by holding on to a chrome support pole. He wasn't smiling. "Are you nuts?"

"Yes." Rachel coughed as she boarded and pushed him aside. "Where's Samantha?"

"Right there." He pointed. "Mind telling me what's going on? Or do you always drive like a maniac?"

Aside from being choked up by the fumes, Rachel was also dizzy and breathless with relief. She wavered, then plunked down next to Samantha, speaking to the wide-eyed child. "I was so worried. This isn't your bus, honey. It won't take you to Mrs. Brody's."

The little girl's eyes grew moist. She blinked. "Oh."

Sean made himself part of their conversation and addressed Rachel. "Then, why did you let her get on it in the first place?"

She raised her gaze, her expression a clear challenge. "I made a mistake, okay? I know that now. I thought I'd be... Oh, never mind." Getting to her feet she reached for the little girl's hand. "Come on, honey. I'll take you home."

Sean blocked her path. "Over my dead body. You're far too agitated to drive. The way you were acting just now you shouldn't even have been behind the wheel of a car, let alone consider transporting kids."

"I beg your pardon."

Facing him, Rachel stood as tall as her short stature would permit and tried to appear formidable. Pitted against his broad chest and wide stance, her effort seemed more pitiful than confrontational. He'd removed his jacket and tie and rolled up the sleeves of his dress shirt. If anything, that made him look even more rugged, more powerful than usual.

"You should beg everybody's pardon, lady."

Before Rachel could reply, Max cut in. "Save your breath, folks. Miz Rachel ain't goin' nowhere. Looks like she's gettin' herself a dandy flat tire." He leaned to the left to get a better look at her car in his rearview mirror.

"That's impossible," she insisted. "I was very careful. And I wasn't speeding."

"Out here it don't matter much," Max said. "You'd best go check before I head on down the road with these here kids. It's a mighty long walk to town."

"Oh, for heaven's sake." She edged past Sean and hurried back to inspect her car. It was definitely listing to one side. Her shoulders slumped. "Oh, no."

Sean had quietly followed. "I'd help you change that tire," he said, "but unless you carry two spares, we'd still be one short."

"What?"

He pointed at one of the rear wheels. "Looks to me like you've got a second tire going flat."

Thunderstruck, Rachel realized he could be right. Her eyes widened. "I don't believe this!"

"I do. I may be from the city but even I know better than to go racing around on rocky roads like these."

"I wasn't racing!" Disgusted with everyone and everything, she let it show in her expression.

"Tell that to your car," Sean said.

"Okay, okay. You don't have to rub it in." Pausing, she considered her current options. "I suppose I could walk to the nearest house and call a garage."

"You could. Or, you could just leave your car where it sits and ride back to school on the bus with us. That way, you and I could take Samantha home in my car, then I could drive you back here afterward."

"What good will that do if there's more than one ruined tire?"

"Simple. We'll take them off, load them in my trunk and find a garage that'll patch them."

Rachel was astounded. "You'd do that for me?"

"No problem. I'm glad to help—as long as I don't have to *ride* with you," Sean chided, ignoring the face she was making at him. "I don't think I'm that brave." He chuckled softly, enjoying her discomfiture. "I don't think *anybody* is."

Chapter Four

By the time Max had dropped off his last regular passengers and returned to Serenity Elementary, it was nearly five p.m. There were only two cars in the parking lot—Sean's black sedan and a silver-colored, dusty van.

Rachel led Samantha up the front walk toward the school office as she spoke over her shoulder to Sean. "Before we go, I need to phone Mrs. Brody so she knows everything is all right."

"I don't think that'll be necessary," he said, gesturing. "We've never met, but I'd say she's just found us."

Oh dear. He was right. She was about to face *another* irate grown-up. Hannah Brody had thrown open the door of the van and was shuffling rapidly across the parking lot, shirttail flapping, bangs glued to her forehead with perspiration. Rachel had never seen the poor woman look more frazzled.

"Hannah! I'm sorry if we worried you," Rachel shouted before she reached them. "Samantha accidentally got on the wrong bus. I was just bringing her back."

"You couldn't *call* me? Let me know?" The older, slightly portly woman wheezed to a stop as she confronted Rachel. "Do you know how hot it got in that there van? I coulda croaked, waitin' on y'all."

"I'm really sorry," Rachel said. "I was worried, too. Guess I wasn't thinking clearly."

Hannah leaned down to focus on the child. "And you. How old are you?"

"F-five."

"So, how did we say you could remember the number of your bus?"

The child stared at the toes of her worn sneakers. "Five. Same as me."

"That's right."

"What a good idea," Rachel interjected, trying to sound upbeat.

Hannah straightened and glared at her, hands fisted on ample hips. "Now you, missy. What do you have to say for yourself?"

"Excuse me?"

"There is no excuse for what you did."

Sean stepped up beside Rachel, clearly taking

sides. "Most teachers would probably have left the child's welfare in the hands of the bus driver. Ms. Woodward, however, took it upon herself to try to put things right. That speaks very well for her, don't you agree?"

For the first time, Hannah took notice of Sean. She gave him a critical once-over. "And who might you be?"

He introduced himself and extended a hand of friendship. The annoyed woman begrudgingly accepted it. Then, instead of stuffing his hands into his pockets the way he initially had when he'd run into the pretty teacher in the hallway, he took half a step closer to Rachel and nonchalantly looped one arm around her shoulders. The gesture was casual yet obviously protective.

Mrs. Brody noticed immediately. Her eyebrows arched. "Oh, I see. You two were too busy playing patty-cake to pay attention to anything else." She grabbed the child's hand and started away. "Well, what's done is done. Come on, Samantha. It's too late to take you shopping for new clothes today like I'd promised. I got to go start supper."

The little girl glanced back over her shoulder, silently pleading with her teacher and Sean to rescue her as Hannah Brody led her away. That soulful look was enough to put Rachel's heart in a twist and leave a lump in her throat.

For an instant she wanted to weep. Instead, she waved, smiled and called, "Bye-bye. See you tomorrow, Samantha."

"Will she be okay with that old grump?" Sean asked softly.

"Hannah?" Rachel glanced up at him while deliberately removing his hand from her shoulder. "Hannah's not a bad person. She gets a little irritable sometimes but she's basically good-hearted. She's been taking in the kids nobody else wanted to bother with for years."

"Samantha's one of those?"

"Apparently. Her social worker did say she was having trouble adjusting. That's probably why they gave her to Hannah."

"I see. What else can you tell me about the Brody woman?"

"Well…" Rachel's smile stayed. "She baby-sat for lots of folks here in Serenity who're all grown up, now. Me included."

"You're kidding! No wonder you let her talk to you like that."

"Hannah means well. And she was right. I should have called her so she wouldn't worry. I was so worried about finding Samantha, I guess it just slipped my mind."

"That's understandable. Don't beat yourself up about it."

"I won't. The only thing that bothers me is the way the small-town rumor mill is going to have fun with us."

"Us?" Sean's expression showed bewilderment. "What *us?*"

With a wry chuckle, Rachel shook her head. "You do have a lot to learn about living in a place like this, don't you. There doesn't even have to be an *us* for people to talk. By tomorrow morning, half the folks in town will be saying you and I are practically engaged. And the other half will be trying to decide if you're good enough for me."

She'd expected Sean to enjoy the lighthearted banter. Instead, he seemed upset. She pressed on. "Hey, don't look so glum. I didn't say it was my idea. It's just how it is in a place where everybody knows everybody else, and half of them are related, besides." That statement brought a further conclusion. "Oh-oh."

"What's wrong now?"

"I just had a horrible thought. Hannah's my mother's second cousin by marriage."

"So?"

"So, I'll bet Mom is the first one she calls."

Sean huffed. "Don't tell me you're still worried about pleasing your mother at your age?"

"Hey. I'm not *that* old."

He deliberately took his time looking her up and

down and fully appreciating what he saw. Chances were good that he was at least seven or eight years older than she was, maybe more, yet they had to be contemporaries in spite of her youthful appearance. For starters, he knew this wasn't Rachel's first year of teaching. A person didn't usually finish college and earn a degree until they were in their twenties at least, so she had to be halfway to thirty by now.

"You don't look a day over sixteen," he finally told her.

"Actually, I'll be eighty-four my next birthday," she said. Struggling to repress a giggle, she twirled in a circle to put herself on display. "Pretty good for an octogenarian, huh?"

"Excellent." Sean was shaking his head in disbelief and laughing softly under his breath. "You certainly had me fooled. What's your secret?"

"Clean living. I never miss a Sunday in church, either."

"Very commendable."

"I think so. Hey! Since you're new in town, how'd you like to come visit my church?"

"Church and I don't exactly get along."

"That's too bad. We won't eat you, you know. We really do accept everybody, even *sinners*." The astonishment in his expression made her chuckle. "That was a joke, Bates."

"I'll laugh later, okay?" He reached into his

pocket for his car keys and jingled them in one hand. "You ready?"

"As soon as I go grab my purse," Rachel said. "Wait here. I'll just be a minute."

Starting away she heard him mutter, "I don't believe it."

She spun around. "You don't believe what?"

"You. You were driving all over the country without your license?"

"Guess I was. I told you Christians aren't perfect. You'd better start believing me or I may have to keep trying to prove it to you."

Rachel's car was right where she'd left it, without so much as a hubcap missing—much to Sean's surprise. A prankster had scrawled "Wash me" and drawn a happy face in the fresh layer of dust coating the lid of the trunk, but otherwise the car was untouched.

He parked as far off the roadway as he could without scratching his sedan on the brambles and small trees growing along the right-of-way, and got out. Rachel followed.

A closer look at her car made her sigh audibly. Her shoulders sagged. "Rats. You were right. I do have two flats."

"Apparently." Sean circled the car, assessing the damage. "Looks to me as if it's going to be dangerous to remove the tires, even if we use both our jacks. The ground is too uneven here. The car wouldn't be stable."

"What do you suggest, then?"

"Calling a tow truck. If we left your car jacked up and drove into town with two of the wheels, any little thing could knock it over and damage the axles. Then we'd have to call a tow, anyway."

Rachel was too exhausted to argue. She yawned. "Fine. Whatever. As long as I can get to work in the morning."

"I don't suppose you happen to know the number of a local garage that does towing?" he asked, reaching into his car for his cellular phone and pushing the power button.

She snorted cynically. "As a matter of fact, I do."

Sean waited, growing impatient when she didn't recite the number. "Well?"

"It wouldn't be my first choice."

"This is not a popularity contest. If this place can come get your car and fix the tires, let's get on with it, okay?"

"Okay, okay."

Rachel gave him the number, then watched as he made arrangements with the garage. To her surprise, Sean knew approximately where they were and gave credible directions, so she didn't have to interrupt to correct him.

That was a plus. So was the lengthening day. If Craig Slocum had already gone home for supper, as she hoped, her personal involvement could be kept to a minimum.

And if not? She clenched her jaw, imagining Craig's superior smirk when he discovered she needed his help. Since their failed engagement, Rachel had managed to avoid him almost completely. If he showed up this evening it would be the first time she'd spoken to him face-to-face since he broke her heart.

Her chin jutted out, her spine stiffened. If she had to face Craig, she would meet the challenge head-on. That man was never going to learn how deeply he had hurt her. *Never.*

Sean noticed Rachel's growing uneasiness. When they heard the approach of a truck, her head snapped around and she stared in the direction of the sound as if expecting a stalking tiger instead of deliverance.

"Want to tell me why you're so jumpy?" he asked.

"I'm not jumpy."

There was nothing to be gained by arguing with her. "Okay. Sorry." Sean smiled. "Maybe you're just hungry. Personally, I'm starved. What do you say we grab a pizza or something while we wait for your car to be fixed?"

Rachel nodded without taking her eyes off the distant roadway as the truck rumbled closer.

Sean decided to test her. "Your treat."

"Sure. Fine."

His resultant laugh finally got Rachel's attention. She frowned. "What's so funny?"

"You are. I could have asked you anything just now and you'd have agreed without hearing a word I said."

"Don't be silly."

"Okay. We are on for dinner, then?"

"Dinner? Oh, sure. Only around here, dinner is what we eat at lunchtime. The evening meal is called supper."

"I'll remember that." He saw the tow truck slowing. Inside the cab, its driver was grinning from ear to ear. The man's eyes were shadowed by the brim of his baseball cap, but it was still evident he was concentrating on Rachel.

"You know him?" Sean asked.

"I told you. Everybody knows everybody around here."

"Let me put it another way," Sean said quietly. "Do you dislike him as much as I think you do?"

She huffed and managed a momentary smile. "Actually, Craig and I used to be engaged."

"Engaged? You were going to marry *him?*"

"Yes." Her frown returned. "Why is that so surprising?"

"I don't know. I guess he just doesn't look like your type."

"Why not? Because he drives a tow truck?" The Slocums owned several lucrative businesses in Serenity and the surrounding area, and Craig drove the tow rig because he liked to, but Rachel wasn't about to explain all that to Sean.

"Listen, Mr. Bates," she said firmly, "if a man does an honest job and is proud of his work, I see no reason to put him down simply because he may not have a college degree like you and I do. If you choose your friends by their level of formal education, you'll miss out on a whole lot, especially around here. There are plenty of very smart folks who haven't had the opportunities you and I have had."

Sean was grinning at her. "You through?"

"I just don't like stuck-up people, that's all."

"Neither do I." He chuckled softly, shook his head. "I was talking about the smug, know-it-all look on the guy's face. I didn't think you'd put up with that kind of attitude for a second. Since you two broke up, apparently I was right."

Chagrined, she wished she hadn't jumped to conclusions. "Sorry about the lecture. Class distinction is a sore point with me."

"So I've gathered." Sean was still grinning.

"Well, here comes your ex-fiancé. Mind if I shake hands with him?"

"Of course not."

"Good." He stepped forward, his hand extended. "I'm Sean Bates. Thanks for coming so promptly. We really appreciate it."

The other man paused to glance at Rachel, then turned back to Sean and gave his hand a pump. "Craig Slocum."

His grip was more than firm, it was crushing. If Sean hadn't known the man's history with Rachel and anticipated the animosity, he would have been taken aback by the overt show of strength. Instead, he met it equally.

"We aim to please," Craig said. "What seems to be the problem here?"

"A pair of flats," Sean answered. "Like I told your dispatcher, we can't safely repair the damage as the car sits. Think you can load it up on your truck and get it back to town for us? Ms. Woodward needs her car in time for work tomorrow."

Craig pushed his cap back on his head and wiped his brow with a red-printed kerchief as he studied the dusty car. Rachel, on the other hand, looked at her feet, at the tree-dotted farmland all around them, at the peacefully grazing cows with their new calves—everywhere except at her former fiancé.

Interested, Sean watched the unspoken interplay between the two. It seemed to him that a spark of romance remained. Then again, he could be imagining things.

Tension hung in the sultry air, blurring the truth like fog on a dewy morning. Slocum wasn't a big man but he was definitely physically fit, Sean noted, which probably appealed to Rachel, at least on a subconscious level. They had undoubtedly made a good-looking couple. Perhaps they would again.

As soon as Craig had winched Rachel's car onto the flatbed of his truck and secured it with heavy chains, he opened the passenger door of the wrecker and flashed her a killer smile. "Ready, hon?"

The expression of panic in her eyes spurred Sean to answer, "We're ready." Taking Rachel's arm, he escorted her to his car and politely held the door for her, behaving as if there was no question who would drive her back to town.

Sean could feel the other man's angry stare. What had he gotten himself into? In town less than a week and already he'd run afoul of one of the good ole boys whose unofficial buddy system ran everything inside and outside of Serenity. These might not be the days of the Hatfields and the McCoys, but Sean knew it wasn't smart to alienate the natives, either. No telling whose uncle or cousin would show up on the school board and wind up voting not to continue funding the counseling program next year. Even a born-and-bred city boy knew that much.

He climbed in beside Rachel and started the car. "You okay?"

"Of course. Why wouldn't I be?"

"No special reason. If you'd explained why you didn't want to call that particular garage, we could have done things differently, you know."

"Slocum's is the best and the fastest. It made sense to use them."

"Not if running into Craig was going to bother you."

"The problem is mine, not his."

"You're the one who broke up with him, then?"

"Not exactly. It was mutual."

Puzzled, Sean glanced over at her as he slowly followed the tow truck, keeping his distance so he wouldn't get a rock chip in his windshield. "Then, why do you say the problem is yours?"

She pulled a face and quickly looked away, embarrassed to admit, even to herself, that she hadn't been able to forgive her former fiancé the way the scripture taught.

Staring out at the passing countryside she said, "Because he's over it and I'm not."

Chapter Five

The drive back to Serenity ended sooner than Sean wanted it to. Rachel had said very little more after her telling comment about her failed relationship with Craig Slocum, and there was no way Sean could hope to help her cope unless she chose to open up to him. Then again, she hadn't asked for that kind of help, had she. So why did he feel compelled to give it? *Good question. Why, indeed?*

Because I'm a "fixer" at heart, he told himself. *Always have been, always will be.*

Though he'd failed to help his own family, that didn't mean he couldn't help others, like Rachel— or the children he'd been trained to work with. That way, at least something good would come out of his troubled childhood. Such assurances gave him solace when he was foolish enough to think back on the trauma of having been raised in a household where he was the only one who wasn't a problem drinker.

Sean parked in front of the service station garage and started to get out. "I'll be right back. I just want to tell Slocum where we're going and when to expect us back." He grinned. "Uh, where are we going and when will we be back?"

"I'm not sure. There won't be any real restaurants open tonight. I suppose we'll have to settle for Hickory Station if we want to eat this late. We passed it on the way in. It's not much to look at but the food's pretty good."

Frowning, Sean glanced at his wristwatch. "What do you mean restaurants won't be open? It's not even seven yet."

"No, but it is Tuesday." Rachel had to laugh at his obvious puzzlement. "This place isn't like Little Rock. Or Cleveland either, I imagine. Folks around here seldom eat out in the evening except on Friday and Saturday nights, so those are the only nights most restaurants stay open past late afternoon."

"You're kidding!"

"Not at all. Breakfast and lunch are different, of course, because people are out and about then. By evening, everyone is home relaxing and getting chores done. We don't stay up late in the country." She smiled broadly, her vivid blue eyes twinkling.

"And we don't waste money eating out unless it's payday or we're celebrating the weekend."

"A guy could starve to death around here."

"Unless he had a local guide like me." Rachel peered out at where Craig was unloading her flat-footed car. "Tell him we'll be back in about an hour. There's no need to be more specific. Nobody ever is."

"Kind of puts a whole new spin on the word *casual*," Sean said with a lopsided grin. "Okay. Hang loose. I'll be right back."

Rachel watched him jog away from her. He was good-looking all right, but awfully restrained for a knight in shining armor. The poor guy was totally out of his element in a place like Serenity. He was game, though. And he had a decent sense of humor. That would probably carry him through, as long as he didn't make too many local enemies right off the bat. Country folk were some of the most loving people there were, yet they also remembered every slight, every error in judgment. It didn't take much to alienate a whole community.

"Guess it's up to me to shepherd him until he gets the hang of things," Rachel murmured to herself. "Humph. Just what I need. Another people project." The thought made her smile.

Sean climbed back into the car. "All set." He paused to glance at her. "You look pleased with yourself. What's up?"

"Nothing. I was just thinking."

"About good old Craig?"

The smile vanished. "Don't be silly."

Busying himself backing out and turning the car around, Sean avoided making eye contact with her. "Hey, you don't have to keep up appearances for my sake. I'm neutral, remember? Think of me as your shrink. Anything you want to tell me will remain privileged information. If you're interested in making up with him, I'll be glad to help." Sean was warming to his subject. "You know, give you pointers from the male point of view, stuff like that."

Stunned, Rachel stared over at him. "Let me get this straight. Are you offering advice on my love life?"

"One professional to another. No charge."

"That's big of you." She folded her arms across her chest and stared straight ahead. "You're starting to sound just like my mother. What makes you think I can't handle my own problems?"

"I never said you couldn't. I like to see folks happy, that's all."

"I assure you, Mr. Bates, I'm as happy as a kid in a candy store." Her voice rose. "As a bee in a rose garden. As a hound dog baying at a full moon. As…"

"Okay, okay, I get the idea. You forgot 'Happy as a pig in a mud hole.'"

"I skipped that one on purpose." Making a face

at him Rachel felt the beginnings of another smile twitching at the corners of her mouth. "I was trying to keep my analogies from getting too earthy."

"So, you do care what others think of you."

"Of course I do."

"Good. In that case, I should mention that your former boyfriend threatened me back there."

"No way. Craig doesn't care what I do or who I'm with."

"I wouldn't be so sure about that. He told me that if I didn't treat you right, he was going to break every bone in my body." Sean grinned over at her. "Sounds to me like he still cares for you. Either that or he took an instant dislike to me for no reason."

"That's ridiculous."

"If you say so. Nevertheless, the guy looks like he could bench-press a bus axle, so I'd appreciate it if you didn't complain about me in front of him. I value these bones."

And nice bones they are, Rachel thought, eyeing him surreptitiously. Considering how good-looking and appealing Sean was, it wasn't hard to imagine that Craig had been jealous. Even if he didn't want her for himself anymore, she supposed he wouldn't want to see her interested in an outsider.

"I still think you're overreacting, but I'll talk to Craig when we pick up my car and make sure you don't have anything to worry about." Rachel pointed out the car window as a busy quick-stop came into view. "There's Hickory Station. The red-and-white building on the right. Pull in anywhere. We'll go inside to eat."

"It's a gas station."

"Among other things." Rachel had to laugh at him. "You'd better get used to not having candlelit dining rooms, linen tablecloths and highbrow waiters, Bates. This is rural Arkansas, not some metropolis."

She led the way to the door and stepped aside so Sean could open it for her. Thankfully, he had that part of Southern manners down pat.

Tantalizing aromas immediately caught and held her attention. The front cash register was located at the end of a deli counter where fried chicken, potatoes and corn dogs stood in trays under heat lamps. Beyond that array was a pizza oven, and a separate service area with tables and benches for those who wanted to eat there instead of taking their food home.

Rachel recognized one of the cashiers as a young woman she'd gone to school with but had never gotten to know well. The two employees manning the kitchen were older members of her church. Fortunately, no one else with close personal connections to her was present, which helped her relax.

"I'm going to go get myself a soda," she told Sean. "Want me to get one for you, too?"

"Sure. Anything." He was gravitating toward the enticing aroma of freshly baking pizza. "What would you like to eat?"

"Food. Surprise me. I'm hungry enough to eat cardboard."

"Me, too."

By the time Rachel brought their drinks to a table, he was waiting for her. She slid into the opposite side of the booth, taking care to gather up the extra folds of her skirt and tuck them neatly beside her.

"They were all out of plain cardboard, so I ordered a deluxe special," Sean said. "Hope that's okay."

"It's wonderful." Sighing, Rachel took a deep draft of her icy soda. "I didn't know how tired I was until now. Guess I've been running on adrenaline."

"Me, too."

Weary, she let down her guard enough to reach over and pat the back of his hand where it rested on the table. "Thanks for all you've done for me. I really am grateful."

He froze, glanced at her hand atop his, then withdrew from her touch with a terse "You're welcome."

Rachel giggled. "Hey, I wasn't making a pass at you."

"I never said you were."

"No, but you acted like it."

"I did not."

"Did so."

"Did not." His eyes narrowed. "You're the one who warned me about the local gossip mill. It's going to be pretty hard to convince anybody we're not involved if word gets around that we were holding hands over a pizza."

"Okay. You've made your point," Rachel said. She settled back against the hard plastic of the booth. "For the record, I want you to know I'm not looking for romance—or anything like that."

"Glad to hear it. Neither am I."

That piqued her curiosity. "Any particular reason?"

"Many. All good."

"And private, I suppose."

"Very."

She began to smile over at him. "You don't mind quizzing me about *my* love life, though, do you."

"That's different."

"Oh? In what way?"

"Because I'm in a position to help you if you'll let me."

"And I suppose I'm not smart enough to do the same for you?"

Sean snorted derisively. "You do have a way of twisting whatever I say, don't you. All I meant was—"

"I know exactly what you meant," Rachel countered. "You have the degree in psychology and you come from a cosmopolitan background, so naturally you're much more enlightened than a simple country girl like me."

She tossed her head, swinging her hair back over her shoulders, her chin jutting out proudly. "Don't make the mistake of selling us country folk short, Mr. Bates. We may not be as sophisticated or as professionally educated as some people you've met, but we're not stupid. I'd lots rather be stranded on a desert island with an Arkansas hillbilly than with a college professor."

Sean chuckled. "Are you through?"

"Yes." Folding her arms across her chest she faced him boldly, defiantly.

"Good. Then, just sit there. I'm going to see if dinner's ready. Okay?"

Rachel pulled a face and said, "Not dinner. *Supper.*"

She watched Sean shake his head and laugh softly to himself all the way to the counter. When he turned around with the pizza tray in his hands his amusement was so evident that it brightened his whole face.

In retrospect, Rachel didn't know how she'd managed to get through the remainder of the long day. By the time she and Sean had reclaimed her car and she'd driven home, she was so exhausted she'd simply fed her hungry pets, showered and gone straight to bed. Even the knots of tension in her shoulders and neck hadn't kept her from sleep.

By morning she felt almost human again, which was a good thing, since she had another full day ahead of her.

She'd decided on a simple skirt and blouse and was rummaging through her small closet, looking for matching sandals, when the telephone rang. That was when she noticed the blinking red light on her answering machine. She knew who had called—and who was on the line this time.

"Hi, Mom."

Martha Woodward didn't bother with a greeting. "Where *were* you?"

"It's a long story."

"So I heard. What was wrong with your car?"

Rachel sighed. If her mother knew that much, she knew the rest of the story. "Flat tires."

"I heard that, too. I'm glad you called Craig. He's such a nice boy."

"I called the tow truck, Mother. Craig just happened to be driving it." *Good thing he wasn't there when we went back to get my car.*

"The Lord works in mysterious ways," Martha said.

"I hardly think God assigned Craig to tow truck duty last night just so he could look after me."

"Why not? Stranger things have happened. Besides, I understand you needed rescuing. Who better to do it than the man you were planning to marry?" She sighed wistfully. "You two make such a lovely couple."

"*Made.* Past tense, Mom. I'm never going to be a Slocum, so you might as well give it up."

"If you weren't so stubborn, I'm sure you and Craig could work out your differences."

Boy, am I glad I didn't tell her everything, Rachel mused. *I'd never hear the end of it.* "That's between Craig and me, Mom. I don't want to discuss it."

"I know, I know. Which reminds me, I talked to cousin Hannah yesterday. Who's the new man at your school? She says he drives the bus."

"He's just a guy. Nobody special."

"That's good, dear. I'd hate for you to get a reputation for taking up with any man who paid you mind. Especially since you and Craig broke up so suddenly."

"Mother…"

"Okay. I'll try to quit worrying. But you'll always be my little girl, no matter how old you get. You know that."

"So you've said. Listen, if I don't get a move on I'm going to be late for work. As it is, I'll be lucky to have time to grab a bite of breakfast."

"Too bad you didn't bring home the leftovers last

night," Martha drawled. "You used to love cold pizza for breakfast. Bye, dear. Have a nice day."

To Rachel's delight, Samantha arrived wearing new, clean clothes. Hannah Brody delivered her to the classroom door and stepped inside to make sure the child was okay.

As soon as Rachel had greeted the little girl she turned to Hannah. "Thanks for seeing that she made it."

The older woman made a sour face. "It was my fault yesterday. I'm sorry. My diabetes had kicked up that morning and I felt like a limp dishrag, so I sent her on the bus. She's a bright little thing. I never dreamt she'd get herself all turned around like that."

"We all made mistakes," Rachel said kindly. "How are you feeling today?"

"Much better, thanks." She swiped at her damp brow. "It's gonna be another hot one, though."

"I know. I've been leaving the air conditioner on at home so my poor animals don't cook while I'm gone."

"You still got that cute little wiener dog?"

"Schatzy? Yes. It's been two years since I brought him home, and Muffin is still sulking. I don't think she'll ever get over having a dog living under the same roof."

"Reminds me of some of the kids I've looked

after over the years." Hannah glanced toward
Samantha. "This one's sweeter than most, but she's
got some strange ideas, that's a fact."

"Oh? Like what?" Stepping closer for privacy
Rachel cocked an ear toward the veteran foster
mother. Hannah's instincts had been honed over the
years and whatever observations she made were
bound to be useful.

"She sees things that ain't there," the older
woman whispered. "I can't tell whether she's just
got a good imagination or if she really believes it."

"Like what?"

"She says she can see guardian angels."

Angels? Again? "I know," Rachel said. "She told
one of the other kids there were angels in the classroom. His mother got mad at me because she thought
I was teaching spiritual ideology. Anything else?"

"Not that I know of. She's only been at my place
for a few days. If I figure out any more, I'll let you
know."

"I appreciate that. And if I learn anything that I
think will help you, I'll do the same."

Hannah patted Rachel on the shoulder. "You're a
good girl. I knew from the time you was little you'd
make a wonderful teacher. Always readin' to the
other kids and makin' sure they could write their
names. Like it came natural to you."

"I guess it did." She surveyed her busy classroom

with a blissful smile. "There's nothing I'd rather do. No place I'd rather be than here."

"I can tell. Well, I'd best be goin'. Now that I know what size our little darlin' wears, I can pick her up a few new outfits on my way home. Just happened to have that blue one she's wearin' in a box of extra clothes. I try to keep nice things on hand. You never know when a new kid'll show up or how long they'll stay, and I can't always get out to go shopping." She chuckled under her breath. "Had to throw those old shorts of hers into the wash machine to get her to stop wearin' 'em. She said her mama gave 'em to her. I didn't think I was ever goin' to get her out of 'em. Not even to sleep."

"Well, one step at a time," Rachel said as Hannah started for the door. "Will you be coming to get her this afternoon, or shall I put her on the bus?"

The older woman held up one hand, fingers splayed. "The bus. Number *five*."

Laughing, Rachel nodded. "I don't think I'll ever forget that. I imagine I'll be having flashbacks about yesterday afternoon for years to come!"

Hannah paused at the open door and gestured with a jerk of her head. "Speak of the devil. Look who's here."

It wasn't necessary for Rachel to be told that Sean was nearby. Her thudding pulse had informed her of his presence the moment she'd heard him call a greeting to someone else on the playground. That, coupled with the judgmental expression on Hannah's face, was plenty of forewarning.

"He works here," Rachel alibied, fighting to keep her tone even. "I'd expect him to be on campus."

"More's the pity. Well, take care. Tell your mama hello for me when you see her, y'hear."

"Of course."

Though Rachel was bidding the foster mother goodbye, her attention was riveted on Sean. He seemed especially chipper today. There was a spring in his step, a twinkle in his eyes. He looked happy. Too happy. It was disconcerting.

When he got closer and his focus narrowed on Rachel, she chanced a cautious smile. "Good morning."

"It certainly is," Sean said brightly. "I saw Mrs. Brody bringing Samantha. Is everything okay?"

"Fine. She's fine. None the worse for yesterday's trauma."

"Who? Samantha or Mrs. Brody?"

Rachel laughed. "Actually, both of them. Hannah'd been having some trouble with her health but she's better today. And Samantha is wearing a pretty new dress, so I'm sure she feels better, too."

"That's great. Well, guess I'd better get to work." Sean turned to go, then paused. "Oh, by the way, I stopped at Slocum's to gas up my car this morning and had a nice, informative talk with your friend,

Craig. You'll be glad to hear he's not going to murder me, after all."

No, but I may. "What *kind* of nice talk?"

"Oh, nothing much. I just assured him I wasn't dating you. He seemed pretty relieved. The guy's still nuts about you. Maybe you should give him another chance."

Watching her expression harden, her lips press into a thin line, Sean was beginning to get the idea she was anything but pleased he'd made peace with Craig. He leaned to one side as if studying her pearl earrings.

"Oops."

"Oops, what?" Rachel absently fingered each stud and found nothing amiss.

"I think I see steam coming out of your ears."

"That's highly possible."

"Then, this must be my cue to exit. See ya!"

"Not if I see you first," Rachel muttered. To her surprise and chagrin, Sean grinned back at her.

"I should warn you. I have excellent hearing," he said.

Embarrassed, Rachel felt warmth infuse her cheeks. "Just as long as you can't read my thoughts."

"Would I like what I learned if I could?"

"That would depend upon whether you'd minded your own business lately," she told him. "As they say around here, 'If it ain't broke, don't fix it.'"

Sean continued to grin at her. "Ah, another bit of folk wisdom for my files. I'll make a special note of it. Thanks."

She would have loved to come up with a witty retort to put him in his place and give herself the last word. Unfortunately, no insightful gems popped into her head.

Slamming the classroom door she leaned her back against it and fought to steady her ragged breathing. What was it about that particular man that set her nerves on edge? He'd been nothing but pleasant to her—even helpful—yet half the time she found herself snapping at him as if they were sworn enemies. Life was too short, too precious, for that kind of attitude toward anyone. Besides, it wasn't her nature to be shrewish. If anything, she was too easygoing, too accepting of those who marched to a different drummer.

Some of that attitude she'd learned by becoming involved in a local church that welcomed everyone equally, no matter what their social or financial status. And some had come directly from her late father. In Rachel's opinion, any man who could put up with Martha Woodward for over thirty years was a candidate for sainthood.

"I still miss you, Daddy," she whispered, looking wistfully at the children milling around in the class-room. *And if I miss you, how much worse must it be for a child like Samantha? She lost both parents at once. No wonder she feels the need to imagine angels watching over her.*

Rachel blinked back unshed tears of empathy. More than once she'd wished for a similarly comforting vision. Like the day her stalwart father had passed away unexpectedly when she was hardly more than a child herself.

Or the night Craig had informed her he wasn't going to marry any woman who couldn't promise to give him the sons he needed to carry on his family name.

Chapter Six

Completing that first week of the fall semester left Rachel so drained she almost didn't get up early enough on Sunday to make it to church. If she hadn't laid out a favorite jacketed sundress the night before, she might not have managed to pull herself together in time.

Sunday school was nearly over when she dashed through the door to the main sanctuary and plopped down in a rear pew to wait for the morning worship service to begin. She'd barely caught her breath when her mother joined her, accompanied by Hannah Brody.

"Mom! Hi." Rachel gave Martha a brief hug, then glanced past her to speak to the other woman, too. "Good morning, Hannah. How are you?"

"Fair to middlin'," the heavy-set woman said.

"Did you bring Samantha with you?"

"Sure did. If there ever was a kid needed Sunday school teachin', it's that one. She's 'bout to drive me crazy."

Rachel leaned closer and took care to speak very softly. "Is she still seeing things?"

"That, and more," the foster mother said. "Now she's sayin' that you and that Bates fella are angels, too! I've never seen the like."

"Me? An angel?" Rachel snickered. "Not hardly."

Martha was smiling, too. "I can vouch for that."

"Thanks, Mom."

"Anytime. Want me to have a talk with the little girl and tell her what a trial it's been to raise you?"

"I think we can skip that much frankness," Rachel said with mock cynicism. "Teachers are supposed to set good examples. I wouldn't want you to destroy my positive image."

"Of course not." Martha reached over and patted her daughter's hand. "Hannah tells me that that poor baby has been through some heavy trials. I suppose it's natural for her to latch on to you. I'm glad you can be there for her."

Martha's sentence had trailed off, leaving Rachel wondering what had remained unspoken. She prodded, "But…?"

Sighing, Martha stared off at the distant altar as if making a decision, then answered. "But, you need to remember that you can't always be a part of her life the way you are now. It's not wise to let yourself get too attached to any of your students, honey. I've seen you do it before. Letting them go when the year is over is always a lot harder on you than it is on them."

"If I didn't have compassion, I wouldn't be nearly as good at my job."

"Maybe so. And maybe the opposite is true." Martha took her daughter's hand. "You also need to be fair. Can you really do that if you're overly fond of one or two of your students?"

"I'm not overly fond of anybody," Rachel argued. "My whole class is important to me. Teaching is my life. I wish I could make you understand that."

"I do understand it," Martha replied. "I felt the same way when I was your age. My job at the county clerk's office gave me a wonderful sense of accomplishment—and more money than I'd ever had growing up. Looking back, I'm still thankful I worked there, but not for those same reasons."

"I know. That's where you met Dad." Rachel had heard many versions of the story and they all led to the same conclusion.

"Yes. But that isn't what I'm trying to say this time. Things change. People change. Chances for added happiness come and go. If I hadn't met your father, I wouldn't have you." She smiled wistfully.

"And I wouldn't give *that* up for anything. Until you've had children of your own, you'll never understand how special you are to me."

Children, again. Rachel's heart twisted. Buried disappointment gave her voice a sharper edge than she'd intended when she said, "If you wanted grandchildren, Mom, you should have let me have the brothers and sisters I kept asking for." The distressed look that suddenly came over Martha was a surprise.

Glancing beyond her mother, Rachel saw Hannah give a barely perceptible shake of unspoken warning.

Thoughtful, Rachel sat back in the pew, eyes forward and hands folded in her lap as if the service had already begun. *How odd.* In all the times she and Martha had argued the merits of motherhood, she'd never seen her get teary-eyed before. Was it possible she'd wanted more than one child?

Was it possible she'd been unable to conceive a second time? Or a first? Rachel's breath caught. *Was I adopted?*

Her head snapped around and she stared at Martha. No, that wasn't the problem. It couldn't be. She and her mother looked enough alike to be sisters, taking into account their age difference. So why was her mom suddenly acting upset? Too bad this wasn't the right time or place to ask.

Resigned to wonder, at least for the present,

Rachel glanced at her watch, then smiled at the women beside her. "It's getting late. I think I'll wander down the hall toward the Sunday school rooms and pick up Samantha so she doesn't get lost in the rush. Be back in a flash."

Rather than give anyone a chance to object, she quickly got to her feet. The sanctuary was filling up, as usual, and there was a hum of muted conversation as families milled around in the aisles, searching for enough unoccupied space so they could all sit together.

Being short, Rachel couldn't see past the nearest parishioners. She smiled, offered an all-inclusive "Excuse me," and stepped out into the crowded center aisle.

Someone jostled her. Touched her arm from behind. Her first thought was that Sean Bates had changed his mind and come to church, after all! Excited in spite of herself, she turned and looked up with an expectant, jubilant smile.

The smile quickly faded. Standing there, grinning down at her like a sated cat with bird feathers still clinging to its whiskers, was Craig Slocum.

Rachel was deeply grateful that her concern for Samantha had provided a ready-made excuse to gracefully escape from Craig. His smug expression had instantly made her so furious she doubted she'd have been able to come up with anything else socially acceptable.

By the time she reached the kindergarten Sunday school room she'd pulled herself together. Most of the children had already left. She peered in the open door. Samantha had stayed behind and was helping the teacher straighten the chairs.

"Hi," Rachel said, smiling.

Samantha's eyes widened. She squealed, "Miss Rachel!" forgot everything else and raced across the room.

Rachel bent down to welcome the child and was immediately caught in a possessive embrace. Samantha's thin arms wound around her neck and she clung as if she planned never to let go.

"I'm glad to see you, too," Rachel said. She straightened with the little girl in her arms and balanced the extra weight on one hip. "Did you like Sunday school?"

"Uh-huh. How come you're not my teacher?"

"I am. In regular school. Don't you want me to have a little time off?"

"I guess so." Samantha's eyes remained bright and curious. "Is this where you live?"

"At church?" Rachel laughed softly, her tone gentle. She was used to having students ask her if she lived at the school because that was where she was every time they saw her, but she'd never been asked if she lived at the church. "No, honey. I live in a regular house. Why?"

"Just wondered."

"Oh." Remembering Hannah's earlier mention of Samantha's angel fixation, Rachel assumed that might be the underlying reason for the question. Since angels were spiritual beings, they might live in a church—it was a logical conclusion for a five-year-old.

"Would you like Mrs. Brody to bring you to see my house someday? I have a dog, Schatzy, you could play with."

"You have a dog? Really?"

"Yes. And a cat. Muffin. But she's pretty old so she isn't nearly as much fun. She gets kind of grumpy sometimes."

"Mrs. Brody is old, too."

Amused, Rachel followed the childish reasoning. "And grumpy?"

"Sometimes."

"Well, I know she doesn't mean to be."

"I wish I could come live with you," Samantha said. Her grasp on Rachel's neck tightened.

"I'm afraid that's impossible. If I took my whole class home with me, poor Schatzy would go crazy. Besides, you see me in school every day."

"What if I have to move? I do that a lot, since…"

"I know, honey," Rachel said, gently stroking her

back to comfort her. "Don't worry, okay? Everything will be fine."

"Promise?" There was a quaver in Samantha's voice.

"I promise."

Rachel knew she had no business promising happiness to anyone, let alone a child caught in the midst of life's trials. Yet she couldn't help herself. Not in this case. There was no way to make a five-year-old understand that sometimes bad things happened for good reasons. Convincing grown-ups of that concept was hard enough, even though it had a basis in scripture.

"Humph," Rachel mumbled as she made her way back to the pew where her mother and Hannah waited. *Grown-ups is right. I believe that God is in charge of my life, yet half the time I don't understand why bad things have to happen, so how can I hope to explain it to anyone else, let alone a child?*

She looked up. Her steps slowed. *Speaking of bad things...* Apparently, it wasn't even safe to come to church anymore. Not with her mother and Mrs. Brody in the same congregation.

Assessing the situation, Rachel stared. Martha and Hannah had scooted farther into the pew to make more room. The problem was, Craig was now sitting with them and the only empty space left was right next to him! Well, it was going to *stay* empty.

Continuing to hold Samantha, she approached the others. "I've decided to take my little friend to Children's Church."

"You're coming back, aren't you?" Martha asked with a sidelong glance toward Craig.

"Probably not," Rachel said. "You know me. I get along with kids better than I do with adults. I'll probably stay to help whoever is running the program this morning."

That said, she spun around and headed back down the aisle toward the haven beyond the official sanctuary. There was nothing wrong with worshiping the Lord in the company of children, she assured herself. After all, their faith was pure, not all cluttered up with ritual and hidden agendas the way many adults' was.

"Mine included," she murmured.

Samantha noticed. "What?"

"Nothing, honey." Rachel gave her a parting hug, bent to set her back on her feet, then released her and took her hand. "Come on. You and I are going to a special church service just for kids."

"I know," the child told her, looking up with innocent adoration. "Angels always do."

By the time the main worship service concluded and Rachel rejoined her mother, Craig was nowhere to be seen. She couldn't help showing relief.

"Here's your purse and your Bible," Martha

said, holding them out. "You left them here when you ran off."

"I didn't run anywhere," Rachel said. "I walked."

"There's more ways to run than with your feet," her mother argued. "Well, no matter. Craig's long gone. You missed your chance."

"Thank heavens for small favors."

Martha sighed. She eyed the petite blond girl clinging to her daughter's hand and gazing up at her lovingly. "Speaking of small, how did you two like Children's Church?"

"We had a lovely time, didn't we, Samantha?"

The child nodded.

"Hannah and I were talking about going out for Sunday dinner at Linden's Buffet," Martha said. "Would you like to join us?"

"What about Hank?" Rachel asked. She knew Hannah's husband well enough to be sure he wouldn't appreciate being left out of any meal, let alone an all-you-can-eat buffet.

"Went fishin' out to the lake," Hannah said. "Serves him right for leavin' me home alone. 'Sides, he took every bit o' the chicken I'd fried. Didn't even leave me a cold ole drumstick."

"In that case, I think you definitely deserve a restaurant meal," Rachel said, smiling. "I'd love to come along." She felt the child's grip on her hand tighten. "We both would. Wouldn't we, Samantha?"

"Okay," Hannah said. "But she rides with me. That's the rules. I been at this fostering business long enough to know better'n to break 'em." She held out a hand. "Come on, Sam. Let's go."

The little girl hesitated. Rachel looked down kindly. "She's right, honey. She's responsible for you. I'll meet you at the restaurant. I promise."

Instead of arguing as she'd expected, Samantha went straight to Hannah. *She trusts me,* Rachel thought. *Completely. And because of that she also trusts Hannah.* That was a new development, a very welcome one.

Rachel's eyes met the foster mother's, paused, then went to Martha's. Understanding flowed among them. Everyone knew what had just happened. Rachel rejoiced. What better place than in church to learn that her efforts were being rewarded.

And what better place to give thanks. She blinked slowly, reverently, silently grateful for the clear confirmation that she was doing the right thing in regard to the lonely child. No matter what anyone said, she knew she'd been meant to help Samantha. And that was exactly what she intended to continue doing.

Linden's Buffet was located in a strip mall in East Serenity, well away from the older part of town. On Sunday mornings the restaurant opened at eleven to accommodate the after-church crowd, then closed early. With such a brief window of opportunity, the buffet was always swamped, especially right after noon.

Martha rode over with Hannah and Samantha. Rachel thought it would be best to reinforce the foster mother's authority by driving separately. Slowed by the only traffic light in the entire town and unable to find a parking place on her first circuit through the Linden's lot, she entered a few minutes after the others. They'd already been seated. Samantha and Hannah were on one side of the table. Martha was alone on the other.

Breathless and grinning, Rachel joined them. "Whew! Thanks for saving me a seat. I've never seen this place so busy."

Martha made a face. "You don't get out much, do you."

"Not on Sunday mornings. You know very well I usually go straight home after church, change clothes and work in the yard. My garden gets away from me if I don't." Her smile widened. "Which reminds me. I have another batch of ripe zucchini for you, Mom."

"Oh, goody." There was no doubt of the older woman's sarcasm.

Rachel giggled. "I knew you'd be thrilled. I suppose I can spare a few vine-ripened tomatoes to go with it, providing you'll promise to take the squash off my hands, too."

"'Course I will." Martha winked at Hannah. "The last squashes she gave me were big enough to use as baseball bats!"

"I'll take some if you really have too many," Hannah said.

"Sure do." Rachel laughed at the scrunched-up face Samantha was making. She leaned closer to say, "It's very good for you," but the child's expression didn't improve. Obviously, there were some barriers that even a pseudo-angel couldn't overcome, zucchini consumption being one of them.

"Well, shall we go fill our plates before all the food is gone?" she asked.

"I'll wait here with the purses and order our drinks when the waitress finally gets around to us," Hannah offered. She gave the little girl beside her a pat and a kindly smile. "You can go ahead with Miss Rachel if you want to, Sam."

Rachel mouthed a silent *Thank you,* and held out her hand. Samantha immediately latched on to it, and they both followed Martha toward the steaming buffet tables.

"I'm going to start with salad," Rachel said, looking down at the child to check her reaction. It was predictably negative.

"Not me," Martha said, grinning. "I'm going

straight for the pizza and the Mexican stuff, like tacos." She reached out toward the child. "Anybody who doesn't want to eat rabbit food can come with me."

Samantha didn't ask Rachel, she merely looked up at her to request permission with her eyes.

"Go ahead," Rachel told her. "I don't mind."

The child shyly accepted the older woman's hand. Watching them walk off together, Rachel was struck with an impression: her mother behaving like a grandmother. She would make a wonderful one, wouldn't she. No wonder she was so eager to see the next generation come into being.

"What I need to find is a man who already has kids," Rachel muttered under her breath. "Like that Mitch guy Brianne Bailey married last year."

The biggest problem was the scarcity of handsome, eligible widowers with small children. It had been years since Rachel had encountered anyone who fit that description—and she was in the perfect job to spot such a man because she'd probably meet his children first.

Slowly filling her salad plate, she let her mind wander. It wasn't until Martha hurried over and grabbed her arm that she realized she'd been holding up the line by daydreaming.

"Did you see her?" Martha asked.

"See who?"

"Samantha. One second she was right next to me and the next she was gone."

Rachel frowned, forced herself to concentrate. "Calm down, Mom. What do you mean, she's gone? She can't be gone. She wouldn't just leave us like that."

"Then, she's been kidnapped! Oh dear. Oh my. It's all my fault. I only took my eyes off her long enough to pick up a slice of pizza."

"She hasn't been kidnapped," Rachel assured the panicky woman. "She's around here somewhere. She has to be. Maybe she went back to Hannah. Come on. Let's start by looking there."

Though she was outwardly calm, Rachel couldn't help the telltale tremor in her hands as she carried her salad to their table and set it at her place.

Hannah asked, "Where's Sam?"

"We were hoping you'd know," Rachel said. "She was with Mom a second ago, then she disappeared. I thought maybe she'd come back to you."

The portly woman stiffened and began to scan the surrounding tables. "Nope. I haven't seen her."

By this time, Martha was near tears. She sank into her chair with a moaned "Oh, no."

"All right," Rachel said, taking charge. "Mom, you and Hannah keep an eye on the front door. I'll go check the bathrooms. If she's not in there, I'll find the manager and get us some help."

Whirling, she managed to take one quick step before crashing into the man who had quietly approached behind her.

Rachel gasped. "Oh—" It was Sean! And Samantha was holding his hand.

"Now, now," he warned, smiling. "Watch your language. There are children present."

"I wasn't going to say anything bad. At least, not until I got a chance to talk to you alone," Rachel snapped. She gestured to include Hannah and Martha. "Do you have any idea how badly you scared us all?"

"Me? I just came in for a peaceful meal and got dragged over to your table." Still smiling, he looked down at his five-year-old companion. "It probably surprised me as much as it did you." He stepped up to the table and nodded an all-inclusive greeting. "Hello."

Rachel took over the introductions. "You remember Mrs. Brody," she said. "And this lady who looks like she's about to faint dead away is my mother, Martha Woodward. Mom, this is Sean Bates. We work together at the school."

Her mother proceeded to look Sean over, all the way from his sport shirt to the toes of his loafers. To Rachel's chagrin, Martha was acting as if she thought she'd seen the poor man's picture on a wanted poster and was trying to decide whether or not to turn him in and claim the reward money!

Finally, the older woman conceded. "Hello, Mr. Bates. I've heard about you. You're not from around here, are you?"

"No, ma'am. I'm from—"

Rachel purposely interrupted as he and Martha shook hands. "He's just moved to Serenity, Mom. Now that you two have met, if you don't mind, I'd like to eat. I'm starving."

"Oh dear. I was so dithered when Samantha ran off, I think I left my plate over there. I'd best go get it. I'll be right back."

"I'll go, too," Hannah said. She slowly pushed herself to her feet and ambled off, leaving Rachel and Samantha alone with Sean. The little girl continued to grasp his hand.

"And I'd better go see if I can find an empty table," Sean said, scanning the crowd. "This place came highly recommended, but nobody warned me I'd better get here early."

"Most churches let out at noon," Rachel explained. "You have to think like a Southerner to figure out our schedule. Which, by the way, is why I stopped you from telling Mom you're from Cleveland."

"I wondered why you'd interrupted me like that."

"Because you were about to admit to being a Yankee. Mom was already upset with you. I didn't see any reason to compound the problem."

"Are you serious?"

"Very. Arkansas may be considered the Midwest by some folks but it's the South to us. We're not all as set in our ways as my mother is, but it's still best to let people get to know you before you announce that you're from up north."

"That's unbelievable."

"I know. Humor the old-timers, okay? They're not mean. They're really sweet people. They're just proud of their heritage."

Samantha tugged on Sean's hand. When he looked down, she said, "You can sit by me."

"Well, I…"

What choice did Rachel have? Since she'd just gotten through extolling Southern manners and virtues, how could she gracefully counter the child's invitation and send him away?

"I suppose we can add another place," Rachel told him.

"I don't want to be a bother."

Too late for that. "There's an extra chair right over there. Bring the silverware, too, so we don't have to ask the waitresses for it. They have enough trouble keeping up with their customers on Sundays."

Sean checked with those seated at the neighboring table and got their permission to remove an empty chair. He was about to settle it in a place farther from Rachel, when Samantha took over and started tugging. The chair's legs collided with those of others—and of people—as she struggled to work it between the closely placed tables.

"Say 'Excuse me' when you bump into some-body," Sean told the eager little girl.

"'Scuse me," she announced loudly, speaking to no one in particular while continuing to awkwardly tug on the chair.

"Here. Let me do that," Sean said. "Where are we going with this?"

Samantha was beaming. She pointed. "Over there. By me."

Since the child's place was directly across from Rachel's, that left only the space at the end of the table for Sean, which meant he'd be seated between them with little elbow room. Judging by the look on the teacher's face, she wasn't pleased.

"Tell you what, Samantha," he said lightly. "Let's put you here, on the end, because you won't take up as much space as I do, and I'll sit in your chair. That way you can be right next to Miss Rachel, too."

"Okay!" Samantha hopped into the chair Sean had been carrying as soon as he slid it into place.

His glance caught Rachel's and held it. "Is that better?"

"Fine. Whatever. It makes no difference to me." Giving a shrug she glanced at her untouched salad.

"Since I seem to be the only one who's managed to find anything to eat yet, why don't you two go fill your plates. I'll hold the fort till everybody gets back."

"Sounds good to me," Sean said. He held out a hand. Samantha grabbed it and jumped down.

"Watch her every second," Rachel warned as they started away. "When Mom tried to take her to the buffet table, she ran off and picked up a stray. No telling who or what she might bring back next time."

The noise level in the room kept Rachel from hearing Sean's reply with his back turned, but the slight, rhythmic shaking of his shoulders told her he was laughing.

Chapter Seven

It didn't take Rachel long to decide she'd have been just as well off to allow Sean to sit next to her as to have him directly in her line of sight. She couldn't continue to stare at her plate and ignore the pleasant dinner conversation around her forever. Soon, somebody was bound to question her inordinate interest in her food. Every time she raised her gaze, however, there was Sean, seeming larger than life and definitely paying way too much attention to her.

I'm being ridiculous, Rachel told herself. *I'm not afraid of him. Or of my mother's interference.* The two elements brought together, however, might prove embarrassing, especially if Martha ever got it into her head that Sean Bates would be a good candidate to take Craig's place. Or, worse, that both men might make suitable sons-in-law!

Rachel was about to excuse herself early, on the pretext of needing to get home, when Samantha announced, "I'm gonna go see Miss Rachel's dog. It got shot."

Martha was so astounded she grabbed her daughter's forearm and almost caused her to drop her fork. "What? You never told me about that!"

"There's nothing to tell," Rachel insisted with a puzzled frown. "I don't know where she got such an idea. I just said she could come and visit. I never said Schatzy was hurt."

Sean began to chuckle. "Listen to yourself. I know exactly why Samantha is confused."

"Of course!" Rachel rolled her eyes. "I said Schatzy and she heard something else." Leaning closer to the wide-eyed child, she explained, "Schatzy is his name, honey. He hasn't been shot. He's fine."

"Really?"

"Really."

"Are you still gonna make me cupcakes?"

Though Rachel had always prided herself on figuring out the convoluted reasoning of young children, she was lost again. "Cupcakes? I don't remember saying anything about that, either."

"Uh-huh. You did so," the little girl insisted.

"Okay. If you're sure."

To her right, Martha was giggling behind her napkin. "I'll bet she means your cat this time."

Sighing and nodding, Rachel had to admit her mother was probably right. "Are you thinking of *muffins,* honey?"

"Yeah. Those. With frosting."

The image that that suggestion brought to Rachel's mind made her laugh, too. "I wasn't talking about baking anything, Samantha. My cat's name is Muffin. I'm afraid she wouldn't like it much if we spread frosting all over her."

"Oh." The five-year-old's lower lip was starting to quiver and moisture was pooling in her bright blue eyes.

"But you can help me feed her if you want," Rachel offered quickly. "Muffin loves to eat. And Schatzy loves to play ball. Maybe Mrs. Brody will let you come over this afternoon. Once you get to know my animals, you won't get their names mixed up again."

A tear trickled down Samantha's cheek as she looked at her foster mother and asked in a quavering voice, "Can I?"

That emotional plea would have melted a heart of stone—and Hannah Brody's was as soft as a marshmallow to start with. "Don't see why not. Hank's not due home yet, and I've got no chores to do till he drags in a mess o' fish—if he catches any." She looked across at Rachel. "Okay if we stop by your place on the way home from here and save me a trip back? I have to drop your mama off, anyway, so we'll be right close."

"Sure," Rachel said. "It's pretty hot to be running around outside in the yard, but Samantha and Schatzy can play fetch in my hallway without hurting anything."

Samantha brightened. "Goody! *Everybody* can go."

Before she could stop herself, Rachel's gaze snapped up and locked with Sean's. *Everybody?* Oh, that certainly wasn't what she'd had in mind when she suggested they stop by her house on their way home from dinner.

Smiling, Sean said, "You have that deer-in-the-headlights look, Rachel. Don't worry. I'm not inviting myself. I have plenty of things of my own to do today."

"Like what?" Martha asked sweetly.

"Well, I…"

"Just as I thought," she said, clearly pleased with herself. "You haven't lived in Serenity long enough to be involved in much besides your work at the school. If you get bored at my daughter's you can always come over to my house for a glass of sweet tea or lemonade. I only live a couple of blocks from her."

"Thank you, ma'am, but I really can't."

"Nonsense. You and I can have a nice chat. I've

been wanting to ask you more about your background, anyway. Are your people related to the Bates family that founded Batesville?"

"I doubt that very much, ma'am." His glance at Rachel was an unspoken appeal for rescue.

Rachel knew exactly how he felt. There was only one thing to do—provide a distraction. She jumped to her feet and abruptly changed the subject. "Today's dessert is pineapple cake. I'm going to go get mine. I'll bring some for everybody. Come on, Sean. You can help me carry the extra plates."

Without waiting for a reply, she started off, weaving between the tables like a skier headed down a slalom course. It wasn't necessary to turn around to know that Sean was right behind her. She could sense his presence in every nerve. Even the roots of her hair tingled.

He didn't speak until they reached the dessert table. "Thanks."

"For what?"

"For getting me away from your mother."

Rachel chuckled softly. "You're not away from her yet. Mom can be very persistent."

"So I've gathered. Between her and Samantha, it looks like you and I will have our hands full."

She handed him two small plates and balanced three others herself. "No pun intended, but we already do—and I'm not talking about this cake."

"How do you mean?"

"Life in a small town. I tried to warn you about it before. You'll manage okay if you remember that only part of whatever you hear is true. Think of the rest as misunderstanding, embellishment, wishful thinking or downright lies. Mom usually falls into the 'wishful thinking' category."

"What does that have to do with me?"

"Plenty. For instance, if you were foolish enough to stop by my place this afternoon when the others do, you'd just provide more grist for the rumor mill."

"I see. And that would come between you and Craig?"

If Rachel hadn't been holding the dessert plates she'd have thrown her hands into the air in frustration. She did whirl to face Sean. "No! I already told you. There's *nothing* between me and Craig. It was over long ago."

"Then, why did he try to sit by you in church this morning?"

"What…? How…?"

"Your mother told me. She can be very informative."

"Terrific. Did she bother to mention that I didn't stay with them after he got there?"

"No. She left that part out. What happened?"

"I refused to be manipulated."

"I see."

Rachel arched an eyebrow as she studied his face. "Somehow, I doubt you do."

"Oh, I don't know. It does prove that my first impression of him was right. The man's still interested in you. Otherwise, why did he act jealous when he saw us together? And why would he purposely face rejection by trying to sit with you and your mother this morning?"

"You're beginning to sound just like her."

"Sociable?"

"No, crazy."

Sean laughed. "You're not the first person who's told me that. And I doubt you'll be the last."

Rachel had never dreamed Sean would ignore her well-meant warning and show up at her house, anyway. True, Samantha's insistence that he come along had undoubtedly played a big part in his decision. What he wasn't considering, however, was what Rachel might have to endure as a result of his stubbornness.

To make matters worse, Hannah had opted to drop Samantha off to play with the dog first, then make a quick trip to take Martha home before returning to pick up the little girl.

"Okay. Outside," Rachel ordered when she realized she and Sean were about to be left alone with no one but the child for a chaperone. "Everybody on the front porch. Now."

Samantha's whining protests were not enough to change her mind. Only Muffin ignored the marching orders.

Acting pleased and relaxed, Sean sauntered outside and made himself at home on the glider, while Rachel plunked herself down on the top porch step with the little dachshund and Samantha. When the dog finally stopped trying to lick her face and rolled over in blissful submission, the child started scratching Schatzy's tummy.

"Is it always this hot this time of year?" Sean asked.

"No. Lots of times it's hotter." Rachel eyed the black sedan parked noticeably in her driveway. "It's your fault we have to sit out here."

"So the neighbors won't get the wrong impression, you mean?"

"Exactly."

Sean chuckled softly to himself. "Listening to you talk about Serenity makes me feel like I've been zapped back to the 1950s. I can't believe anyplace is actually as antiquated as you say this one is. Not these days."

"We aren't backward here, if that's what you mean. Maybe I am being too sensitive about gossip, but remember, I do teach impressionable children.

I'm also a product of my mother's upbringing, so I'm bound to be at least half a bubble out of plumb."

"Half a what?"

"You know. Like, two sandwiches short of a picnic? Three bricks short of a load? A few squares shy of a whole quilt?"

When he continued to look confused, she explained further, gesturing for emphasis. "Picture a carpenter's level. The bubble inside the glass capsule has to be right in the middle, between the marks, to ensure that whatever he's building isn't crooked or leaning. Half a bubble out of plumb means 'not quite normal.'"

Sean grinned. "*That* I can understand."

"I thought you would."

"Of course, if you'd listened to my professors you wouldn't think any of us were normal. That's a pretty subjective term." He grew pensive. "If you were to ask my family, they'd swear they were the normal ones and I was the oddball."

"I take it you disagree."

"Yeah."

A scowl knit his brow, and Rachel could see the muscles of his jaw clenching. Apparently, their innocent conversation had touched a tender spot. "Want to tell me about it, Doc?"

"Mutual psychoanalysis?" Sean began to lose his angry look. "I don't think so."

"Why not? You might feel better if you unloaded."

"What makes you think I have anything to unload?"

"Your expression. Your attitude." Rachel smiled sweetly. "The way your mood changes the minute you mention your family."

"It's that obvious?"

"Sticks out like a sore thumb. How long have you been estranged from them?"

"I wouldn't put it that strongly. We just don't see eye to eye. I figured it would be best for everybody if I got away from them, at least for a while."

"Your parents?"

"And my brothers," he said with a slow nod.

"They're still in Cleveland?"

Another nod. "Dad runs a hardware store in the Heights. My brothers work for him."

"Maybe they're jealous that you went on to college?" Rachel suggested.

"No. We all had the same opportunities. Paul and Ian are both older than I am. They had degrees in business administration long before I got mine."

"Was that when you drove a school bus?"

Sean took a deep breath and released it slowly. "No. I didn't do that till I went back to school again later, after I was on my own."

"Which explains why you seem older than most recent college graduates."

He managed a wry smile. "Sometimes I feel downright ancient."

"Well, my offer stands. If you ever decide you need a real person to talk to, remember I'm available."

"Thanks but no thanks. I'm fine. I don't need anybody."

"Everybody needs somebody," Rachel countered. "A friend, a mate, God. For me, it was the good Lord."

"Spoken like a true resident of the Bible Belt."

"That's absolutely right," she said, refusing to allow herself to become upset over his cynical tone. "And proud of it. There have been times in my life when I might have done something really stupid if I hadn't had my faith to fall back on."

"I don't need a crutch."

Rachel laughed lightly. "I'm not talking about stumbling along with a broken leg, Sean. I'm talking about being so uplifted, so enthralled with the wonders of life, you feel like your feet aren't even touching the ground."

Before he could answer, Samantha looked up from where she'd been playing, smiled at them both and said, "I know. Angels always fly like that."

If Schatzy hadn't jumped up and yipped, tail wagging, no one would have noticed Hannah's return a few minutes later.

She leaned out of the van and yelled at Samantha. "Come on, Sam. Hank's home. He caught me at Martha's. We gotta go."

"Awww…" The child immediately began to pout.

"You can come back another time," Rachel said firmly. "And we'll see each other in school tomorrow."

Acting as if there was no chance of her being disobeyed, she ushered the unhappy little girl to the van and helped her climb into a rear seat where she could be belted in for safety.

Rachel was standing in the driveway, waving goodbye and watching Hannah and Samantha drive away, before she fully realized she had one remaining guest. The uninvited one.

Her conscience added, *the lonely one.*

Oh, why had Sean revealed so much about his family?

Because you asked him, dummy, her heart answered. *You're a terrible softie who doesn't know enough to keep her mouth shut.*

That much was true. It was also true, however, that at least a portion of her empathy was a gift from God—a sensitivity that she knew He expected her to use to His glory.

Which didn't mean she was supposed to climb on her soapbox and start to preach, she reminded herself as she started back toward the porch where

Sean waited. *Too bad.* It would have been a lot easier for her to lecture him, then walk away, than to continue to befriend him. Friendship meant personal involvement. Commitment. It also meant she'd probably have to reveal a portion of her inner self that few people ever saw, in order to show Sean it was safe to do the same.

"Why?" she muttered, casting her eyes heavenward. "Why me?"

Sean was already on his feet, waiting, as she approached the porch. "Sorry. I didn't catch that. What did you say?"

"Oh, nothing important. I was just talking to myself."

He chuckled. "Do you do that often?"

"All the time."

"I suppose you answer yourself, too."

"Uh-huh. Doesn't everybody?"

"No, but I promise not to tell the school board that you do it."

"Thanks." Rachel made a silly face at him and sighed. "Well, here we are. What now?"

To her surprise, his cheeks reddened as if he were blushing. Was that possible? She faced him boldly, fists on her hips, her head tipped to one side.

"A penny for your thoughts?"

"No way." His color deepened.

"That bad, huh?"

"You'd probably think so."

"Maybe not. You never know," she said.

Sean's resulting smile reminded her of the one Craig had displayed in church. That was *not* a good sign.

Rachel had remained at the top of the porch stairs. Sean approached her slowly, then passed by and took one step down. When he turned to face her, they were close to the same height.

"I was thinking about how beautiful you are," he said. "And I'm not talking about your looks."

"Hey, thanks a bunch."

He gently clasped her arms, holding her so she couldn't turn away. "I'm trying to give you a compliment, Rachel. You have the sweetest nature of anyone I've ever known."

Awed, she was speechless. Her eyes searched his for any sign of insincerity. There was none. Sean Bates might like to kid around a lot of the time, but right now he was being serious. Too serious.

Rachel managed a smile. At least, she thought she did. Given the charged atmosphere between her and Sean she wasn't positive of anything, least of all her own reactions. The sensation of his warm hands caressing her upper arms reminded her of the first time they'd accidentally touched—when he'd tried to open the office door for her. That unexpected encounter had nearly destroyed her composure, just when she'd needed her wits about her for Samantha's sake.

This time, however, there was no one to consider but herself. And Sean, of course. The intensity of his gaze made her toes curl, her pulse hammer. It took her breath away. Without giving the action any conscious thought she parted her lips. They were trembling slightly.

Sean saw the telling reaction and his heart overruled his head. He bent slowly, purposefully, giving Rachel time to order him to stop. She didn't. On the contrary, she closed her eyes, raised her chin and leaned closer.

Before he could change his mind and behave sensibly, he followed through and kissed her.

Chapter Eight

Rachel's eyes popped open the moment he ended the kiss. She stared up at him, dumbfounded.

If Sean hadn't kept holding on to her arms, she knew she would have crumpled into a little pile of nothingness at his feet the instant their lips met. Wouldn't *that* have impressed the neighbors! From intelligent schoolteacher to inert dust bunny in three seconds flat. Imagining that vivid illustration made her giggle.

Clearly puzzled, Sean studied her expression. "I've had my face slapped before, but this is the first time a woman has laughed at me for making a pass at her. Was I that funny?"

"No!" She tried to compose herself and failed. The giggles continued. "I—I think I'm just stressed. You know, with school starting, and my mother making waves, and Samantha's awful situation, and Craig showing up in church this morning, and, and…"

"I get it," Sean said. There was a tinge of wounded pride in his voice. "One little kiss pushed you over the edge and now you're going to blame me if you end up getting hysterical."

"Something like that." Rachel's grin was so broad her jaw ached. The hurt look on his face helped her decide to reach out and gently pat his cheek. "Hey, don't sulk. It was a very, um, nice kiss. Really."

"'Nice?' Is that all you can say?"

"Well…" Once again, Sean's perturbed expression tickled her funny bone. "Oh, all right. I liked it, okay? It was great. Stupendous. So wonderful I'm about to keel over in ecstasy." Which wasn't all *that* far from the truth.

He frowned as he released her. "You don't have to exaggerate. I get the general idea."

I'm grateful you don't, Rachel thought. She said, "Well, good. I'm glad we have that all settled. Now, as I was saying before you got carried away—what next? Can I fix you a glass of iced tea or something?"

Sean took another step backward down the porch stairs, his hand sliding down the railing. "No thanks. I think it's high time I left."

It's long past the time you should have left.

Instead of voicing that opinion she offered a plausible pretext. "I do have quite a few chores to do before nightfall. Stopping at Linden's after church kind of messed up my schedule. I usually catch up on yard work Sunday afternoons."

"I meant to tell you what a beautiful place you have," he said.

One more step took him to the level of the lawn, where he paused to casually scan her yard. There were low, lush flower beds lining the front of the house. Two shade trees between there and the street were ringed with bright pink and white blooms that stood out boldly against the strong green of the grass. If there were weeds hidden among the plantings, he certainly couldn't tell. The only chore he could see that looked like it needed doing was to mow the lawn.

"I suppose it does take quite a bit of work to keep everything looking just right," he said.

"Thank you. Yes. It does. But I enjoy puttering. Flowers never sass me like some kids do, or argue with me the way Mom does." *Or kiss me when I'm not expecting it.*

Sean struck a nonchalant pose, hands stuffed into the pockets of his slacks. "So, what's on today's agenda?"

"I have to mow the—" Rachel stopped herself the moment she saw an eager glint in his eyes. It was too late.

"That's what I figured. I'm a whiz at pushing a mower. Since it's partly my fault that you're late getting started, let me cut the grass for you."

"I don't push my mower," she countered. "I ride around on it. Actually, it's lots of fun."

"Great!"

"I mean, it's fun for *me*. I like mowing the lawn."

"Honest?"

Rachel raised her right hand, palm out, as if taking a sworn oath. "Honest."

"Okay." Sean shrugged and started to turn away. "I'll see you tomorrow, then."

"Right. Tomorrow."

Watching him saunter to his car she was struck by how strongly she wanted him to stay. It wouldn't do to reveal that urge, of course. Now that she'd finally gotten him to agree to leave, she'd be twice the fool to ask him to change his mind and hang around longer. Still, the idea was appealing. Foolish, but appealing.

Sean wasn't sure why Rachel seemed so determined to get rid of him but he could tell when he wasn't wanted. Clearly, he'd overstayed his welcome—and then some.

He was getting into his car when a mud-splattered, red pickup truck came roaring down the middle of Old Sturkie Road and skidded to a stop at the end of the driveway, blocking his only exit. He tensed. Unless Rachel had other former jealous boy-friends he didn't know about, there was little doubt who had just arrived.

Staying focused on the truck for only a few seconds, Sean glanced back at the porch. Rachel was no longer smiling. She was standing her ground, yet clearly not thrilled to see Craig Slocum. One hand was clamped tightly to the stairway railing and the other was squeezed into a fist at her side.

Sean hesitated. There was no way he was going to drive off and leave Rachel at the mercy of the angry-looking man who was now climbing out of the red pickup and heading his way. Besides, as long as his car was penned in, he couldn't make a graceful exit even if he wanted to.

Slamming the car door, Sean welcomed his rival with a smile and an amiable "Hello, again," his right hand extended.

Slocum didn't respond verbally. He merely closed the distance between them, gritted his teeth and swung.

The unexpected punch caught Sean off guard. He grabbed his chin and staggered back against the side of his car. Before he could gather himself for the melee he was sure was coming, Craig had spun around and stalked back to his pickup. The truck's tires squealed, throwing loose gravel, then caught.

Rachel ran up and grabbed Sean's arm as Craig sped away. "Are you okay?"

"I think so." He gingerly wiggled his jaw. Surprisingly, it still worked.

"I can't believe he did that!"

"I can. I kept trying to tell you he was jealous."

"I know, but… Why hit you? That's not fair. We've never given him any reason to…" She took a ragged breath. "Somebody must have seen you kiss me!"

"News travels *that* fast? I doubt it. Not even around here." Sean glanced up and down the narrow road. "I have an idea he was watching us himself."

"That's ridiculous." Shaking her head she studied Sean's face. "Move your hand and let me see your chin."

"I'm not sure I should let go of it until I decide if I'm still in one piece," he quipped, wincing. "Your boyfriend packs quite a wallop."

"I told you…"

"I know, I know. He's not your boyfriend. He means nothing to you. Maybe you should tell *him* instead of me. I don't think ole Craig has figured it out on his own."

"He should have. We had a big enough argument the night we broke up."

"Then, it's probably an ego thing. Most men are like that. We aren't exactly rational where our women are concerned." His eyes met Rachel's and darkened. "Figuratively speaking, of course."

"Of course." She looped her arm through his. "Come on. You and I are going into the house to put some ice on your face. Otherwise, you're liable to look like you were in a fight."

"I was," Sean gibed. "I just didn't find out about it in time to participate."

Looking up at him with a smile she said, "Oh, I think you participated plenty."

Seated at Rachel's kitchen table, Sean held a cold pack to his jaw as he watched her preparing fresh lemonade. She'd kicked off her shoes and was standing with her back to him, giving him the opportunity to enjoy looking at her without embarrassment.

He'd always thought of petite women as delicate, which she was, in a way. Yet she was also strong. Any lack of size was more than made up for by her spunky attitude and obvious intelligence.

When he started to grin, the pain in his cheek muted his good humor. If he was going to convince Rachel he was fine, it was apparently going to have to be done straight-faced.

"I could squeeze those lemons for you," Sean said. "The guy didn't cripple me, you know."

Rachel turned, pitcher in hand. "I know. But

there's no need. I'm all done. If we finish this batch, you can squeeze the lemons for the next one, okay?"

"Sure." Sean tried a lopsided smile and was happy to find it didn't cause undue pain.

"What's so funny?"

"You are. The way you say things sometimes. I know you don't mean to, but it comes out sounding like you're talking to little kids."

"It doesn't!"

"Oh yes, it does. There's a kind of cajoling tone you use that reminds me of the way you deal with Samantha when she's pitching a fit."

"Oh dear."

Rachel placed the pitcher on the table, went to the cupboard to get tall glasses, then filled them with ice from the freezer before returning. She stood till she'd poured them each a glassful of lemonade, then sat down across from him.

"I think it's kind of cute," Sean told her.

"And I think I've been spending too much time exclusively with children."

"Possibly. You've definitely found your niche, though. I admire that. You know what you want to do and you do it. There are times when that can take a lot of courage."

"No kidding." She smiled over at him. "Speaking of courage, how's your face?"

Sean chuckled. "I hardly notice it." In order to

drink he'd had to lay aside the towel they'd wrapped around the ice cubes to pad them. Now, he canted his chin toward her. "How does it look?"

"Kind of red. Could be from the cold instead of a bruise. We'll have to wait and see."

"Suppose it's too late for me to grow a beard to cover it?"

"Probably. Although I did notice a little stubble when—" She broke off, suddenly all too aware of the intimate way she'd caressed his cheek when she'd been so worried about his welfare.

"Yeah." He rubbed his hand over the unhurt side of his face. "I guess I do need a shave. Too bad my hair isn't darker, like my brother Paul's. He can go from clean-shaven to looking like a bum in a day."

Rachel had noticed a definite stiffening of her companion's posture as soon as he mentioned his brother. That was the second time. Whatever had distanced Sean from his family clearly had left hard feelings that he had yet to deal with.

"I like the color of your hair," Rachel said. "It's kind of brown and kind of red at the same time. Very unusual."

"My genealogy is part Irish and part German with some unknown ancestors thrown in for interest. Guess you could say I'm a mutt."

"We all are." She took a slow sip of her lemonade and licked her lips before continuing. "According to family legend, one of my great-great-great-grandmothers escaped from the Trail of Tears."

"When the Cherokees were marched across to Oklahoma?"

"That's the time. There were actually several different trails. The one that came through northern Arkansas was called Benge's Route, named after the army officer who was in charge of that detachment."

"How interesting."

"I thought so. There were supposedly about twelve-hundred Cherokees in that particular group, although nobody kept very accurate records of the tribes back then."

"So, what makes you think your grandmother escaped?"

"Family legend. In those days, folks didn't talk openly about things like that, so there's really no way I can prove it—but I'd like to believe the story is true."

"Can't you trace the genealogy somehow?"

"Not without more details. I don't even know her original name. I'm assuming she anglicized it. Supposedly, she hid out on a local farm till the army gave up looking for her. Later, she married a boy from around here and they lived way back in the hills where nobody bothered them."

"That's fascinating."

"I always thought so. And she wasn't the only one to break away from the band. Folks around here say that's why there are so many dark-haired, blue-eyed natives. There were a lot of blue-eyed Cherokee."

"Really?" Studying her face he noted—not for the first time—the striking effect of dark lashes shadowing the vivid blue of her eyes. "I had wondered why your eyes aren't brown like your hair."

He'd paid that much attention? Oh!

Rather than admit to herself that she was flattered, she continued with their discussion of history. "I just wish the Native Americans hadn't been forced to hide their origins in order to live away from the reservation. Think of the stories they could have told."

"They probably did pass on their oral history to some extent. Otherwise, you wouldn't have known anything about your ancestor."

"That's true. So, tell me more about your family."

"There's nothing to tell."

"No skeletons in the closet? No big secrets?"

Sean huffed, gave her a derisive look. "The skeletons in my family are more likely to be found in a bar than in a closet."

To Rachel's dismay he abruptly got to his feet and carried his half-empty glass to the sink.

"I'd better be going."

"You should keep ice on that bruise," she cautioned.

"I have ice at home."

"I know. But you still have to get from here to there. Where do you live, anyway?"

"East Serenity, in the new apartments. That's why I was eating at Linden's when we ran into each other. It's close to home."

"I see." Rachel rolled the kitchen towel more tightly around what was left of the ice cubes she'd given him and held it out. "Here. Take this with you."

"I don't need it."

"Humor me." She was following him to the back door, towel in hand.

"Since when do you need humoring? I don't think I've ever seen you mad at anybody."

"I was plenty mad at Craig Slocum about half an hour ago."

Sean managed another crooked smile. "I wasn't too crazy about him, either. Next time, remind me to duck."

"If I have to remind you," Rachel said with a soft laugh, "maybe he hit you harder than we thought."

"It wasn't bad. I've taken lots worse."

The comment hadn't been specific, yet she couldn't help assuming he was still referring to his family. Though she hadn't grown up with siblings, she had had friends with brothers and sisters. They'd never admitted that rivalry within the family had led to physical clashes, but she knew that kind of thing happened. It was certainly more likely among boys.

And, as the youngest, Sean might have been cast as the scapegoat. That unfortunate tendency was one she'd dealt with before in her students. It wasn't all that rare for one child to be singled out to bear the brunt of an angry parent's outbursts, which often led siblings to behave in a similar fashion and produced an atmosphere of ongoing abuse.

Rachel laid her hand on his arm to stop him as he started through the open door. When he looked down at her, whatever she'd intended to say fled from her mind and was replaced by "There's only one place to find unconditional love and acceptance, Sean."

She hadn't meant for her concern to be so evident or for her words to be so bold. In truth, she'd had no forewarning that she was going to say anything that alluded to God's perfect love. Which was just as well. If she had planned to present a plea for her Christian faith she'd probably have gotten so uptight she'd have stammered something unintelligible and ruined the whole thing.

His frown wasn't as puzzled as it was off-putting.

"If you mean *church,* you can forget it. I already told you that."

"No, not church." Smiling benevolently, Rachel shook her head. "You don't have to be in a special building to open yourself to the possibilities God offers. Jesus said that all the time. I know it seems far-fetched to think that a Heavenly Father can love you just the way you are, but I happen to know from experience that He can and does."

"Right. I suppose you believe in Santa Claus and the Tooth Fairy, too."

"I used to. Then I grew up and searched for the truth myself. Faith isn't a gift I can just hand you, or I would. It's an inside job. Like love. You can't see that, either, but you believe it exists, don't you?"

"Maybe. Maybe not." He pushed through the door. Before turning to head for his car he said, "Thanks for the lemonade. I know you were risking your reputation by taking me in to doctor me. I appreciate it."

"No problem. The next time you get clobbered you'll know where to come for first aid." To her relief, that quip brought his crooked smile back.

"I don't intend to stand still and be Craig's punching bag again," Sean said firmly. "There aren't any more unhappy guys waiting to deck me, are there? I hate surprises like that."

"Nope. He's it. One's enough, don't you think?"

"One is plenty." Sean backed away toward his waiting car.

Schatzy followed, barking bravely and nipping at the air by Sean's ankles, as if his ridiculous efforts were the real reason the man was leaving.

When Rachel caught up to the little dachshund she scooped him into her arms for safekeeping and held him close while he wiggled, stretched and licked at her earlobe in pure adoration.

"I'm glad he's not a mastiff," Sean said as he started the car.

"Me, too. He'd be awfully hard to cuddle if he was."

"Right."

Watching Sean back out of the driveway, she wondered if the redness on his cheeks was from the blow he'd received or if he was blushing again, simply because she'd mentioned cuddling.

Either way, she was the cause, Rachel reasoned.

To her chagrin, that concept didn't bother her nearly as much as she thought it should.

Chapter Nine

By the following morning, Sean's face showed little sign that he'd been punched. He did notice a few school staff members whispering and sneaking peeks at him, but he figured that was normal, given his newcomer status. Moving to any strange area would have been the same. Serenity might be a tight-knit community, but there wasn't anyplace that didn't have its cliques. Here, they just didn't make any bones about it.

Sean chuckled to himself. He'd only been in town for a week or so, yet he'd long ago lost count of the number of times someone had looked him up and down and drawled, "You aren't from around here, are you?" It was as if he'd had "Outsider" tattooed across his forehead!

Well, at least he finally had an office—of sorts.

Vanbruger had had maintenance clear out a large storage closet directly behind the main offices and had fit it with a desk, chair and single upright filing cabinet. It was certainly not much, but he couldn't fault the school district for that. He'd known when he applied for the counselor's job that it was a part-time position, which was why he'd suggested he become their standby bus driver. Chances were good he'd been hired partly because of his versatility.

He'd removed his jacket and was trying to decide how best to arrange the cramped room, when a knock on the door startled him. "Yes?"

Rachel opened the door, stuck her head through, looked around and grinned. "Hey, cozy."

"You could call it that." He dusted off his hands. "Come on in. I'll give you the fifty-cent tour."

She obliged, laughing softly. "I don't think it should cost more than a dime at the most." Crossing to his desk in three steps, she ran her hand over the scarred surface. "Nice furniture. I love antiques. Where did they get this one?"

"From storage, I assume," Sean said. "I've already cleaned a mouse nest out of the bottom drawer." The memory of all the dust made his nose itch again and he sneezed.

Rachel had circled the desk and was pretending to admire it. "How lovely. It came with its own science project. Just like my refrigerator."

"You have mice in your refrigerator?"

"No, silly. Science projects. You know, moldy things I can't identify that have gotten shoved to the back of a shelf and been overlooked."

"Whew." Sean made a face and pretended to wipe his brow. "I'm glad you explained. I ate something you fixed from that refrigerator and I was getting worried."

"You didn't eat, you drank," Rachel said.

"Lemonade," he added. "I drank lemonade. When you just say I *drank,* it sounds like you mean something else."

"Sorry." She studied him out of the corner of her eye while she made a point of looking elsewhere. "You have a nice view from here, too."

To her delight, that ridiculous observation made Sean laugh. "I think you have to work here longer than I have to rate a window. I thought I might get one of those fake ones. You know, the frame is real and then you put an outdoor scene behind it so it looks like you do have a view."

"Well, don't buy one," Rachel said quickly. "When I remodeled my house I stacked all the old wooden window sashes out behind the toolshed. You can come pick out whatever you want from the pile and we can rig it to hang." She rapped on the paneling. "This sounds hollow. Maybe you should screw the frame right to the wall for support."

"Uh-huh." He sighed pensively. "Too bad I don't have access to power tools the way I used to at the store. It would be much easier to drill holes for the screws."

"I have lots of tools at home. You're welcome to borrow anything you need."

"You do?"

She found his amazement amusing. "Yes, I do. Why? Did you think men were the only ones allowed to own tools?"

"Not exactly. It's just hard for me to picture you with a framer's hammer in your hand, banging in sixteen-penny nails." Pausing, he added, "Sixteen-penny is a size, not the cost per nail."

"I know that." Rachel made a face at him. "You have a lot to learn about country girls, mister. Some of us even drive tractors and help with the haying before we're out of grade school."

"Did you do that?"

"Well, no. But I have friends who did. The closest my folks got to farming was to keep some beef cows and raise a few calves every year. We either traded for what little hay we needed or bought it. Most of the time there's plenty of grass for grazing, as long as you don't run too many head on a small plot of land."

Sean offered her his only chair. When she chose to remain standing, he perched on the edge of the battered desk. "I can see I have a lot to learn. The kids won't respect my advice in other areas if I come across as ignorant about things like farming."

"Don't worry. You're bright. You'll catch on," Rachel assured him. "And you'll be able to give them pointers about someday surviving in a big city."

"I suppose a lot of them do leave here once they're grown."

"Not as many as you'd think. Some go away to college, of course. I've found that the majority of the families who've lived in the Ozarks for generations try to talk their kids into staying fairly close by. Kind of like your father did when he involved you and your brothers in his business. What made you pull away, anyway?"

Sean got to his feet and circled the desk. When he was on the opposite side he turned and faced her. His jaw was set, his gaze penetrating. "You might as well stop bringing up my family, Rachel. I never should have mentioned the store or my brothers in the first place. I don't intend to discuss anything about them—or my past. Period."

Flustered, she said, "Don't be shy, Doc. Speak right up. Tell me what you *really* think."

"I just did."

"No kidding? Well, enough chitchat. It's almost eight. I'll have a passel of five-year-olds looking for me any minute." Backing toward the open door she felt behind her with one hand till she made solid contact with the jamb.

"Rachel…?"

There was a poignancy in his tone that would have made her stop even if she hadn't been aware that she'd just jogged a tender spot in his memory. "Yes?"

"I'm sorry I came on so strong just now."

She smiled agreeably. "No problem. I have broad shoulders."

Sean returned her smile. "You're so tiny you barely have any shoulders at all. Maybe that's why I was so surprised when you told me you owned power tools. Is the offer still good? Can I come get a window or two and maybe borrow a drill once I decide what I need?"

"Of course. Just give me a call ahead of time to make sure I'm home. You know where I live. The number's in the book."

"I think I'll call Slocum's Garage and send my buddy Craig on a wild-goose chase, first," Sean joked. "He's not a real rational guy when he's around you."

"He never was. That's one of the reasons I decided not to marry him—no matter what."

"Whoa. I thought you said you weren't over him."

"It's a long story," Rachel said. "Actually, Craig did me a favor by breaking our engagement."

"How's that?"

"He helped me admit that I didn't need marriage to make me a complete person."

Given Rachel's undeniably maternal nature, Sean was taken aback. "You really don't want a family? Kids of your own, I mean."

Waiting for an answer, he sensed her withdrawal. It didn't take a degree in psychology to see that she was shutting him out. Rachel Woodward might put on a good act most of the time, but there was definitely some unspoken outrage hidden beneath the persona she presented to the world. Whatever it was, it was bad enough to negate her normal good cheer. Of that, he was positive. He'd just watched it happen.

"You're starting to sound like my mother again," she said.

Sean carefully schooled his features, presenting a tranquil, amiable facade. "Tell you what. If you'll promise to stop mentioning my family, I'll try to avoid saying anything that reminds you of Martha. Okay?"

"Okay. Deal."

Rachel knew it was well past time to beat a hasty retreat. Whirling, she headed straight for the haven of her classroom. Sean had misunderstood her when he'd assumed she meant that he, personally, had reminded her of her mother. On the contrary. Being around him brought far different thoughts—thoughts that related directly to Martha's wish that her daughter would someday fall in love and marry.

That was one of the reasons why Rachel's conscience had twisted so uncomfortably when Sean mentioned having children. It was evident that having a family was high on his list of priorities, the same as it was on Craig's, which was a typical male trait. Women took on the care and nurturing of their children while men strutted around and bragged about what extraordinary kids they had produced.

"I'm happy single," she muttered to herself. "I like my life. I *love* my life. And I don't intend to complicate it by falling in love with anybody."

In her heart, she heard one word echo silently. *Liar.*

With so many students to look after and teach, Rachel wasn't surprised that the rest of the day seemed to pass quickly. When the dismissal bell rang, however, she realized how exhausted she was. It was definitely quitting time.

Samantha lagged back, remaining with her teacher instead of boarding the bus immediately. She gave Rachel's skirt a quick tug to gain her attention. "Can I come play with Schatzy today?"

"Today? I don't know. It's awfully hot again."

"I don't care. I don't have to take that old bus. I could go home with you."

Rachel already knew she'd made a grave mistake by inviting the little girl to visit in the first place. Yet when Samantha raised those big blue eyes and gave her such a needy look, she couldn't bear to refuse without offering a possible alternative.

"I can't take you home with me, Samantha. It's against the school rules. You have to ride the bus. I suppose it would be all right if Mrs. Brody wants to bring you over later, after I get home, though."

The little girl was bouncing up and down like a doll suspended from rubber bands. "Yeah!"

"But...if she decides she's too busy tonight, I don't want you to make a fuss. Understand?"

"*You* tell her. She'll do it if you tell her to."

"We *ask* when we want someone to do us a favor," Rachel instructed gently. "We don't tell them what to do. That isn't polite."

"But you can make her do it," Samantha argued. "You can make anybody do anything."

Rachel laughed. "I think you give me too much credit, honey. I don't have any special powers of persuasion."

"Yes, you do. Angels can do lots of things. I saw them."

Crouching beside her so she could look her straight in the eyes, Rachel asked, "What did you see?"

"Angels. I told you."

"When?"

Expecting the child to mention the classroom incident involving the weeping boy, Rachel was shocked when Samantha said, "When my mommy and daddy went to heaven."

Rachel had done her best to control her astonishment at Samantha's declaration about encountering angels. Nevertheless, she knew she'd reacted too strongly because the child had refused to explain further, even when she'd probed for details.

As soon as bus five pulled out, Rachel went in search of Sean. She found him coming out of his office. "Hi."

"Hi. What's up?"

Rachel stepped closer so they could converse privately, even though the hallway was now nearly deserted. "I think I just made a big mistake."

"You? A mistake? Perish the thought."

She playfully punched him in the shoulder. "Knock off the jokes, Bates. I'm trying to be serious here."

"Sorry. What's the problem?"

"It's Samantha."

"Don't tell me she took the wrong bus again."

"No. I made sure she got on number five and stayed there. It's something she said while we were out front waiting. She told me she'd seen angels—when her parents died."

"Go on."

"That's all I could get out of her," Rachel said with a sigh. "The minute I started asking questions, she clammed up. I thought maybe you could give me some pointers about what to say the next time she brings up the subject."

Sean pressed his lips together, his brows arching. "That's a tough one. It's not the kind of thing you can rehearse ahead of time. You just have to feel your way along. Were you careful to allow her to express herself without condemnation?"

"I hope so. I was trying to act nonchalant. I know I did fine until she mentioned her folks. After that, I'm not so sure. I couldn't believe how matter-of-fact she sounded."

"Children are like that," Sean said. "They accept death a lot easier than adults do. Samantha may have imagined angels were involved to help cushion the loss."

"Maybe. Maybe not." Rachel's voice was barely a whisper.

Head cocked to one side, Sean leaned closer and strained to hear. "What?"

"Never mind. I was just talking to myself," Rachel said. She couldn't help noticing how his nearness was speeding up her heartbeat and taking her breath away. It was bad enough that the afternoon humidity was stifling. Now, her emotions were kicking into high gear, too. The combination made her dizzy.

Sean touched her arm. "You okay?"

"I don't care for the heat, that's all."

"A fine Native American you make," he teased. "Come on. I'll walk you back to your classroom."

"That's not necessary."

"I know it isn't. But how are we going to generate enough gossip to keep everybody occupied if we don't give them fresh news to pass around from time to time? We wouldn't want them to get bored."

She gave a wry chuckle. "Perish the thought."

His grasp on her arm was firm and gentle—more than a caress but less than forceful. There was an unexplainable assuredness to it that gave Rachel moral as well as physical support. Perhaps friendship between them wasn't out of the question, even though he had overstepped its bounds when he'd caught her by surprise and kissed her.

Remembering that precious moment didn't help Rachel's dizziness one bit. Neither did the touch of Sean's strong hand on her bare arm. Heat or no heat, she wished she'd kept her jacket on instead of leaving the classroom in only her sleeveless cotton dress. The sheath was appropriate for summer wear, it simply didn't cover her upper arms enough to keep his hand from making direct contact with her skin.

They reached her classroom quickly. Sean ordered her to sit down while he fetched her a cup of water. "Drink."

"Let me sip it, okay?"

"Okay. I didn't see you in the staff room at lunch-time, today. Did you eat?"

"I needed to get art supplies ready for the afternoon lesson, so I ate a bite in here, while the kids were gone."

"A bite? Or a real lunch?"

"Well…"

"That's what I thought. No wonder you're woozy. Probably have low blood sugar. You didn't take nearly enough at Linden's the other day to get your money's worth, either."

"I happen to love salads."

"You still didn't eat enough to keep a rabbit alive."

"I'm not a rabbit."

One eyebrow arched and he grinned. "No kidding. If I'd had teachers who looked like you when I was a kid, I might have done better in school."

That confession surprised her. After taking a few sips of water she asked, "You weren't a good student?"

"Not at first. It took me till I was out of high school to figure out that the only way I was ever going to make it on my own was to improve my education. Even then, I didn't go about it right."

Rachel finished the cup of water and held it out to him with a smile and a "Please?" While he was refilling it at the classroom sink, she questioned him further. "What did you do wrong?"

"I didn't follow my heart. My brothers had majored in business so I did the same. That was my first mistake. The second was trying to work with them. We fought all the time about how the store should be run. It wasn't until I was totally fed up that I realized I was a big part of the problem."

"Because you weren't doing what you really wanted to do?"

"Exactly." Smiling, Sean handed her the refilled cup. "How did you get so smart? I thought I was the psychologist around here."

"Horse sense." When he looked puzzled she amended her comment. "You know, plain old common sense."

"Right. The moment I met you I sensed you had intuitive capabilities. That's one reason I doubt you said or did anything to make Samantha wary of confiding in you. I suspect she'll come around and tell you the whole story when she's ready. In the meantime, she's been assigned as one of my first cases."

"That's wonderful. I'm so glad you're working

here. I don't know how many times I've wished for a professional opinion about a student and had to muddle through myself, instead. I'll feel much better knowing I'm not struggling with Samantha's problems alone."

"Good. Happy to help." Sean took a backward step toward the door. "Well, I'd better be getting back to my office. Our esteemed boss was supposed to drop in after four and look over what I've done with the place. Not that that overgrown closet gives me much opportunity to be creative. I do still want to make one of those fake windows, though. Okay if I stop by your place on my way home today and pick one up?"

"No problem. I'm always home by five. If you get there ahead of me, just help yourself."

"And be shot as a trespasser by one of your gun-toting neighbors? No, thanks. If I don't see your car, I'll just park out front and wait for you."

So much for avoiding him by dragging my feet, she thought ruefully. It figured. The way the past few weeks had been going, she was liable to wind up with a house full of guests this evening when all she really wanted to do was kick off her shoes, grab a tall glass of iced tea, plop down in front of the air conditioner and veg out till bedtime.

Rachel sighed. "Okay. You can come tonight as long as you don't make it too late. Once the sun sets I'm usually ready for bed."

"I'll get there early. Wouldn't want to accidentally catch you in your jammies," he teased. "I'll bet they're cute. Do they have bunny feet? No, I don't suppose they would in the summertime."

Rachel's eyes widened, her cheeks suddenly aflame. This wasn't the first time her creative imagination had run amok and toyed with notions of intimacy where Sean Bates was concerned. Yes, she knew it was wrong. As a Christian she wasn't supposed to let her innermost thoughts amble in that direction. However, she was also human. Those two elements of her being weren't mutually exclusive, but they did sometimes clash. Like now.

Wresting control from her daydream and forcing herself back to reality, Rachel stood, chin up, shoulders square, spine straight. "Don't worry. You're perfectly safe. I never get ready for bed until I'm sure I won't have any more company."

Laughing, Sean started toward the classroom door. "That's comforting. Well, see you later."

He was almost out the door when she called after him, "And I *don't* wear pajamas with bunny feet."

Chapter Ten

Physical exertion had never left Rachel as weary as the mental calisthenics she'd been doing lately. Exhausted, she shed her dress and donned shorts and a tank top as soon as she arrived home, then wandered out onto the shaded front porch with Schatzy. It was always soothing to stroke the little dog and swing slowly back and forth in the old glider. As long as there was a breeze to fan her, Rachel much preferred being outdoors in the evening when the temperature started to drop a bit.

Sighing, she pushed her bare feet against the plank floor of the porch to set the glider in motion. Oh, how she wished it were that easy to smooth out her tumbling thoughts. No matter how often she told herself it was useless to reflect seriously on any man, let alone one she hardly knew, her mind refused to stop dwelling on Sean Bates. She'd relived every moment with him, every word he'd spoken, so many times it was becoming impossible to separate reality from wishful thinking.

Moreover, she continued to worry about Samantha. All children had fantasy lives. That was natural. The problem was deciding where normalcy stopped and obsession began. Once Sean began working with the little girl, she hoped they'd gain a better understanding of the situation.

And if not?

Thoughtful, Rachel petted the contented dog lying beside her on the padded swing seat. There was no easy answer to that question. The simplest fix, from an adult standpoint, would probably be to get Samantha to admit she'd made up the stories about seeing angels.

On the other hand, if they tried to take away that support system, no matter how far-fetched it was, without providing another, Samantha might falter. Except for seeing things that weren't there, she was doing pretty well. The last thing Rachel wanted to do was knock the emotional props out from under a child who had already been through so much.

Traffic on Old Sturkie Road was rare. Consequently, Rachel noticed Hannah Brody's van as soon as it turned the corner off Main and started up the street.

Weary, she sighed and scooped up Schatzy so he

wouldn't get excited and dash in front of the approaching vehicle. By the time Hannah pulled into her driveway, the little dog was wiggling all over with joy and Rachel was getting the underside of her chin licked. Smiling, she waved.

"Hi there."

Hannah rolled down the driver's window to lean out. "Evenin'. I tried to call and ask if this was all right. You must not o' heard your phone."

"I just got home a few minutes ago. I didn't notice any messages on my answering machine."

"Won't talk to them things," Hannah said flatly. "Real folks is bad enough. You don't answer your phone by four rings, I hang up."

Chuckling, Rachel paused on the lawn to appreciate the cool feel of the grass beneath her feet. "Well, you're here now so Samantha may as well stay to play a while."

"What about your supper?" Hannah asked. "You had time to eat a bite?"

"I'm fine. I don't get very hungry in hot weather, anyway. I'll grab a snack later."

"Okay. If you say so. How about I run down to the market and get us some ice cream?"

Rachel heard Samantha's shrill voice yell "Yeah!" from inside the van. The child's enthusiasm was contagious.

"That sounds great to me, too," Rachel said.

"Why don't you leave your co-pilot here? We'll get some dishes out and set up a picnic on the porch while you're gone."

That said, she opened the rear sliding door of the van and helped the little girl climb down.

"Long as you promise not to tell that Heatherington woman," Hannah cautioned.

"I won't. I promise." Rachel took Samantha's hand, holding tight to both her and Schatzy to keep them safe while Hannah backed out into the street. Just then, a familiar black car turned off Main and headed their way.

Hannah stopped and leaned out of the van to shout at Rachel, "Looks like I'd best make it a double order. What flavors does he like?"

"How should *I* know?" Rachel retorted. "I barely know the man."

To her chagrin, Hannah laughed. It was a cackle of disbelief if Rachel had ever heard one.

Sean pulled into Rachel's driveway, parked and got out. As he came around the rear of the car, Rachel could see that he'd been home to change after work. Clad in faded blue jeans and a plain T-shirt he looked like an altogether different person. He still hadn't started wearing a baseball-type cap the way most of the local men did, but the rest of him certainly blended in well.

He waved. "Hello."

"Sean!" Samantha was jumping up and down. "You came, too. I knew you would!"

He darted a look in Rachel's direction and shrugged, silently denying any collusion on his part. When Samantha barreled up to him, he caught her and swung her off the ground.

"Hi. How's my best girl?"

The child giggled. "She's fine. Me, too."

"I meant you, you little stinker," he said fondly. "Stop trying to get me in trouble with your teacher."

"Angels never get in trouble," Samantha told him in a stage whisper that could easily be heard all the way to where Rachel stood.

"I've been meaning to talk you about that," Sean said. "What makes you think I'm an angel?"

"'Cause you're nice. And you help people. Just like on TV."

"I see." Sean was beginning to feel a lot better about the child's fantasies. "You mean the program where the angels look just like regular people?"

"Uh-huh."

With a nod and a satisfied sigh, Sean put Samantha down. "Good. You go play now. I need to talk to your teacher."

The eager little girl wasn't about to be distracted. She circled him. "Can I see your wings? Please?"

"I don't have any wings," Sean said.

"But you can still fly, can't you?"

"Sorry. I can't do that, either."

"Not even float? Not even a little?"

"Nope. I'm afraid not."

"Bummer," the child murmured, pouting.

Watching the interplay between the handsome man and exuberant child, Rachel had covered her mouth to hide her smile. Now, she pressed her fingertips to her lips to keep from bursting into giggles.

As soon as Samantha dashed onto the porch in pursuit of her canine playmate, Rachel glanced up at Sean. There was so much merriment in his eyes and on his face, she had to chuckle in spite of her best efforts to contain herself.

"You sure you don't have wings?" she teased.

"Positive. Do you?"

"Not the last time I looked."

He made a silly pout reminiscent of Samantha's, lowered his already deep voice and said, "Bummer."

That was the last straw. Rachel erupted into laughter. By the time she finally regained control of herself there were tears rolling down her cheeks. She dashed them away. "I'm sorry. I tried not to lose it but…"

Sean was chuckling, too. "I know what you mean. I can see her mistaking you for an angel, but I sure can't picture myself that way."

"Thanks—I think."

"You're welcome." Continuing to laugh softly he looked toward the porch where Samantha was playing tug-of-war with the low-slung dog. "Has she asked to see your wings, yet?"

"No." Rachel sobered. "Has she told you any more about seeing angels right after her parents were killed?"

"I haven't broached the subject. I've just let her talk about whatever she wants to, and that hasn't come up."

"Probably because she figures all us angels already know everything," Rachel offered. "Do you think it would hurt if I came right out and asked her for details?"

"It might. Give her time. She'll discuss it more when she's ready."

Sighing, Rachel gazed with fondness at the lovely blond five-year-old. "I wish we knew more about the circumstances behind this obsession she has with angels."

I don't think there's anything to worry about," Sean said. "She apparently got the idea from watching TV. The concept fit her current life, so she used it—that's all."

"Uh-uh." Rachel shook her head slowly, pensive. "It's more than that."

"Now who's imagining things?"

Instead of answering directly, she asked a

question. "What about you? Do you believe in angels?"

"In the supernatural, you mean?"

"If that's how you want to put it."

"Not really," he said with a shake of his head. "I believe in what I can see and touch."

"So you've told me. Have you given any thought to what we talked about right after Craig decked you?"

He unconsciously stroked his jaw. "Ducking faster?"

"No, silly. Things that are unseen, like faith and…" She hesitated, reluctant to mention love again.

Sean had no such qualms. "And love? I remember exactly what you said. It made an interesting analogy, but I have to disagree with your conclusions. Too unscientific."

"I suppose you still believe the world is flat, too."

He laughed. "No. I have it on good authority that the earth is relatively round, as long as you allow for the effect of the moon's gravity as it passes over."

"Gravity?" Rachel folded her arms across her chest and took a firm stance, her eyebrows raised. "How interesting. And just when did you see and touch *that?*"

"I don't have to see it to observe its effects," he argued.

"Exactly. The same goes for faith."

"Not hardly. Since we aren't floating off into space, I have all the proof of gravity I need."

Rachel smiled. "Has anybody ever told you you're as stubborn as a mule?"

"Often. Your point is?"

"Nothing. I give up. I should have known better than to get into a theological debate with you. It's not up to me to convince you of anything. Whatever finally happens is between you and the good Lord. I have enough to worry about in my own life." She glanced toward the porch. "That little girl's future, for instance."

Sean had been feeling strangely uneasy with their former subject and was glad for the change of focus. "What do you think will happen to her?"

"I don't know." Careful to keep their conversation private, Rachel stepped closer to him to continue. "Health and Human Services says she has some shirttail relatives living somewhere up in Colorado. Hannah's convinced they weren't very keen to add to their family when they were told about Samantha. If no one else steps forward to lay claim to her, I assume she'll be put up for adoption. I just don't know how soon."

After a moment of silence broken only by the songs of birds and the cooing of Samantha as she cuddled Schatzy, Sean asked, "How about you? Why don't you consider adopting her?"

The idea wasn't new to Rachel. Neither was her decision. "I've thought about that. It's impossible."

"Why?"

"Because I don't have a proper home to offer her."

He swept his arm in an arc that took in her house and yard. The place was small and quaint, yet more of a home than a lot of children had. "Looks to me like you do. What's the real problem?"

"It's me, okay," she replied, irritated by his probing. "I'm not mother material, and I certainly don't intend to rob that poor little thing of the chance to belong to a complete family. Enough of my students have only one parent. There's no need to add another child who's forced to grow up that way."

"Humph. Funny," Sean said dryly. "I would have thought any permanent arrangement would be preferable to being passed from foster home to foster home the way Sam has been."

"Now you're doing it, too. Stop calling her *Sam*. Her name is Samantha. If you and Hannah had your way you'd have her sounding like a boy."

"Okay, okay." Sean held up both hands in surrender. "I stand corrected. Don't try to change the subject. I can buy the notion that two parents are preferable to only one, but one is certainly better than none. What I don't get is why you say you wouldn't make a good mother." He smiled mischievously. "Except for a stubborn streak and some nutty ideas about destiny, you seem like a perfect candidate for motherhood. What makes you think you're not?"

Rachel was not about to bare her innermost secrets to anyone, let alone a man she hardly knew. Telling Craig the whole truth had been necessary because of their plans to marry. It had also been the hardest thing she'd ever had to do. She wasn't up to repeating that crushing episode, especially since there was no need to reveal her physical shortcomings to Sean—or to anyone else for that matter.

Maybe someday, when she was older and hopefully wiser, she'd get around to telling her mother about the specialist who had warned her that she would never be able to conceive, never produce a family.

And maybe not. Lately, Martha had been so outspoken about the whole subject that Rachel had decided to keep her own counsel. That was certainly better than having her eager mother drag her to every fertility doctor from Little Rock to Springfield—or beyond.

"Look," she said flatly, "if the Lord wants me to have kids of my own, I'll have them, okay?" *Sure, if a miracle happens.* "Until then, I wish you'd stop needling me."

"Me?" Sean looked abashed. "Hey. I wasn't

trying to bug you. I was just making a suggestion—and a pretty good one, too, if you ask me."

"That's the problem. I didn't ask you."

"Right." He stiffened, squared his shoulders. "Well, I didn't come here to bother you, Ms. Woodward. I came to look at those old windows you offered me. I'll pick one out and be on my way before I stick my foot in my mouth again."

His sudden shift to formality took Rachel by surprise. Had she really been that offensive? Apparently. "Look, Sean, I'm sorry if I snapped at you. I guess I have a little hangup where my future is concerned."

"A *little* one?" He chuckled. "Lady, that's the understatement of the year."

"I wouldn't go that far."

"Okay. I don't want to argue. Your quirks are none of my concern. But what happens to Samantha Smith is. I just made the mistake of assuming you cared, too."

Before Rachel could recover from the shock of his comment and tell him how off base he was, he'd whirled and was headed toward her backyard, presumably in search of the old window he'd come for.

Pausing before following him, she called to Samantha and Schatzy. "Let's go, you two. Into the backyard. I don't want you playing out here all by yourselves."

The dog responded immediately, tail wagging and tongue lolling. The child, however, lagged back with a scowl and a plaintive "Awww."

"Now," Rachel ordered. "We'll be close enough to hear Mrs. Brody's van when she comes back. You won't miss your ice cream."

That explanation seemed to satisfy. Samantha skipped across the lawn to join Rachel, grasped her hand and tugged for attention.

When Rachel leaned down to listen, the little girl whispered, "You could show me *your* wings. I won't tell. I know I'm not supposed to."

Amused, Rachel played along with the fantasy. "Who told you not to tell?"

"The big angel who came to get me," Samantha said soberly. "He said not to be scared and not to tell anybody."

"A big angel? Like Mr. Bates?"

"Oh, no. Much bigger." She stretched out her free arm as far as it would go. "Bigger than this, even. He went way up to the sky."

"He did?" Pausing, Rachel bent down to look into the child's eyes. "What did he look like?"

"White, sort of. It was hard to see."

"Why was that?"

"'Cause he was so bright. Like the sunshine, only more. And he was strong, too."

"Very strong?" Awed, Rachel sensed that something profound was about to be revealed. She only hoped she could remain calm enough to listen without distracting the child.

Samantha nodded gravely. "*Real* strong."

Trying to keep from showing excess interest, Rachel fought to control her uneven breathing and willed her racing heart to slow down as she asked, "How do you know he was so strong?"

"You know, silly. 'Cause he picked up the car." A smile appeared briefly on her innocent face, then faded. "I told him to get Mommy and Daddy out, too, but he said they had to go to heaven."

"Oh, honey." Rachel opened her arms and pulled the child into a tight hug. She'd read a brief history in Samantha's file. It hadn't been specific about how the Smiths had died, only that they'd perished together, leaving one daughter. "I didn't know you were with your mommy and daddy that day. You were all in a car accident? Is that what happened?"

The small blond head nodded against Rachel's shoulder.

"And you think an angel rescued you?"

"He did. Honest." She leaned back just enough to look at her teacher's face. "He was real nice. Like you."

Blinking back unshed tears, Rachel gave the child a kiss on her soft cheek. "Thank you, Samantha. That's the nicest thing anybody has ever said to me."

Chapter Eleven

Rachel and Samantha found Sean rummaging through the odds and ends of building materials, old and new, piled behind her storage shed.

"Watch out for spiders and snakes," Rachel warned, taking care to hold tight to the child to keep her out of danger.

He stepped back and dusted off his hands. "Wasn't that a popular song back in the early seventies?"

"How would I know? That was before my time." She grinned. "I'm not *old* like you are."

"Oh, fine. Stomp all over my ego. See if I care."

"I wasn't kidding about the danger, Sean. There are undoubtedly Black Widows and Brown Recluse spiders in that pile. As for the snakes, they'll probably run away unless they feel cornered."

"Thanks for the warning."

"You're welcome. We're about to share some ice cream out on the front porch. When you get finished back here, why don't you join us?"

"And risk getting my nose broken if Craig cruises by again?"

"Hannah will be here, too," Rachel explained with a light laugh. "There should be safety in numbers."

"Well, in that case, maybe I will. I am hungry. Haven't had my—" he pointedly glanced at his watch "—*supper,* yet."

"Good. I see you have learned a few things since you've been here. I haven't eaten either, but right now I'm more concerned with being cool than with good nutrition. Ice cream sounds heavenly. And speaking of Heaven, that reminds me," she lowered her voice till she was almost whispering, "I need to have a private talk with you."

Sean immediately glanced at the little girl by her side, and when he looked back at Rachel, she nodded. "I see," he said. "Okay. I'll put one of these windows in my trunk and meet you out front as soon as I can find a hose to rinse off my hands."

"Don't be silly. Go inside and wash in the kitchen or the bathroom," Rachel said.

"What about your reputation?"

"Humph," she snorted with disgust. "I'm afraid it's too late to worry about that."

"Why? What's wrong now?"

"Look over your shoulder."

Turning, Sean thought he saw quick movement in a window of the house next door. He blinked, frowned. "Who's that?"

"Miss Verleen," Rachel said. "She's a veritable fountain of knowledge. Anything you want to know, she can tell you. And more. Of course, half of it's supposition, but nobody cares about that. All they want is the gossip. Verleen's a master."

"Did you know that when you moved in here?"

"Oh, sure. I wasn't worried. I've always led a straightforward, honorable life." Rachel gave him a wry smile and chuckled softly. "Until I met *you,* I hadn't given her one single reason to talk about me."

"We didn't do anything wrong."

"Not wrong. Just interesting." The expression on his face made her laugh again. "Don't look so surprised."

"I know, I know. You warned me." He was shaking his head. "It's just hard to get used to being around anybody who cares that much one way or the other. Back home, I knew some of my neighbors, sure, but I guess my life was too hectic to spare much time wondering about what they were up to in their private lives."

"They were probably up to plenty," Rachel offered. "You just didn't know it."

"I suppose you're right. People will be people, wherever you go." With a wry grin he looked her up and down, clearly admiring her slim, petite self, then said, "Some of them are just a whole lot prettier than others."

By the time Hannah arrived with the promised ice cream, Rachel and Samantha were waiting on the porch. Sean came out the front door as the older woman was climbing the steps. She had a plastic sack in one hand and was using the other to pull herself up the stairs.

"Here," he said, reaching out, "let me help you with that."

"Ain't heavy," Hannah countered. She raised an eyebrow at Rachel, then glanced pointedly at the screen door.

"Sean was inside washing up," Rachel said. "He got dirty out back, and I didn't see any reason for him to have to wash his hands in the garden hose." Chin jutting out, she faced Hannah. "Do *you?*"

"'Course not. Well, where do you want me to put this?"

Samantha shouted, "Here!" holding out an empty blue plastic bowl. That made all the adults laugh. Even Hannah.

"Over here," Rachel said. "I moved my plants off this table. And here's a scoop and more bowls and spoons." While Hannah emptied her shopping bag, Rachel added, "I think you should dish up Samantha's first, before she busts a puckering string."

"Good idea. You wanna do it?"

"No. Go ahead. I'll be right back. I need to speak with Sean for a minute." The quizzical look on Hannah's face made her add, "About a certain little mutual friend."

To Rachel's relief, the other woman gave a sage nod. "You go right ahead, then. Sam and me, we'll start without you. Come get yourselves a dish when you're ready."

Sean was standing apart from the group, waiting. Rachel led him to the far end of the porch and stopped with her back against the railing so she could watch the child as she spoke and make sure they weren't being overheard.

"I found out more," she said softly.

"Go on."

He stepped aside and lounged against the front of the house, forming a right angle with Rachel so he could glance sidelong at the ice-cream party without being too obvious.

"There was a car accident. She was with her parents when they died."

"You're sure?"

"That's what she said."

"What else?" Sean asked, studying the giggling little girl.

"She told me an angel rescued her."

His head snapped around. "How?"

"Supposedly, this angel lifted the whole car off her and helped her escape."

Sighing pensively, Sean nodded. "It's possible someone came along and did that. There have been recorded instances of bystanders performing feats of enormous strength in times of stress. If a person saw a trapped child he might find it in him to pick up a vehicle."

"That's what you think happened?"

"Of course. What else could it be?"

"A real angel."

"Oh, come on, Rachel. You don't honestly believe in all that hocus-pocus, do you?"

"Why not?" She huffed cynically. "Oh, that's right. I forgot. You don't believe in anything you can't see or touch."

"You make it sound like I'm the one who's delusional."

"Aren't you?" Waving her hands in front of her she quickly added, "Never mind. Forget I said that." A smile raised the corners of her mouth. "It's not your fault. You can't help being blind to the miracles all around you."

"Nice of you to give me the benefit of the doubt."

"Not at all. I sometimes forget that not everyone sees life the way I do. Think of yourself as a lamp with a cord that's not plugged in. You can try to turn that lamp on all you want, but it'll never give light unless it's properly connected."

"Are you calling me a dim bulb?" Sean gibed.

"Oh, no. I think you're one of the brightest people I've ever known."

"Thanks." His gaze narrowed on her, obviously saw the twinkle of mischief in her eyes. "Okay. What's the catch?"

"No catch. I just hope I'm there when you finally discover all you've been missing."

Sean chuckled to himself. "I don't—not that I'm agreeing with you, mind you."

"Why not? You chicken?"

"No. I just hate to be wrong. Once I've made up my mind, it's not in my nature to change it."

"Then, you and I are in for a lot of trouble," Rachel quipped, "because I never back down, either."

"Never?" He pushed off the wall where he'd been leaning and took one step closer to her, then another.

"Well, *almost* never," Rachel said, finding herself suddenly trapped.

Ducking to dodge around him she hurried back to where Samantha was shoveling in ice cream while also entertaining Hannah with stories of previous ice-cream treats.

Rachel grinned at them, hoping she wasn't blushing from her close encounter with Sean. "Well, here I am. What's good? Or should I ask, what's left?"

"I got strawberry!" the little girl announced. "It's larupin'."

"That good, huh?" She laughed, looking to Hannah. "Have you been teaching Samantha new expressions?"

"Maybe a few. She does learn real fast, that's a fact. Be a shame to lose her."

Rachel had the scoop in her hand and was filling it with rapidly softening ice cream. She stopped abruptly. "Lose her? Why? I thought everything was okay."

"So'd I, till this afternoon. I got a call from a lady up north in Colorado, Sam's aunt, by marriage, on her papa's side. She's thinkin' 'o steppin' in, after all."

"What? Those people weren't interested before. Why the change? And why *now?*"

"I think there's an inheritance," Hannah said, turning aside and lowering her voice. "Don't know how big, not that it matters to me. Doesn't take much money to win over some folks, though."

"That's terrible! We can't let—"

Coming up behind Rachel, Sean interrupted by laying his hand gently on her shoulder and saying,

"I'm sure we all want whatever's best for Samantha."

When Rachel turned to look up at him, she couldn't help her unshed tears.

He relieved her of the ice-cream scoop and stepped up to take her place. "You having strawberry, Miss Rachel?"

"Um…yes."

"I see there's chocolate, too. I think I'll have some of that." With a polite smile he went on to ask, "Mrs. Brody? Can I get you something?"

"I'm fine, thanks. Already had a bite of each. But help yourself to all you'd like. It's fixin' to melt, anyway."

"I think it already has melted," Sean said. "I like it that way, myself. How about you, Samantha? Would you like more?"

She held out her half-empty dish. "Yes, please. I want chocolate, like you."

"Would you like it in a separate bowl?"

The child looked puzzled. "Why?"

"No reason," he said with a short laugh. "I was just remembering how my brother Ian used to eat everything. He didn't want any flavors mixed together."

"Oh." Studying the softening scoops in her bowl when Sean handed it back, Samantha paused a moment, then gave the whole thing a quick stir with her spoon and held it up for him to see. "Look! I made a picture!"

"Hey, great."

"Know what it is?" she asked.

Sean glanced over at Rachel, as if hoping for rescue, but she was still fighting back her tears.

"Let me think," he drawled, stalling. "It kind of looks like—um—an angel?"

Samantha giggled behind her hand. "No, silly! It's Schatzy. See? It has a red collar and everything."

"Actually, it looks more like a glob of melted ice cream than anything else," Sean countered, laughing with her. "I think you're teasing me."

That sent the child into a fit of giggles. The laughter was so contagious that even Rachel had to smile. She nodded to Sean. "I think you're right."

"Samantha has a wonderful imagination," he told Rachel. "Remember that when you're talking to her. Know what I mean?"

"I know exactly what you mean." She picked up the dish of strawberry he'd fixed for her and tasted a spoonful, savoring the cool, smooth sweetness before she went on. "I also know what I believe. See that you don't forget that, either."

"Are you likely to let me?" he asked, muting a wry grin and trying to look more serious than he felt.

"Not in a million years, mister."

Sean nodded and smiled amiably, including

everyone in the magnanimous gesture. "Good. I wouldn't know what to do with myself if you quit picking on me."

Rachel's eyes widened. "Picking on you? Me? I've been trying to *help* you!"

If Sean had been the only one to laugh, Rachel wouldn't have been surprised. However, when Hannah also began to guffaw, Rachel's brow wrinkled with confusion. "What's so funny?"

"You two are," the middle-aged woman said. "The way you argue sounds just like me and my Hank used to, back when we started courtin'."

Rachel didn't mind Sean lingering after the others left. Truth to tell, she needed another adult to talk to. Preferably someone *other* than her mother.

When she started to carry the dirty bowls into the house, Sean pitched in and followed. "I'll bring what's left of the ice cream. I'm pretty sure it's not salvageable, though."

"There isn't much. You can dump it in the sink. Just don't let it drip on the carpet on the way to the kitchen."

"Can't we feed it to the animals?"

"Not the chocolate. It's toxic to dogs and cats."

"I didn't know that."

Rachel smiled at him over her shoulder. "See? Stick with me and you'll learn something new every day."

"Is that a guarantee?" he asked, amused.

"Close to it. I was planning to tutor you in country ways, remember?"

"How could I forget?"

Rachel laughed softly, enjoying his wry humor. Then she sobered. "You can do me a favor in return."

"Sure. Name it."

She set the bowls in the sink beside the cardboard ice-cream containers he'd put down, and rinsed off her sticky fingers before turning to look up at him. "I want you to get a copy of the police report on the death of Samantha's parents."

"Why? What good will that do?"

"Maybe none." Pensive, Rachel dried her hands on a kitchen towel. "Then again, maybe the report will give us a better idea of how best to approach her."

"Okay, I'll do what I can. It might take some time."

"According to Hannah, time is one thing we may not have a lot of," Rachel countered. "Look, Sean, I know I'm no expert like you are, but even I can see that Samantha's got some king-size hang-ups. Who wouldn't? Especially since she saw the whole horrible accident."

"If she really did," he replied. "It's also possible that she imagined being there."

"Why would she do that?"

"Maybe because she subconsciously felt she should have been hurt, too. Or maybe because she thinks she could have saved everybody if she'd been with them."

"What about the angel story? Do you really think she imagined all that?"

"Probably. The mind plays funny tricks under extreme stress." He reached for Rachel's hand, meaning only to offer consolation, but the instant he touched her he knew it was more than that. Much more. An undeniable current flowed between them, connecting them in some intangible way.

She grasped his hand in both of hers and held firm, looking up at him with misty, pleading eyes. "I want to help her, Sean. I have to. It's like she was *sent* here to me. Can you understand that?"

Understand? Did he? From an intellectual standpoint, yes. From an emotional one, however, he had to admit he didn't have a clue. If he were to concede that there might be a Higher Power at work in anyone's life, he'd also have to acknowledge that the same Power could be affecting him. That concept was ridiculous, of course. Man was in charge of his own destiny. He, of all people, knew that. After all, he'd been just as apt as the rest of his family to lean on alcohol as an easy escape from reality, yet he'd managed to thwart those inherent tendencies. So far.

"It doesn't matter what I do or don't believe,"

Sean said. "It's what you think that counts. If you want my assistance in dealing with Samantha, I'll be more than happy to help—as long as it's in the best interests of the child."

"I'd never do anything that wasn't," Rachel insisted.

"Not willfully, no. The only thing that worries me is how attached you're getting to her already."

"She needs love. You can't tell me she doesn't."

"Of course she does. We all do." He felt Rachel's grip on his hand tighten and he laid his other hand over hers. "That doesn't mean you have to be more to her than her teacher."

Rachel knew he was right. She also realized it was too late to lock up her heart and keep it from responding to such obvious need as Samantha's, nor would she want to. But what about Sean's needs. What about her own? When he'd told her that everybody needed love, she'd sensed that he was speaking more from a personal standpoint than an objective one. Clearly, he needed somebody to love him unconditionally.

Not me! she immediately countered. She already had her hands full looking after this year's class of five-year-olds and she didn't intend to take on the burden of worrying about a "lost" adult, too. Let him find his own answers, his own niche in life. Hers was already crammed with enough responsibilities to last a lifetime.

Oh, that was real Christian, Rachel, she told herself. *What a wonderful example you make. How proud Jesus must be of you!*

Ashamed of her selfish inclinations, she held tight to Sean's hands and boldly lifted her gaze to meet his. "I want to be Samantha's special friend," she said softly, earnestly. "And yours, too."

He didn't say anything in reply. He didn't have to. The gratitude and fondness in his expression spoke for him, leaving her so deeply touched that she wanted to open her arms and give him a hug of encouragement, of validation, the way she often did her emotionally needy students.

In Sean's case, she knew it wasn't very smart to consider putting her arms around him. It wasn't logical. But it was the right thing to do. And this was the right time.

Rachel didn't care if her nosy neighbors peeked through the windows, misinterpreted her actions and shouted about them from the rooftops. Sean Bates needed a hug and he was going to get one. Right now. From her. So there.

He looked a little surprised when she pulled her hands away, then responded instinctively when she slipped her arms around his waist and stepped into his embrace.

In any other context she might have fretted that her behavior would give him the wrong impression. At this moment, however, she was confident he understood.

Laying her cheek on his chest she held him close and listened to the steady beating of his heart. This was not the breathless, frantic embrace of two clandestine lovers. It was deeper. More poignant. Almost spiritual.

Rachel didn't know whether Sean was surprised or even if he was having the same kind of reaction to their closeness that she was. The only thing she was sure of was that she'd never felt this special, this safe, this *loved,* in her whole life.

Chapter Twelve

In retrospect, Rachel wasn't sure which one of them had made the first move to relax their embrace. She only knew that they had thought and acted as one, perfectly in tune. How very unusual. How awesome!

Stepping back, she tilted her head to look up at Sean's handsome face and was astonished to see traces of moisture in his eyes. Deeply affected, without pausing to consider the possible repercussions, she lifted her hand and tenderly, lovingly, cupped his cheek.

Sean placed his hand over hers, drew it around to his lips and kissed her palm.

Unsteady, Rachel laid her free hand on his chest and felt the pounding of his heart as it raced with her own runaway pulse. Her eyes closed. Her lips parted, trembled.

Lurking unheeded in the back of her mind was the caution that she should break away, should call a halt to what was happening.

She ignored the warning. Even her most vivid fantasies had never shown her this kind of belonging, this purity of devotion and endearment. Stop it? On the contrary—she wanted this wonderful moment to go on forever!

Sean slid his hand around the back of Rachel's neck and pushed his fingers through the silky thickness of her hair. Then he tilted his head and bent to kiss her.

She put her arms around his neck and raised on tiptoe to meet him boldly. This kiss began softly, cautiously, like the one on her front porch had, then quickly intensified until she lost all sense of reality. Instead of seeing the situation clearly, she imagined herself floating off into the clouds just like one of Samantha's angels.

It was Sean who finally tore himself away. He was breathing quickly and gawking at her as if he'd suddenly discovered a total stranger sharing his embrace.

Speechless, Rachel stared up at him. The tingle that had begun in her lips now included her entire being. Nothing seemed real except Sean. Nothing mattered but him. Being near him. Touching him. Trusting him completely. She wanted to ask him a thousand questions, yet her brain refused to cooperate and empower her voice. The loss of that much self-control was so frightening that it helped wake her up and bring her back down to earth—at least partially.

Could this be what it was like to fall in love? Rachel wondered. Or had she suddenly lost her mind? Given her usually levelheaded approach to life, she suspected the latter. A few seconds ago she had been so emotionally unstable she might have done something really stupid—and sinful—if Sean had asked.

Thank the Lord he hadn't! Which proved that Somebody Up There was still looking out for her, she reasoned, although she knew she would have been the one ultimately responsible if she'd lost control and stepped over the line. It was no use trying to shift the blame to God when free will was involved. Clearly, she must never let herself get into that kind of a situation again with any man.

Rachel drew a shaky breath as the truth hit her squarely in the heart. No other man had ever affected her the way Sean just had! None had even come close. Not even Craig Slocum, the man she'd once planned to marry. Following that line of logic, breaking up with Craig had been a blessing, not the disappointing loss she'd imagined it to be.

Her eyes widened. Her jaw gaped. She stared up at Sean, finally managing a squeaky "Oh-oh."

"Yeah. You can say that again."

His voice was rough, raspy. Looking flustered and embarrassed, he cleared his throat as he took a step backward. "I think I'd better be going."

All Rachel could do was nod. She followed him through the small house and out onto the front porch. It was one thing to know she shouldn't try to stop Sean from leaving and quite another to actually keep her mouth shut and let him go. What she really wanted to do was throw herself into his arms and beg him to stay, to hold her and kiss her again, to make her forget everything else.

Acting on that idiotic impulse was out of the question, of course. Seeing him every day at work was going to be difficult enough after this. Letting him know that she had developed a schoolgirl crush on him would make it a hundred times worse, especially since nothing positive or lasting could ever come of a relationship between them. To encourage him romantically would be more than foolish—it would be cruel.

Seeing him heading for his car reminded her of the original reason for his visit. She shaded her eyes against the brightness of the setting sun and called, "Do you still want to borrow my hammer or my electric drill?"

Sean's laugh was coarse, self-deprecating. "No, thanks. The way I'm feeling right now, redecorating is the last thing on my mind."

It only took three working days for Sean to come up with the copy of the accident report that Rachel had requested.

He was thankful he'd managed to avoid running into her at school—probably with a lot of help from her—since their last ill-fated kiss in her kitchen. Now, however, in order to properly do his job, he was going to have to stop dodging her.

He contemplated slipping the report into her school mailbox rather than handing it over face-to-face. Delivering it like an interoffice memo would be a lot easier on him.

It would also be a cop-out, he reasoned, angry with himself for even considering such a thing. Taking care of the children he'd been assigned to was his sworn responsibility. If that meant he had to face the one woman who could tie his insides in knots with a mere smile, then so be it.

Had the report been faxed to the school earlier in the day, Sean could have passed it to Rachel at lunch or on her break. Unfortunately, he didn't receive the pages until well after three in the afternoon. That meant he had to let it wait till the following morning, try to catch Rachel before she went home or follow her to her house. That third option was out of the question. However, since their time to help Samantha was rapidly running out, waiting another day wasn't fair, either.

Which meant he'd better get a move on. He started looking for Rachel on the front lawn by the bus zone. She wasn't there. Hurrying to her class-room, he tried the door. It was locked. The lights were off.

Frustrated, he wheeled and jogged toward the one other place she might be—the faculty parking lot. Until he spotted her getting into her car, he hadn't realized how relieved he'd been when he'd thought he'd missed catching up to her.

He swallowed his pride and waved. "Rachel! Wait."

She paused and looked back, her hand on the door, one foot already inside the car. As Sean drew closer, she straightened and faced him.

"What's wrong?"

"Nothing. I just…" He waved the loose sheets of paper while he grabbed a few quick, extra breaths. "I knew you'd want to see this ASAP."

"What is it?"

"The police report you asked for. About Sam's parents."

Frowning and still gripping the open door, she eyed her car as if it were a lifeboat and the parking lot had suddenly become an ocean of hungry sharks. "You can see I'm on my way home. Why did you wait this long to bring it to me?"

"Had to," Sean said. "It just came."

"Oh." Rachel was chagrined. "Okay. I apologize. So, what does it say? Was Samantha in the car that day?"

"I don't know. Haven't taken the time to read it." He held out the papers. "I've been trying to find you ever since Mary told me this fax was here."

"Well," Rachel said with a sigh, "come on, then. Let's go sit in the shade and read it together. Then we'll both know what it says and we can discuss it intelligently."

"Sure."

Only, Sean wasn't sure. Not about anything. The moment he'd sighted Rachel his heart had leapt into his throat and lodged there, cutting off half his air and leaving him thoroughly disconcerted. He knew it was impossible, yet every time he saw her she seemed prettier. More appealing. Sweeter. Each time he parted from her he'd be positive she could never improve on such absolute flawlessness. But she always did.

Falling into step behind her, he watched her graceful walk, noticed the way fine tendrils of hair had escaped from the pinned-up twist at the back of her head, saw how light her step was even though she had to be weary from a long day. He grimaced. It wasn't fair of her to look that good when he was trying so hard to do the right thing by staying away from her and not letting himself get involved.

Too late, his conscience insisted. *You're already more than involved. You're in love with her, you dummy. Now what are you going to do about it?*

Nothing, Sean countered firmly. A woman like Rachel needed a husband who came from a normal family, a man who wasn't afraid to become a father. Someone who could give her children without worrying about passing on the tendencies toward alcoholism and addiction that had polluted his lineage for generations.

And she also needed someone who fit into her world a lot better than he did, he decided easily. Judging by what he'd already observed, even if he did eventually find his niche in Serenity, he'd never be one of the "natives." That was a state of being a person was born into, not one that could be adopted.

Knowing he was right, Sean's heart ached. Some things were obviously meant to be. Others were not. It was bad enough that he'd kissed Rachel the first time. Repeating that mistake had been totally reckless. Idiotic. He'd let himself follow his heart's leading, and now he was stuck living with the consequences, the memories.

Sean sighed quietly. There was no way to undo

the damage already done, but he could still protect Rachel. She'd be fine, as long as he never let on that he'd fallen head-over-heels in love with her.

Rachel led him into the shade of a broad oak and settled herself on one end of the bench beneath it.

Sean remained standing until she looked up at him quizzically and asked, "Why don't you sit down? You're making me nervous."

"Okay." With a purposely nonchalant shrug he took a seat as far from her as the bench would allow. Leaning forward, he rested his elbows on his knees and laced his fingers together, ostensibly ignoring her.

If Rachel hadn't been so engrossed in the sketchy report she was reading, she'd have stopped right then to question Sean more. For the past few days he'd been acting ridiculous, dodging her as if she were some kind of predator and he were her prey!

The more she thought about it, the angrier she got. After all, she hadn't thrown herself at him. In both instances their kisses had been his idea, not hers. So how dare he avoid her as if everything that had happened between them was her fault?

The instant she finished scanning the report she thrust it toward him with a terse "Here."

He straightened and took it. "What's the matter? Didn't you find out what you wanted to know?"

"The report says Samantha was in the car, just like she told me she was. There's no mention of any good Samaritan lending a hand, like you thought."

"That doesn't mean there wasn't one."

"True."

Sean scowled over at her. "Why are you acting like you're mad at me? I didn't write the stupid report."

"The way I feel right now has nothing to do with that report," she countered. "It's you."

"Me? What did *I* do?"

"Nothing. Everything." Giving in to frustration, Rachel jumped up and began to pace in front of the bench. "You've been treating me like I have the plague."

"Me? You're the one who's been avoiding me!"

"I have not."

"What about the time you got up and left the lunchroom the minute I walked in?"

"I happened to be finished eating. But how about when you were coming out of your office yesterday and I was walking by? You turned around and ducked back in, the minute you saw me."

"I did not. I— I just left something on my desk and had to go back for it, that's all."

"Right. And pigs can fly."

Sean couldn't help smiling as he glanced at the sky and ducked for effect. "I sure hope not."

"It's not funny." Rachel was having trouble remaining irate in the face of his captivating grin.

"Yes, it is. Know what? You're really cute when you're upset."

"Upset? Who said I was upset?"

"Are you telling me you're not? Tsk-tsk. I think your halo is slipping, Ms. Woodward."

"If I have one, it's probably down around my ankles right about now," she countered wryly. "I told you Christians weren't perfect. I keep trying, though."

"If I wanted to keep you all riled up I'd tell you you're *very trying,* but since I've promised myself I'll behave when I'm around you, I won't say it."

"Oh, thanks. That makes me feel *much* better."

"I knew it would," Sean said with a laugh. "And you're right. I have been avoiding you. I thought it was best."

Rachel heaved a sigh and nodded. "Yeah. Me, too. I guess we're being silly. After all, we do have to work together. There's no way we can both occupy such a small campus and not accidentally run into each other."

"I suppose not."

She smiled. "The past few days have been interesting, though. I almost fell this morning when you popped out of your office and I ducked into the ladies' room to avoid you. The floor had just been mopped. For a few seconds there, I thought I was going to slide into the sinks, fall down and break my— neck."

"That sounds pretty drastic," Sean said, "and awfully hard to explain on an accident report. I suggest we both stop acting like kids with grudges and begin behaving like sensible adults."

Rachel pulled a face. "Aww. Do we have to?"

"I intend to try."

"Really? You aren't going to grab me and kiss me again?"

"I certainly hope not." He sobered. "I realize what a terrible mistake that was."

Chin raised, she defended her wounded pride with a terse "It certainly was."

"You hated it?" A muted smile gave away the fact he was teasing again.

"Worst kiss I ever had," she replied.

"Liar. There goes your halo again."

Rachel made a derisive noise and scrunched one corner of her mouth into an exaggerated jeer. "Halo? Ha! As long as I hang around you, I'll probably never even come close to earning one."

"And you blame me for that? Oh, great. Now I suppose I'm responsible for keeping you out of heaven, too?"

"It doesn't work like that." She paused to give him an encouraging pat on the arm, leaving her hand there just a fraction too long before she came to her senses and jerked it away. "I don't believe people can ever be good enough to earn their way into Paradise. I know I certainly couldn't. That's where Jesus comes in."

"He has your admission ticket, you mean?"

Rachel smiled sweetly and said, "Yes. He's got everybody's. Even yours. Bought and paid for."

"I sincerely doubt that."

"I know you do. That's too bad."

"Why? Because you can't talk me into buying your belief system?"

"No, because I like you, Sean. I don't want to see you miss out on all the blessings the Lord has waiting for you."

"Yeah, well, my folks went to church all the time and it never did them much good that I could see. The only time I ever heard my dad mention God was when he was drunk as a skunk and cursing at the top of his lungs."

Once again she laid her hand on his arm, this time with more tenderness, greater courage. "Try not to look at the worst examples. Even good Christians have bad days. We all make mistakes we regret later. The point is, we may be far from faultless but we're learning how to live better lives all the time. That's why I go to church. Think of it as God's School."

"I'd probably flunk out."

"Why? Because your father did?" She ignored the disgusted glance he gave her and went on. "Have you ever asked yourself what he might have been like without his faith?"

Sean huffed. "Don't even go there."

"Why not?"

"Because, thanks to my brothers, I already know. I've watched Paul and Ian all my life. It hasn't been pretty."

"That doesn't mean you're the same kind of person they are," Rachel insisted.

"Doesn't it? Tell that to a geneticist and see what he says."

"I'd rather trust the Lord than rely on scientists. Oh, they have their place. I'm not saying they don't. But they can claim to have all the right answers one day, then turn around and contradict themselves the next. The more they learn, the more they realize they don't really know."

Pausing, she began to smile in spite of the seriousness of their discussion. "The same thing happens to me when I begin to study the Bible. I know I'll never understand everything about it. Fortunately, a person doesn't have to be well educated to become a Christian. Faith isn't reasoned. It's more basic than that."

"How so?"

Rachel laughed at herself and shook her head. "I wish I could explain. All I know is what happened to me after my father got sick."

Sean was studying her expression. Empathetic, he reached for her hand. "Go on."

"I was barely a teenager at the time. Daddy and I were very close. I didn't see how I could live the rest of my life without him if he died. Thoughts of suicide kept popping into my head. That really scared me. Finally, when I thought I was at the end of my rope, I called out to Jesus. I don't know why I did it. I just know that at that moment, everything changed for me."

Gently squeezing her fingers, Sean said, "I'm glad your parents gave you a faith to call on when you needed it."

"Did they?" Rachel raised misty eyes to him and blinked back tears. "When I went to them and tried to explain how happy and relieved I felt, they didn't seem to understand what I was trying to say. It wasn't until just before Daddy died that he told me he'd turned to Jesus the same way I had."

"What about your mother?"

"Martha Woodward is already as perfect as any Christian can get. Ask her. She'll be more than happy to tell you."

"So you're still worried about her?"

"Yes. And no. I did all I could when I told her

about my conversion. I can't coerce her into believing, any more than I can convince you to give God a chance. If you choose not to open your mind to the spiritual possibilities all around you, then that's your choice. It always will be."

Chapter Thirteen

Rachel didn't have to try to get away from Sean after she spoke so boldly. He seemed more than happy to part company with her.

Heading for home, she tried to relive their conversation, hoping to assure herself she hadn't been too preachy. Not only were most of her brilliant comments beyond recall, she couldn't even be sure she was putting the parts she did remember into the proper sequence. For all she knew, she might have alienated him for good, when that was the opposite of what she wanted to do.

That's what I get for praying for the guy. Thanks, Father. But I didn't mean I wanted to be the one to talk to him. I wanted You to send somebody else. Anybody but me. Please?

No booming voice came out of the clouds to

answer, nor did Rachel expect it to. She'd had enough experiences with what she viewed as God's sense of humor to recognize an ongoing satire, especially when she was such an integral part of it. The temptation to try to figure out the Good Lord's plans beforehand was strong, as usual. It was also foolhardy. The more she tried to help, the more likely it was that everything would get worse. Quickly.

So what am I supposed to be doing? she prayed. *Just tell me and I'll do it, Father. I promise.*

Sweet thoughts of Sean were joined by the image of Samantha the first time Rachel saw her. Such a pitiful little thing. So lost. So in need of love. However much time they had left to get to know her, it wouldn't be half long enough.

The idea of some shirttail relative claiming that dear little child made Rachel's temples throb. It wasn't right. The law shouldn't be allowed to interfere and move her. Not when Samantha was finally getting settled, finally acting more like a normal, happy child.

"So, what am I doing going home when I could be headed for Hannah's, instead?" Rachel asked herself aloud.

That was such a good question that she turned right instead of left on Highway 62 and started toward Squirrel Hill Road.

In her heart she knew she was doing the right

thing. The peace of mind that immediately soothed her when she made her decision was further proof she was finally on the right track.

The Brodys were at home when Rachel pulled up in front of their old farmhouse.

Drying her hands on her apron, Hannah came out onto the porch. "Well, hello there. You missed supper, but I think I can scare up a bit more if you're still hungry."

"I don't want to be a bother. I can't stay. I was just on my way home and got this urge to stop by. Hope it's all right."

"'Course it is. You come right on in."

Climbing the front steps to the covered porch made Rachel feel as if she were returning to a beloved home. Hannah's house had been her refuge on more than one occasion, especially in the difficult months after her father's death. In retrospect, she supposed if she'd been older at the time she'd have been more tolerant of her mother's vacillating moods.

"Is Samantha busy?" Rachel asked.

"That child is always busy. Never sits still for more'n a minute or two." She gave a satisfied sigh. "Right now, I suspect she's out in the chicken house collectin' eggs for the third or fourth time today. Poor hens can't stay ahead of her."

Laughing softly, Rachel remembered doing the

same chore for Hannah as a child. "That used to be a favorite job of mine, too. I swore I could tell those hens apart. Even had names for them."

"I know. You used to say they talked to you, too. Always did have a wonderful imagination. I 'spect that's why you cotton to kids the way you do."

"Which reminds me," Rachel said. "Sean got me a copy of the accident report about Samantha's parents. She was in the car with them when they wrecked, just like she said. According to the investigator, she was thrown clear."

Thoughtful, Hannah nodded. "Could be."

"Yes, it could, only she didn't have a scratch on her. The car was totaled. It rolled over and over, then landed upside down at the bottom of a ravine."

"Maybe she fell out before it happened."

"That was my first thought." Rachel raised her eyebrows and shook her head slowly as she explained further. "Samantha was found at the bottom of the cliff right next to the flattened car. If she did fall out, it wasn't until the major damage had already been done. So why wasn't she hurt?"

"You thinkin' what I'm thinkin'?"

"That her guardian angel actually did rescue her?" Rachel shrugged. "I don't know. The report also said that it looked like her seat belt might have been cut to free her, which contradicts the theory that she was thrown clear. She's small. If she was wearing a belt and riding in the back seat, that might explain how she survived when the car was crushed, but it still doesn't explain how she managed to free herself while she was hanging upside down, then wiggle out without getting cut on broken glass or jagged pieces of metal."

"Well, never you mind," the older woman said. "What's done is done. Don't matter to me if she crawled out or if the good Lord pitched her out a window. Our little angel was spared and that's all that counts."

"True."

The sound of an approaching car caught their attention, bringing an "Uh-oh" from Rachel and, "Well, well, well, looks like I got more company" from Hannah Brody.

"I'd better be going." One quick look told Rachel the oncoming car was Sean's.

"Nonsense. You didn't drive clear out here just to tell me about the accident report, did ya? Don't you wanna see Sam, too?"

"Well, I did, but…"

"Then, don't go runnin' off just because *he's* here," Hannah cautioned. "Hank and me'll protect you from him."

Rachel huffed. "Who's going to protect me from myself?"

As she'd expected, her candid comment made Hannah laugh.

"I 'spect I will," the older woman said. She opened the screen door and ushered Rachel inside. "You go on out in the kitchen and make yourself at home. I'll send Mr. Bates to the chicken house to fetch Sam. That'll give you time to pull yourself together and act natural."

"Okay."

With a sigh of resignation Rachel made her way through the house to the old-fashioned farm kitchen. The room was the largest in the house, plenty big enough to cook for a slew of farmhands or set up a home-canning operation at harvesttime. Now that the need for that much extra space was long past, Hannah had replaced the wood cookstove with a modern range. The round stovepipe opening in the wall above it was capped but could still be seen, a reminder of the hard work previous generations of women had done on that very spot.

Finding the kitchen empty, Rachel gravitated to the rectangular table in one corner, took the same seat she'd often occupied as a child and unconsciously brushed her hands across the plastic tablecloth to smooth it. The lingering aroma of home cooking made the place seem even more appealing. Her stomach growled.

Hannah breezed in the back door with a broad smile. "Stay right where you are. I'm fixing to feed you."

"That's really not necessary," Rachel said. "I didn't come here to mooch a meal."

"Nonsense. Where'd my Southern hospitality be if I didn't offer? Besides, your Mr. Bates has agreed to eat a bite with us, too."

"He's not *my* Mr. Bates!" Eyes wide, Rachel peered past Hannah to see if Sean had followed her inside. Thankfully, he hadn't. "Where is he, anyway?"

"Outside, talkin' to Hank and Sam." Hannah began pulling plates and bowls of leftovers out of the refrigerator and placing them on the table. "You two sure coulda fooled me. Miz Slocum tells me her son's real upset over what's been goin' on."

Rachel jumped to her feet. "Nothing's been going on!"

"Oh yeah? Then, why're you and Sean seein' so much of each other?"

"For Samantha's sake, of course."

"Pooh."

"Pooh, nothing. She's in my class and Sean's been assigned to counsel her. It's perfectly logical that he and I would want to compare notes—especially since you said there was a chance she'd be leaving here soon."

Hannah reached out to pat Rachel's hand. "That's a fact. But don't you fret. There's lots 'o mixed-up kids these days. Once Sam's gone, I'm sure you can find another reason to keep seein' your new fella."

"Ugh!" Rachel was beside herself with frustration. "I meant what I said. There is *nothing* between me and Sean. Nothing. And I'm not fixin' to start anything. Okay?"

"Okay. Just remember, you aren't gettin' any younger. You'll have to settle down one day soon. Any man lucky enough to snag you will be the envy of every bachelor in town."

"No, he won't." Somber, Rachel shook her head for emphasis. "I don't care what lies Craig told his mother, he was glad to be rid of me. That's why I don't understand what made him haul off and hit Sean the way he did."

"Jealousy."

"That's impossible," Rachel said. "Craig doesn't want me."

"You sound like you think nobody does. So you had a problem with Craig. So what? He's not the only deer in the forest, you know. You'll find somebody else."

"I don't *want* to find anyone else. That's what I keep trying to tell my mother. I'm never getting married. Period."

Confused, Hannah stopped bustling around the kitchen and paused to study her companion's expression. "Why on earth not?"

Rachel had long ago made up her mind that such

a personal query deserved no answer. This time, however, she was too overwrought by all her conflicting emotions to listen to her own sensible warnings. Of all the people in her life, Hannah Brody was probably the best choice as a confidante—and the one most likely to keep her secret.

Making a final decision, Rachel looked around to be certain they were still alone, took a deep breath and blurted, "I can't have children, okay?"

Hannah's eyes widened. "What? You sure?"

"Positive. Well, almost," Rachel said. "I've been to three specialists and they all told me the same thing." Sighing, she added, "Please keep this to yourself. I've accepted the idea but I know my mother won't."

"Why not? You come by your problems naturally, Rachel. Martha was the same way. She'll probably be hoppin' mad at me for tellin' you, but it's time somebody did."

"Is that why you gave me that hush-up look in church? Did Mom try to have more children besides me?"

"Never quit. Not till your daddy passed on. After that, I guess she started thinkin' more like a grandma. She's always loved children, probably as much as you do."

"Then, why didn't they adopt a brother or sister for me?"

"You know why. Folks around here set a lot of

store by kinship, by blood ties. Always have. Likely as not they always will. That's why I'm glad Sam's relatives are comin' for her, after all. I'll be sorry to see her go, but it'll be for the best. Family should stick together."

Though she disagreed, at least in Samantha's case, Rachel kept her opinions to herself. She understood the mind-set that had led to Hannah's conclusion. Everyone she knew had grown up believing that blood relationships were more important than anything else. That kind of thinking was part of their culture. In fairness to Craig, he wasn't acting any differently than most men would—than her own father and mother apparently had.

Which was all the more reason for her to remain single, Rachel reasoned. Clearly, Martha wanted a grandchild by birth, just as she'd wanted only a child who was born into the family—which did answer one nagging question.

"Then, there's no chance I'm adopted?" Rachel asked.

Hannah cackled. "Silly goose. 'Course not. Your mama would never of agreed to somethin' like that."

The back door banged. Rachel's head snapped around. Sean! She'd gotten so caught up in the emotional discussion she'd temporarily forgotten he was nearby! She was thankful there was nothing in his expression to imply he'd overheard what she'd just told Hannah. Matter of fact, he wasn't even looking at either of them. Instead, he was focused on the pretty little girl he carried.

Samantha had one arm around Sean's neck. In her other hand was an empty basket for gathering eggs. Giggling and talking a mile a minute, she was monopolizing him as only an enthusiastic child can. Sean was grinning, nodding and giving the little girl his rapt attention.

Rachel smiled. Seeing two people she loved, together like that, was such a beautiful, dear sight that it brought tears to her eyes. What a wonderful father Sean would make some day!

For an unguarded moment Rachel let herself imagine being the third party in the make-believe family portrait. More tears gathered, wetting her lashes and threatening to spill over. She had to admit the futility of a dream like that.

Not wanting anyone to notice how unhappy she was, she quickly looked away.

The last thing she glimpsed before she turned her head was an unspoken question in Sean's eyes.

With Hannah controlling most of the adult conversation during the impromptu meal, and Samantha so excited to have both her teacher and counselor there that she babbled incessantly, Rachel didn't have to participate often. When she did choose to speak, she kept it short and to the point. She didn't see how she could get into much trouble with "Please pass the gravy," although the way her life had been stirred up lately, there was no telling.

To her consternation, Sean seemed to be taking the whole encounter quite calmly, even when Hannah began to quiz him about his background. And, to the Brodys' credit, they didn't react negatively to his announcement that, yes, he was a Yankee. Amused, Rachel came to the conclusion that true Southern hospitality knew no bounds. *Well, almost none.*

Allowing herself a moment to appreciate her roots, she dropped her guard, smiled and glanced over at Sean. He was looking straight at her! Instantly he broke into a wide grin, eyes sparkling. Rachel wanted to avert her gaze but she was mesmerized by the sight of his apparent bliss.

He leaned back and sighed with contentment. "I believe that's the best meal I've ever eaten," he said. "I couldn't hold another bite if you paid me."

"Not even a piece of homemade apple pie?" Hannah was beaming with pride.

"Homemade?"

"Made it myself just this mornin'."

Rachel had to laugh at the funny, distressed look on Sean's face. "Hannah's famous for her pies. If you're really too full to eat it now, maybe she'll let you take a piece home with you."

"That would be great!" He looked to his hostess. "Ma'am?"

The older woman acted as if she didn't care, but Rachel could tell how pleased she was to have been asked. "Oh, I 'spose. No sense lettin' it go to waste. I'm fixin' to bake cookies tomorrow, anyway." She smiled down at Samantha. The child had crawled up in Sean's lap as soon as he'd pushed away from the table. "Gotta get 'em done afore my little friend leaves."

Rachel stiffened. "Leaves?"

Hannah looked ashamed. "Sorry. I shouldn't of talked out of turn. Not when we're all havin' so much fun." She stared pointedly at the child, then turned to Rachel with a warning shake of her head. "Nothing's definite."

That was a lie if Rachel had ever heard one. She knew Hannah well enough to see right through her, especially since the older woman's eyes had grown suddenly misty when she'd mentioned Samantha's imminent departure.

Needing moral support, Rachel looked to Sean. He, too, was showing concern over the unexpected disclosure. He leaned down to whisper something in Samantha's ear, then set her on her feet and stood as if preparing to leave.

Rachel didn't want him to get away until she'd had a chance to speak privately with him, yet she also wanted the opportunity to find out exactly what Hannah was holding back. She took the initiative.

Starting to stack plates she said, "We'll help you clean up these dishes, won't we, Sean?"

To her delight he pitched right in and grabbed the bowls that had held potatoes and brown gravy. Rachel pointed to the meat platter. "Shall I put the roast away on this plate or do you want to put it on something smaller?"

"You two young folks just leave that table be," Hannah ordered, fists on her ample hips. "You're my guests. We'll see to the dishes. Hank always helps me soon as he gets the stock fed, anyways." She smiled fondly. "Sam, why don't you take your teacher and her friend outside and show 'em the chickens? I've been lettin' one old broody hen run loose and I figure she's made her a nest. See if y'all can find that, too. But leave it be if you do. I'd like her to raise a batch."

That notion made Rachel frown. "Isn't it pretty late in the year to be starting baby chicks?"

"Nope," Hannah said, shaking her head in silent warning.

Rachel understood. "Okay. We'll be right outside if you need us. But before I go home, you and I are going to have a serious talk."

"'Fraid so. Now, scat, the three of you."

Leading the way and talking nonstop, Samantha

let the screen door bang behind her and skipped on ahead to start her search.

Sean held the door for Rachel, then followed her out onto the back porch. Pausing, he took a slow, deep breath and released it as a sigh.

"I'm beginning to think I may have made a mistake when I chose this career."

"Why?"

"Because I don't seem to be able to stay objective."

"About Samantha, you mean? I know. I'm having the same trouble. When Hannah slipped up and told us she was leaving pretty soon, I felt awful."

Sean reached for Rachel's hand, grasped it gently, then said, "We have only a very short time."

"What?" She clasped his fingers tighter. "How do you know?"

"Hank told me. I caught him out here before dinner and he filled me in. I mean before *supper*."

"Dinner, supper—who cares?" Rachel stared up at him, her eyes pleading. "Exactly how much time did he say we had left?"

"Less than a week."

"Oh, no. Oh, Sean…"

Suddenly, it no longer mattered that she'd vowed to keep her distance from him. There was solace in his embrace and she needed that moral support a lot more than she needed to maintain her stupid pride.

Releasing his hand Rachel stepped into his arms, knowing he'd accept her and hoping he'd understand that her motives were innocent.

Sean pulled her close and laid his cheek against her silky hair, breathing in the sweetness of it and allowing himself to relish the tender moment. Like it or not, they shared a love for a special little girl and were about to experience a mutual loss when she was sent away.

Under those circumstances, leaning on each other, literally and figuratively, couldn't be wrong. Ill-advised maybe, but certainly not wrong. Saying goodbye to Samantha—for good—was going to be rough on everyone involved.

That realization had already settled in his heart and made it ache. How much more was it going to hurt when Samantha left them. And if he was so miserable, it must be a lot worse for a loving, maternal person like Rachel.

Filled with empathy, he turned his head a fraction and kissed her hair, finding the spot damp from his own silent tears.

Chapter Fourteen

Samantha's excited shout brought Rachel and Sean to their senses. By the time the child dashed around the corner to rejoin them, they were standing apart and trying to appear unaffected.

"I found it!" Samantha grabbed Rachel's hand and dragged her away. "Come see! Come see!"

Still fighting to maintain what little was left of her dignity, Rachel glanced back to tell Sean, "You'd better come, too, in case she's right. Broody hens can be pretty testy if they're disturbed."

Several long strides brought him even with the woman and child. "Think you'll need protection?"

Rachel looked up at him. "Tall. We need tall and you're it. If a hen starts to kick up a fuss, anybody close to the ground is going to get scratched. Including me."

Sean chuckled. "Are you saying you want me to pick you up?"

"No! Of course not. Just grab Samantha and keep her out of harm's way."

"Okay." In one fluid motion he scooped the little girl into his arms and held her while she protested, "Let me go! I wanna show you."

"You can show us from up there," Rachel said calmly. "Mama chickens can be really mean. Tell me where you think you saw the nest, and I'll check it out for you."

Samantha pouted. "No fair. I found it first."

"And we'll let you look again, just as soon as I've made sure it's safe. I know Mrs. Brody wouldn't have sent us to look for a nest if she'd thought we'd actually find one."

"There," the child said, pointing. "Under that big bush."

"This one?" Cautious, Rachel pushed back the lower branches of a thick crepe myrtle and peered through the greenery to the ground. The straw Hannah had used for mulch was slightly concave in one small spot but there were no eggs in sight. The depression certainly didn't resemble any nests Rachel had seen chickens scratch out before.

She relaxed. "You can put her down," she told Sean. "There's nothing under here."

"Yes, there is!" Samantha hit the ground running

and dived under the shrubbery before either adult could stop her. Her shrill voice cried, "See? Right here. Oh," then went very still.

Rachel crouched. Sean dropped to his hands and knees and edged forward. They both heard Samantha cooing.

"Look," the child whispered. She turned, cradling something tiny and brown against her chest. "It's so soft."

"Aww, that's a baby bunny," Rachel gently told her. "You should put it back so its mother can take care of it."

"Maybe it doesn't have a mother," Samantha argued.

"Of course it has a mother. Everything does."

"Uh-uh. Maybe she got killed. Like my mama."

Overcome with guilt for having spoken so carelessly, Rachel didn't dare say anything else right away. Not without the catch in her throat making her voice break. She was grateful when Sean filled the gap.

"Tell you what," he said. "Let's put the baby back in its nest and I'll help you check on it every day after school. If it looks like its mother is really missing, then we'll give it something to eat. Okay?"

"There's two of them," Samantha said. "Twins."

"All the more reason to put it back. You wouldn't want its brother to be lonesome, would you?"

"It's a sister," Samantha announced. "They're girls. I know 'cause they're both so pretty and soft."

Smiling, Sean cast Rachel a sidelong glance. "I'm glad we cleared that up."

"Me, too." Rachel couldn't help but return his grin. "I knew better than to ask."

She held a group of branches back so the little girl could reach the hidden nest more easily. Samantha tucked the bunny next to its sibling beneath the loose straw and reemerged looking forlorn.

"You did the right thing," Rachel told her. "It's the job of people to take good care of all the animals."

"Like Noah did?" Samantha asked.

"Yes. Kind of."

Already eagerly following another train of thought, the child said, "Noah had lions and tigers and stuff. I saw pictures in Sunday school. I did. And giraffes, too. They stuck their head out the windows of the boat."

Rather than try to explain the immense scope of the actual ark the way the Bible did, Rachel merely said, "That's right. He had two of everything."

"I never saw a real giraffe," Samantha said, "or lions and stuff, either. My daddy was going to take me but…"

"I'm so sorry." Pulling her close, Rachel gave her a long hug before she let go and straightened.

"I'm sure you'll get to go to the zoo someday, honey."

Eyes twinkling, Samantha grabbed her hand. "I know! *You* could take me. You and Sean!"

Rachel's gaze darted to his face and found her own surprise mirrored there. "I don't think so."

Sean shrugged, smiled. "Why not? You're a teacher. You're allowed to take kids on field trips, aren't you?"

"Yes, but it can take weeks to get a trip authorized."

"Okay. Then, we'll go privately."

"Hannah can't permit that," Rachel argued.

"How about if she goes along, too?"

"Are you saying we should take her with us?"

He wasn't about to back down. "Sure. Why not?"

"If we're going to do that, why not just give Hannah some money and send her while we're both at work?"

"And miss all the fun? Not me," Sean vowed. "I haven't been to a zoo in I don't know how long."

"Well, I'm not about to play hooky from school, if that's what you have in mind," Rachel said flatly.

"Don't our contracts say we get personal leave days or something like that?"

"Yes, but…"

"No more excuses, then. It's settled. We're going to the zoo. All of us." At his feet, the excited little girl was jumping up and down and squealing with delight.

Rachel wasn't quite as thrilled. She stared up at him. "Okay, smarty. When?"

"Soon."

"Not if we can't officially get the time off. I'd never ditch school. What kind of example would that be for my class?"

"A lousy one," Sean said with a sigh. "The question is, how badly do you want to keep from disappointing poor Sam."

Glancing around the immediate area, Rachel said, "Speaking of which, where did she go?"

"Probably ran inside to tell Hannah the good news."

"Terrific."

Shaking her head incredulously and staring off into the distance, Rachel wondered absently how she'd been coerced into agreeing to participate in such a crazy scheme. It didn't take her long to admit the truth—she wanted to go with Samantha and Sean so badly she could taste it.

So much for maintaining emotional distance from her students! She grimaced as her thoughts spiraled further. *Students?* Ha! They were nowhere near the worst of her problems. No, sir. Her biggest dilemma stood six feet tall and had enticingly mischievous eyes, not to mention an inherent kindness and the sort of physique that lonely women's dreams were made of.

Sean tapped her on the shoulder to regain her attention. "Hey there. Anybody home?"

"Nobody sane," Rachel quipped. "If I were, I'd have told you I wasn't going anywhere with you, let alone to the zoo."

"But you didn't," he countered, grinning. "And you know how important it is to keep a promise to an impressionable child. Shall we plan on the day after tomorrow?"

"Will that be soon enough?"

"Barely," Sean said, sobering. "Just barely."

By the day of the trip Rachel was convinced that the Lord must have had His hand in their outing. Otherwise, how could all their plans have panned out so beautifully? Standing in Hannah's yard, waiting for Sean to arrive, she said as much.

"Know what ya mean," the older woman agreed. "When I told Mr. Vanbruger that Sam would be leaving soon, he said she could keep up with her schoolwork at home till then. 'Course, it ain't like you give her much homework in kindergarten."

Rachel laughed lightly. "True. But we learn new things every day. What I can't believe is how easily he approved my request for time off, even though the year's just beginning. I hope he was as generous with Sean."

"You didn't ask him?"

"I haven't seen him. Not to talk to. The closest I've come to that man since we ran into each other over here the other night was a few glimpses of him in the hallways at school. He didn't bother to telephone me, either. If it hadn't been for you, I wouldn't even have known what time we were supposed to be leaving or where we were going to meet."

All Hannah said was "Hmm," before she turned away and went back into the house, leaving Rachel free to concentrate more fully on her innermost thoughts.

The thing that surprised her was her own level of enthusiasm for the trip. From the moment she'd awakened that morning she'd felt like a child herself. At first she'd assumed she was merely happy on Samantha's behalf, but now that she'd had time to look deeper into her heart she had to admit that much of her joy was personal.

Such a sudden awakening brought Rachel up short. It wasn't right to let herself make believe that her life could turn out differently than she knew it would. Yet she desperately wanted one day—just one day—when she could pretend there was hope, that she might someday become someone's mother. Someone's wife.

Her breath caught. She stood very still, listening to her racing heart and acknowledging the whole truth. She didn't dream of being just anyone's wife—she dreamed of belonging only to Sean Bates, and he to her.

"But I love him, Father," she whispered. "I can't do that to him. I can't deny him a family. What am I going to do?"

For a moment she considered asking God to change her body so she could feel complete. It wouldn't have been the first time she'd begged for healing. When Craig had taken the news of her physical lack so hard, she'd fallen on her knees as soon as she was alone and wept an unspoken plea. At that time, the Lord had granted her peace instead. To continue to ask Him for something else seemed ungrateful. Wrong-hearted.

Before Rachel could pursue that conviction further she heard a car approaching. The screen door banged behind her. She intercepted Samantha flying down the porch steps and used the child's momentum to swing her around twice before cautiously releasing her with a gentle warning.

"Slow down, sweetie. Let the poor man park before you mob him, okay? You know it's not safe to run out in the road when a car's coming."

Samantha acted as if she didn't hear a word. As soon as Rachel let go of her, she barreled up to Sean's car and tugged on the handle of the driver's door.

Grinning, he opened it and gave her a hug. "Hi, there, kiddo. You ready to go?"

"Yeah!"

He looked past the wiggling child to the woman standing at the base of the stairs. "Looks like you are, too. Very nice."

Nervous, Rachel smoothed the hem of her knit shirt over the waistband of her shorts and smiled. "Thanks. I know we'll have a lot of walking to do and it's bound to be hot today. I wanted to be comfortable."

"Hey, don't apologize to me," Sean said. "I think you look great."

Modesty made her counter, "With these short legs?"

"They reach the ground, so they must be long enough," he teased. "Is Hannah ready to go?"

Rachel nodded. "She just ducked back into the house a minute ago. Stay there. I'll go get her."

Watching the petite woman whirl and dash up the porch steps, Sean was taken with her youthful exuberance and upbeat attitude. Such qualities were definitely a gift, he reasoned, although he wasn't quite ready to credit the Almighty as the giver.

He did have to admit there was something odd about living among so many believers, though. Most days, not an hour went by that someone didn't mention a Higher Power. Christianity was such an integral part of everyone's life here, it seemed that even those who didn't profess a particular denominational faith knew the Bible and gave credit to God for even the smallest blessing. Speaking of which…

Sean heard Samantha babbling about the baby rabbits she'd found and saw her gesturing wildly toward the nest. "What?"

"They're gone," she told him. "I looked and looked. Maybe they got lost."

"Or got big enough to leave home. Maybe it was time for them to go to kindergarten, like you."

Hands on her hips, the child made a silly face. "Bunnies don't go to school!"

"Are you sure?" Sean couldn't help laughing at the way she was posturing. It reminded him of the way Rachel acted whenever she was miffed.

"Positive."

"Okay. If you say so." He glanced up with an expectant grin as the front door opened again. "Here comes Miss Rachel and Mrs. Brody. Time to go. Get in the back seat, and I'll fasten your safety belt."

"I want Miss Rachel to ride with me!"

"That's what I was afraid of," Sean murmured. "Okay. This is your trip. We'll do it your way."

By the time he'd secured Samantha's belt, however, only Rachel had come as far as the car. She was frowning. Sean looked from her to Hannah and back. "What's the matter?"

"Hannah says her blood sugar is too high again. She doesn't feel well enough to go with us."

"Oh-oh."

Rachel nodded sagely. "Oh-oh is right. *Now* what are we going to do?"

"Well, I don't know about you, but I'm going to the zoo."

"We shouldn't."

"Mrs. Brody doesn't seem to mind. See? She's waving."

"I know. I suggested we take Hank, instead, so we'd have an authorized foster parent along. She just laughed at me."

"No wonder. Can you imagine old Hank at the zoo? He'd probably spend all his time telling the keepers they weren't taking care of the animals properly."

Rachel smiled at his accurate assessment. "Probably." She leaned down to look at the child already ensconced in the back seat of Sean's car, then sighed noisily as she conceded. "Okay. I'll go. But if I get in trouble over this I'm going to blame the whole thing on you."

"Fair enough. Want me to tie you up, sling you over my shoulder like a pirate and throw you in the car to make your story more convincing?"

He burst out laughing when she gave him the Samantha Smith pose of indignation and said, "No, thanks. I'll pass."

There were two large zoos within a reasonable driving distance of Serenity—one in Little Rock and one in Memphis. Both were a three-hour journey. Sean decided to go to Memphis because he also wanted to give Samantha the opportunity to see the Mississippi River. Long before they reached the Tennessee/Arkansas border, however, she'd fallen fast asleep in the back seat.

"I'm glad you rode up front with me," he told Rachel. "Our little friend has conked out. Guess I'll have to show her the Big Muddy on our way home."

"I had to sit where I could see out," Rachel replied. "The road between Hardy and Blackrock is way too crooked. It always makes me dizzy."

"Sorry. Do you get seasick, too?"

She shrugged, taking care to keep her eyes on the road in case there was a curve ahead. "I don't know. The only boat I was ever in was a canoe. A friend and I floated down the Strawberry River. We went so slowly I hardly noticed movement."

"Someday we'll have to take a trip in a real boat, then."

When she didn't comment, Sean glanced over at her. Her hands were clasped tightly together in her lap. Her jaw was clamped shut. Her beautiful blue eyes were staring out the windshield, concentrating as if she were the one driving.

Wisely, he dropped the subject. It had been stupid to talk to Rachel about the future. She was right. There was no use prolonging the agony by pretending they had a chance as a couple. Thanks to his big mouth, she already knew he came from a dysfunctional family—one she'd not want to even consider joining. Nor would she want to bring into the world children who might exhibit that same propensity for addiction.

Geneticists were still split on whether or not such leanings were inherited, but Sean wasn't about to chance finding out they were. So far, he'd escaped the insidious addiction that had swallowed up his father and brothers, yet they all came from the same ancestors. If he ever let himself slip, no telling how far down he'd slide before he hit bottom.

His hands tightened on the wheel, his knuckles whitening from the effort. No way was he going to involve an innocent woman like Rachel in such a terrible life. She deserved better. Much better than he could ever offer.

To distract himself before his musings made him too depressed, he handed her a Tennessee road map. "Here. I checked before we left, and I think if we get off on Poplar we can take it all the way to the zoo. See if that's right, will you? The off-ramp should be coming up pretty soon."

"Okay. As long as you don't go around any corners while I'm not watching the road."

"If any come along I'll straighten them just for you," he quipped, quickly adding, "Oops! Hang on. Corner coming up."

She blinked and focused on the roadway as best she could. It was several long seconds before her equilibrium returned to normal. "Whew! That was fun. Remind me not to eat anything for a couple of hours before we start home."

"*Eat?* What if the zoo doesn't sell rabbit food?"

"Very funny. I don't eat salads all the time. I happen to love hot dogs. Ice cream, too, although I don't usually indulge when I have my whole class along on a field trip."

"Why not?"

"Because it's not fair to give myself a treat when my students can't have the same thing. It's way too messy. Bus drivers really hate it when you bring twenty-five or thirty sticky kids back on board for the ride home."

"Speaking from experience, I have to agree." Sean nodded toward the back seat. "Tell you what. If you and Sleeping Beauty promise to wash afterwards, you can both have all the ice cream you want."

Rachel raised an eyebrow. "I'm so relieved to have your permission, Mr. Bates. Thanks bunches."

"You don't have to get sarcastic. I was just trying to make polite conversation."

"I know. Sorry. When you mentioned driving the bus it made me think about school again. Neither of us may have jobs if the authorities find out Hannah didn't come with us. I guess worrying about that has made me a little cranky."

"You? Why should you worry? Everybody I meet keeps telling me God will take care of them. Don't you believe the same thing?"

She gave a derisive huff. "It's not that simple. If I suspect that what I'm doing may be wrong, then for me it *is* wrong. I can't count on divine providence to step in and rescue me if my own folly has gotten me into trouble."

"What we're doing here can't be wrong," he insisted. "This is our last chance to show Sam a good time, to let her know we care about her. No matter where she goes or what happens in the future, she'll always have today to remember."

So will I, Rachel mused. *So will I.*

Remembering was going to be easy. It was forgetting that was going to be hard.

A child and a zoo are more than compatible, they're symbiotic, Rachel thought, watching Samantha run from one exhibit to the next with Sean in tow. It had only taken the bright child a few attempts to figure out that she could get a much better view of everything if she asked Sean to hold her up instead of begging Rachel for a boost.

The only time that additional height wasn't helpful was in the tropical, walk-in aviary, where all the brightly hued birds flew freely overhead, as if still at home in the jungle. The rest of the zoo followed a stylized Egyptian theme, in keeping with the Memphis name, and featured gardens brimming with flowers between each exhibit. No matter how many times Rachel visited there, its beauty always enthralled her.

Sean led the way to the elephant enclosure. Samantha was balanced on his shoulders, pointing and babbling. "She only loves me for my height," he said aside to Rachel.

"Speaking as someone who's been hanging out pretty close to the ground her whole life, I can understand that fascination," she replied, smiling. "I dare you to leave her up there while we eat the ice cream you promised us."

"Only if you pick a flavor that doesn't clash with the color of my hair."

Rachel laughed. She'd smiled and giggled so often since they'd been together that the muscles in her cheeks actually hurt. What a day this had been! What a marvelous, blessed day. If she were running the universe, the sun would never set. This very same day would go on forever and ever. And so would her happiness.

Their *shared* happiness, she corrected. From the outset, Samantha had acted as if being with the two of them was as routine as being with her former parents. And Sean played the part of father-shepherd with a natural grace and quiet wisdom.

Though Rachel had done her best to fit in, there were still unguarded moments when she felt like an outsider, a pretender, and had to hide behind her sunglasses to blink back tears.

If Sean noticed, he kept the observation to himself. Rachel was glad he hadn't quizzed her about it. Under the circumstances she had no intention of baring her soul. Especially not to him. Clearly, Samantha was delighted with the zoo trip, and Rachel didn't intend to do or say one single thing that might spoil it.

She smiled to herself, accepting the inevitable with a dollop of cynicism. Yes, she'd miss Samantha. Terribly. And she'd always think of this outing with Sean as a high point of her life. But the tears weren't all for them. Not even close. Rachel's tears were for herself, for the one thing she wanted that she could never have—love and commitment.

Truth to tell, her mother had been right all along. A job wasn't enough. Being with Sean and Samantha all day had convinced her of that.

Like it or not, she did want a family of her own. Desperately.

Chapter Fifteen

The drive back to Serenity seemed to take hours longer than the drive the other way. Rachel yawned. "Sorry. It's been a long day."

"Hang in there. We're almost to the Brodys'."

"I know." She smiled wistfully as she glanced at the dozing little girl in the back seat. "You shouldn't have bought her that enormous stuffed animal. It was way too expensive."

"Had to. This was my last chance to spoil her."

Rachel sighed. "I'm really going to miss her."

"Me, too."

Glancing sidelong at Sean she was certain she saw a glint of moisture in his eyes. "Do you think they'll let her write to us, or maybe phone if we tell them to reverse the charges?"

"Maybe," he said. "I suppose it all depends on

whether they're taking her because they really want her or because of her inheritance. Wait till they learn it's been placed into a trust fund so it can't be squandered."

"Hannah did mention something about money coming to Samantha. How did you find out so much?"

"I asked. I'm surprised you didn't."

"I suppose I should have. I just kept telling myself I couldn't do anything to change what would eventually happen, so I ought to stay out of it. Stupid, huh?"

"Avoiding heartache? No, that's not stupid. It's normal. Nobody goes out looking for dragons to slay unless they find monstrous footprints in their own backyard."

Rachel's brow knit. "Huh?"

"Some people are born crusaders," Sean explained. "Others aren't. Your talent happens to be teaching and you do that well. You said you recognized the gift when you were very young."

"Yes, I did." She was surprised he remembered a casual comment from so early in their relationship.

"Then, don't beat yourself up about not being gung-ho to do something else. You have character, Rachel. If you saw an injustice that needed righting, I know you'd try to right it. When there's nothing that can be done, staying out of the affairs of others is the smartest choice."

"But I haven't. Not really," she said softly, in confidence, with a quick peek at the back seat to make sure Samantha was still asleep. "I was involved up to my eyebrows the minute I set eyes on that little girl."

All Sean said was "I know exactly what you mean."

The sun was set by the time they pulled into the driveway of the Brody house and parked. Apparently no one had thought to turn on the outside lights, leaving the yard dark except for the glow from the living room windows and a waxing moon that was starting to rise above the treetops.

Dimness suited Sean just fine. It matched his sinking mood. Leaving his hands resting on the steering wheel, he sighed and looked over at Rachel. "Well, I suppose we'd better wake her up and get this over with."

"I suppose so." She managed a smile. "I want to thank you for talking me into going along. I had a wonderful time. I'm sure Sam did, too."

"Hey!" Sean said, brightening. "You called her Sam. That's a real breakthrough."

"Better late than never, I guess."

Slowly, deliberately, Rachel turned in her seat and got to her knees so she could lean over the back of the front seat and gently rouse the weary child.

She touched Samantha's shoe, wiggled it. "Honey? Wake up. We're home."

Samantha snuggled closer to her stuffed panda and rubbed her cheek on its soft fur. Still asleep she murmured, "Mama."

Tears sprang to Rachel's eyes. Hiding her ragged emotions she quickly got out of the car and stood with her back to it, arms folded across her chest. When Sean came up behind her, laid his arms over hers and pulled her close, his tenderness cost her the last vestiges of her self-control and she began to weep.

"I...I'm sorry," she said. "I wasn't going to do this."

"It's okay. I have broad shoulders."

"No kidding."

As he slowly leaned down and kissed the top of her head, she dashed away her tears, turned and said the first thing that popped into her mind. "You missed."

"I what?"

"You missed." Through her misty gaze she saw understanding dawn as she pointed to her trembling lips. "It goes there."

"Does it?" Sean whispered. "Are you sure?"

"No. But do it, anyway."

He bent his head, more than ready to give her the kiss she was asking for. He'd been longing to end their marvelous day together in exactly that loving way. Only the belief that Rachel wouldn't welcome the romantic overture had stopped him. Now that she'd removed that obstacle, he was overjoyed to oblige.

Rachel rose on tiptoe, waiting, anticipating, remembering. She could feel Sean's breath, warm on her face, see the flicker of desire lighting his eyes. One more chapter in the fairy tale, she promised herself. Just one more and then it would be all over. For good.

Her lips parted. Her hands slipped around his neck. The moment she sensed his strong arms around her, she trusted him completely, and felt him raise her enough to lift her feet off the ground. Lost in that precious moment, Rachel started to close her eyes.

Bright light suddenly blinded her. Sean started and almost dropped her.

She staggered, fighting for balance and calling upon her heightened perceptions to make sense of whatever had just occurred. Floodlights illuminated the front yard, trapping them in the shadow thrown by his car. Rachel was instantly glad they'd been standing on the side opposite the house instead of sharing their kiss on the porch where they'd be easily seen.

Shouting and cursing was coming from the direction of the house. It built to a cacophony of deeply disturbing sound. The front door slammed, then slammed again.

Still blinking against the brightness, Rachel shaded her eyes with one hand. When she reached out to touch Sean's arm with the other she felt his muscles flex beneath her fingers. "What's going on?"

"I don't know." He tried to maneuver her behind him. "Stay back till we find out."

She resisted. "Don't be silly. Hannah wouldn't let anything bad happen to us here. Neither would Hank. He may be old but he's strong as a bull."

Peering up at the porch she counted five adults. Hannah and Hank were there, of course, arm in arm. The only other person Rachel recognized was—oh, no! It looked like Heatherington! Now the fat was in the fire for sure!

A middle-aged couple Rachel had never seen before broke away from the others and started down the porch steps toward the car. The smartly dressed woman left her portly mate lagging behind, stomped straight up to Sean and wagged a long finger in his face.

"How dare you! Do you know how late it is? We've all been worried sick. Field trip, my eye. I'll see you're *fired*. Both of you."

Sean kept his voice low. "We're very sorry you

were inconvenienced, Mrs...." He tried Samantha's last name. "Smith, is it?"

"You know very well it is," she screeched. "No alibis. You tried to steal my niece and you're not going to get away with it. Not if I have any say in the matter."

Rachel stepped forward, still squinting and shading her eyes. "That's not what happened at all. We just wanted to show her a good time before she left us."

"Don't give me that. Ms. Heatherington told these people we were coming all the way down here to pick her up, and you didn't even have the courtesy to have her here." The woman muttered a curse. "Good thing you came back when you did. I was about to call the cops. Maybe I still will."

"That won't be necessary," Sean said calmly. "Apparently there was some mix-up about the exact time of your arrival." He gestured at his car. "As you can see, Samantha's fine. She's right here. Safe and sound."

"Then, give her to me. I don't intend to stand around all night and argue."

Rachel opened the car door and leaned inside.

Standing close by, Sean heard her mumble, "You could have fooled me," before her tone changed to gently rouse Samantha. "Come on, honey. Wake up. We're home. And there are some new people here I want you to meet."

Sean was proud of the way she put aside her own needs to do what was best for the child. If it was tearing him up to think of handing Samantha over to the rigid, unforgiving person they'd just encountered, what must poor Rachel be thinking? One quick look at her face told him exactly what she was going through, and it made his heart ache for her.

Clinging to her beloved teacher the child rubbed sleep out of her eyes while Rachel stroked her thin back and urged her more awake. She looked as if she was about to hand Samantha to her new guardian when the woman reached out, grabbed the little girl's wrist and wrenched her away!

Rachel screamed, "No!"

Sean put his arm around her in consolation and restraint.

Hannah Brody had been hanging back, watching. Now, she bustled up and started to call the other woman every nasty name Rachel had ever heard—and a few she hadn't—while Samantha wailed at their feet and the social worker dithered in the background.

The Smith woman paused only long enough to tell the child to shut up, then said, "Come on, Robert. Bring her," and stormed off.

"Yes, Daphne." With a shrug, the man held out his hand. Instead of taking it, Samantha clung to Rachel.

The little girl's weeping had intensified almost to the point of hysteria, and Sean was worried about her mental state. He had begun considering intercession the moment he'd encountered Samantha's new guardians. Now that Daphne Smith had demonstrated such a horrific lack of compassion and tact, he was beginning to think they might actually stand a chance of heading off the change of custody. It was worth a try. Staying with the Brodys indefinitely would be far better for Sam than going to live with the part of her extended family he'd just met.

Rachel was on her knees trying to soothe the weeping child when more shouting began. Hank and Robert were getting into it now. Younger and heavier, Robert threw a punch at Hank. He missed. Hank fell, anyway, when he staggered backward to escape the blow. Yelling, Hannah launched herself, fists flailing, into the midst of the melee.

Sean wasn't far behind. He pulled Hannah out of the fracas, but she dove back in before he had a chance to rescue Hank.

Clearly, someone should telephone the police, Rachel decided—but who? Hank, Hannah, Sean and the Smiths were all part of the problem. And it didn't look like Ms. Heatherington was in any shape to help, either. The usually staid social worker stood frozen in place, her mouth agape, staring at the near riot from the relative safety of the porch.

It was evidently up to Rachel to make the call if anyone was going to. What the whole group needed was a cooling-off period, and she knew she wasn't big enough or tough enough to send them to separate corners the way she did her kindergarten students when they misbehaved.

Preparing to go inside to use the Brody's phone, she straightened and reached for Samantha's hand so she could keep her close. The child must have misunderstood. Instead of meekly taking her teacher's offered hand, she jerked away and dashed down the dirt driveway.

Rachel was caught off guard. "Samantha! Wait!"

The little girl didn't pay any heed. Already in a frenzy, she increased her speed. The last good glimpse Rachel got of her before the night swallowed her up was the bobbing of her blond curls and the dusky white of her tennis shoes.

"Sean!" Rachel hollered at the top of her lungs, then took off in pursuit without waiting to see if he'd heard.

The driveway was dark and winding. There were no streetlights along Squirrel Hill Road, either, so the farther Rachel got from the Brody house the more the countryside blended into a murky blur, lit only by a sliver of the moon.

"Samantha!" she shouted. "Wait! Please."

Behind her she heard Sean's voice echoing her

calls. Just knowing he was following gave Rachel confidence. Her legs were already tired from a whole day of walking. The muscles throbbed, threatening to fail. She tripped. Faltered. Recovered.

"Oh, please, Lord," she prayed aloud. "Help me!"

Arms held out in front of her, she groped along, hoping she wouldn't accidentally bump into one of Hank's barbed-wire fences and praying Samantha knew enough about the lay of the land to keep herself safe, even in the near dark.

By Rachel's reckoning there was only the cement crossing over the wet-weather creek left to negotiate before she reached the road. The smack of her rubber-soled shoes hitting the hard concrete of the swale confirmed that conclusion.

She stopped there, fighting to hold her breath long enough to listen for Samantha's footsteps up ahead. Instead, she heard the pounding of a runner's stride somewhere behind. Sean was coming! Thank God!

A quick breath later she heard another sound. The way noise echoed in the narrow, wooded valley it was hard to tell what direction it was coming from, or even what it was. She listened carefully. The roar was growing more definable. It had to be a car or a pickup truck. And it sounded like it was headed their way on Squirrel Hill Road!

Panic chilled Rachel to the depths of her soul.

Even the most levelheaded five-year-old was liable to forget safety rules in a moment of excitement. Samantha was unlikely to remember anything, let alone an admonition to stay out of the street.

Rachel sprinted for the road, praying all the way. The car's motor was getting louder and louder.

She could see headlight beams now, brilliant and blinding. Between her position and that of the speeding car she caught a glimpse of a small, moving shadow.

It might be a deer, her subconscious insisted. And what if it wasn't? With no thought for personal safety, Rachel ran out into the road, waving her arms wildly over her head and shouting, "Sam! Look out!"

Behind her, Sean gave a guttural roar when he saw her luminescent silhouette aglow in the glare of oncoming headlights.

The driver braked. Skidded. The car started to slide sideways, tires screeching.

Sean lunged for Rachel. Everything seemed to be moving in slow motion. Airborne for what seemed like ages, he finally got his arms around her. He twisted to use his own body to cushion her fall and they landed in a heap by the side of the road. The vehicle came to rest mere feet away in the same shallow ditch, its lights blurred by tall grasses and brush.

Irrationally angry, Sean bellowed at her, "Are you *crazy?* What did you think you were doing?"

Rachel was wobbly when he helped her to her feet. "Sam," she gasped. "Samantha. Did you see her?"

"No. Where?"

He scanned the darkness beyond the car. In the distance he could see small lights bobbing down the driveway from the Brody house. It looked as if several people were sensibly using flashlights to guide them.

"I don't know where," Rachel said. She sagged against him. "I thought I saw her just before…before the crash."

Refusing to let go when he knew he'd come so close to losing her moments before, he said, "Okay. Show me what you think you saw. We'll look together. Then I'll come back and see about the driver." He sneered in the direction of the car. "The guy's probably feeling no pain. I can smell the booze from here."

"Over that way." Rachel pointed with a shaky hand.

Sean didn't like the tremulousness of her voice. He'd never heard her sound so weak, so dispirited. "Can you make it?"

"I'm fine," she lied. "Hurry."

"Looks like the cavalry's almost here," Sean told

her, indicating the Brody driveway. "Let's wait. We can borrow their flashlights instead of stumbling around in the dark."

Rachel wasn't willing to delay. She grabbed his hand and forged ahead. "No. I'm sure I saw something. I…" Her legs suddenly gave way.

Sean caught her before she fell. He didn't have to ask what was wrong. He could see for himself.

They'd found Samantha.

No one argued with Rachel when she was chosen to accompany the unconscious child to the hospital. Her own bumps and bruises from the near miss with the out-of-control car were her ticket to ride in the same ambulance. She'd have suffered the injuries gladly to earn the opportunity to comfort the poor girl.

Unfortunately, Samantha remained unconscious. Patting her cool, limp, little hand, Rachel kept asking the paramedics, "Why doesn't she come to?"

"We won't know till we get some tests run," one of them answered. "We're taking good care of her. Why don't you lie down until we get to the emergency room, ma'am?"

Rachel was adamant. "No. She needs me."

"There's nothing you can do for her right now. You'd better take care of yourself so you'll be able to look after her when she wakes up."

"I'm fine. Just cold," Rachel said, shivering.

"That's from shock." The medic gently wrapped a gray blanket around her shoulders, guided her to the spare gurney and lifted her feet to swing her whole body around.

The appeal of a moment's respite was so strong that she let him ease her down onto the pristine sheets and pillow. "Thanks."

"You're welcome," he said. "I understand how you feel. I've dealt with lots of mothers and they all act the same way when their kids get hurt."

Bone-weary and beyond responding, Rachel closed her eyes and turned her face to the wall to hide her silent tears.

Chapter Sixteen

Sean had lingered at the accident scene just long enough to make sure Rachel and Samantha were safely aboard the ambulance, then headed for his car.

What he wanted more than anything was to be reunited with Rachel. To comfort her as best he could. If things didn't turn out okay for little Sam he didn't know what either of them would do. He'd been so angry when that drunk driver was pulled out of the wrecked car and arrested he'd wanted to strangle the guy with his bare hands. It had taken several police officers—plus Hank Brody—to keep him from trying.

Right now, the ambulance bearing Sean's loved ones was headed for an emergency facility near Salem. He'd been told that if more specialized care was needed once initial assessments were made, one or both patients would be flown by helicopter to Little Rock. He was determined to get to them before that. He had to. Nothing was more important.

His hands clamped the car's steering wheel, every muscle tense, as he raced on through the night. How totally helpless he felt! This was a situation where a strong belief in God, like Rachel had, would sure come in handy.

If there is a God, he countered.

But suppose there was? What would he say to Him?

Sean had no idea, nor did he think the Almighty would be inclined to listen to the prayers of a cynical guy like him. Why should He?

Maybe for Rachel's sake, Sean answered. For Rachel's sake he'd have to try.

Keeping his eyes on the road ahead he first drew a deep breath. "Hey, God? You up there?" he began. "It's me. No, forget that. I'm not asking for myself, I'm asking for Rachel. You know Rachel. She's one of Yours. She's probably too traumatized to ask for help herself right now so I'm asking in her place. And for Samantha, too. Okay?"

Sean felt silly talking to an invisible being. Next thing he knew he'd probably be seeing guardian angels the same way Samantha said she did.

Angels? A vivid recollection of the accident leapt into Sean's consciousness. He'd never forget the sight of Rachel bravely trying to flag down that oncoming car. Reflected light had played tricks with her appearance, making her waving arms look like wings in motion. That was how he'd known where she was. It was that glowing image he'd jumped for when he'd come running out of the Brody's driveway.

His heart started to pound erratically. That was *exactly* what had happened. No question about it. He was positive. So how had he and Rachel landed at least three car lengths up the road from the end of the drive, instead of beneath the wrecked car? If there was a logical, scientific explanation, he sure didn't know what it might be. Unless…

The urge to dismiss the notion of divine intervention was strong. Stronger still was his assurance that he'd been an unwitting part of something amazing.

His hands trembled on the steering wheel. His heart felt lodged in his throat. "God?" he whispered. "Jesus? Are You really out there?"

Though no audible answer came, Sean was certain there had been one. He was finding it hard to see the roadway through eyes misted by tears of intense gratitude. Cautiously he slowed his frenetic driving pace, while his heart threatened to pound its way out of his chest.

As the beginnings of faith touched him he sensed a subtle change in his outlook, a kind of peace he'd never felt before. It flowed over and through him like the passing of a warm wind or the rising of a blush to one's cheeks.

"Okay," he said, nodding resolutely. "You win, God. If You want me, You've got me, although what You'd want with the likes of me, I sure can't imagine. Just keep taking care of the people I love, will You? Please? That's all I care about."

Sean had barely finished speaking when he realized he'd arrived at the hospital. He cut the wheel hard to the right and drove straight to the emergency entrance. As he climbed out of his car it occurred to him that he'd just turned more than one hard corner to get to where he found himself right now.

Sean barged past the receptionist without asking anyone's permission and straight-armed the swinging door. The treatment room was crowded. He spotted Rachel pacing in front of a closed curtain. She had a blanket wrapped around her shoulders, her hair was a mess and her cheeks were pale and dirt-smeared, but she still looked wonderful to him.

He hurried across the room. "Rachel!"

She didn't hesitate to step into his embrace. "Oh, Sean."

For a long moment he just held her, breathing in her familiar scent and giving silent thanks that she was okay. Finally he loosed his grip and looked at the curtain.

"Is Sam in there?"

"Yes."

"How is she?"

"I don't know. They won't let me see her. The doctors are with her right now. I've been trying to listen to what they're saying but it's too noisy in this big room."

"At least they got to her right away. Have they checked you out yet?"

"No. I'll be fine as soon as I know Samantha's going to be all right. I've been going crazy, waiting and worrying."

"I'm here now. We'll wait together."

He turned, keeping one arm protectively around her shoulders. "Come on. Let's sit down. You look awful."

"Oh, thanks a heap."

Sean gazed down at her tenderly. "That's my girl. When you snap at me like that, I know you're okay."

"I didn't snap at you for no reason," Rachel argued. "You said I looked awful."

"You've never looked better to me." There was a definite catch in his voice.

"Really?"

"Really." Once again realizing fully how close he'd come to watching her die, he couldn't convince himself to stop touching her, holding her close, so he sat down first and urged her onto his lap.

Rachel willingly settled there, wrapped in her warm blanket and the comforting arms of the man she loved. Tomorrow there would be plenty of time to explain why they ought to stop seeing each other. Right now, all she wanted was to retreat from reality by cuddling up to Sean.

"I wish…" he began.

She raised her face to him. "What do you wish?"

"Nothing. You rest. Now's not the time to talk about it."

"Hmm. I wonder. After what happened tonight it seems to me that waiting too long to do *anything* can be a mistake."

"Maybe you're right this time."

"Maybe?" One eyebrow arched. "And what do you mean, *this time?*"

Rachel had intended her remarks to distract him and lift his spirits. She might be showing signs of stress, as he'd said, but so was he. If she looked half as world-weary as he did, it was no wonder he'd commented on it. To her relief, he smiled.

"Okay. Maybe you have been right more than once. And I have to admit I've been wrong—at least about a few things."

"Like what?"

"Kids, for one thing."

Rachel stiffened. "What kids?"

"Sam, to start with," Sean said. Rachel was just beginning to breathe again when he added, "and maybe having some of my own someday, too."

"That's nice."

"I thought you'd agree." He gave her a quick squeeze. "So, how about it?"

"How about what?"

"Kids? A family? You and me?"

She pushed herself away from him and struggled to her feet. "No, thanks."

The dejected expression on his face, in his eyes, hurt her to the core. The truth wouldn't wait. It wasn't fair to leave Sean wondering why she'd turned his proposal down flat. No matter how hard confession was going to be, he deserved to hear her reasons.

Drawing the blanket closer as a symbolic shield, Rachel stood at his feet and spoke softly. "I can't have children, Sean. You need to find a wife who can."

He stared up at her. So, *that* was it. No wonder she'd acted so upset when her mother had kept needling her about grandchildren. Martha must not know.

"Have you told anyone else?"

Rachel grimaced. "Only Hannah. And Craig. You know how that turned out—he dumped me."

Sean slowly got to his feet. There was a lopsided smile on his face that confused Rachel. He reached for her. She backed away, tripped on the dragging tail of the blanket and nearly fell. Sean righted her just as the curtain around Samantha's bed slid open.

They froze, staring at the emerging doctor. He was stripping off his gloves as he announced, "Your daughter's going to be fine."

Rachel was glad Sean's arms were around her shoulders again because her knees felt suddenly wobbly. She started to tell the doctor, "Samantha's not..." then felt the tightening of Sean's grip and realized there was a definite advantage to being considered the little girl's parents. There would be time enough to set the record straight after they'd spent some time at her bedside.

"She's not badly hurt?" Sean asked, filling in the gap in Rachel's response.

The doctor shook his head. "Doesn't appear to be. I'm going to go ahead and order a few tests, just to be sure. I really don't think you have anything to worry about."

"Thank God," Rachel breathed.

Beside her, Sean said, "I already did."

Samantha was wheeled to a private room as soon as the tests were completed. Rachel and Sean stood at her bedside, holding hands and watching her sleep.

"I can't believe she's going to get to stay in Arkansas," Rachel said. "What did Robert tell you while I was in being examined, anyway? Why the change of heart?"

"Apparently, Daphne didn't want the responsibility of a child in the first place. Being related, Robert felt guilty so he insisted on trying, but when he saw his wife with Sam he decided he'd made a big mistake and called everything off."

Rachel sighed. "Well, that's one worry behind us."

"Actually, it's *two*," Sean said quietly. He stepped closer to the woman he loved and gently caressed her shoulder. "You see, all along I've been bothered by the idea of having kids of my own. If you'd been listening closely, instead of worrying about your own problems, you might have figured that out."

"But…"

He laid a finger across her lips. "Hush. Let me finish. It took me a while to think it all through but I finally saw the light—in more ways than one. God knew what we both needed. He went out of His way to bring us together." Sean glanced briefly at the sleeping child. "He provided our first little girl, too."

Awed, Rachel could hardly believe her ears. She placed her hands flat on his chest and felt the rapid beating of his heart. Her own pulse wasn't exactly dawdling, either. "Do you think we'd have a chance," she breathed, "really?"

"Well, there is a catch. I'm afraid we'll have to get married."

"I could probably manage that," Rachel told him. "If you asked me properly."

A stirring from the bed prompted them to glance at Samantha. Though her eyes were still closed, Sean suspected she'd been listening. He leaned over her to whisper, "I'm about to ask Miss Rachel to marry me, kiddo, so pay close attention."

"Do you think she can hear us?" Rachel asked.

"Let's find out, shall we?" Sean dropped to one knee. "Ms. Woodward, would you do me the honor of becoming my wife?"

"Yes!" She couldn't help giggling. "Now get up before the nurses think there's something wrong with you."

Sean immediately took her in his arms and swung her around, feet off the ground. "You said *yes!* What could possibly be wrong with me? I feel wonderful!"

From the direction of the bed came an answering giggle. Then a small voice asked, "Can we go home, now?"

Epilogue

Rachel stood at the rear of the crowded church, her bouquet in one hand, Samantha holding tightly to the other.

"Now?" the excited child asked.

"Very soon." Rachel smiled down at her. "Remember what you're supposed to do?"

"Uh-huh. I throw flowers and stuff. On the floor." Her blue eyes widened. "You sure I won't get in trouble?"

"Positive." Rachel laughed softly. "I'm the bride and I get to do anything I want today. Even make a mess in church so I can walk on flower petals."

"Okay." Samantha giggled. "I'm gonna do that when I'm a bride, too."

"I'm sure you will." Love glowed in Rachel's eyes as she looked from the child to the wonderful man who had just joined the pastor in front of the altar. "There's Sean. See? It's almost time. Are you ready?"

"Uh-huh."

Bending, she kissed the child's warm cheek, then took her by the shoulders, turned her so she'd be facing the right direction and made a last-minute adjustment to the circlet of fresh flowers atop her blond curls.

"Okay. The music is starting. Let's go. I'll be right behind you."

Watching the two most important people in his life approaching, Sean was in awe. Rachel's elegant white gown accentuated her delicate but regal stature, and her flowing skirt barely brushed the floor as she glided toward him.

Walking slowly in front of her and grinning from ear to ear, Samantha was taking evident pleasure in scattering handful after handful of rose petals. When a few of those petals fluttered down and landed outside the aisle runner, the little girl dutifully followed and stomped them flat with her brand-new patent leather shoes, bringing titters of laughter from wedding guests who were close enough to see what she was doing.

Samantha paid them no mind. As Sean watched, he saw her pause and lift her gaze to the highest part of the vaulted ceiling. Then she smiled, nodded and continued straight to the front of the sanctuary, where she reached for Sean's hand as if she'd just been reminded of the solemnity of the ceremony.

Those who had been observing her progress looked up at the empty rafters, then at each other, with curious interest.

Sean's gaze met Rachel's. Mutual understanding held it. They didn't have to wonder what Samantha had seen or heard. They knew she believed guardian angels had blessed her with a new family—and that was fine with them. After all they'd been through, they weren't about to question the simple, un-shakable faith of their very special little girl.

* * * * *

Dear Reader,

I checked the cyclopedic index in my Bible and found sixty-seven listings concerning angels—and that's not counting the forty-seven more in the concordance!

I don't presume to understand everything about angels, but I do know Jesus spoke plainly about the jobs they do here on earth and in the heavens, and that's a good enough reference for me.

Could a child with a special need actually see an angel the way Samantha does in this story? I think so. Children had a special place in Christ's heart, and there's no reason to believe that has changed from then to now.

Have I ever actually seen an angel? Maybe I have and just didn't realize it. Either way, my faith is not based on things seen, as this story explains. Faith is a gift with two sides: intellect and choice. Each of us has the inner need to believe in a Higher Power, but that's only the beginning. Choosing to surrender to the will of God and follow Jesus is what makes the difference. That part of faith cannot be reasoned out like a puzzle; it can only be embraced wholeheartedly. That, I *am* sure of.

I'd love to hear from you. You can write to me at P.O. Box 13, Glencoe, AR 72539-0013, check out my Web site at www.ValerieHansen.com, or e-mail me at valw@centurytel.net.

Blessings,

Valerie Hansen

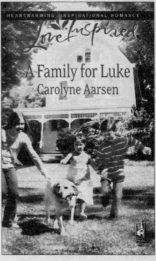

REQUEST YOUR FREE BOOKS!

2 FREE INSPIRATIONAL NOVELS
PLUS 2
FREE
MYSTERY GIFTS

Love Inspired®

YES! Please send me 2 FREE Love Inspired® novels and my 2 FREE mystery gifts (gifts are worth about $10). After receiving them, if I don't wish to receive any more books, I can return the shipping statement marked "cancel". If I don't cancel, I will receive 4 brand-new novels every month and be billed just $4.24 per book in the U.S. or $4.74 per book in Canada, plus 25¢ shipping and handling per book and applicable taxes, if any*. That's a savings of over 20% off the cover price! I understand that accepting the 2 free books and gifts places me under no obligation to buy anything. I can always return a shipment and cancel at any time. Even if I never buy another book, the two free books and gifts are mine to keep forever.

113 IDN ERXA 313 IDN ERWX

Name	(PLEASE PRINT)
Address	Apt. #
City	State/Prov.	Zip/Postal Code

Signature (if under 18, a parent or guardian must sign)

Order online at www.LoveInspiredBooks.com

Or mail to Steeple Hill Reader Service:

IN U.S.A.: P.O. Box 1867, Buffalo, NY 14240-1867
IN CANADA: P.O. Box 609, Fort Erie, Ontario L2A 5X3

Not valid to current subscribers of Love Inspired books.

Want to try two free books from another series?
Call 1-800-873-8635 or visit www.morefreebooks.com

* Terms and prices subject to change without notice. N.Y. residents add applicable sales tax. Canadian residents will be charged applicable provincial taxes and GST. Offer not valid in Quebec. This offer is limited to one order per household. All orders subject to approval. Credit or debit balances in a customer's account(s) may be offset by any other outstanding balance owed by or to the customer. Please allow 4 to 6 weeks for delivery. Offer available while quantities last.

Your Privacy: Steeple Hill Books is committed to protecting your privacy. Our Privacy Policy is available online at www.SteepleHill.com or upon request from the Reader Service. From time to time we make our lists of customers available to reputable third parties who may have a product or service of interest to you. If you would prefer we not share your name and address, please check here. ☐

LIREG08R